Cry of the

White Moose

Alex McGilvery

Cry of the White Moose

Alex McGilvery

Cover Design by Matt Kehler

Copyright © 2018 by Alex McGilvery

For information contact:
http://alexmcgilvery.com

ISBN 978-1-989092-04-0

Chapter One

On the other side of the field from where the hunters sat huddled in a bush, a ghostly animal wandered out of the dark and began chewing on the willow growing in the meadow.

"Damn, look at that!" Bob whispered and pointed into the dusk.

"We only have about ten minutes of hunting time left," Frank peered into the dimming light. "Don't waste it."

"But the moose is white!" Bob said, "Maybe it's diseased."

"It don't look diseased," Frank sighted through the scope of his rifle. "Look at the rack on it.

Bob lifted his rifle up to look through the scope. The antlers were immense. He imagined himself in a picture standing beside the beast, probably in an outdoors magazine with hunters all over just screwed up with jealously that he got the shot. He lined his sights up extra careful. The pair had been out every day for a week and this was the first time they'd seen anything other than cows or footprints.

"Don't take the shot," came the voice of their guide through their radio. "That's a sacred moose, a spirit moose."

"Screw that. I paid five thousand dollars for this trip. I'm going home with a moose." He pulled the trigger. The .300 Win Mag banged against his shoulder and he thought briefly it was dislocated. The voice over the radio was saying something again, but he couldn't hear it over his whispered cursing.

Frank had his rifle up and he took his shot. The moose turned its massive head toward them then went back to eating the willow. Frank cycled his rifle and aimed for another shot, but then the moose went down on its knees before falling to the ground.

"Hot Damn," Frank said, "We got it."

"You mean you got it." Bob rubbed his shoulder. "I missed."

"Hell no. I could see the bullet hole through my scope. I just took a backup shot." He slapped Bob on the shoulder and laughed when Bob swore. "I told you the .300 Win Mag was too much gun for you." He stood up and stretched. "Let's go check it out."

The hunting partners picked up their gear and checked their rifles, as always, very safety conscious. They prided themselves on being responsible hunters. It was almost full dark now so walking across the field took some time. Their guide caught up to them as they reached the moose.

"I told you not to shoot. This is a spirit moose." Their guide frowned at them. "A messenger from the Creator."

"I'm sorry." Frank shrugged his rifle into a more comfortable position. "We didn't hear you."

"Like hell you didn't hear me," the Cree guide said, "you just wanted to kill a moose."

"Damn right I wanted to kill a moose." Bob pointed at the guide. "I paid five grand for a week's hunting and a chance to shoot a moose. This is the only one we saw all week. I wasn't going to pass up a chance to bag an animal. I'm sorry you don't like it, but tough. You should have found us an animal sooner and your precious sacred moose would be safe.

"Roger, go get the swamp truck," The fourth man in their group joined them.

"Sure thing, Rivers." The guide stared at him for a long moment then disappeared into the darkness.

"Well, boys," the new man said, "you got your moose. I hope you enjoy it." Something in his voice put Bob's back up, but the man pulled out a camera out of his pack and got them to pose with their kill.

In the dark all Bob could see was the ghostly shape of the fallen giant, but when Rivers showed them the photographs on the camera screen the flash made the blood stand out stark against the snow-white hide of the moose.

"Look, Rivers." Bob looked down at his feet. "I'm sorry I killed your people's spirit moose, but this is the only time I'll be able to afford this."

"It's done. Whatever message it may have had for my people is lost." He pulled a hunting knife out of his pack. "I'd better dress it."

"Let me," Bob stopped Rivers, "My kill, my responsibility."

***

"Yes," Rivers stared at the white hunter from the south. What did he know about responsibility? "You're right."

He let Bob step up to the carcass. When the hunter knelt beside the white moose, Rivers leaned over and casually sliced open Bob's throat with his hunting knife. Frank stood in shock, still with his gun in hand. Years of training himself to never point the muzzle at a human being meant he didn't think about using the rifle in self defense until after Rivers buried his hunting knife in the man's heart. Frank went down like the moose; first to his knees, then falling to one side.

Roger was pissed off enough he'd take as long as he dared bringing the swamp truck back, so Rivers didn't feel rushed. Methodically, and with the ease of years of practice field dressing game, Rivers hung the men up in the trees beside the murdered spirit moose. He would like to have skinned them, but he didn't think he'd have enough time. He contented himself with gutting them out and spreading their ribs to allow the air to cool their corpses.

He heard the swamp truck approaching as he laid the hunters' hearts beside the moose.

The Spirit Moose had brought its message. River had heard it as the great creature breathed his last. It was time.

The war had started.

He vanished into the trees as the lights of the vehicle lit up the meadow.

Chapter Two

Acting-Staff Sergeant Jim Dalrymple looked at the members sitting across from him in the tiny office he used in the detachment.

"It is important we set an example to the community. That example means we work together and not get caught up in the trap of racism."

Cam Turcott opened his mouth to argue, but Jim held up a finger and the member shut his mouth again. Jim might only be Acting-Staff, but he was still the Staff-Sergeant and arguing with Staff about calling another member racist names was never a good idea.

Jim nodded at Cam and looked over at Darren. Darren had been working with them for a few years. He arrived at the tail end of a mess that had almost cost Jim his life. The Cree officer had been invaluable in building bridges with the First Nations community since then. They almost trusted the RCMP now. Jim didn't want to jeopardize that because a couple of members couldn't grow up and deal with each other.

"Darren, I've heard from several sources you've been baiting Cam here. Constable Turcott may be too green to control his mouth, but I expect better of you. If I had my way I'd put you in the same car and you'd learn to deal or die trying, but Division Command has suggested I put you on different shifts and assign you to some remedial training. So Cam, you're on shift two now. I've put your assignment in your cubby. You will find some required reading and course material. I suggest you take some time and get familiar with it because at some time in the next week I'm going to expect you to know it. Dismissed."

Constable Turcott nodded and left the office.

"Darren," Jim said, "You should know better than to lose your temper around people who don't like you."

"Sorry, Staff," Darren rubbed his forehead. "The man's a prick. I don't know how he got into uniform."

"That's beside the point, isn't it?" Jim leaned on the desk. "He isn't the only prick in uniform. He has friends in places that can cause you trouble. As the more senior officer I expect you to have some sense. Stay away from him and stop trying to poke holes in him. If I want him deflated, I will take care of it myself."

"Sorry, Staff," Darren said again. "I'll keep that in mind."

"Staff," Carol knocked at the door. "You'll want to take this." She handed a dispatch radio to him.

"SB Detachment." Jim picked up the radio. "Go ahead, dispatch."

"There is a call from the Loon Lake Lodge requesting immediate police assistance," dispatch said. "Two of their guests have been murdered and a guide is missing."

Jim went over to the map on his wall. Loon Lake was a fly-in camp. "Ten-four dispatch, we'll get there as soon as we can."

"Carol call the airport and see who's available for immediate flight to Loon Lake. I'll take Darren with me. Call Pat in to hold things down until I get back. Cam has been moved to shift two, so Amber will have to move to shift one. Tell her I'm sorry, but that's the way it is. Then put in another request to Division. I need at least two more members up here to manage the basic shifts if we want to do more than just sit in the detachment and wait for trouble."

He grabbed his gear bag with everything he'd probably need and headed out the door. Darren already had the truck running. Jim climbed in and they headed out to the airport. *It isn't really an airport so much as an airstrip with delusions of grandeur.* Not much there other than the fuel storage tanks and a vending machine backed against a metal shed to store equipment for clearing the runway in the winter.

A plane and a pilot waited for them so it wasn't long before they were flying over the black spruce forest to the hunting lodge. The pilot landed them on the water and taxied them into the dock. The lodge owner met them.

"Thanks for coming. I'm Jack Fritz." He led them up to the lodge. "We had two hunters out last evening on their final hunt of their stay. We got a radio call just after sunset saying they'd shot a moose. That would normally mean they'd be late getting in. The guides would wake me if they needed to, but otherwise I go to bed since I cook breakfast. None of them were back at breakfast, so I sent one of my other guys out to the site to check on them. Sometimes the hunters will choose to spend the night out. He came back looking sick and told me to call you guys." Jack pushed a door open and ushered them into his office. "This is Dusty, officers."

Dusty looked to be a younger guide, probably his first or second year at it. His clothes still had a bit of stiffness showing he hadn't broken them in completely. He still wore the blaze orange vest and hat required for hunters and guides in the province.

"Tell us what you need to," Darren leaned against the wall. Jim moved over to be out of Dusty's line of sight.

"I went out to find Roger and his pair. They were Americans, he was hoping for a good tip, but they hadn't shot anything so I didn't think it was likely. They kept talking about how much money this cost so I figured them for stiffing Roger at the end."

"This morning, Dusty," Darren said.

"Mr. Fritz asked me to run up to the meadow they were hunting last night, and check on them. I thought I'd find them drinking coffee and bullshitting about what great hunters they were. We knew they'd made a kill, 'cause Roger had radio'd in."

"What did you find?"

"Ravens all over the place which was all wrong. Roger'd never let them leave stuff to attract ravens or other scavengers. That's just asking for trouble. I come up and they flew up into the tree and the men were hanging there, gutted like deer." Dusty gulped and looked like he wanted to throw up.

"Take your time."

"The hunters were hanging there and that's what the ravens were about. Their guts were just about gone and the birds had started on their faces. This big white moose lay on the ground beside them. The birds had hardly touched it. I've never seen anything like it. Roger must have been mad as hell. You should have heard him go on about that white moose they shot in Nova Scotia, I'd never thought we'd see a spirit moose here."

"Was Roger there?"

6

"No, he was gone. The swamp truck was there and it looked like it had run out of gas. Like it had been running all night."

"So is Roger the kind of guy who'd kill someone for shooting a spirit moose?"

"I don't know. I didn't think so, but they were dead and strung up and he was gone."

"Alright, you'll need to take us out there."

"I'll send you with some extra gas to get the swamp truck running. That will be the best way to get the bodies back here." Jack led them out to the back. "You'll have to ride double on the quad so one of you can bring the quad back."

"Fine," Jim said, "Let's go. There will be a lot to do out there before we bring any bodies back. He looked up at the sun. It and his stomach told him it was past noon.

After almost an hour of tortuous riding, Jim spotted the black cloud of ravens ahead. They got to the spot and the ravens flew up to roost in the trees and called down to them.

"You didn't tell us someone had skinned off the moose," Jim said.

"They hadn't," Dusty said, "Not before I was here. That's how I knew it was a spirit moose. You can't tell with the hide and the head gone." He looked around nervously. "Someone was watching me. I'm lucky they didn't shoot me."

"You didn't shoot the spirit moose," Jim said. "They had no reason to be angry at you."

He got out his gear bag and started taking pictures. The hunters hung from their ankles. They wore their clothing, but a knife had sliced them open and their guts had been removed. One of the men had his throat cut, the blood on the other man's shirt suggested a stab to the heart. The coroner would face a challenge with no organs to work with. Both men had almost no face left from the depredation of the ravens.

Once all the pictures were taken, they wrapped the bodies in corpse bags before letting them down to the ground. Dusty had filled the swamp truck with gas, so they loaded the bodies, adding whatever other gear lay around. The rifles probably belonged to the men, and a camera with the batteries and the memory card missing. Once it was all loaded, Dusty drove the swamp truck while Jim and Darren followed on the quads.

7

Jack had a meal ready for them when they got back, which Jim and Darren ate gratefully along with the pilot. Jim had seen him around here and there, but hadn't had the time to talk much with him.

Tim had been a pilot since before Jim was born and was full of stories.

"This is sad," he said, "but I've seen worse. A village died because they got sick and I was grounded by bad weather and couldn't get medicine to them in time. There were too many to bury so I had to just leave them. Somewhere in the wilderness their bones still sit. Probably covered with moss now. Most of my flying now is hunters, but there are still a few old prospectors trying to find a big ore body to make them rich. I've heard stories. The best stories come from Zeke Hamilton. He looks like a wild man, but he speaks seven languages and has a handful of university degrees. He spends most of his time in the bush looking for signs of a deep ore body. Last time I flew him he said he'd found one. Was going to turn the town around and make everybody rich again. He wouldn't say anything else until he'd file the claim."

They finished the meal, loaded the body bags and gear into the plane and flew back to Spruce Bay.

"I'm sorry it was such a sad reason," Tim said, "but I'm glad to be of help." He left them to unload their gear and the bodies into the ambulance that would take them to the hospital where Dr. Diat would examine the remains.

It was getting dark by the time they'd finished and Tim had come back to secure his plane. Jim hoped Leigh's day had gone better than his.

Chapter Three

Leigh sat in the Principal's office and breathed deeply. It felt like foreign territory. She'd spent two years building a working relationship with Mr. Ryckle, but he'd retired at the end of the last school year. Ms. Taladut was made acting-principal while the board dithered over hiring a replacement. Ms. Taladut was also the self-appointed expert on the special needs students.

"Sorry to keep you waiting," Ms. Taladut said as she sat down behind the desk. She pulled Ryley's file out and opened it front of her. "I see Ryley is having some troubles again."

"I have suggested to Mr. McRoy several times that Ryley does not do well under pressure. If he's not disrupting class, it is better to let him follow at his own pace. Ryley wants to learn, but his capacity for learning is severely limited." Leigh focused on staying calm.

"I understand that." Ms. Taladut caressed the folder in front of her. "I really do, but Mr. McRoy runs a very strict classroom and having one student doing whatever he wants while the others work…" She let her voice drop off and shook her head. Leigh wondered why the woman didn't squeeze out a few tears as well.

"I'm not suggesting Ryley do whatever he wants." Leigh twisted her hands in her lap. "I'm suggesting he be allowed to follow at his own pace. That is quite a different thing. If he is having such a difficult time with Ryley, I'd be glad to put him back in my class."

"Ryley isn't the only one of your students to be having problems in subsequent years."

"Excuse me?" Leigh's hands locked and her chest started aching. She knew if she didn't escape quickly, she would soon start shaking and having a hard time breathing.

"Macky, for one," Ms. Taladut said, as if Leigh hadn't spoken. "He is being very disruptive, almost as bad as Ryley–"

"Is this discussion about Ryley or about my teaching?" The question came out much sharper than Leigh intended. Ms. Taladut looked wounded.

"Since we are here," she said, "I felt it to be a good use of time to discuss your other ... problems."

"You know you can't do this," Leigh said. "We are either talking about Ryley, or we are talking about me. We can't bounce back and forth like this."

"Very well," Ms. Taladut shut the file with a snap. "Let's talk about you, shall we?"

Leigh stood up.

"Not without my union representative present we don't." She fled the room and walked as fast as she dared to her car in the parking lot. When she got to the car, she locked the door and let the shakes come. She didn't indulge her weakness very long before she started the car and drove away toward home. She couldn't afford having Ms. Taladut find her like this.

Jim's truck was in the drive, so Leigh parked beside it and forced her hands to stop shaking. He had enough problems trying to run the detachment shorthanded. He didn't need to be worried about her too.

The house welcomed her with light and the smell of chili cooking.

"Hi," Ryley said before he went back to staring at the TV. The screen had a fascination for him Leigh didn't understand. If she turned the TV on in the midst of one of Ryley's outbreaks, he would immediately sit and stare at it. It didn't matter how upset he'd been getting.

"Hi, sweetheart." Jim gave Leigh a kiss and a hug. "If you set the table, I'll pour milk for everyone." Leigh smiled and hugged him back. She missed the days of late suppers as they satisfied their desires, but she wouldn't trade her present for anything.

"Ryley help." Ryley took the cutlery from her hands and carefully arranged it on the table. He made sure every knife, fork and spoon lined up exactly straight. He wouldn't set the table with just forks or spoons either. It had to be everything. Leigh set the plates down in their places and Jim put the glasses of milk on the table.

They sat and ate in quiet, sometimes Ryley would talk, more often not. As soon as he finished eating he walked back to the TV.

"Rough day?" Jim asked as he gathered up the dishes.

"You could say that," Leigh leaned against the counter and took a long deep breath. "Acting-principal Taladut tried to segue from Ryley to my teaching methods." Leigh could feel the shaking start. "I invoked the union rep clause and ran away."

Jim put the dishes down and wrapped his arms around her and held her until the shaking stopped.

***

Leigh got to her classroom early to get ready for the day. Though Thanksgiving had passed, they were still wrapping up their exploration of different harvest festivals from the cultures represented in the class. She found a paper with a note attached with a paperclip.

This is the schedule for your class. I expect you to keep to the schedule from now on. T.

Even Allan at his worst in the first year Leigh had worked at the school hadn't gone this far. Leigh crumpled the schedule and the note up and threw it away. Then she stopped and picked them out of the recycling bin. She smoothed the schedule out and looked at it more closely. It looked like it had been pulled from a first-year teacher's handbook. Leigh put it in a folder and locked it away in her desk. Ms. Taladut had been appointed to be an administrator while the School Board decided how to replace Mr. Ryckle. She had quickly started taking on more of the supervision duties, but the Board wouldn't reign her in. If they wouldn't, then Leigh would have to.

She sat and practiced her breathing as she waited for the bell. Dr. Hallace had got her using yoga techniques to deal with the trauma and anxiety that was the fallout from Mr. Henry's murderous rampage.

"Did you get my memo?" Ms. Taladut stood in front of Leigh. She hadn't noticed the other woman come in.

"I got it. I will be discussing it with the union." Leigh watched the acting-principal's face go through several emotions. Ms. Taladut finally decided on friendliness.

11

"You know once the union gets involved, things can get way out of control. Let's just keep this between us. I don't want to lose a teacher."

"It has already got out of control," Leigh said, "I have a meeting with the union rep scheduled." She smiled and stood up. "Almost time for the bell. If you excuse me I need to get ready for my class."

Ms. Taladut either had to force Leigh to stay in her seat or get out of the way. She backed up and let Leigh move out in front of the desk.

"This isn't done," Ms. Taladut lost her smile.

"No," Leigh said, "It is just beginning." The bell rang and she heard the shouts of students coming in from the yard. The other woman turned and left the classroom almost bumping into the first of the students to enter.

"Hola! Mrs. Dalrymple," Marc waved at her. He was a third grader and bilingual in Spanish and English. Leigh suspected he was a long way toward being fluent in Cree as well.

"Hello, Marc."

"What did Old-Tell-Us-What want?" He immediately put his hand over his mouth. "Sorry, Mrs. Dalrymple. Respect."

"Apology accepted Marc," Leigh pointed to his seat. Other students came in and found their seats. As in the past two years they were a mix of third and fourth grade. The School Board never managed to hire a full slate of teachers so classes were large and mixed. Leigh loved it. The students challenged each other and she got two years to get to know them and their strengths.

"*Tansi,* class." Leigh said.

"*Tansi,*" the class said in chorus.

"Good morning children," Ms. Taladut's voice came over the PA. "Let's stand for O Canada."

Leigh dove into the teaching and let the schedule and the visit from Ms. Taladut fall from her mind.

They meandered from math to reading to social studies. The children's questions drove them to learn new things and to find new ways of learning those things. It was what Leigh took up teaching to do. She thought of the schedule sitting in her desk and almost snorted.

The recess bell rang and they streamed out of the class into the yard. Leigh had yard duty so she followed them at a more sedate pace.

"Hi, Mrs. Dalrymple," Georgia was no longer the short, overly-smart girl Leigh taught in her first year in Spruce Bay. Over the summer Georgia had gained some inches in height making her an even stronger player on the basketball team. She was growing some curves, causing more than one boy to try to gain Georgia's attention. They had a tough task, as one of the brightest students in the school, she didn't suffer fools gladly.

"Hi Georgia," Leigh smiled. "New look?" Georgia looked at herself as if surprise to find herself wearing these clothes.

"Dad was in Winnipeg and went shopping. You like it?" She spun in place for Leigh. A wool cap tamed her black hair and a bomber jacket managed to both hide and emphasize her changing shape. Jeans and bright orange running shoes finished the picture. Leigh spotted Ryley watching not too far away. Fortunately, Georgia didn't mind Ryley's attention. She was the only person besides Leigh herself who could calm the boy down when he got upset.

"Looks great," Leigh said. "Your dad has great taste."

"You better believe it." Georgia grinned. "You should see the dress she picked up for herself!"

"I can't wait."

"I'll tell her that it's time to invite you over for dinner again."

"I'd love that."

Georgia ran off toward a group of students huddled by the fence. She waved at Ryley on the way past and he waved back with a grin. Leigh watched her join the other Spruce Bay Wolves. Tom, Steve, Jaime and Anna were Cree, Macky had bright orange hair and a huge crush on Georgia. There were some new members Leigh didn't know as well. One of the boys looked like he might be in Grade Eight or even Nine.

The Wolves were working on building better relationships between the many groups in town. They had also decided, at Tom's suggestion, to try to stop bullying in the school yard. This was a new venture for them and Georgia had told Leigh there was a lot of disagreement about how to do it. Leigh was sure they'd figure it out.

13

After recess the class headed to Fran Dupuis' room for French class while Leigh had a spare. She went to the staff room and looked up the name of their union rep; a high school teacher, Craig Ballan. Leigh left a note in his box saying she wanted to meet about union issues. Having set things in motion, she went back to her room to decide where to start when her class returned.

Chapter Four

Leigh waited a week for Craig to get back to her. Jim was involved in a nasty case which had him traveling to far flung communities by air, and often not making it home at night. She sat with Ryley while he stared at the TV and read to him. It didn't matter to Ryley if the sound was on or not, so the blue glow of the TV was a constant. From things he said, Leigh thought he was listening to what she read. It was the best she could do.

Thursday night she watched a cop show and tried to keep from worrying. It seemed the things her mind wanted to worry about were multiplying. There was her concern for Jim, the problems with work, both her argument with Ms. Taladut, and the union reps lack of response. Then there was Ryley. Leigh wasn't sure what she had been thinking when she asked to be Ryley's foster-mother. She had no illusions of ever having a normal mother/son relationship. Sometimes she felt guilty for using the TV to keep her home calm, but the workers at Ryley's center told her it didn't do him any harm and did her a lot of good.

The biggest worry was her anxiety. The last two years she'd had it under control. Mr. Ryckle had given her the space she needed to feel safe and welcome at the school. When he retired, she lost that space. Ms. Taladut had no patience for what she saw as Mr. Ryckle getting soft in his last years. Now the almost panic attacks were getting to be common occurrences. She would talk to Dr. Hallace about it on their next trip to Thompson, but that was close to a month away.

She got up and stretched. Time for bed even if the show wasn't done. As she turned the sound on the TV off she saw some shadows run across the lawn. Her heart pounded and she felt the shakes coming on. Children had been twisted and used as weapons against her. Ryley shared her scars from that experience.

Leigh checked all the door and the windows, but still she couldn't stop shaking. She sat in the kitchen and gasped for breath. Whispers of demented children sounded in her head. She put her head on her knees and tried to control the desperate gasping for air, but nothing she did worked. She'd have to wait it out. Tears leaked out of her eyes and soaked her knees. Her chest ached, while her stomach tied itself in knots. She didn't have the strength even to sit on the floor anymore, so she let herself fall to the side and curled up in a ball.

She felt the warmth at her back before she heard any words. Ryley's arms wrapped around her and gradually she heard what he was saying.

"Ryley help," the boy said over and over like a mantra. Leigh felt the panic relax and break, but she lay on the floor, and let her son's care flow over her. He stroked her hair and talked to her - exactly what she did when life overwhelmed him and he had one of his episodes.

"Thank you, Ryley." She finally sat up. He crouched across from her and looked at her.

"Mom, OK?" he asked.

"Yes," she said, "I am OK. Let's get you back to bed and then Mom will go to bed too."

"Ryley read Mom a story." He went to his bookshelf, picked a book and followed Leigh to her room. She crawled under the covers, clothes and all and he pulled the covers up and tucked them around her, just like she did for him. Then he opened the book.

"Frog was sad," he read, "be - cause Frog did not get an-y let-ters."

Leigh fell asleep clothes and all. She thought she felt his lips on her forehead, but she wasn't sure.

She woke up feeling exhausted and sick. She took a long hot shower and got dressed again. When she went out into the kitchen Ryley was already dressed and watching TV. He had the sound on and was laughing at the cartoon antics. It looked to be a good day.

She made lunches for them both, and then set toast and peanut butter beside him so he could eat while he watched.

She drank her tea, some of the blend of native plants Anna's kohkom had given her. Ella, one of kohkom's friends kept her supplied now kohkom was gone. The tea had a calming effect. The attack last night was the worst one yet. Only Ryley had kept it from being worse. Leigh looked at the boy. He was big for his age. Nobody could say how old he was. The doctors guessed at about twelve, maybe thirteen. His thinking stayed at a much younger age, but every once in a while he'd surprise her. Like last night, coming to her rescue with exactly what she needed. She couldn't remember him ever volunteering to read before.

She drove them to school a little early. Time to track Craig down and find out what was going on. Ryley wandered over to the yard where a couple of other kids played. He crouched down by a tree and looked like he was watching something. Maybe a bug or the like.

Leigh walked through to the High School side of the school and looked for Craig Ballan's room. A younger teacher, last year was his first year, Leigh thought she remembered. He was marking papers, but he put his pen down when she came in.

"Good morning," he said, "I should remember who you are, but I have to admit, I've forgotten."

"Leigh Dalrymple." She put out her hand. He looked a little startled but shook her hand with a firm grip. *Not Cree, but definitely First Nations.*

"Haida," he said.

"Ah," Leigh felt herself blushing and shook herself. "I don't know much about the Haida."

Craig shrugged. "What can I do for you?"

"Did you get my note about wanting a meeting?" Leigh asked.

"Note?" Craig looked puzzled. "Why would you want a meeting with me?"

"You are the union representative," she said, feeling a little annoyed now.

"Damn," Craig shook his head. "I took the job because they promised me I'd have nothing to do." He grinned at her. "I'm guessing you have something for me to do."

"It won't help much if you don't know what you are doing," Leigh headed toward the door.

17

"Tell me what the problem is and I will check with some folks," Craig came to stand beside her. "I may have taken the job because no one else would, but if you need my help, you have it."

"OK." Leigh breathed to regain her calm. "Here's the problem." She told him about Ms. Taladut and the schedule as well as the sliding from parent meeting to talking about performance issues.

"I can see the issue," Craig said. "I'll get back to you on Monday about what our next step should be." He opened the door for her and put his hand on her arm. "Try not to let her get to you."

Leigh nodded her head and walked back to her classroom.

Marc was waiting for her.

"Ryley's in trouble in the yard," he said. "I thought I'd better come get you."

Leigh sighed and followed the hispanic boy out to the yard. They'd arrived in town last year. She'd taught his sister Maria last year before she'd move on to Mr. McRoy's class. Now Maria WAS nose to nose with Ryley, screaming at him in Spanish. Ryley looked more confused than upset. Leigh could see Ms Talabut coming from the parking lot.

"Let's back off and calm down," Leigh pulled Ryley back to create space between the children. "Maria, tell me what the problem is."

"He dug up some nasty bones and shoved them at me. They're gross."

"Ryley?" Leigh looked at him. He held out his hands and they were indeed filled with bones; small and delicate with bits of skin and sinew still attached. Leigh thought they were interesting, but she could understand Maria's view point.

"Those are nice bones, Ryley, but not everyone likes bones. You scared Maria."

"OK," Ms. Taladut said as she arrived. "Ryley come with me."

"Ryley sorry," he said.

"It's too late to be sorry now," Ms. Taladut said. She took Ryley's collar and tried to pull him with her.

"NO!" Ryley shouted and pulled away from her. "Ryley sorry, Ryley sorry."

18

"Come with me now," Ms. Taladut repeated much louder and took another grip on Ryley's collar. Leigh took a breath to warn her, but it WAS too late. Ryley swung his arms wildly and flung her off. Unbelievably the acting-Principal tried a third time to pull Ryley away by force and this time one of his hands connected with her face with a heavy slap.

"No, Ryley," Georgia had arrived and threw herself between Ryley and Ms. Taladut who held her face, bleeding from between her fingers.

"Marc." Leigh fought back her anxiety. "You and Maria take Ms. Taladut to the nurse's office." The children helped the woman to her feet.

Georgia was still talking to Ryley, but he put his hands over his ears and ran off.

"You really can't try to pull Ryley like that," Georgia said, "He doesn't like it."

"Don't talk to me like that, you stupid girl." Ms Taladut pushed Marc and Maria away and walked off to the school.

"Thanks for your help, Georgia." Leigh smiled at the girl. "You tried."

"I didn't mean to make so much trouble, Mrs. Dalrymple," Maria was almost in tears, "He just scared me. I hate bones."

"It's OK, Maria," Leigh patted the girl on the shoulder, "This wasn't your fault."

"I'm going to go find Ryley," Georgia glared at Maria, but didn't say anything.

Great, how can this day get any better?

Chapter Five

The police constable showed up while Leigh was chopping vegetables for the variety of meals she cooked on Saturdays to heat up through the week. That explained her answering the door with a large knife in her hand. The police officer took several steps back and put his hand to his gun.

"Sorry," Leigh said, and put the knife on the step. "If I leave a knife on the counter Ryley likes to play with it."

"That sounds dangerous, ma'am." The constable took his hand away from the gun.

"Not really, but you haven't seen a dull knife until you've tried to cut with one someone's used to cut up lego blocks." She backed away from the door. "Come on in."

He picked up the knife and carried it into the kitchen and put it in the sink. Leigh rinsed it off and placed it in the knife drawer. It clicked when she closed it. Ryley wouldn't open that drawer.

"What can I help you with?" Leigh asked once the knife was safely stowed away. "You're Cam Turcott, right?"

"Yes, ma'am," he said. "We received a complaint from a Ms. Taladut that Ryley assaulted her before school yesterday."

"He gave her a bloody nose," Leigh said, "but she tried to physically force Ryley to move. That isn't a good idea."

"She states she ordered Ryley to follow her to her office and he hit her."

"More or less true," Leigh was glad she'd locked the knife away. An irrational desire to go after the woman with the chef's knife made her hands twitch. "What she has left out is that I was already there already dealing with the situation between Ryley and another student, Maria Horate. Her brother Marc had fetched me. Ms Taladut stepped in and tried to physically move Ryley. She did so three times even after Ryley reacted badly to her first attempts. Fortunately, another student intervened before the situation got worse."

"Why another student?" Turcott took notes. "Why didn't you stop your son?"

"I was prepared to try, but Ryley is unpredictable. I can calm him down most days, but the only person Ryley will never hit is Georgia Cassidy. They've had a special bond for the last two years."

"Would Georgia lie to protect Ryley?"

"I doubt Georgia would lie for anyone, but I can't prove that statement."

"I talked to Maria, she said was too scared and didn't see what happened. Her brother insisted the teacher hit Ryley first. He was clearly antagonistic toward Ms. Taladut. I will talk to Georgia and form my own opinion, but I think from what I have there is no cause for charges."

"Thank you for your diligence, Constable," Leigh said, "I appreciate you being fair about the whole thing. I feel very badly that Ms. Taladut was injured. Do you want to talk to Ryley?"

"How much is he able to communicate?"

"He has his good days and his bad days."

"In the interest of being fair, I should try then."

"Come with me," Leigh led the constable into the living room where Ryley sat looking at the TV.

"Ryley," she said, "the policeman would like to talk to you."

Ryley looked around, then stood up and saluted.

"He salutes everyone in uniform," Leigh said.

"Hi Ryley," Turcott knelt so he was on eye level with the boy. "You had a problem at the school yesterday."

"Maria doesn't like bones," Ryley shook his head.

"That was the initial problem," Leigh said. "She screamed when Ryley showed her some bones he found."

Turcott nodded, but didn't look away from Ryley.

"What happened next?"

"Ryley sorry." He put his head down. Turcott put his hand on Ryley's shoulder. Leigh could see Ryley tensing, but Turcott just let his hand rest there.

"What are you sorry for?" Turcott asked.

"Maria scared."

21

"What about the teacher?"

Ryley started getting more anxious, but Turcott left his hand resting gently on the boy's shoulder.

"Ryley scared, Ryley sorry."

"OK, Ryley, it was an accident." Turcott stood up and backed up a step. Ryley turned and went back to watching TV.

"Thank you for your cooperation," Turcott said to Leigh. "I don't see him as dangerous under normal circumstances. He certainly didn't attack me. I think he's lucky he has you." He closed his notebook and put it in his pocket. "I'll let myself out and you can get back to your cooking. I've heard about your Chinese food dinners and I'm looking forward to trying it out."

Leigh walked him to the door and closed it after him. She went back to chopping. She had a sense Turcott was a problem at the detachment, but from what she saw of him, she approved.

Jim arrived home just after she'd put the last of the bags in the freezer. She told him about the visit.

"He's a mixed bag," Jim said. "Sometimes he's a fantastic officer and I want to give him more responsibility, then he does something that makes me want to wring his neck."

"So he's pretty much normal then," Leigh said and Jim laughed.

"What about this teacher who complained about Ryley?" he asked.

"She's an incompetent baboon," Leigh snarled and Jim raised his eyebrows.

"The Board hired her to do administration, but she's decided she can interfere with the teachers, even though she has no teaching degree and no experience. The Board is terrified of doing anything after the fiasco a couple of years back. They won't reign her in. I've started talking to the union rep, a teacher in the High School named Craig Ballan. He's young, but he insists he will be able to do the work of representing the teachers in this situation."

"Hmmm," Jim frowned, "union fights can get messy, especially if neither party knows what they are doing. Be careful."

"I'm not letting someone push me around. Even if she were the principal and not just acting, she'd have no right to dictate to me this way."

"I'm not saying don't do this." Jim put his hand on hers. "I'm just saying be careful. It will be stressful and you will have to make sure you have the supports you need in place."

Leigh ground her teeth, even Jim was against her. She forced herself to rewind the conversation. Not against her, just worried. Leigh wished he didn't have so much reason to be worried. She hated being so weak.

"Can you watch Ryley and get him to bed?" Leigh hugged him. "I'm going to go out and line up some of those supports."

"Sure," Jim said, "we'll be fine."

Leigh put on her coat and drove down to the old trailer court where Don Beauchamp lived. Anna answered the door when Leigh knocked and she grinned.

"Hey Uncle, Leigh is here."

"*Tansi,*" Don said, "You want tea?"

"Thank you, Don," Leigh followed Anna into the trailer. "I'd love a cup."

"I hear Ella's keeping you in stock of ma's special tea," he said from the kitchen, "If you need some, I have it here too."

"That's sort of why I'm here," Leigh said when he came in and sat down. Anna sat in a chair and looked attentive. *Well, let her listen.* "I'm feeling the need for another sweat. I can't travel for it since I don't have any days off, so I was hoping you knew someone who wouldn't mind coming here."

"Aah," Don looked over at Anna and raised his eyebrow in question.

"Let her stay," Leigh said, "but Anna, you can't talk about this at school or with your friends."

"It's medicine," Anna nodded firmly. "I get it."

"So, what do you need to sweat out?" Don asked.

"I'm having some trouble with Ms. Taladut," Leigh looked down at her feet. Anna snorted and Don frowned at her.

"Sorry, uncle." Anna blushed.

"I think she means well, but she is interfering with my teaching and making life hard for Ryley, as if it wasn't hard enough already. I've started a complaint through the union, but that means it's going to get worse before it gets better. I need all the strength I can muster. Whenever I do a sweat, I feel balanced, I really need that balance."

23

"I will talk to some elders," Don went into the kitchen and came back with a tray with mugs of tea and some cookies.

"You want warrior's medicine," he said after he sat down.

"I don't want to make a bigger fight than I need to," Leigh said.

"No true warrior does," Don looked at her. "but you must be ready if the fight comes to you."

"Yes, I want to be ready." Leigh pulled a pouch out of her pocket and gave it to him. "A gift of tobacco for the elders." Don nodded and tucked it into his shirt pocket.

Leigh took a sip of tea and sighed, the mood in the room shifted. Anna told her about the project she was working on with Tom and Steve.

"We're collecting stories from the elders. Some of them let us video tape, but some we need to listen and write down. We are talking to the white elders too. There is this old prospector Mr. Hamilton. You should hear his stories. He says he's found the next big gold mine and it's going to change Spruce Bay back to being rich and busy.

"I hope he's right," Leigh said. "It sounds like a great project. It's important to know our history from all kinds of people."

They talked about the project and which people the trio had interviewed and who they could add to their list.

"This is going to take years," Anna said, "It is just supposed to be a project for school."

"There's no reason you can't hand in your school project, then keep working on it in your spare time." Don smiled at her over his tea.

"No, you're right." Anna picked up a cookie, "and it gives me an excuse to hang out with Tom."

"I didn't think you needed an excuse to hang out with Tom," Anna blushed a little. "I like Tom, you should bring him by more often."

Leigh left soon after with Don's assurance he would get back to her as soon as he'd talked to the elders.

Leigh slept deeply wrapped in Jim's arms. She felt safe and loved.

Sunday morning, they had breakfast and it was such a beautiful day Leigh decided they should go out to enjoy it. The three of them drove down to the lake and spent the day fishing and just enjoying the quiet of the wilderness. Ryley found more bones and showed Leigh. This time a skull, probably a rabbit, according to Jim. Leigh let him bring it home to put on his shelf.

The light on the answering machine was flashing so Leigh hit the play button as she got out dishes for supper.

This is Ms. Taladut, the message said, we have a zero tolerance for violence at Spruce Bay Community School. Because of Ryley's outburst on Friday, the Board is suspending him for three days. If it happens again, we will have to consider expelling him. Please make suitable arrangements for his care as he is not to be on school property during his suspension. Thank you for your understanding.

Leigh snarled and banged the dish she was holding onto the counter. It shattered into countless pieces. She looked at the fragments. Don had it right. She was going to be a warrior. Taladut didn't know what she was starting. Leigh had survived the wendigo; this woman wasn't going to take her down.

Chapter Six

Jim got to work Monday morning still angry about Ryley's suspension. Leigh had got hold of Jen McCrey and she would watch Ryley for the three days. The change in Ryley's routine upset him, but as long as Jen had a TV, he'd be fine.

He took a moment in his office to review the files on his desk. They'd run into a dead end on the murder of the American hunters. Roger Dupreis was the last person to see them alive. He had been their guide and presumably watched them shoot a white moose. Darren explained a white animal was a spirit messenger for many of the First Nations peoples and Roger would have been very upset they shot it.

They couldn't find Roger Dupreis at any of the places he normally lived. He hadn't been home to see his girlfriend, he wasn't at the lodge, none of his relatives had heard from him. It didn't feel like they were covering for him either. Darren insisted they looked genuinely worried.

In the meantime, there were other cases to look at. Ralph Ellers had filed a complaint that someone was stealing fuel from the depot at the airstrip. Ellers owned the airstrip and a large share of a junior mining company exploring north of town for a viable mine. Jim hoped they found something. There was some concern that Ellers was prospecting on reserve. Unfortunately, Ellers refused where he was drilling, and without a clear location there nothing anyone could do about it.

Jim made a note to send Darren to the reserve to see what he could pick up. Ellers was accusing the Cree and Cam supported the theory. The only thing they had going for them was generic footprints and a cut lock. Jim decided to see if he could track down some of the pilots and talk to them. Maybe they'd seen something.

Tim Hadstadt had flown them to Fritz's lodge. Jim found him in the Coffee Shop at the mall. He bought two coffees and slid in across from the pilot.

"Yeah," Tim said, "Ellers would blame the indians for his problems. He's one of those racists who has a reasoned argument for being an asshole. Just as likely one of the pilots who couldn't get hold of Ellers to buy the fuel helped themselves. It wouldn't be the first time. Mostly they pay up when they get back. Ellers only makes a fuss if you aren't as white as he is."

"So checking his records against his inventory might be a good move?"

"It wouldn't hurt," Tim said, "I wouldn't deal with the guy at all, except there's no one else unless you want to go all the way to Thompson to buy your fuel."

"What other pilots are around?" Jim pulled out his notepad.

"Not many." Tim swirled his coffee. "Moose season is done so a lot of the guys have buggered off South until the winter and we start flying supplies to the isolated reserves. There's not much sense in maintaining an expensive airplane and paying storage fees if there's no business to pay for it."

"You don't go South?"

"I live here. There's nothing South for me. I never had time to get married or have kids. Besides someone has to hang around for emergencies. I get to fly your guys around and we have a great time."

"Thanks for your help, Tim."

"Thanks for the coffee."

Jim walked along the mall to the detachment. The Coffee Shop was the only place selling prepared food in town. Someone made pizzas and delivered them on Saturdays, but Jim suspected they used frozen pizza. He didn't care. The grocery store was usually well stocked, but there were odd gaps at times. He walked past the clothing/hardware/gift shop and waved at the girls at the cash. The pharmacy was across the way beside the Library. There used to be a craft shop and learning centre but Sandra and her family had moved away after the wendigo case.

A lot of people had moved away then. They had some people coming in, but not as many. A sign caught his eye and he went over to read it. Though it had been empty for years there was

27

space for another restaurant in the mall which acted as the downtown street in Spruce Bay. Someone planned to open a Mexican food place. Jim wished them luck. Probably the Horate's. They were an enthusiastic family very invested in the town. The mom worked as a nurse. Jim didn't know what the dad did. *Looks like Mexican cooking.*

The detachment had a door into the mall as well as the door to the parking lot. They were beside the Council offices. Jim always wondered why they didn't have a direct connection between the hospital and the mall, but you had to go outside to get to the main doors of the hospital. It was the same with the school, though a single steel door beside the library gave emergency access to the Mall. It had felt strange at first, walking through a mall instead of along a main street, but now it felt good. Jim liked to interact with people as they just walked or did their shopping. One good thing that came out of the wendigo thing - the barriers between folks started breaking down. Cree and white and black all met and talked. There was still some separation between generations but some young kids worked on breaking that down too.

Carol welcomed him with a smile and a pile of phone messages. Half of them from Ellers wanting to know if they'd arrested the indian who stolen his fuel. Jim put them in the file and tried to come up with a way of asking to see Ellers' sales and inventory records which wouldn't set the man off.

Jim kept the radio in his office turned on loud enough he could follow what was going on. Something grabbed his attention.

"SB 2," Darren's voice came across the radio, "I have a license check, Alpha, Bravo, Zulu, 993."

"Stand by SB 2," dispatch responded. "No wants or warrants," she said after a minute, "Brown Escalade registered to Ralph Ellers."

"Ten-Four," Darren said. Jim imagined him getting out the car and crunching along the gravel to ask for Ellers' license and registration- walking back to his squad car. He'd fill out whatever offense Ellers committed, probably speeding. The man drove like a teenager. He would take the ticket along with the license and registration back to the Escalade and pass them through the window along with a suggestion to drive more slowly in the future. He would walk back to his car and do his paperwork. Then call in --

"Dispatch, SB 2, clear."

Jim let out a breath he hadn't realized he was holding. He didn't know how Ellers would take to getting a speeding ticket from a Cree member of the RCMP. Darren didn't sound any different than he normally did, so there probably wasn't any problem.

He found Cam's report on the incident at the school. Jim read through it carefully, but as Leigh told him, it looked like he'd done an admirable job of investigating something which should never have come to them. He found himself hoping Darren would find some excuse to give Ms. Taladut a ticket.

Jim sighed and pushed the thought away. He started on the paperwork. Being a cop was about doing paperwork. If he wasn't taking notes, he was writing them up for a file. If he got done with this, there were always other files to read and make notations. As a Sergeant, Jim had to do all that plus check on the work of the other members under his command.

He had an even deeper respect for Anne who had been the Staff Sergeant when he arrived. She'd retired and moved to British Columbia with her husband, Bill. Rob, who Jim thought a shoe in to be the next Staff Sergeant, transferred to Ottawa, and John hadn't written his Sergeant's exam. Jim was put in as acting Staff Sergeant. It would have been nice if they'd sent him more officers to go with the title. John wrote his Sergeant just last month and transferred to Fort MacMurray. Amber had a few years under her belt, but Pat was almost as green as Cam.

Short staffed as they were, they rode one member per car and had the video system in the cars. Not much good in a fire fight, but the cameras had made more than one case for them.

Jim had worked through the case files and was considering starting on the reviews due on Amber and Cam in the next couple of weeks. He was rescued by Carol knocking on the door.

"There's a gentleman here to make a complaint," she said.

Jim set down his pen and followed her out to the front area. Her use of gentlemen may have had a little bit of exaggeration to it. The man stood probably a few centimeters over Jim's height,

29

but he was thin and his clothes hung on him like he'd once been much bigger. Grey hair fell in a tangle to just above the coat collar where it was cut raggedly. The man's beard almost reached his stomach and it had a couple of twigs and leaves caught in it. Jim thought the pants and jacket might be wool, but it was hard to tell.

"I'm Jim Dalrymple, acting Staff Sergeant," Jim said when he got to the window. "How may I help you?"

"Zeke Hamilton," the man said, "Someone's been messing with my claim markers."

"Do you want to come in back here and I'll take a report?"

Zeke just nodded and walked through into the office.

"Nice, looks better than the old set up, Grimwald had the detachment in his living room. It's hard to get folks to take you seriously when everything is covered with doilies. He knew what he was doing though. You couldn't fool Grimwald."

"I'd heard about those days. I'm happy to have the detachment." Jim led Zeke to the interview room and waved him to a seat. He took a seat that let him take notes on the desk without putting it between them. "Let me get the details out of the way first. You're Zeke Hamilton, and your birthdate?"

"I'm not sure," Zeke shrugged. "I think it was in the forties. My parents died in a fire and all the family records burned. Turned out they never registered me, probably 'cause I was born in a canoe on native land. Never saw a white face until I was five and got sent to my aunt's to go to school in the south."

"OK then, tell me about the problem with your claim markers."

"I have a claim a ways north of here. It's going to be the biggest mine this century. I got the claim file proper and marked on the ground. Never had a problem until last week. I was up getting some samples and found my marker had been moved a hundred meters west."

"How did you know it had been moved?"

"GPS coordinates," Zeke grinned. "I may be an old geezer, but I know a good thing when I see it. GPS works fine where I'm at so I have points marked at the edges of my claim."

"So GPS doesn't work all the time?"

"Nope, there're some places out there depending on a compass or GPS will kill you. I don't know what does it, but you

30

get turned around all backward. You have to follow the lay of the land or mark by the stars there."

"Could you show me on the map?" Jim asked, "It sounds like something important to know if I have to send my people up that way."

Zeke peered at the map for a bit.

"I'm not completely sure," he said, "but I think it's around here between these two lakes. I try to stay out of there. It's strange country in other ways too. Just crawling with spirit animals like the moose those damn fools shot a week back. Damn fools they may be, but they didn't deserve what they got."

"How do you know about that?" Jim asked, "We haven't made the details of the case public."

"Seen the pictures. The young men on the reserves, especially the more isolated ones, they pass them around. If the buggers weren't already dead, there'd be people out for their blood."

"What do the pictures show?"

"They show the fools posing with the white moose. Then there's the ones showing them hung and gutted with their hearts beside the moose. Nasty those ones."

"How did you get to see them?"

"Well, I'm just old Zeke, I could be as indian as them if I weren't white. They talk to me and I see things."

"I see," Jim looked at Zeke and remembered what Tim had said about him. "How would you suggest I go about getting copies of those photos?"

"I'll ask," Zeke said, "They'll likely give 'em to me. They like me, 'cause they know if I strike it big, I'll give them a big slice off the top. It's their land."

"That would be very helpful," Jim said. "Now to get back to your claim. I'm guessing you have registered it with the ministry so what good would moving the stakes do?"

"It could confuse the matter." Zeke frowned. "They argue I filed the wrong location with the mines people, then they can argue they should get a slice of whatever I find."

"How would they know where your claim is? Tim told me you're keeping that close to your chest."

31

"Damn right I am, but that's only the exact location. They could drop a drill bit down there and hit the bubble dead on. It's a big claim, they can look up where the claim is easy enough, but trying to find the bubble in all that rock and swamp is tougher."

"So, you think it's someone who knows a bit about prospecting?"

"I figure I know who it is, but I haven't any proof." Zeke leaned in close to Jim. "I got trail cameras set up now, and I'll get you proof."

"Could you give me coordinates of the cameras?" Jim asked, "If something happens I'd like to be able to send someone to the place without you disturbing anything."

"Give me your card and I'll email them to you." Jim handed Zeke a card and watched the man leave. His head was spinning a bit. He found an old-fashioned prospector who used email and GPS a little disconcerting. He wondered how much of Zeke was an act. For all his clothes looked dirty, the only thing Jim had smelled while they shared the interview room was spruce and tobacco.

Chapter Seven

Nothing like clients dying to drive a business down. Jack Fritz cursed the damn fools. There was no guarantee of getting a moose. He made it clear on his website. If there were guarantees, it would be shopping. He did his best and his guides did their best. The idiots had to go shoot a spirit moose and get themselves murdered. None of his guides would come back and his customers cancelled bookings as fast as they could.

Everywhere else in the world people had read the story and maybe thought 'too bad they shot the moose', or maybe 'too bad they got murdered for it. Jack bet not one of them thought 'too bad Jack Fritz was going to go bankrupt because of them'.

Jack loved this place. He'd helped build the lodge himself as his retirement present to himself. He'd invested smart and spent little. When everyone else was into big houses and big cars he'd stayed small. His ex-wife hadn't appreciated it, not until she saw the size of his investment account. She'd almost changed her mind then. But she'd have hated it here. She like the city same as he hated it. Instead they parted amicably. He'd given her a decent settlement and a promise she'd get the rest when he died.

"Sorry, Jane," he said, "looks like we'll both be a lot poorer after this." He considered calling her, but he didn't want to spoil her day. She probably just got home from some concert or party. She'd taken his advice and stayed small when everyone else went big, so she could still afford to have fun with her life.

Jim got up and walked through the lodge. Tim would come to pick him up tomorrow. Everything was closed down for the winter; the water off, the windows shuttered. Even if he had no bookings, he still had the lodge. Maybe he could tough it out next season. Offer a sale or two. It was still a prime location.

A knock on the door interrupted his thinking. A guest would help distract him from his problems. Sometimes some of the Cree hunters would drop in to chat, or ask him to get a message back for them. Sometimes he even let them use the satellite phone. Three dollars a minute for a dad to sing to his daughter on her birthday was a good investment when he came to guide for a season. Jack didn't understand the people who hated the Cree. They were people, some good, some not so much. He opened the door and let a young Cree man in.

"Can I get you a cup of tea?" Jack asked as he headed for the kitchen. The generator still ran and he had a jug of water to last him 'till morning. Enough for tea. He didn't feel the knife stab into through his back into his heart and died before he hit the floor.

Rivers looked around at the lodge; a pleasant enough building. They could have used something like this on the reserve. They didn't have it. They didn't have anything on the reserve. Nothing but drugs and violence and despair. If he'd been able to, Rivers would have moved the lodge to where it would do some good.

He found the fuel for the generator and poured it around the inside of the building then put trails to the outbuildings too. There were fuel drums in the shed with the swamp truck and quads. He tipped them over and watched the gas spill.

Back at the lodge he lit the fuel covering the floor. The fire spread quickly and enveloped the wood building in flame. Rivers moved to the edge of the woods and watched as the fire moved to the other buildings. The shed went up with a thump and flames leaping high into the air. He stayed until the fire died down to smoke and embers. Then he headed back into the forest. Other lodges in the area profited from taking hunting rights from his people. They'd be burning tonight too.

Roger had followed him the first night, then recruited people to help torch the lodges. Rivers hadn't expected that. The pictures of the sacrilege had gained them more followers. Soon they'd be an army. Soon the people who had stolen their land would know they were at war.

Chapter Eight

Jim stood and looked at the ashes of Jack's lodge. The fire crew had found a body in the kitchen area. It was no accident. He could see the fire trails to the outbuildings. The gas in the shed must have been tipped over because little was left of that building but splinters and the blackened hulks of the machinery.

It didn't make any sense. Nothing had been taken. All the machinery was accounted for. Jim had Dusty with him and as far as the guide could tell everything was there. Dusty found something else odd as well. While he checked the buildings, he'd found a track leading to the woods. He showed Jim.

"Right there." Dusty pointed at a spot on the ground. "Someone stood and watched the fire before walking away. I could follow the trail a little way, but I lost it when he crossed some rock".

"Show me." Jim checked his gun, thinking of the moose being skinned between Dusty's visits to the scene. No one attacked. Dusty pointed out the minute signs of passage which vanished at the large expanse of rock. The only new thing Jim learned was the trail went North.

"What's North of here?" Jim asked.

"Nothing," Dusty said, "just rock, tree and water until you run out of trees. There aren't any reserves on this line. They're all a little east of here where the big rivers are."

"So where would he be going?"

"I have no idea. A lot of us hunt this area, because it's good for moose. Mr. Fritz always welcomed folk who dropped in. He was always helpful and friendly. Not like some who bellyached we were taking all the game as if there weren't enough for everyone."

"Thanks, Dusty." Jim headed back toward the lodge. The crew had done everything they could which wasn't much. The body had been placed in a bag and loaded on Tim's plane. Jim climbed on and smelled the burnt flesh. The rest of the crew would fly out in shifts between Tim and a pilot who came up from Thompson to help.

Jim got back to his office and found a stack of paper work to do. He was deep into reports and evaluations when Carol knocked on his door. He looked up and saw her face was white.

"What's happened?" Jim had visions of accidents and death

"Tim needs to talk to you," she said, "Take your gear, you'll be going flying."

Jim grabbed his bag and walked out to find Tim standing in the office with tears on his face.

"What's wrong?" Jim asked.

"They're gone," Tim said. "All of them."

"What are gone?"

"The lodges." Tim took a deep breath, "all the lodges are burnt. I saw a smoke trail when I was bringing the last of the crew home. We flew over to check and found another lodge burnt to the ground. I dropped the crew in Spruce Bay and fueled up. I took a quick tour and found four more burnt out lodges. That's all six fly-in hunting and fishing lodges gone."

"Would there be people at the other lodges?"

"God, I hope not," Tim said, "but you never know. Someone might have stayed to do repairs or finish getting ready for winter. Some of them double as snowmobile lodges in the winter."

"So you're going to take me to check." Jim hefted his bag. "Let's go. Carol, call Division and let them know what's going on. We need some more people as soon as they can send them."

"Yes, Staff," Carol headed for the phone.

"Dispatch," Jim said into his radio, "SB 1, I'm going to check on multiple arsons, alert members in the field to take special precautions.

"Ten-Four SB 1," dispatch replied.

"We'll only have time to get to the nearest one before dark," Tim said. "We don't have great lights on the strip and I don't feel like flying to Thompson tonight."

"Are any of the lodges accessible except by air?"

"If you don't mind spending eight hours on a quad you can ride to the one we're headed to. The others have trails, but it

36

would be an overnight trip. One is on an island and you'd need a boat."

Jim climbed into his truck and followed Tim to the airstrip. The pilot checked his fuel level and did a quick walk around, then they strapped into the Cesna and took off. It wasn't a long flight. This lodge had a strip dozed in the woods not far from the lodge. They landed and walked to the burnt-out building. Jim walked around the edge of the building. The same fire tracks led to the outbuildings. He didn't see any bodies in the ashes. He'd get a fire crew up here to double check here and the other sites.

Without saying a word Jim followed the pilot back to the plane and they flew home.

Help in the form of a couple of helicopters from Natural Resources and hydro showed up the next day. Crews from Thompson flew out to each of the sites to evaluate the situation and look for bodies.

Jim stayed in the detachment and took reports as they came in. Three of the sites had no bodies; two dead at one, and they found a terrified man in the woods at the last site. They were bringing him in to be checked out at the hospital. Jim picked up his notepad and pen from his desk and walked around the outside of the mall to the hospital. He heard the helicopter approaching and watched it land.

The crew helped a large man out of the helicopter and walked him over to the emergency entrance. When the man saw Jim, he walked over to him.

He was dressed in camo that barely fit. The man was also covered with ash and soot.

"It's them indians," he said to Jim. "They're on the warpath." He reached into one of his pockets and handed a camera to Jim. "I got them on video." He turned and followed the rescue crew into the hospital.

"I don't know," one man said as he watched the rest go through the doors. "He showed me the video and it's mostly black. There's one place where you might be able to see a face. He told us he went out to pee and the indians came and kicked in the door. He stayed where he was and watched as they burned the place down. He happened to have his camera in his pocket so he recorded them until the battery died." The man shook his head.

37

"You might want to get him to stay a little quieter about the warpath thing. He won't make any friends accusing the First Nations of going to war."

"I'll see what I can do," Jim said, "but he's clearly in shock. He'll be hard to keep quiet short of locking him up."

He went into the hospital and let the staff know he'd like to interview the man when he was ready. While he waited, Jim reviewed the video on the camera. The rescue worker was right. It was mostly black. One bit looked like it might show a face, but it hard to tell on the tiny screen.

"Is there a computer I can hook this to for a better look?" Jim asked the woman at the admissions desk.

"There's a computer in the office there not hooked into the network yet. You could use that." She pointed to an office behind her.

Jim turned on the computer and waited for it to boot. He took the time to think about his next move. No possible way his understaffed detachment could handle the multiple arson cases. He was sure they were connected, but had no evidence to prove it. He really needed a scene of crime team for each site and a half dozen extra members to do interviews of the owners and managers of the lodges.

The computer finished booting and he put the SD card in the slot. He saw pictures of the man in camo fishing and hunting at different places. Jim scrolled down until he saw a video that looked black. He hit play.

He could hear the man's breathing and the roar of the fire. He must have taken a few minutes to think of the video. There was no picture of any one exiting the main lodge. Jim kept watching, the frame he looked for came near the end. A silhouetted figure wandered through the burning camp. It looked like they were checking to make sure everything was burning well. Just before the video ended the figure turned and the flames lit his face. Jim recognized it immediately. He'd had members looking for this man for the past week.

They'd found Roger Dupreis, and it looked like he was an arsonist as well as a murderer. The question now was who set the other fires? Dupreis must have been able to recruit more people to his cause with the pictures of the dead spirit moose. That worried Jim, he didn't think they'd be content with burning the lodges. There was more to come, but he needed to be able to convince Division.

Convincing Division of the need for help would also mean telling them he couldn't handle it on his own. It meant the end of his run at being Staff-Sergeant. In spite of the disappointment sitting heavy in his gut, he knew he needed to make the call.

"Hey, Jim," Brenda Cassidy stood in the door. "The man they brought in wants to talk to you."

"Be right there, Brenda." Jim ejected the card and found an envelope. He sealed the card in and placed the envelope in his pocket.

The man sat on the bed. He'd stripped at least a few layers of clothing off and didn't have as many bulges. Jim thought his eyes looked haunted. He knew how the man felt.

"I'm Jim Dalrymple, acting Staff-Sergeant of the detachment here in Spruce Bay. I'd like you to start by just telling me your story."

"I'm Norm Dardell," the man said, "I've being going to Cold Lake Lodge for at least ten years. Fred lets me stay a few days after moose season closes. I shoot a few grouse and try to get photos of moose. Never had any luck at that. When I was done, I'd call and get someone to pick me up." A tear ran down his cheek. "Best part of my life was spent there." He fell silent and Jim waited.

"Like I told the rescue guys, I needed to water a tree. The plumbing was shut down, so I went outside. I heard the door being kicked in, so I stepped around the tree into the dark. I just watched. I heard banging from inside the lodge, then I saw the flames. Someone came out and went to the outbuildings. He lit them on fire too. He didn't take anything, just burned it all. Fred had a brand-new side by side in the garage and it just went up in flames.

"You know, I've never been so scared in my life. I thought about my little camera and took the video. I know it's crap, but it was all I could do." More tears followed the track of the first one.

Jim handed him a tissue from the box and waited for Norm to work through his emotions.

39

"He left when everything was burning. I'm sure I saw paint on his face. I know I babbled to the rescue guys the indians were on the warpath. I'm sure they thought me a fool."

"He did have paint on his face," Jim said, "though I would ask that you not spread that fact around."

"The video?"

"There are some good images near the end. I'll get our people to work with them." He gave Norm the camera. "I'm going to hold on to the memory card for a while, but I'll get it back to you when we're done with it. Norm just nodded. Jim sat on the stool and rolled over to Norm.

"That's all I need from you as a cop, but I want to talk to you about your experience. I've been in that situation." Norm looked directly at Jim for the first time. "I can't tell you the whole story now, but I didn't think I'd live. Someone came and rescued me and the only problem I had was my hands are extra-sensitive to the cold. That and waking up with nightmares for months afterward. I'm lucky, I have access to some very good counsellors through the RCMP. I'm going to give you a card, and when you need to call someone to help you get through this, I hope you call them. My number is there too, and you can call me if you need to. It isn't weak to have panic attacks and nightmares. It just means you're human. Ask for help, and the sooner the better."

Norm took the card like it was made of gold. He put it carefully in his wallet.

"I'm an insurance salesman," he was. "The only reason I can afford that lodge is because Fred buys his insurance from me and gives me a deal. I go up there and pretend I'm tough and able to deal with anything. The rest of the time I wear a suit and tie and let my wife tell me what to do."

"Norm," Jim put his hand on the man's shoulder. "You are tougher than you think. Your video is going to be very helpful to us. You survived. Remember that, and when all this is done you'll have a story to tell your grandkids to make their eyes go wide."

"I'd like that," Norm smiled briefly. "The only thing my grandkids want from me now is money from my wallet."

"You take it easy. We'll get you back down to the city safe and sound. Use that card and you will be OK."

40

Norm shook Jim's hand, then hugged him. Jim hugged him back. The man was just beginning to learn how tough he was.

Once Jim was out of the room he called Cam.

"Cam, I'd like you to hang around the hospital and keep an eye on Norm. Make sure he gets safely back down to the city. Go with him if you have to but I want him back with his family safe and sound."

"Sure thing, Staff," Cam said, "I'm on my way over now."

Jim waited until Cam arrived before heading back to the detachment. He wrote up his notes and copied the video to his computer. He burned the rest of the pictures to a CD and left it with a note for Carol to mail it to Norm at his home address. He watched the video again and paused it to look at Roger Dupreis in his paint. It only took a minute to look up John's email in Ottawa and send him the video. John's specialty now was video enhancement. It was outside of proper channels, but it would be faster than doing it properly.

He went to another page and placed a request for a commendation for Norm. He thought it would help with the grandchildren. He had done everything he could think of to delay the inevitable. He picked up the phone and made a call to Division at a special number going straight to an office high up in the command. They told him over and over when they made him acting Staff-Sergeant. 'Call for help if you need it'. He'd also heard the stories of the people who'd called for help and been transferred somewhere quiet, safe and well off the track for promotion.

"Hello," he said when someone answered the phone, "this is acting Staff-Sergeant Jim Dalrymple of the Spruce Bay detachment. We have a crime beyond the scope of our detachment and I'm requesting special help from Division."

Damn, I really like it here. It's going to suck to have to move.

41

Chapter Nine

Ryley went back to school with Leigh. He'd spent three days with Jen and Joe. Joe took him out fishing and hunting rabbits. Ryley had been very excited and exhausted at the end of each day. Fortunately, he had no incidents, and Leigh was grateful for the rabbit stew they sent home with Ryley.

She knew Jim was up to his neck. She didn't know any more than the rest of the town, but everyone knew the lodges had burned and more than one person blamed the First Nations people. Tension in town hadn't been so high for more than a year. It didn't help loud mouths on both sides proclaimed the obvious guilt of the other side. Ellers pointed to the fires as proof indians were stealing his fuel. The Chief on the reserve just outside of town claimed the fires were an insurance scam meant to cash in on the lodges while blaming innocent First Nations people.

Leigh knew better than to comment on either opinion, though privately she sympathized with Mike Tremblant on the reserve. The Cree got blamed with no evidence other than a racist's overly loud mouth.

The bell rang and Leigh heard the students clomping up the hall toward her room. It had snowed a few centimeters last night so winter boots made an appearance.

"*Tansi,* class," Leigh said as they sat down. They listened through the announcements then Leigh started them on their math work. She wandered up and down the aisles to watch them and to force herself to focus. She was worried about Jim and her anxiety coiled close to the surface. She breathed deeply as she walked and soon was immersed in the instruction of her class.

Once math was done, they were ready for some lively discussion, so Leigh leaned against her desk.

"We've finished with Thanksgiving and harvest," she said. "What's next on the calendar?"

"Halloween!" several voices shouted.

"*Dia de muertos!*" Marc shouted.

"What's that?"

"Speak English," Sandra, a fourth grader said.

"Speak Cree." Sam, a Cree boy in third grade, retorted. The class laughed and Leigh waited for them to calm.

"*Dia de muertos*," Marc grinned broadly. "Day of the Dead."

"You mean like zombies?" Bill was a fourth grader who drew horror pictures whenever he had spare time.

"No, not zombies," Marc rolled his eyes. "We celebrate the people we love who've died and have a party in the cemetery and eat sugar skulls."

"Do you dress up?" Sandra asked.

"Sure, we paint our faces to look like skulls."

"Oooh," Bill said, "I like that."

"Can we do Halloween too?" Chelsea asked.

"Why not?" Marc said, "You do Halloween up here and we do *Dia de Muertos* in Mexico. I want to learn more about your Halloween."

"Can we?" The class turned to Leigh.

"I don't see why not," Leigh said, "You will need to figure out what you need for each. Find out what is similar and what is different. It is ten days before Halloween and *Dia de Muertos,* so you'd better get started."

Ms. Taladut stood at the door with a frown on her face. Leigh nodded to her then moved through the groups of children who made notes or looked up things in books or crowded around Marc as he told them about the Day of the Dead.

"It's not on the curriculum," Ms Taladut's fingers tapped on the door frame.

"It's on mine," Leigh said, "They are learning research skills, cooperation, they will discover new art techniques and we'll be talking about family origins and the importance of tradition. I suggest you go do your job and allow me to do mine."

"I forbid you to take this nonsense any further. You have the curriculum. You will follow it."

Leigh clenched her fists and tried to slow her breathing, but dark shapes flitted past the edges of her mind laughing at her.

"Go away," Leigh said. "Now."

43

"I am not going to stand here and allow you to continue to let your class run out of control." Ms. Taladut was almost shouting and Leigh could hear the whispers of the class behind her.

Leigh tried to say something but the shadows stole her words. The only sounds she had left were curses and she wasn't going to let them escape. Instead she closed the door in the acting Principal's face and forced a smile on her face as she walked to the front of the room. She could hear the pounding on the door as Ms. Taladut screamed at Leigh. *Good thing I locked the door, if that was the way the woman was going to talk in front of the class.*

She couldn't remember what she wanted to say to the class. Leigh sat at her desk and stared blankly at them. One of the girls, Chelsea, Amber's daughter, with beautiful black curly hair came and stood in front of her.

"Are you OK, Mrs. Dalrymple?" she asked. Leigh tried to answer but the words wouldn't come, instead tears started flowing down her face.

"I'm calling 911," Sandra announced. She went to her cubby and pulled a cell phone from her coat. Leigh wondered when Grade Four students starting carrying cells.

"Hello," Sandra spoke calmly into the phone, "Our teacher is sick and the Principal is crazy." She started to answer the questions the dispatcher asked. Leigh closed her eyes. It was out of her hands now. That was strangely comforting. The other children gathered around her and murmured encouragement. Leigh just let them. These were her kids and they were all good kids.

There was more noise at the door and it slammed open. Ms. Taladut started to enter with her finger pointed at Leigh. Mr. Kwali stood behind her looking apologetic.

"Stop," Sandra held out the phone like a gun. "I called the police and if you come in here they're going to shoot you." Leigh heard a siren approaching fast and Ms. Taladut paused in the door. Some of the children stayed with Leigh while the rest filled the space between Leigh and the Principal. They didn't say anything, but they wouldn't move either. The siren gave a final cough and Leigh heard the thud of boots coming up the hall. The police woman came up behind Ms. Taladut.

"Move please," Amber said and stepped past the Principal. The children let her through and closed up behind her.

"Can you tell me what's happening?" Amber asked Leigh. The children all started talking at once and Leigh let Amber sort through their stories. "It sounds like a panic attack," she said, and Leigh nodded. "Well let's get you out of here." Amber helped her up and led her toward the door. The children gave a chorus of 'get betters' as she went.

"Who's going to teach this class if she leaves?" Ms. Taladut asked.

"You're the principal," Amber said, "you'll think of something." She led Leigh past the dumbfounded woman and out into the hall. The last thing Leigh heard was Ms. Taladut trying to silence the shouted good byes of the class.

Give her hell, Leigh thought to her class. Then the doors shut behind her and cut off the sound.

***

Dr. Kwali checked her out at the hospital and sighed sympathetically.

"You've been under a lot of stress and this kind of thing is going to happen. You're lucky you are such a good teacher. Your class knew just what to do."

"I'm never going to be able to work like this," Leigh said. "What if it happens again?"

"What if it does? You'll deal with it. You aren't a danger to the class, far from it. Just take a few days off then you will be able to go back and be just fine."

Amber insisted on driving Leigh home. She told Leigh she'd already informed Jim everything was fine. The house felt empty with Ryley still at school and Jim at work. The light on the answering machine was blinking. Leigh almost decided to ignore it, but then thought it might be Jim.

"Leigh Dalrymple," Ms. Taladut's voice said out of the machine, "you are obviously incapable of teaching. You are suspended until further notice. I will discuss with the Board whether you should be allowed to return."

Leigh felt like crying, but then decided she was just too tired. She lay down on the bed and fell asleep.

She dreamed. She knew she was dreaming, but she couldn't wake up and soon the dream had her in its clutches and she forgot.

The wendigo sneered at her calling her weak. It inhabited Mr. Henry's body, but she could see the vague shape of it around him. Parts of him fell off and were replaced by dark smoke until the only thing left beside the smoke were his eyes, but they started to glow yellow. His smoke hands gripped Leigh's arms and sucked the warmth out of her. The voices in her head chattered with glee. Leigh tried to escape, but the cold made her weak. She couldn't move, she couldn't push away the voices.

Then a wolf bounded up and sunk his teeth into the wendigo and shook it like a rabbit. It came apart and the yellow eyes vanished. The wolf growled at the voices and they retreated in fear. Leigh huddled on the ground and the wolf came and curled up beside her.

"Ryley help," it said.

Leigh woke to find Ryley curled up beside her on the bed.

"My hero." She ran her fingers through his hair. Ryley stirred briefly and made a noise that might have been a growl. Leigh let her eyes close. She was safe now.

Chapter Ten

Georgia walked up and down her living room and ranted at her parents. She knew it wasn't their fault, but they were there.

"That woman is a menace," she shouted, "first she sets Ryley off in the schoolyard, then tries to blame Ryley for her stupidity. Now she's trying to make Mrs. Dalrymple crazy."

"I told you," her mom said, "sometimes people have panic attacks. It just happens."

"It didn't just happen." Georgia clenched her fists. "Maria told me Marc said she was yelling at Leigh and banging on the door. Sandra called the police! Then when she was gone Ms. Taladut yelled at the class and told them it was all their fault. She tried to teach them but she got everything all wrong. Half the class was in tears by lunch time! We have to do something. She told the class Mrs. Dalrymple was too sick to come back."

"There's nothing we can do," Georgia's mom said, "She's the Principal. It's her job to run the school."

"But she isn't running the school. She's wrecking it. Can't you do anything?"

"I don't know. It's up to the School Board."

"Why is it always someone else's job?" Georgia shouted at them and ran to the door. She put her coat and boots on and went out the door.

Why couldn't adults see? What Ms. Taladut did to Leigh was wrong. It was obvious. Everyone had excuses about it being someone else's job. Well let them, Georgia would do something about it, but she needed help.

Alastair didn't live very far from her home, but the night air was cold and damp. Georgia walked as fast as she could with her hands in her pockets. She had to be careful, cold air could start her coughing and she didn't need that right now.

Alastair answered the door when she knocked.

47

"Uh, hi," he said, "you want to come in?"

"Sure." Georgia stepped past him into the house.

"Ma," Alastair shouted, "Geogia's here."

"That's nice," an answer floated down from the upstairs.

"I think I could tell her Frankenstein was here and she'd just say *That's nice*. Come on, Sandra's downstairs. He led her down to a room with the largest TV she'd ever seen. Sandra was watching some show with a laugh track.

"Hi Georgia," she said without turning from the TV.

"Hi Sandra."

Alastair sat where he could look at Georgia and see the TV from the corner of his eye. Georgia tried not to let the larger than life faces distract her.

"Maria told me about today with Mrs. Dalrymple," Georgia said.

"It was horrible," Sandra said. "We were learning about the Day of the Dead and Halloween and Old Tell-you-what came and gave Mrs. Dalrymple the evil eye. She started telling her what she should teach and Mrs. Dalrymple was getting all upset. She closed the door in Tell-you-what's face. Then she looked all weird and she couldn't talk. I thought she was having a stroke so I called the police."

"Maria said Marc told her that you said the police were going to shoot Tell-you-what. That was brilliant."

"Yeah well, Mrs. Dalrymple was crying and couldn't talk and Tell-you-what was going to be mean to her. I had to do something."

"I think you were brilliant. Then Chelsea's mom came and took Mrs. Dalrymple to the hospital?"

"Yeah, she wasn't having a stroke, it was some kind of panic thing."

"If she had been having a stroke, you'd have saved her life."

"For real?"

"For real."

"So now what?" Alastair asked. "They won't be able to let Mrs. Dalrymple come back. What if she goes crazy and kills someone?"

"Mrs. Dalrymple is the best teacher I've ever had, but she has anxiety problems. She explained it all to us when I was in her

48

class. It isn't being crazy. It's like her brain doesn't always work right and she needs to rest and let it start working right again."

"Like rebooting my computer," Alastair nodded.

"I guess," Georgia shrugged.

"I don't want Old Tell-you-what teaching our class. She's mean. I'd rather have Mrs. Dalrymple anxious than her being mean."

"But if they don't let Mrs. Dalrymple back, you'll be stuck with her," Alastair said. "Sucks to be you."

"Maybe I'll just stay home." Sandra stuck her tongue out at her brother, "So there."

Georgia felt the idea land in her mind fully grown like a gift from the heavens.

"What if you did stay home?" She got up and paced around the room. "What if all the kids stayed home? They'd have to let Mrs. Dalrymple come back."

"We'd get in trouble," Sandra frowned. "They'd give us detention for a year."

"What if we *all* stayed home?" Georgia grinned broadly. "They can't give us all detention."

"Cool," Alastair pumped his fist.

"They call it a strike," Georgia said, "My dad told me about it. If everyone goes on strike, then they have to listen."

"So when do we start?" Sandra asked.

"Now," Georgia said. "Do you have a phone?"

All three of them had phones so they started calling their friends and telling their friends to tell their friends and brothers and sisters. There were two parts to the message. "Don't go to school, and don't tell the adults."

***

Ms. Taladut stood at the front of the class. She dreaded the bell. The horrible children would come in and ask questions and whine and complain. It was all that Dalrymple's fault. If she didn't spoil them so much, they'd have proper respect for authority.

The bell rang and she wiped her hands on her skirt. *Be firm* she told herself, *show no fear.* She didn't hear any approaching feet. She went out to the hall and looked down it. There were no children. One child pulled the door open and saw her.

"Oops." The girl stuck her tongue out at Ms. Taladut. She ran away giggling. Ms. Taladut walked down to the primary grades. The Kindergarten children were there in their usual chaos, but the Grades One and Two missed almost half their students. Mr. Jackson and Mrs. Hall taught the remainder as if nothing strange were going on. She walked the other way and found Mr. McRoy in the hall with a bemused look on his face.

"I believe today sets a new record low for attendance," he said. "At least I'll be able to get caught up on my paperwork." He went back into his room.

Ms. Taladut found Mlle Dupuis sitting in her chair reading a book.

"Where are the children?" Ms. Taladut asked.

Mlle Dupuis looked around as if she'd just noticed there were no students in her class.

"If I had to hazard a guess," she said, "I'd say someone has organized a strike; very effectively too."

"A strike?"

"You know, common action by a group to achieve a common goal, usually a matter of refusing to work, or in this case refusing to be made to work."

"But why?"

"I'm sure they will let you know. Or if you're in a hurry, you could go ask them."

"Ask them?"

"Certainly, I saw a bunch them going into the mall."

Ms. Taladut walked down the hall to the door marked emergency exit. *Well if this wasn't an emergency...* She pushed the door open and the fire alarm went off. When she stepped through the door she saw the faces of children and adults look at her. She squared her shoulders and walked up to the children.

"Whose idea was this?" she asked. She didn't expect an answer so was taken aback when Georgia stood up.

"That would be me, Ms. Taladut."

"You know you can get into a lot of trouble for this?"

"Really." Georgia tilted her head. "Why?"

"You are supposed to be in school and all your friends too. You aren't allowed to just decide not to go to class."

"We didn't just decide not to go to class," Georgia said. "We're on strike."

"That's ridiculous," Ms. Taladut walked up to Georgia. "You get yourself back to class right now."

"No," Georgia sat down with the rest of her class, though somehow Alastair and Sandra sat on either side of her.

Ms. Taladut reached down to pull the little snippet to her feet.

"I hope you aren't planning to use force on that child," Constable Amber McKendal spoke from where she leaned against the wall watching.

"Officer tell these children to go back to school this instant!"

"Children," the constable said, and Ms. Taladut was sure she winked at the little brats, "Go back to class."

"NO!" the children shouted.

The constable shrugged.

"I'd arrest them all," she said, "but the jail isn't big enough to hold them. As long as they behave themselves, I'm not going to do anything."

"What do you want?" Ms. Taladut said to Georgia. She had to snap her teeth down on the words she wanted to say.

"We know you yelled at Mrs. Dalrymple yesterday and she had a panic attack. We aren't going back to school until she does."

"She's an incompetent teacher and a menace," Ms. Taladut clenched her fists behind her back. "I am not going to let her back in the class, and if you don't get back to school I'm going to fire her right now!"

To Ms. Taladut's horror, Georgia just shrugged and turned her back. Ms. Taladut looked around for support, but didn't see any friendly faces. Mr. McRoy walked out from behind her followed by Mlle. Dupuis.

"I have to admit to a certain sympathy for the children. Do you mind if I join you?" he asked the crowd of children.

"NO!" they shouted. He sat down on a bench and relaxed. Mlle Dupuis didn't say anything, but sat beside him. The fire alarm cut off abruptly and the door behind her clanged shut.

"You can't think this will change my mind?" Ms. Taladut shouted. No one answered, but the children just stared at her. She

51

turned to leave, but the door had locked again. She had to walk around to the door of the school.

The next day not a single student or teacher showed up in either the Elementary or High School side of Spruce Bay Community School.

Chapter Eleven

Jim looked out at the mob of children in the mall and didn't know whether to laugh or cry. They were there for Leigh. Students who had never met her sat chatting or playing on their cell phones. Amber had suggested strongly if they remained orderly he just leave them alone. He noted the teachers who sat drinking coffee also kept an eye on the crowd.

The real ring leader was Georgia. Somehow she'd put this together overnight and challenged authority with a calm and poise belying her age. She and her friends wandered through the mall providing some conversation here, a little trouble shooting there. Anna taught beading with the help of Mai Dupreis, Fran's sister. Tom made snowshoes and had his own group of watchers. Steve tied flies. Jim shook his head, right there was the future of Spruce Bay. He figured it was in good hands.

"They'll be landing in about twenty minutes," Carol said.

"OK," Jim sighed and straightened his belt. "It doesn't look like they will riot today. I had better go meet the brass."

"Jim," Carol stopped him with a hand on his arm. "You are doing the right thing. Not everyone sees asking for help as weakness. It can be a sign of wisdom."

"We'll see, won't we?" Jim headed out into the cold rain. Jim thought snow would be better, but not until after the plane landed. He climbed into the truck and drove out to the landing strip. He had Hank out there with the bus he used to take people into Thompson who didn't have their own cars. Pat sat on the bus ready to welcome the task force.

The bus would be warm and dry. Jim hadn't been told who they were sending. After a couple of phone calls, he had been told only that a task force would come and to give them his full cooperation. Since he'd asked for them, he was determined to do exactly that.

53

The lights of the airplane appeared through the rain and it made an easy landing. The plane taxied close to where the bus and Jim's truck waited. He grabbed an umbrella and went to meet the task force.

The door cracked open and dropped to become the stairs. The first person out of the airplane was John. Jim grinned and shook his hand.

"Why don't you head over to the bus. No sense in standing about in this weather."

"I had to be crazy to come here this time of year," John slapped Jim on the back.

Jim didn't recognize the other members who climbed down. He directed them to the bus where they would be comfortable. The final person out was an older man in an Inspector's uniform. Jim saluted.

"Welcome to Spruce Bay, sir," he said. "I'd give you the full speech, but we'd die of hypothermia before I was done. If you'd join me in the truck, I'll fill you in."

"Thank you, Staff Sergeant," the Inspector said, "Lead on," Jim tried to shelter them both with the umbrella, but the rain soaked him enough he had to towel his face off before he drove.

"Good to find a man who put common sense ahead of ceremony," the Inspector grinned over at Jim. "I'm Wilf Grenfell. The rest of the introductions can take place where it is comfortable."

Jim put the truck in gear and led the way back to the mall. He parked and they walked the short distance to the detachment. Pat brought the rest of the group in and Hank waved as he drove away.

"This way." Jim waved to the group. "We don't have space in the detachment for a group your size, so I've arranged for you to use a store front." He led them to the store Sandra had used for her crafts before moving away. It still had the chairs and tables and other furniture. He'd had the mall staff cover the windows with white paper. He decided he would ignore the mob of children and people in the mall. What he didn't take into account was whether they would ignore him.

A murmur ran through the crowd as they saw the group of uniformed RCMP officers enter the mall. Someone, probably

Georgia stood and soon the entire group was standing. Another person started clapping and the task force walked to their office to a standing ovation.

When the last person had come in. Jim turned to face them.

"I want to thank you for coming. That's the community of Spruce Bay out there and they thank you for coming. This is your headquarters. If you need something, talk to me and I'll find it for you. We have accommodations at the apartments for you that have cooking facilities. We don't have a restaurant in town, but if you don't want to cook there are lots of people who would be happy to feed you."

"I am sure they weren't expecting us," Inspector Grenfell said, "What are they doing out there?"

"The children are on strike protesting the unfair treatment of one of their teachers," Jim said. "One of the children started it. As long as they behave themselves, I'm not going to interfere."

"Good man," the Inspector slapped him on the shoulder. Jim's shoulder looked likely to take a beating over the next while. "Let's get down to business. Janice, see if you can get some tape and put the maps up the window. John, you know this place, can we get the network hooked up in here? I want it hard wired if possible. The rest of you set up your areas wherever you can find space. Save a corner for me. Play nice." He looked at Jim. Is there a place we can grab a coffee and talk?"

"There's the Coffee Shop just down the way,"

"Hey, what am I supposed to do with these knitting needles?" Someone called from the back.

"You could always knit me a sweater," Janice said as she taped a map on the window. Jim followed the Inspector out to the sound of laughter.

They walked along the mall toward the Coffee Shop, Georgia came up to Jim.

"How is Mrs. Dalrymple today?" she asked.

"She's doing better," Jim said, "but she's afraid coming here would be too much for here. Why don't you drop by the house later and say hello? She'd like that."

"Thanks, Sergeant Dalrymple." She looked at the Inspector. "Welcome to Spruce Bay, sir."

"Thank you." The Inspector nodded at her. "I'm guessing you're the chief organizer here."

"I have my friends to help," she said, "We're a team."

"Good." His hand twitched as he stopped himself from slapping her shoulder. "Carry on."

Jim showed him to the booth at the back of the Coffee Shop and brought two coffees over.

"I'm glad you're here, sir," he said.

"That makes you a sensible man." The Inspector added creamer to his coffee. "You asked for help, and you've got it. It looks like you've given us a good set up to work from. So, this is how it is going to play out. You're the Staff-Sergeant here. You run the detachment and do your job. You let us do ours. If you learn something which might be helpful, you let us know. If I think it will be helpful to tell you what we learn, I'll let you know. Mostly John is going to be the liaison between our offices. Any problem so far?"

"No sir," Jim said, "That's pretty much what I'd hoped for. With you carrying the ball on the arson, I'll be able to manage the rest."

"You didn't mention you're short staffed."

"No sir, I didn't, my staffing isn't your problem. Six lodges burning down with three dead people is your concern. I don't want to distract you. I've managed for the last six months; I'll manage a while longer."

"Look, Staff-Sergeant, I like you, so I'll be honest with you. A lot of people they call for help, then they resent the help when it comes, or they want us to solve a lot of problems that aren't what they asked us to solve. You do your job and let us do ours and I'll make sure you come out smelling like a rose. Get in my way and I'll bury you."

"Understood, sir." Jim sipped at his coffee. "I'll give you a quick synopsis of what I know so far so you can do what you need to do. If you have questions, ask. We had two American hunters, nice guys by all accounts, come up to do a moose hunt. It was the trip of a lifetime for them. They shot a white moose. The Cree believe white animals are spirit messengers, sacred in other words. Constable Darren can probably explain better. As far as we can tell their guide, a Roger Dupreis killed them, then hung

56

and gutted them like animals before just walking away leaving everything behind. Guns, equipment, everything. The only thing missing that we could tell was a memory card from a camera. We found the camera. I have reason to believe Roger Dupreis is using the pictures of the hunters with the moose to recruit other people to his cause.

"Six lodges were burned down the same night. They are in a two hundred kilometer circle, so it took some careful coordination. The evidence at the scenes suggests the arsonists walked into the camps. I didn't see any evidence of mechanical transport. There was a survivor at one of the lodges, He's back in the city, but I have his full statement and he'll go to meet your people if they have more questions. Norm took some video of one of the arsonists. I'm thinking since John is here, you've seen the video. From pictures of Roger Dupreis, I'm certain the man in the video is him."

"You left out one Mr. Ralph Ellers," the Inspector said. "What can you tell me about him?"

"He's the owner of the airstrip where you landed. He's accusing the Cree people generally of stealing his fuel. The only evidence we've found is a few footprints and a cut lock. He's also been a loud voice shouting the 'indians' are dangerous and should be dealt with. I'm thinking he wouldn't be adverse to just exterminating them."

"That would explain the complaint against your Constable Darren Little. Apparently, the constable stopped him when he was driving ever so carefully, then berated him and threatened to scalp him if he didn't leave the indian lands alone. After that the Constable wrote him a speeding ticket and drove off cursing at him." The Inspector's tone of voice made it clear Jim had no need to defend his Constable. "There isn't a hole deep enough for the likes of Mr. Ellers, but make sure your Constable stays out of his way. No more traffic stops unless there is imminent threat to life and limb. I don't want a three-ring circus happening around us while we work."

"I will pass that suggestion on to Constable Little."

"We are going to get along just famously." The Inspector leaned back. "John's been telling us your wife is a great cook. If she's up to it, I would love to meet her."

57

"She is well enough for a dinner for you and the whole task force, she is just concerned that her showing up here will set off events she won't be able to handle."

The Inspector nodded and sipped his coffee.

"While I'm waiting for the crew to finish all the hard work, how about you tell me about the case a couple of years back, Anne told me it was a wendigo."

"Well," Jim said, "yes and no…"

Chapter Twelve

Jim hadn't realized how frustrating it would be to have the task force take over the investigation of the arsons. It became like having an itch he couldn't scratch. To distract himself he pushed his detachment to get back to as close to standard as they could manage. That meant having an officer out on patrol at least during the day times.

Cam was back from escorting Norm home and reported he'd personally reinforced Norm's hero status with his family. Jim watched him talk to Darren and apparently, they came to some kind of agreement, because there were no more arguments. Jim set up three shifts, Cam and Pat, Darren and Amber formed shifts which rotated evening and morning. Jim patrolled through the day while Carol worked in the office. He still needed more officers, but he wasn't going to complain while the Inspector and the task force busted their tails next door.

Leigh had made a brief appearance at the mall, and to her surprise hadn't fallen apart. The School Board decided not to be cowed by the student protest and refused to reinstate her. The parents were supporting the protest now and brought snacks and supplies to the mall. From what Jim could see, the kids learned more now than they ever had in the school. After the first ovation, they didn't give the new officers any more attention than anyone else got.

Jim climbed into his truck to patrol for a few hours. The weather stayed damp and sloppy. He couldn't decide if it was raining or snowing. He drove out to the reserve, Spruce Bay Cree Nation. The chief had been complaining of a lot of petty theft. Jim drove up and down the streets more or less at random. The housing wasn't as good as in Spruce Bay, even on the Grid side of the town. Windows were plywood or screens. Graffiti covered every available surface - depressing. He drove for a couple of

59

hours and then on the way out of town he saw something that made him pull over and scrape the snow off the back of the SBCN sign. A white moose had been spray painted over all the other graffiti. He took a couple of pictures with his cell phone and forwarded them to John.

He drove back to Spruce Bay. It made sense they were recruiting in SBCN, but it still unnerved him. These were people he'd served for the past two years; relatives of people he counted as friends. He worried the divisions which had begun healing were going to get torn open again.

Just as he reached town a brown Escalade fishtailed out on the road in front of him and took off toward the airstrip. He didn't know why Ellers was in such a hurry, but he didn't feel like dealing with the man. He let it go and turned back in toward town.

He hadn't got there when dispatch came on.

"SB 1," dispatch said.

"SB 1, go ahead."

"Report of a robbery in progress at the airstrip. Please attend."

"Ten-four," Jim turned around and put his siren on. If Ellers could be that fast in his Escalade, Jim would match his time in the truck. He pulled up to the airstrip and saw the Escalade with door open and Ellers nowhere to be seen.

"My twenty is the airstrip," he said, "any update?"

"Negative, SB 1."

"I'm getting out to investigate. Switching to channel four, maintain radio silence."

"Ten-four SB 1. Channel 4."

Jim loosened the gun in his holster and tried to figure where Ellers might have gone. Probably toward the fuel depot. He pushed his way through what was definitely snow now, and tried to see the fuel tank. Being white it vanished into the snow fall. Jim wondered how Ellers had seen the fuel tank never mind a thief.

He reached the tank and saw the lock was cut off again. He left it there for now. To his left and rear was the runway. Unlikely someone would go that way. To the right stood the shed and the vending machine. They weren't likely either. If the thief was on foot how were they getting the fuel away? They needed a quad with a trailer, or maybe a side by side, even a pickup. He hadn't passed a vehicle coming here, so they would have to have gone away from him. What was behind the airstrip? A fence, and on the other side the town landfill. It was possible someone had cut a hole in the fence and drove through. He couldn't recall if they'd checked the fence.

The snow stung his face and his hands started to ache. The thin gloves he had on were no match for the damp cold. If he wasn't careful they'd turn into balls of pain and be useless for days. Jim kept going. He needed to find Ellers. He'd worry about the thief later. If Ellers was injured out here he wouldn't last the night. Jim wasn't ready to start shouting for him yet.

A figure leaped out of the snow screaming and swinging a club. Jim pulled his gun and side stepped the attack. He tripped his attacker and watched him go down. Not a club, but a huge pair of bolt cutters.

"Freeze!" Jim shouted.

"Damn you stupid incompetent fool." Ellers picked himself up off the ground and glared at Jim. "You let him get away."

"Who?" Jim lowered his gun.

"The thief you idiot. I chased him up this way. Some damned indian." He picked up the bolt cutters. "I found these by the fence." He walked away back toward the truck. Jim holstered his gun and followed. Ellers threw the bolt cutters into the back of the Escalade and sped away. Jim climbed into the truck and peeled his gloves off.

"SB 1," he said, "All clear.'

"Ten-four SB 1."

Jim sat and let his hands warm up slowly. Ella had taught him sudden changes in his hand temperature would cause trouble. Slow was better. The others might laugh, but Jim was going to carry his full winter gear from now on.

As soon he could hold a pen, Jim made some notes. When he'd finished, he headed back to the detachment. A shape moved in the snow, but even though he stopped and watched for a while he didn't see it again. Probably his imagination.

He headed back to town. The weather was getting worse and he had to take it slow. He parked in front of the detachment and shook his hands and arms out before going inside the detachment.

"Inspector would like to see you," Carol said. Jim couldn't decide if she looked worried. He just nodded. He hung his coat in his office then headed over to the task force. Leigh waved at him from where she sat reading a story to a mixed group of children and teens.

The store front had been transformed. Maps of the surrounding area covered the walls and windows with hieroglyphic marks on them. Cables ran across the ceiling and dropped down to computers. The team huddled around a computer at the back. John pointed to the Inspector's corner and shook his head slightly. Trouble.

"Staff-Sergeant," the Inspector said without looking up from a folder on his desk. "I thought I made it clear I didn't want Ellers causing me problems."

"You did, sir."

"He was banging on our door demanding to speak to me." The Inspector looked up, frowning at Jim. "I can't have that, not good for security. He claimed you almost shot him."

"That is correct, sir."

The Inspector let a smile show ever so slightly on his face.

"If you are given another opportunity, you might want to consider pulling the trigger. It will be less trouble than if he bothers me again. Understood?"

"Yes, sir."

The Inspector waved his hand at the chair.

"Sit down and tell me about it."

Jim sat and explained the events at the airstrip, to the Inspector's delight.

"I probably would have shot the bastard, you did well to trip him and disarm him. You're letting him push you around though. There's no way he should have just walked away without you putting a scare in him. You don't want to be a hard ass, but you have to make sure you get the respect your position deserves." The Inspector leaned back and thought for a minute. "What was he doing at the airport in this weather? I think it's a bit fishy."

"I didn't see a vehicle and no tracks by the depot, of course in this weather they wouldn't last two minutes. He came from where the fence separates the airport from the landfill. It is possible a quad may have come from the landfill through a hole in the fence. It would still be awkward to transport any fuel. By the time they'd finished, stealing the fuel would cost more than just paying for it."

"So we're thinking that Ellers is trying to pull something over our eyes?"

"I've considered it, but I doubt he'd get much if any insurance out of stolen fuel since he'd have to document the inventory against sales and show the difference and he'd still have to convince them it was stolen."

"Maybe I'll put Mr. Ellers on my radar. He deserves if for annoying me. Now what can you tell me about Zeke Hamilton?"

"I think a lot of the back woods thing is an act. He was in my office for an hour and he looked properly unwashed, but he didn't have the smell. Tim Hadstadt, our pilot, suggested Zeke has several university degrees and speaks seven languages. He uses modern technology as well as anyone else I know. I think he uses the look to let him keep his cards close to his chest."

"We went looking for him since your report mentions him seeing pictures of the moose being used for recruiting. Couldn't find him."

"I think he spends as much time out in the bush as he does in town. I'll let you know if I see him. He's supposed to email me copies of those pictures, but I haven't got them yet. Speaking of moose pictures though," Jim pulled out his cell phone and showed the Inspector the white moose graffiti. "I saw this today while I was patrolling."

"So?" the Inspector asked, "What am I looking at?"

"As I'm sure you know, gangs used graffiti to mark their territory. It is the same here. This is new, and it was on top of the other gang tags. Under normal circumstances that would be an invitation to a war. I'm wondering if they are recruiting in the gangs and this is a sign they're on board."

"You might be right." The Inspector rubbed his chin. "We'll keep an eye on it. Do you have anybody in the gangs who could tell us for sure?"

"The Cree gangs are hard to turn. The wendigo thing also involved the gangs. I'll put the word out, but unless we get lucky it will be a challenge."

63

"You look like a man who likes a challenge," the Inspector said. "You're local, so you have an advantage over us. Do what you can, and let me know what you learn."

Chapter Thirteen

Inspector Wilf Grenfell watched Jim walk out of his office and sighed. The poor bastard didn't stand a chance. This investigation of the arsons wasn't going anywhere. The video of Dupreis in war paint had lit a fire under some people in Ottawa and they put together a high-powered task force and sent them to Spruce Bay to uproot what might be a First Nations' terrorist threat. Wasn't the first such task force. Even if Jim hadn't called they would have shown up and taken over. His call just made it easier.

What would doom Jim was they hadn't learned anything new. They had fancy maps; they'd been to the scenes. Autopsies of the victims showed the three bodies had died before they burned. But the perpetrators had just vanished into the wilderness. Not a peep out of them. None of their people in the reserves had seen the photos this Zeke Hamilton mentioned. The white moose graffiti bore investigating, but it was easy to make a stencil and put white moose all over the place. One person could cover the town.

If they had to pack up and go home without anything to show for it, Ottawa would have to blame someone and it wouldn't be Wilf. That left Jim, which was a damned pity because Wilf liked the man. They needed more members like him. Too bad this mess was going to drag him down.

Wilf went out to check on his crew.

"Anything new?"

"There's a little chat on the radical boards. Nothing definitive. Someone mentions not dissing the WM, but on the whole, it's the usual crap. Nothing centered in this area. Most of the radicals are where industry intersects native land claims." Janice looked at him and shrugged.

"We have confirmation the paint on Dupreis is probably war paint. It is very individualized and interpretations change and

65

shift, but they can't think of any other reason for painting up." Pete rolled his eyes.

"I have people watching for the white moose graffiti, but nothing definitive yet." John took his turn reporting no news. The team didn't like the lack of information and action any more than Wilf did.

"I'm going to go talk to some of the rabble," Wilf said. "We need some new sources of information and we aren't getting them here. I want you in civvies, don't hide you're RCMP, but don't advertise it either. Listen and see if you hear anything that sounds like it's worth flagging. Listen particularly for any talk of gangs or white moose. I want to hear what people are saying about Ellers too. No questions, no fuss. I don't want to spook anyone. John, you hold the fort here."

The team split up and headed for the apartments. Jim had arranged a couple of trucks for them. The five headed out on the fishing trip would fit well enough.

Wilf wandered out into the mall and looked for Georgia. The crowd was dispersing quickly, maybe he should have waited until tomorrow. He shrugged, it didn't matter, a few more days and Ottawa would pull the plug. He saw the girl talking with a group of kids about her age. They were a mix of Cree and white. Interesting. He meandered through the mall, looking at what little was on display in the windows.

"… patrol tonight. There's some kids running about. No graffiti yet, but we should know who they are at least. This strike is going better than I thought, but if there is any trouble, we'll get our heads torn off. Maria, Marc if you stick with the new kids, anyone who came since last year. Don't get heavy with them, just let them know we're around and we'd rather be friends than not. Tom, Steve see if your brothers have heard anything about people making trouble in town. This is someone's turf so they may know if someone is marking it up. Anna, I'd like you to come with me and we'll do walkabout."

"What about me?" That sounded like an older boy. Wilf hid a smile, probably trying to hide a crush on Georgia.

"You and Sandra are into the texting and chat thing. Just listen, see if anyone is bragging or hinting."

"About what?"

66

"About anything." Georgia sounded a bit sharp there. She obviously expected her crew to keep up with her. Wilf wondered what Ottawa would think about putting a twelve-year-old on the payroll.

The meeting disbanded and Wilf sat looking at the display in the library. He felt someone sit beside him and looked over at Georgia. She was sizing him up.

"What do you want?" she said.

"What makes you think I want anything?"

"You don't look like the type to be reading the newest romances," She waved at the window in front of them. "but it is a good place to listen in on conversations and watch what is going on."

"Is it now?"

Georgia made a face at him. It came and went so quickly he wasn't sure what he'd seen. He had the impression he'd dropped a notch or two in her opinion.

"I'm not some stupid kid." The sharpness evident in her voice. "I knew you were listening. I wanted you to know we take care of our community."

"So what happens when you catch someone?"

"We aren't vigilantes, if that's what you're asking. Most of the trouble comes from kids who are bored. We can help them find something constructive to do. This is about making a better community; you can't do that by force."

Wilf found himself nodding. He decided he needed a change in tactics. No one would put anything over on this one. He wondered if the other adults in town knew just how scary she was. Probably not.

"I need your help," he said. "We are looking for information and we aren't finding it. You have a network in place that could be very productive."

"What do I get out of it?"

"You get the pleasure of serving your community."

Georgia snorted and rolled her eyes.

"Nice try," she said, "I'll help you, but you need to make sure Sergeant Dalrymple doesn't get blamed for this mess."

Wilf raised his eyebrows. "What makes you think --"

67

"That's twice." She frowned at him. "Treat me like stupid kid a third time and I walk."

"I will do what I can," Wilf said, "somebody needs to take responsibility."

"I don't want to lose them." For a moment, she sounded like a normal kid about to tear up. "Mrs. Dalrymple is the best teacher I've ever had, and Sergeant really cares about what he's doing. He shouldn't be punished for it."

"You know how dangerous it is to care though, don't you?" Wilf said. "No promises, but I will do my best to deflect the worst of what's coming down the pipe."

"How long?"

"Another couple of days with nothing new and Ottawa will be frothing at the mouth. No manufacturing crap either or the deal's off."

"It will be Halloween in six days. If there is going to be trouble it will be on Halloween. Sergeant always has all hands on deck the whole day and night. The one before him did too."

"The wendigo thing started on Halloween."

"Yeah, anyone stupid enough to have an axe in their display is going to find it's gone missing."

"Right," Wilf sat and calculated for a few moments. "I think I can hold off the wolves until Halloween."

"That's what we call ourselves," Georgia bared her teeth at him. "We're the Wolves of Spruce Bay. Do you have a number I can text you at?"

Wilf gave her his card and wrote a number on the back.

"This is my private cell. You get information, you text me. Don't give the card to anyone else."

Georgia put the card in a pocket and zipped it up. Wilf had the feeling she wouldn't look at it again.

"One last thing." Wilf caught her eyes. "These people I'm after. They're dangerous. They've killed at least five people and maybe more. They won't care you're just a kid. If they catch you, you're dead. I don't want that on my conscience, so nothing stupid. Here me?"

"Yes, sir."

Georgia got up and he watched her transform back into a normal twelve-year-old kid. She ran over to the girl she'd called Anna and the two of them went off whispering and laughing.

Wilf walked back to the office. He needed to plan how to cover Jim's ass. That was one kid he didn't want mad at him. She was going to be far too useful to disappoint.

Chapter Fourteen

Georgia pretended to the others she'd just been talking with the old RCMP guy about stuff because she was interested in the force. That part was true. She hated playing the psycho kid, but she wanted to protect Sergeant Dalrymple. This guy was the only one here who could do that. Not that Jim would thank her for it.

If she was honest with herself, she had just the slightest bit of a crush on the Sergeant. Too bad he was the same age as her parents and married to her favourite teacher. Alastair mooned about her. He was nice enough, but so slow! Though to be truthful, since she was in mood - *everyone* was slow.

She arranged to meet with Anna after supper, then went home. Her dad wore one of her new dresses. She looked stunning. Georgia was glad she was going out. He was going to try and seduce her mother again. It was painful to watch. Maybe she should just tell her dad that being a better looking woman than mom wasn't earning him any points. She didn't know what to suggest in its place.

Her dad was a woman in a man's body. Georgia had never had a problem with it. Her little brother was clueless. He'd grown up with two women and called them both mom. He would be in Mrs. Dalrymple's class next year. Or he would be if Georgia could save her job.

She decided again to keep her advice to herself. Unless she had a different strategy, she didn't think either Dad or Mom would appreciate her interference.

Georgia ate supper and barely noticed it. Her mind planned how to keep her side of the bargain she'd made with the old guy. After putting on the psycho kid act, she didn't think he would buy any attempt at *I'm just a kid*. She needed results and results meant risks. The scar on her hand ached. It always did when she contemplated something stupid.

Georgia went out into the night with coat, hat, scarf and boots. Her mitts were gauntlets reaching up to her elbow. Though she was covered from head to toe, the outfit proclaimed to anyone in the know she was the leader of the Wolves. She'd chosen the name in defiance of the wendigo's wolf pack, but now she wished she'd chosen something a little less aggressive. Some kids joined the group thinking they took a much more active role in running the community. Mostly they did what Georgia called walkabout. They just observed. Who was running wild? Who had parents that didn't care? What graffiti was showing up? The kids who thought it boring soon went on to other things.

Georgia put the information together and occasionally tracked down a particular troublemaker to offer some suggestions about more positive ways of expressing themselves. Now she wished they were a little more active. Talking to some of the kids on the fringe might give her information on what the gangs were doing. They knew gang members who were older siblings or even parents.

What she planned to do instead was visit a hangout. The Wolves knew it was there and they chose not to interest themselves. Even would-be gang bangers deserved some place they could be themselves without interference. It was part of an unwritten truce. She and her friends stayed away from the hangouts, and the kids at the hangouts left the wolves alone.

Georgia knew she had a reputation because she had trapped the wendigo's wolf pack. Her voice still rasped a little and her hand ached where a wolf had sliced it open. She also knew she was lucky. It could have been much worse. She succeeded because the wolves were easily led and not very smart. The kids at the hang outs were different. Much smarter and they wouldn't be easily fooled.

Georgia was going anyway and she knew Anna would give her heck for it. That was the price of taking risks. Your friends told you they disagreed. Georgia could deal with it.

She saw Anna waiting for her under the streetlight, also dressed as warmly as possible. It was one of Georgia's conditions for being part of the group. Dress warm, stay in the light, don't confront, don't fight, report only when absolutely necessary to the authorities. Georgia was about to break most of her own rules.

71

"Hi, I made something for you." She handed Georgia a tiny leather bag on a shoelace. "I had a feeling you might need it." Georgia put it on without comment. If she was the leader of the pack, Anna was their wise woman. She'd been trained by her kohkom until she died. Now she waited patiently for her next teacher to appear.

"Thanks," Georgia said. "You were right."

"So what crazy stunt are you planning tonight?" Anna asked.

"I thought we might swing by the shed for some conversation."

"So that's why you sent the boys walkabout."

"I don't need anybody getting protective and upping the ante."

"Right, and if the guys at the shed up the ante for you?"

"The risk is mine. You stay far enough back to escape if you need to. I'll take whatever bruises are coming to me."

"What if they decide to give you more than bruises?"

"No kid has been involved in killing someone since the wendigo. I'm hoping no one plans on changing that tonight. I don't think it is a huge risk."

Anna shook her head, but started walking toward the equipment shed which used to hold gear for maintaining the trails running through and around the town. Now it was the hang out of choice during bad weather. They walked in silence. Georgia planned strategy. She didn't know what Anna was thinking. One of the reasons she liked Anna so much was she wasn't transparent. Not like the boys, especially Alastair.

To reach the shed they had to leave the road and walk along one of the paths. Lots of footprints led the way. At least they wouldn't arrive and find no one there. Georgia felt her stomach clenching and her hand was aching. They stepped off the road and onto the path. The darkness surrounded them like a live thing. First rule down.

After a few minutes of feeling their way along with their toes and hands, they could see the outline of the path. Georgia led the way now. She could see the light from a fire in a garbage can.

"Wait wherever you are comfortable." She told Anna. "Don't try to rescue me if it gets bad. Just leave. If it gets really bad, you know who to call." She walked forward into the light of the flame. She could feel Anna stop behind her. Georgia walked up to the barrel and let the warmth seep through her clothes. The night held damp more than cold and she appreciated the heat.

"What the fuck are you doing here?" That sounded like Gavin, he was in Grade Eight, but only because he'd failed twice.

"The fire looked warm." Georgia rubbed her gauntleted hand together.

"You know what I mean."

"I came for some conversation." She felt the weight of Gavin's friends? followers? around her.

"We don't want prissy, little girls here."

"Good thing I'm not prissy, Gavin," Georgia was much smaller than him and she didn't want him thinking she might not be that little any more. Two rules.

He grabbed her shoulder and threw her to the ground. Georgia rolled a couple of times then stood up. She didn't want to look like she was challenging him. He closed the gap and pushed her to the ground again.

"Stay on the ground, little bitch." Laughter came from the others. Georgia took the opportunity while Gavin basked in their applause to look around. She didn't see anything out of the ordinary. She'd been here a few times to look things over. Each time approaching carefully to make sure no one was around. Information meant power.

She came to her feet again and slid around to where she could see the rest of the clearing. A couple of lunks stood beside Anna. *Shit, change of plan.* Whatever she came in for, she didn't want Anna getting hurt.

"I prefer the fire." She moved back toward the barrel. He came at her a third time, but this time she side-stepped. More laughter from the audience, a snarl from Gavin. He pulled a stick from the fire and held it carefully by its unburnt end. It still looked plenty hot. She guessed where he was going with this. She hoped her gauntlets would survive. She liked them.

As she figured, he shoved the stick at her. Whether he meant to scare her or really burn her, she didn't care. She grabbed the flaming stick with both hands and wrenched it out of his grasp. Georgia stepped to the side and tossed the stick into the fire.

73

Gavin looked like he was deciding whether to try another tack. Georgia waited.

"OK, I think that will do." Another boy stepped out from the crowd.

"But -"

"Are you arguing with me?" the other boy said. Georgia was trying to place him. She'd seen him with Daniel, Jaime's brother, at the mall. He was Cree, but lived here in town.

"Brad, she was asking for it."

"It's your funeral." Brad shrugged and looked carefully casual. Georgia couldn't tell if he wanted her to get hurt, or if he wanted her to fight back and hurt Gavin. Maybe he didn't care. This had to be more interesting than just hanging out and blowing smoke.

"Do you watch movies?" Georgia asked.

"Yeah, I like to watch the ones where the bitches get it hard. You want it like that, little bitch?" Gavin leered at her.

"I was thinking more of educational movies," Georgia said. "I read you can learn kung fu from watching Bruce Lee movies."

"What, you're Bruce Lee now?" Gavin made some kung fu poses and laughed at her. Then he lunged forward. Georgia feinted another side step, but he was ready for it and swung his arms wide. So she stepped in and planted her, she hoped, still hot gauntlet on his face and twisted him just so. Hard to practice in her bedroom by herself. She didn't get it quite right. Instead of flipping him she just turned him off balance. Fortunately, he got his feet tangled and went down in a heap.

"That's my bro, bitch!" One of the boys guarding Anna lunged toward Georgia. She was too off balance to get out of the way, but Anna swung her leg hard and caught him between the legs. He went down hard on his face.

"Do you want a piece of me too?" She asked the other boy who stood beside her. "I'm sure all the filth your friend was talking is turning you on." The boy backed up in a hurry. Anna walked up to Gavin who was still untangling himself.

"You know who I am?" She planted herself in front of him.

"Why should I?" he said, but Georgia saw him move away just a little.

"Go after my friend again and I will either kick you so hard you'll be able to suck yourself from inside, or I'll put a curse on you that it will never stand up again."

Gavin scrambled back until he was well out of range. His rescuer lay groaning in the snow.

"Don't say I didn't warn you," Brad sauntered forward and made a grand sweep of his arm. "Welcome to our fire. I usually like the bitches to know their place, but you're new, so I'll make an exception, this time."

"Thank you," Georgia went back to warming herself at the fire. Anna stood across from her. Georgia smiled at her, she'd saved Georgia some bruises.

"So what brings you out to our fire?"

"Like I said, I'm looking for some conversation."

"So, you were talking educational movies," Brad said. "What do you watch besides Bruce Lee?"

"I like movies where people cobble together things to make weapons or gadgets."

"Like what?"

Georgia looked around.

"I bet cell signal here sucks."

"The whole town sucks," Brad said, "It's a fucking black hole here."

"Do you have some insulated wire? Not too heavy?"

One of the crowd went rummaging through the shed and came up with a length of wire, probably for lights on a trailer.

"That's great." She peeled off one piece and handed the rest back. She pulled a twig out of the fire and wrapped the wire around it leaving one end with about five straight centimeters. It was already stripped, bonus. She pulled the wire off the twig and gently tugged until the coil spread out more.

"Can I see your cell phone?" she asked.

"Aren't you a little young to be asking for my number?" Brad said, but he pulled out his cell. "Hey, what if you blow it up?"

Georgia took her phone out and handed it to him.

"I blow up your phone, you keep mine."

"Sweet, go ahead and blow it up."

Georgia found the external antennae port and carefully put her makeshift antennae in. She handed the phone back to Brad. He shrugged and tossed hers back.

"Wow," he said, "Three bars, I'm impressed. What else can you do?"

"I don't want to give away all my tricks in one night." She smiled at him.

"So you come here and show off a little. What do you expect from us? We're not about to fall at your feet, and frankly, you're way too young for me."

"Those arsons at the lodges," she said without looking at any of them. "That was a lot of potential income up in smoke. Those American are good tippers when you point them in the right direction."

"Shit, girl," Brad's tone shifted. "There's no messing with those fuckers. I don't know what your game is, but it's going to get you killed."

"You know these people?"

"Hell no, they're bat shit crazy. I heard one guy crossed them and they nailed him to a tree and pulled his guts out while he was still screaming. I like you, you're mouthy, but you're entertaining. Take my advice and leave the war to those who are stupid enough to fight it."

Georgia stared into the flames, she felt Anna looking at her. Time to go. Now they just needed to get away.

"I appreciate your advice, Brad," Georgia said. "I don't want to get caught up in any war, and speaking of war, if I'm late my parents are going to declare war on me."

"So," Gavin said, "just how freaky is it having your Dad decide he was a bitch? Do they still do it?"

"Do yours, Gavin?" Georgia responded, "Do you watch them, or did they give it up after seeing what kind of moron they produced?"

"Down, boy." Brad put his hand up to block Gavin. "She's off limits. You fuck with her and I may decide to see how long your guts are." He turned to Georgia and Anna. "I'd better walk you to the road. Keep you safe and all that." He put an arm around each of their shoulders and half guided half pushed them toward the path to the road.

They reached the road and Brad looked at Georgia.

"Maybe in a few years," he said. "I'd never be bored." He handed her an envelope. "Your dad helped me get an apprenticeship. I don't care what he wears. I wasn't kidding about these guys. They're seriously fucked in the head."

He turned and walked back into the darkness.

"Anna." Georgia let out a long breath. "Thanks."

"You want to do this again," Anna said. "I'll slap you silly."

"Thanks, I think." They walked back toward where they met up. "What you said to Gavin, where did you get that line?"

"You're not the only one who watches educational movies," Anna grinned. The girls laughed. Georgia said goodnight and went home to see how badly her dad had failed this time.

Chapter Fifteen

Leigh sat in the mall and read. She'd been reading steady for the last two days. Coming to the mall had been scary, but nobody made a fuss over her. She was welcomed, then ignored. The protest had gone beyond how one teacher had been treated badly. Leigh listened while she took breaks, and she heard stories of how other teachers felt abused by the School Board. Ms. Taladut was the latest symptom, but she wasn't the problem.

The children who laid or sat around Leigh ranged from Kindergarten students to teens in high school. Something about a story being read out loud drew people. She'd noticed a few adults sitting close enough to hear as well.

For all that she was having fun, Leigh worried about how long this was going on. The Board had stated its position, then refused to talk to the strikers. All the teachers had received letters that put them under discipline for refusing to work. The children were learning, but not the entire curriculum. Time for somebody to move, but it wasn't her fight. Georgia was there every day with her friends, encouraging and organizing. She had to know there needed to be a next step.

On one of her breaks, Leigh wandered over and tapped Georgia on the shoulder.

"Join me for a drink in the Coffee Shop," she said. Georgia immediately nodded and left Tom to take over the discussion apparently about the use of the washrooms.

Leigh bought coffee for her and drink for Georgia, then they sat in the back booth.

"I've never sat in this booth," Georgia said. "I've always seen it as a spot for the elders."

"Leaders," Leigh said, "and you've taken on a leadership role. Now you need to decide what you are going to do next. We can't stay in the mall all year."

"I know." The girl shook her head in frustration and Leigh reminded herself Georgia was still a kid. A very smart kid, but a kid. "I've been sending daily emails to the Board asking to meet and I get the same response every time. They've stated their position. We have no legal standing and they won't negotiate."

"Perhaps it is time to go over their heads," Leigh sipped her coffee. "They are accountable to the Ministry of Education for how they run the School District. It wouldn't hurt if the media happened to get word of what is going on. They always like a story about a good fight."

"What do I say?" Georgia twisted her cup in her hands. "I know about the strike because of Dad's stories, but I wouldn't know what to say to a Minister of Education."

"Talk to her the way you'd talk to me. Tell her about what is happening and why it is happening and what you'd like to do to see it resolved. You can always copy it to someone in the media so it is harder to ignore."

"I see." Leigh could almost see the wheels turning, "I'm going to go talk to a few people." Georgia finished her drink, "Thanks, Mrs. Dalrymple." She left Leigh to sit and finish her coffee. Before she finished John slid into the booth across from her.

"I'm on a coffee fetching mission," he said. "I want you to pass something on to Jim. Someone slid an envelope of very disturbing pictures under the door this morning. I'm certain the Inspector knows who left them, but he's not talking. The result is that we've managed what may be a break in the case. The danger is it is going to be very political and Jim is directly in the line of fire on this one. Someone has lit a fire under the Inspector, but it may not be enough. Jim needs to figure out how to cover himself on this. He doesn't want to be the guy who called the heavies on a First Nations group, but he also doesn't want to be seen as a lightweight who lets First Nations get away with shit because he's afraid of them. I can't say more and the Inspector would have my jewels if he knew I'd said this much." He slid out of the booth and picked up the box with coffee and some snacks and walked out.

Leigh felt the anxiety return. There were too many ways everything could go wrong. She went back out into the mall and

79

read to the children, but the back of her mind urged her to run and hide. She had long practice at ignoring the voices.

That night at supper she looked at Jim. She hadn't really seen him for days, she'd been too caught up in her own stuff. Her heart twisted with guilt. There were lines she was sure hadn't been there before this mess started, and she wasn't sure if it was the light or grey hair appearing amongst the black.

"John dropped by with a message," she said, "more of a warning. He told me the task force has some new information which makes this situation even more of a political time bomb."

"Did he say anything useful?" The bitterness in Jim's voice was new. Leigh worried even more for him.

"He said you want to present a balance between respecting First Nations and making sure you were seen to be upholding the law."

"Oh, that's a lot of fucking good." He pushed away from the table. "It doesn't matter what I do, I've been screwed from the moment I asked for help with the arsons. I just couldn't do what I needed to do, so my career is going down the toilet. If we're lucky, I'll just get reassigned somewhere and we can rebuild."

"John thought you could do something about it, or he wouldn't have suggested it."

"Yeah, it's easy enough for him. He's the brilliant analyst everybody needs."

"If he's such a brilliant analyst, isn't he worth listening to?"

"I don't have the luxury of an excuse," Jim shouted at her. "I'm not sick, I'm just a failure!"

Leigh stared at him, feeling the impact of his words. She'd been thrown from a horse and this had the same disorienting pain to it. She knew she hurt; she knew the world didn't look right from this angle, but she couldn't connect that reality to what should be real.

"When you're done being a failure and feeling sorry for yourself, you come and talk to me." Leigh walked away. She half expected to shatter like glass on the floor, but she held together until she got to her office. That's when she recognized she wasn't hurt. She was furious. She'd never felt anger like this. The voices whispered to her she was broken. *Shut up*, she thought and let the rage loose on the voices. They retreated.

Jim would have to deal with his own problems. She needed to face hers. She was letting a twelve-year-old fight for her. Wanting to stay out of Georgia's way was an excuse for not fighting for herself. It ended tonight.

She called Craig Ballan.

"Hello, Craig," she said when he picked up. "I think this farce has gone on long enough. It's time to talk to the Union about a grievance. I want to throw everything we can at the School Board. Forget, Ms. Taladut. She's an incompetent; it is the Board who is backing her up and acting contrary to the contract and the law. I want to ratchet up the pressure until they break. Now, yesterday, last week. We should have done this as soon as she stepped out of the role she was hired for and the Board didn't reel her in. Don't wait for tomorrow, search some names and talk to people tonight. By tomorrow I want the school board to wonder what hit them."

"Right, I'll get on it." Craig responded.

"Great, tomorrow then." She looked up to see Jim standing in the door. She'd never seen him look so lost. Leigh went and hugged him.

"I don't know how," she whispered into his ear, "but we are going to get through this. Whatever you need to do, I'm behind you. All those years I leaned on you, well now it's your turn. I'm here and I'm here for good and I will never stop fighting for you."

"I have an idea," Jim said. "How do you feel about cooking Chinese food for my staff and the task force?"

"How's tomorrow night? It just so happens I have a bit of time on my hands."

Ryley went to Jen's for the evening and all the RCMP in town gathered in Leigh's living room. Cam and Pat had drawn the short straws and drank iced tea. It didn't appear to be dampening their spirits. There was a tacit agreement not to talk about the investigation, but there was plenty of shop talk.

Jim and John told the task force about the wendigo, while the Inspector recounted stories of his own days on the margins of Canadian society. Leigh had out done herself and John had told her the biggest thing he missed was her Chinese nights. Leigh wondered how Anne and Bill were handling Anne's retirement.

"Do you mind if I turn the TV on for a moment to check the score?" one of the task force members asked. "I have a bet on the game with my brother."

"Gambling is frowned upon," the Inspector said. "What spread do you give him?"

"Two and a half points for Boston," the other man said. "Loser hosts Christmas with all the family."

"Hosting a Christmas dinner doesn't sound too bad," Janice said.

"You haven't met my family have you?"

The TV got turned on and the news had just started.

"Turn the sound down until they get to the sports," John said.

"The small northern town of Spruce Bay …"

"Wait!" the Inspector held up his hand.

"… today is the center of a controversy over whether a beloved teacher is allowed to return to work. At this time neither the School District nor the Ministry of Education would comment on the story, though the Ministry did confirm they were looking into the situation. The Teacher's Union issued a statement in support of the teacher, Mrs. Leigh Dalrymple and the right of the students to protest. According to the Union, the entire school has been out in protest over the suspension of Mrs. Dalrymple after she had a panic attack. The Union stated they are also investigating allegations of interference on the part of the Board in the work of the teaching community. They note this isn't the first issue from Spruce Bay to come to their notice.

"One of the students who organized the protest, Georgia Cassidy, spoke to us by phone. Ms. Cassidy, what made you decide to organize a strike of the students in your school?"

"We have some very good teachers in our school and they all have their own style of instruction. I watched as certain teachers were singled out and pressured to teach in a much more rigid format which made it hard for certain students to learn. When Mrs. Dalrymple was suspended, I realized somebody needed to speak up. Since none of the adults had, the students decided we would."

"What do you know of allegations that Mrs. Dalrymple suffered a panic attack and might present a risk to the student population."

"The first year, Mrs. Dalrymple taught at Spruce Bay, she explained she had an anxiety disorder. She told us she took medication for it and that it was unlikely it would ever be a problem at school. She said if it did happen that it wasn't dangerous. It is no different than a person who has epilepsy."

"But if she has an attack, then she won't be able to care for the class."

"Please, that is why we have principals and other people, so they can back each other up. An anxiety disorder is no different than a physical illness. It's just people get scared and stupid when it comes to mental illness. If we can deal with it, why is it so hard for the adults?"

"Thank you, Ms. Dalrymple. So, what is next in your protest?"

"The School Board needs to sit down and listen to us. They've refused to say anything to us, other than treating us like kids."

"But you are children."

"So? That's no excuse for refusing reasonable discussion. You can't educate children by behaving worse than they do."

"Right. So, there you have it. We will be following developments as they appear. Now on to the sports, George?"

"Well once again the Leafs have managed to snatch defeat from the jaws of victory, losing four - three to Boston after leading for two and a half periods…"

The TV was turned off and the members pretended sympathy for their colleague. Leigh saw the Inspector looking at her and she raised her eyebrow. He lifted his glass to her.

"That's right," John said, "a toast to families and Christmas and may everyone make it through the day without any calls to 911."

In the morning Craig called to say the School Board contacted him to negotiate a resolution to the situation.

"The Chair tried to make it sound like they were being gracious even talking to me, but I think they're scared. Nobody wants to be on National TV as the opponent to a bunch of kids."

Leigh walked to the mall since the weather had turned nicer and the main subject of conversation was the upcoming meeting with the Board.

83

"The day before Halloween." Georgia rolled her eyes. "At least is isn't Halloween. There is someone from the Ministry coming and the news is sending someone as well."

"Congratulations," Leigh smiled at her. "It looked like your move broke the log jam. A great interview on the news too."

"I didn't sound too dorky?"

"You impressed the commentator - definitely not dorky."

"I have to talk to the others and plan what we're going to say."

"Sounds like a good idea."

"I didn't contact the Teacher's Union," Georgia said. "I should have thought of it too."

"I couldn't let you do all the work," Leigh said.

"Thanks, Mrs. Dalrymple." Georgia hugged her. "You'll always be my teacher."

"And I think you'll always be mine," Leigh said as Georgia ran to gather her friends.

Chapter Sixteen

Georgia spent the day writing speeches and answers to all the questions she thought anyone would ask. She'd also invested a lot of time convincing Tom, Steve and Anna they should do some of the talking. The boys especially were hard to convince and she had to draw a rosy picture of what appearing on TV would do for their popularity with the girls.

She would have liked to have more students involved, but there just wasn't time to organize them. She wanted kids who had been taught by Mrs. Dalrymple so they could speak to the value of her teaching. She got a call from the news people to comment on the announcement the deputy minister would be coming to the meeting. She hoped she'd made sense.

Nothing seemed to have changed because of the envelope she slipped under the door. It was sealed when Brad gave it to her, and she decided she didn't need to see its contents. She hoped she'd at least get a wink from the Inspector, but the RCMP had all gone off to the Dalrymples.

The news about the upcoming community meeting drove it out of her head for a while, but lying on her bed with words still spinning through her head brought her back to it. Brad had been genuinely scared. Georgia wondered what her Dad had done to make him risk his neck for her. She'd replayed the confrontation in her head and decided Brad had things under control the whole time. Gavin might have bruised her, but nothing else.

She wondered what it would be like to have a boyfriend in high school. She was only twelve now, but it wouldn't be that long before she was sixteen and he wasn't the kind who moved away when they finished school. Her phone startled her when it rang and she fumbled it.

"Hello?" she said when she'd finally picked it up and answered.

"Hi, little girl," Brad's voice said, "Were you thinking about me?"

"Are you going to university?" she asked, then smacked her forehead.

"Not likely," Brad said, and laughed. He didn't sound mean though. "So you *were* thinking about me. I'm glad I haven't lost my touch." His voice shifted and dropped. "You know the track to the old ski lodge?"

"Sure," Georgia said.

"Be there in ten minutes," Brad hung up.

Georgia got dressed and went out the door without letting her parents hear her. She didn't want to run and show up hacking and coughing, but she had to walk briskly. Couldn't he have chosen a place a little closer? On second thought she decided maybe she was happy he hadn't.

Brad stepped out of the shadows as she reached the path. He wrapped his arms around her and pulled her into a hug.

"Play along," he whispered in her ear. His lips tickled and she got too flustered to say anything, but she put her arms around him and leaned her head against his chest. She had to admit it felt nice. Her heart pounded harder than it had when she'd gone out to challenge the wendigo's wolves.

"There's big trouble coming to town," he whispered. "Don't ask how I know, I won't tell you. All I know is something is going down because the deputy minister and the news is here. It is going to be big and bloody. For God's sake let your pet Inspector know and convince him to do something."

"I will," Georgia could feel Brad shaking and she didn't think it was from overwhelming desire. She was a kid and nothing much to look at.

"Your Dad listened to me when no one else would." Brad said. "He saved my life." Georgia felt him step back. On impulse, she tilted her head up and kissed him. Brad's arms tightened again and he kissed her back. She had wondered what it would be like. She hadn't expected her knees would shake, while she was sure Brad could feel her heart beating. She could feel his.

Georgia closed her eyes and just let the moment happen while she fixed her mind on remembering every detail from the hint of chocolate on his tongue to the sudden warmth she felt in her stomach. He broke it off and grinned crookedly at her.

"God, I hope you wait for me," he was. "just a couple years and you'll be in high school."

Georgia thought he got it backwards, since he'd should be the one waiting, but he turned and walked away quickly. Georgia walked home slower and savoured the tingle on her lips.

She got home and slipped in without getting caught. Her parents were talking in the bedroom again. They put on a good face, but it was rough. She didn't think it was getting easier on them. She went up to her room and texted the Inspector. She took three texts to get all the information she wanted to tell him. She wanted to sit back and think about the kiss, but there was work for her wolves to do.

Anna picked up on the first ring and Georgia explained what she'd learned.

"Be careful," Anna said.

"You too," Georgia responded, but she wasn't sure they meant the same thing. Anna sometimes knew more than Georgia wanted her to. Tom and Steve were easier. They just accepted the warning as coming from their leader. Each of them would pass the word along, but not, Georgia emphasized, to cause panic. They wanted to be prepared.

"Prepared for what?" Tom asked.

"I wish I knew," Georgia said. "Imagine the worst thing that could happen and try to figure out how to keep everyone safe if it happens. If we have a plan, they will follow us. They're already used to doing that."

She tried to call Alastair, but he didn't answer his phone. It was too late to call Sandra, so she had to leave him out of it. Maybe she'd get a chance to talk to him tomorrow.

She decided she had one more call to make.

"Sergeant Dalrymple," she said when he came to the phone, "I have something to tell you. I can't tell you how I know, but I trust it and it scares me."

"Go ahead, Georgia," the Sergeant said. "I trust your judgment."

"Something is going to happen. Something bad. While the deputy minister is here and the news people. I don't know anything more, but if I find out I'll let you know."

"You need to talk to the Inspector, Georgia."

"I have already." Her phone buzzed in her hand. "That's him now. Look, don't depend on him to make your plans. You know the town better. He's smart, but I trust you more."

"Thank you, Georgia."

She hung up and answered the Inspector.

"Yes, I trust my source. I don't think he knows any more, but I know he's scared. You know better than I do what these people are like."

"I can't go on high alert on the word of a kid," the Inspector said.

"Why the heck did you ask for my help if you weren't going to listen?" Georgia refrained from banging the phone. "They don't know your source is a kid. This is your job. It's what you wanted. Don't mess it up." She hung up.

Georgia sat on the bed and started shaking. She'd just hung up on the Inspector, after she snapped at him like a puppy wanting to join the wolves. She crawled under the covers and tried to think of something else, anything else.

The only thing she came up with was to wish Brad was there with her.

***

The Deputy Minister arrived at the airstrip on the morning of the thirtieth. The RCMP turned out in uniform to welcome her. Georgia watched from the bus as the VIP walked along the path lined by the police. Some other people walked behind her. They ignored the honour guard and talked about something on one of their cell phones. Georgia was expecting disaster, but nothing happened. The woman reached the bus and smiled at Georgia. She sat across the aisle from her while the others walked to the back.

"You must be Georgia Cassidy," she said. "I read your briefing and I must say I'm very impressed. You sounded much older than you look."

"I get that a lot," Georgia put a smile on her face. She decided the Deputy Minister was going to get a variation of the psycho kid she played for the Inspector. She'd be friendlier, but she wasn't pulling any punches. Georgia was aware of the news crew who clambered on the bus and pointed the cameras at her and the Deputy Minister. They had arrived in a long line of cars and vans earlier in the day.

"My name is Grace Hampton," the Deputy Minister shook Georgia's hand. "You call me Grace and I'll call you Georgia."

"OK, Grace." It felt strange calling an adult by her first name but she wasn't going to argue in front of the camera. She wondered what it would be like to always have the camera there, to always think carefully before she spoke. Hard, she decided.

"So tell me about what makes Mrs. Dalrymple such a special teacher."

"She listens," Georgia said, "and she cares about what you say. I've heard her encourage kids to do things they would never have imagined. She didn't abandon me because I was smart; she made me work harder than anyone else, then got me to help the others. There were kids in the class everyone else had given up on and she didn't."

"She sounds pretty incredible."

"She is, but people get all weird because her brain chemistry is a little off. She explained to us. I didn't think then how much guts that took, but she wanted us to know she was all right and not to be scared."

"But some people are scared."

"They don't know her like we do. She's not crazy she's just sick sometimes. There's a difference."

"So what do you want to get out of this?"

"I want Mrs. Dalrymple to be able to teach. Other kids should get what I had. It isn't fair what they did. There are rules."

"What happened?"

"I wasn't there," Georgia said, "so I can't really comment. I know some kids who were there and you can ask them." She thought she saw a tiny nod of approval from Grace.

They arrived at town and Grace was whisked away by the Town Council. Georgia sat on the bus and watched. She found it harder than she'd expected.

"Hey, Georgia," one of the reporters stood by her seat. Georgia slid over and he sat down. "You did good, kid. I know practiced politicians who wouldn't do as well. You sounded passionate, but still reasonable. That's a tough combination to find these days. Oh sorry, I'm Matthew Wolf, you sent your brief to me. Like the Deputy Minister said, impressive. I'd like to do a little bit of background on you if you don't mind. Just things like what you like at school and where you learned to be an organizer."

"Sure, I guess," Georgia shrugged. "I'm free until the meeting."

Mark laughed and they did a taping. He went back a few times to change the questions he asked slightly.

"I want to look like I did my homework," he said. "Where can a starving reporter get something to eat?"

"There's The Coffee Shop, but it's probably crammed full. We don't have much in the way of services. Why don't you come to my place, and I can make you a sandwich. Just leave the cameras here, I don't want to freak out my parents."

"OK, as long as your parents are home."

"Mom's off shift today. She'll be home, if you like I'll call and check."

While she called home, Matthew had his cell phone out and frowned at it.

"You guys have the slowest service I've ever seen," he said.

"Welcome to Spruce Bay, the land of *You can't get that here yet*," Georgia said, "We're on the old network technology. It takes forever to upload or download anything and costs a fortune if you do. They keep promising upgrades, but not enough people live here for them to bother doing anything.

"Anyway, Mom and Dad are home and said to bring you over. It's just a quick walk from here."

They walked the short distance while Georgia gave a running commentary on the town.

"Matthew," she said when her Dad answered the door. "this is my Dad, Ruth, and that's my Mom, Brenda in the kitchen."

"Thanks for the hospitality," Matthew replied without a blink. "Not everyone would allow a reporter into the house, never mind a crew."

"You're welcome." Her dad waved them in.

90

"Where are your cameras?" Paul asked as he ran out from the TV room.

"You must be Georgia's brother."

"I'm Paul," he said before he ran back to the TV.

The conversation ranged far and wide as Matthew told stories of all the ways he'd embarrassed himself.

"It's an occupational hazard, but it's worth it to meet so many interesting people."

"I saw your segment on the trans community in Winnipeg," her dad said. "I was impressed."

"I would like to have seen more about the other people whose lives change," her mother said. "I know it isn't easy." She put her hand on Ruth's shoulder. "It would be nice to hear someone else's story."

"I've been thinking about doing a follow up story," Matthew said, "Maybe you'd consider coming to Winnipeg and being part of it."

"I would like that." She nodded and smiled. "I would like that a lot."

Matthew and his crew ended up staying for supper. Georgia was impressed at how few questions he asked. She guessed when he wasn't being a reporter that questions got old quickly.

She looked at her watch.

"Time to go."

Chapter Seventeen

Georgia walked into the Council Chambers. She remembered standing on a chair so people could see her. That had been a few years ago. She wouldn't be standing on any chairs tonight. She'd taken special care with her appearance for this meeting. She didn't want to look too casual, but neither did she want to look like a little girl dressing up to impress the adults. She compromised on a pair of dress pants and a favourite sweater. Her dad wanted her to wear one of her necklaces, but she decided to put on the little leather medicine bag Anna gave her. To make her dad feel better she wore one of her bracelets.

The Chambers were already full when she got there. Tom waved her over.

"We've saved you a seat." He was standing very close to Anna and Georgia had to hide a grin.

More people packed in and they had to open the doors and give people space to stand in the mall. The Deputy Minister, Grace, came out of the RCMP detachment. *Clever, there aren't any safer places in town.*

The Chair of the School Board made sure Grace was comfortable in her seat. They sat behind the tables the Town Council used so it looked like she was on their side.

Once everybody was arranged to the Chair's satisfaction he banged the gavel on the block.

"We're meeting tonight to review Mrs. Dalrymple's fitness —"

"No, we're not." Georgia stepped forward. "Mrs. Dalrymple's ability as a teacher is not the question. The question is whether you acted correctly in allowing her to be suspended and whether your action against the other staff is fair."

"Excuse me, little girl," the Chair frowned at her, "don't interrupt. You don't know what you are talking about. Please sit down."

"The legislation around discipline of teachers and the treatment of people with mental illness and other disabilities is clear. I can quote you the sections if you'd like. For you to discuss personnel issues in a public forum such as this is in clear violation of those statutes and the labour code of the province."

The Chair looked like he'd been slapped by a fish. He shook himself and tried again.

"I will have you removed if you don't behave -"

"Perhaps it is time I stepped in." The Deputy Minister lifted her hand. "I and the minister's staff have reviewed the case at hand including reports submitted by Ms. Cassidy and the Teacher's Union. She is quite correct in her statements. I did not fly up here to listen to a good teacher being maligned. If there are issues of her performance, there are proper procedures and channels to address those concerns. There are issues of justice which concern our government and it is my responsibility to see that those issues are respected. Now unless you plan to tell me to sit down and be quiet, I suggest we listen to Ms. Cassidy and hear what solution she proposes."

"But she's just a child," he sputtered.

"No, she is not just a child. She is a representative of a group of people under your care who feel justice is not being done."

The Chair sat down looking shocked.

"If you would continue, Georgia."

"Thank you, Deputy Minister." Georgia hid her triumphant grin. "Mrs. Dalrymple is an exceptional teacher, but even if she were not the process leading to her suspension was not correct. The question is not whether she is able to teach. She had a contract to teach, and part of the contract, signed by the School Board is she is not subject to discipline without due process. Mrs. Dalrymple was told by a message on her phone that she was suspended. No cause was given."

"There was good cause," Ms. Taladut interrupted, "She had some kind of fit in class."

"So you suspended her because she was sick."

"Exactly, who knows what she might do if she has another fit?"

"Suspension or dismissal on the basis of illness or disability is discrimination and forbidden by the Charter of Rights." Georgia kept her voice even, when she wanted to scream at the woman's ignorance. "But to address the concerns of Mrs. Dalrymple having 'some kind of fit' and being dangerous. Marc would you explain what happened?"

"We were going to learn about *Dia de Muertos*," he said, "but Ms. Taladut said we weren't allowed 'cause it wasn't part of the circus something. Mrs. Dalrymple said we should because we were going to learn stuff and have fun. Ms. Taladut started yelling at her, so she closed the door. She was crying and we were all scared. Sandra called 911 and we told Mrs. Dalrymple she was going to be OK."

"Were you scared?" The Deputy Minister asked.

"Sure, we thought Mrs. Dalrymple was having a stroke. That's what Sandra said, and Ms. Taladut was banging on the door screaming at us."

"What did Ms. Taladut say after Mrs. Dalrymple left?" Georgia asked.

"She said Mrs. Dalrymple was sick in the head and would never come back."

"Thank you," Georgia said. Marc sat down.

"As you heard, Mrs. Dalrymple wasn't the scary person." The crowd laughed and Ms. Taladut frowned.

"What I stated at the beginning and what I say now is that Mrs. Dalrymple should be able to teach her class. She should be able to teach it the way she wants to. My teacher Mr. McRoy teaches his class the way he wants and nobody complains. We want to learn and we want to learn in different ways. That's what school should be about. I'm not going to say anything about the other teachers, because that's their business."

The room erupted in applause and Georgia sat down and tried to hide the shaking in her hands. Anna patted her knee and she felt a hand on her shoulder. Brad sat behind her and he gave her a thumbs-up. Georgia felt herself turning deep red. She was going to hide her face, but then she decided she didn't need to. Maybe people would think it was because of the applause. She looked at Anna and her friend wasn't fooled. Anna smiled at her and patted her knee again.

"Thank you, Georgia." Grace stood up again. "I think it is fair to say it is the Minister's opinion that Mrs. Dalrymple should be immediately re-instated and paid for the days she has missed. The other teachers acted in support of their colleague and as long as they resume their duties in an orderly manner, no further discipline is needed. The minister has ordered a review of the School Board with a view to ensuring they follow due process and the legislation as it is laid out in the Education Act. During that review, the School Board will not act without the permission and input of the Ministry. We realize this is an inconvenience for everyone, but we ask that you be patient during the interim.

"The Trustees of the School Board are elected officials and we don't interfere in their work lightly. I hope you understand."

"So when do our children go back to school," Joe asked from the back of the room.

"If the teachers are willing, there is no reason the students can't return to school tomorrow morning."

"We'll be there," Craig spoke from where he sat with some other high school teachers.

The room erupted in applause again.

"I think that is it, then," the Deputy Minister said. "I suggest we adjourn the meeting and give the teachers some time to get ready for their day tomorrow."

Georgia hung back to talk more with Grace. Brad gave her another thumbs-up and went out with his friends. Georgia noticed Gavin wasn't among them. The Chair accosted the Deputy Minister.

"You can't do that," he said. "This is our district."

"You have no idea what I'm allowed to do." The Deputy Minister frowned severely at him. "You are elected and sworn in to fulfill a very defined role. If you chose not to work with the Ministry we have the right to have you removed and call an election for new Trustees. And let me tell you, if I get the slightest hint of any kind of retribution against any of the teachers or the students you will be removed from office before I go home for the day. Let me give you some advice. Listen to Zack Cooper very

95

carefully and don't do anything without his approval. He will be here next week and I have personally given him his instructions."

The Chair frowned but left without any more argument.

"Georgia, my dear." Grace turned with a grin. "You were fantastic. The kid from her class was brilliant. It was a great bit of public education. If you want some advice from an old hand. Be humble about your victory. The School Board made a mistake they're fixing it, blah, blah blah. You don't want people thinking you're full of yourself." She hugged Georgia.

"I'm going to let you get home and get ready for school tomorrow, and I have to write a report to the Minister so she can make a statement to the press. I probably won't see you in the morning, but if you're ever in Winnipeg, stop into my office at the Lege."

Georgia went and found her parent talking to Matthew.

"I've have to get back to work," he said, "Everyone knows reporters drive where Deputy Ministers fly."

Georgia shivered and she wrapped her arms around herself.

"Hey, you look good in that sweater," Alastair came up behind her.

"Why didn't you answer your phone last night?" Georgia said.

"I got into trouble with my Uncle. He's a bigwig General in Ottawa and it was his birthday yesterday so I sent him this text message. Only he didn't think it was that funny. I wasn't even supposed to have the number, but he called me once for my birthday. He told me to erase the number but I never got around to it. I think he was in a meeting and had to explain how his fool nephew somehow had access to a classified number."

"Sounds rough," Georgia said. "So how long have you lost your phone for?"

"According to my Uncle, until I'm dead, according to my mom, long enough for her brother to get into some other crisis and forget about it."

"I'll see you tomorrow."

"Really?" Alastair's face brightened.

"Tomorrow, Alastair."

Georgia tried to remember what had sent that chill through her, but she was tired and decided to go home. Maybe she'd remember in the morning. At least Grace was safe tonight surrounded by Mounties at the apartments.

Chapter Eighteen

Halloween day dawned clear and bright. Jim called his team in.

"All hands on deck today. I've heard warnings there may be some form of attack so be on the alert. Anything unusual report it to me. I want you using cell phones, not police frequencies. Make some standard chatter on the police band so everything sounds normal. I want you to use extreme caution responding to any situation. Wait for backup. The Inspector's team is running security for the Deputy Minister, but I want a sweep of the airport road and of the landfill. Go, and we'll all hope my sources were wrong."

The four officers went out to their vehicles and headed out. Jim knew they would sweep the roads several times before patrolling the town and reserve. There was just too much area to cover. The roads barely scratched the surface, but they had to do something.

He walked over to the school and did a walk through. He looked in every classroom and cupboard, but nothing looked out of place. It was empty and waiting for the students to return to class. At least something was going right. He had to give Georgia and her friends credit, but the mob scene in the mall was trouble waiting to happen. They got lucky.

The first students arrived and hung out in the yard. It was cold but not unreasonably. He liked seeing the yard full again. He got into his truck and started his sweep of the area the Deputy Minister would go through. He noticed something unusual and went back to check. As parents dropped their children off they'd drive away to home or work. Today many of them, especially the Cree parents, stayed and watched. The cars formed a barrier around the edge of the school yard.

Jim observed for a few minutes, then put his truck in gear and went to do his work. There were a lot of cars on the road, but he recognized the drivers. People were cruising the town. He finally stopped Joe when he saw him.

"What's going on Joe?"

"We got word it would be best if we left town today," Joe said, "A couple of anonymous phone calls. Some people left, the rest of us decided if anyone wants to cause trouble they'll have to go through us."

"Good God, do you know the kind of risk you're taking?"

"Yes," Joe said, "I think we do, but this is our town too."

"OK, I don't have time to argue, but if you see something, anything out of the ordinary, you call me. Use my cell, you have the number."

He got back into the truck but his stomach churned with acid. He hated this feeling. The convoy had just lined up when he reached them.

"There's a lot of traffic on the road," Jim reported. "Response to some anonymous threats. They'll stay out of our way, but I'll lead as I know every vehicle in this town. Anything I don't recognize I'll flag for you."

"Good man," the Inspector said, "You take point then. Keep the speed steady, not slow, but safe. At least the media people all left early this morning. We don't want this on the evening news if it turns out to be nothing."

Jim led out of the parking lot. They weren't using the bus today. The Deputy Minister and her staff each rode in a different vehicle. The plan was simple. Get her to the airport, put her on the airplane and get her out of town.

The trip to the airstrip wasn't a very long one, but it seemed to take forever. Even knowing his people had swept the area several times he expected an attack at every place his vision was obscured.

Jim was never so glad to get to the airstrip. It looked as bleak and desolate as it always did. The air moved the wind sock fitfully. The cars formed up beside the plane and the pilot came out to talk with the RCMP. Two of the members boarded the plane and did a sweep. Jim could see their heads pause at each window. They were checking the overhead bins and under the seats. Jim waited and schooled himself to patience. To pass the time he did a visual sweep of the strip. The shed was locked with a brand new heavy padlock. Ellers was increasing security. Jim still didn't know what was going on with the fuel. The plane was parked by the fuel depot. Something was missing. Jim looked again. No lock. He saw a glint in the snow a few meters away from the fuel tank.

"Get away from the fuel tanks," he yelled. "Someone's tampered with them."

The Inspector grabbed the Deputy Minister and pulled her away from the plane. The other RCMP went on high alert and ordered the other civilians away from the plane. They would check the fuel tanks and assess the situation. Far to the west he saw a glint of light; he filled his lungs to yell a warning but something slammed against his shoulder and he fell back against his car. He was still trying to shout a warning when the fuel tank exploded. The world became unbearable heat and sound as the airplane's tanks ruptured and burst into flame as well. The entire area became a burning hell.

That's when Jim figured out what bothered him. The Cree wouldn't have to leave town if the only attack was against the airstrip. Jim fumbled out his phone and dialed the last number to call him.

"They're attacking the town," he yelled. "Get back there." He coughed from the smoke and the pain in his shoulder flared up. He couldn't hold the cell phone any more. He couldn't talk. He lay in the melting snow and tried to breathe.

***

Mr. McRoy was in the middle of an explanation of the Pythagorean theorem when Georgia heard the explosion. She could see the fireball through the window. The rest of the class started shouting and screaming.

"QUIET," Mr. McRoy thundered, and the noise stopped. Georgia could hear the screams from the other classes. She also heard her cell phone. She ran to answer it.

"They're attacking the town." She heard the Sergeant's voice. "Get back to town." *He must think he called his detachment.* She didn't have time to worry about that, they had to get the students to safety.

"Tom, Steve," She stood up and pointed at them. "One of you take this class, the other one go get the rest of the sevens and

100

eights. Maria, primary area, take them to the gym. It only has one outside wall and no windows. Anna get the threes and fours. Hurry.”

“Listen,” Mr. McRoy said, “we need to remain calm and stay here. There’s no danger from the fire.”

“The phone call I got was the Staff Sergeant trying to reach his people to say the town is going to be attacked. We have to get away from the windows.”

“What do you want me to do?”

“Go to the office and warn the High School. No panic, but they have to get to the gym or away from windows.”

Georgia pulled out her phone as she followed the class, making sure there were no stragglers. There were always stragglers. Ryley. He wasn’t here. Georgia hoped he was at home as she dialed 911 and tried to explain to a skeptical operator that the town of Spruce Bay was under attack and they needed all the help they could get. Then she didn’t have time for them. She heard an engine revving and then a crash.

“Move,” she shouted, “We don’t have time.” The floor shook as an explosion rocked the building and ceiling tile fell on the children. They screamed and ran for the gym because their leaders had told them to. Georgia heard another explosion behind her and the building shook again sending her slamming into a wall. She picked herself up and hoped they weren’t leading the entire school to their deaths.

***

Dispatch called Carol at the Detachment.

“Some kid claims your town is under attack.”

“There was an explosion just minutes ago,” Carol said. “I’d say we’re under attack. Call the off-” With crash, a truck came through the security doors to the parking lot. She had just enough time to see a face painted in terrifying shapes before the truck exploded. The detachment blew apart and into the council offices next door.

***

Harold had run The Coffee Shop since they built the mall back when the mine was booming. When the mine left, he stayed. There was always a need for good coffee. He felt more than heard the first explosion and went to the doors to see what had happened. He was there when the first car crashed into the cars lined up between the school and the parking lot. He heard the crash and explosion to his right where the Detachment was. Another car drove straight for him. He turned to run.

Harold wasn't a young man, but fear gave him speed and he just rounded the corner as the car smashed through the doors and skidded into the mall. When it exploded, Harold was blown down to the other end of the mall, then the roof fell in. He couldn't hear anything or see anything. His head rang like a bell. He didn't know if he was dead or not, but he prayed he was.

Chapter Nineteen

The junker passed Darren on the road into town throwing up a cloud of snow leaving him blind. He almost went into the ditch before he could see again. Staff had ordered them not to engage anyone unnecessarily, but damn it that idiot was asking for it. Besides it would provide some of the chatter Staff asked for.

"Dispatch," Darren said, "In pursuit of a vehicle of indeterminate age and colour, will advise." He put on the lights and siren and floored the truck. He thought the car was going fast, but all he could see was the snow trail blown up by the car's passage forcing him to follow behind barely able to see the road.

"All units, all units, explosion reported at Spruce Bay airstrip, respond immediately. Use extreme caution.

"Fuck caution." Darren gunned the engine and drove into the artificial storm. He was going to stop that car if it killed him. He steered by instinct and his memories of two years of patrolling these roads. This one was used by hunters and drug runners. It ran to an abandoned mine and further away became little better than a track. This part was graded semi-regularly since it gave access to trails and lakes for fishing.

Darren had no idea how close he was to the car. The snow got thicker and the truck rattled over potholes and corduroy. He couldn't be far from where it joined the paved road. Magically the snow vanished and Darren saw he sat right on the tail of the car. He tried to nudge it, but unbelievably the car accelerated out of his reach. Darren would have called in a warning, but he couldn't take his hands off the wheel. He had the gas pedal to the floor, but was losing the race.

The car reached the point at which it would need to turn to enter town or continue at its mad speed toward the airstrip. Darren guessed since the airstrip had already exploded the car would turn into town. He decided to gamble and swung his wheel. The truck

103

left the road and fish tailed in the ditch. Darren steered up the incline on the other side and prayed he'd got the timing right.

The truck blasted through the brush and onto a trail, narrowly missing the large spruce on either side. The trail was snow and ice, but it led straight from here to the road. The trail made the turn into town just a little less sharp so he could carry more speed. He kept the pedal down and gripped the steering tighter. If he was right, he should see the car now. The junker roared past the opening of the trail, a hair faster than Darren expected. Instead of t-boning the car he clipped the bumper. The car spun in circles on the road while Darren's truck slewed through the snow-covered park on the other side of the road. He smashed a bench into splinters before he could get the truck pointed toward the road again.

Unbelievably the driver of the car had recovered control and accelerated toward the town centre. Darren pushed his truck to its limits and followed. He heard the first explosion as the car he chased made a drifting turn onto the road to the hospital. Two other explosions followed quickly. He kept the gas pedal down even though he knew the last turn was sharp. No way he'd make it at this speed. It held true for the car too.

At the last second he saw the brake lights of the car go on as the driver tried to negotiate an impossible turn. The car drifted into the turn, but Darren didn't slow, driving hard into the back of the car and sent it careening out of control. He didn't have time to watch. He hit the brakes, but they hardly gripped before his truck crashed into the bush behind the hospital. Trees smashed at the truck and showered Darren with glass before the truck hit a tree that refused to break.

The seat belt dug into him as the airbag blew up in his face. Somehow in the midst of the crash he heard another explosion. Then he sat in the seat of a wrecked truck gasping for air. He thought maybe a rib or two had broken. He felt worse than when he'd lost that bar fight in his first year as a cop.

Darren undid the seatbelt and looked for how he could get out. The side doors were crumpled and jammed against trees. A huge spruce stood in the middle of the engine compartment. He turned and crawled into the back. The flashlight made quick work of the rear window and he scrambled through into the truck bed.

The pain sent white flashes through his head, but he climbed out of the truck and stumbled toward the hospital.

***

Brenda Cassidy felt the explosions and wanted to panic. It would be so easy to panic, but she knew Georgia needed her, Ruth needed her. She pushed the fear away and focused on what she knew. She was an emergency nurse and when all this was done they would be flooded with victims. She stood in the emergency entrance giving orders when the car came down the road too fast and missed the corner. It slammed into a tree.

"Down, get down," she screamed as she dove for the floor. The car exploded and glass from the windows and doors sliced into anyone who moved too slow.

Brenda jumped to her feet.

"Someone get a broom and clear the glass. Call out if you're injured or the person next to you is. This is just the beginning people; we have work to do!"

***

The entrance to the hospital was in shambles; but he saw people moving inside. The remnants of the car were jammed against a tree in front. The bomb had torn branches off twenty feet up and blown out windows, but nothing else. He walked through the doors into the organized chaos of the emergency room.

"How bad are you?" Brenda Cassidy asked him.

"I'll live," he said.

"Fine, over there," she pointed to where some other people were standing and sitting while bandaging cuts.

"Dispatch," Darren spoke into the radio, but no one replied. The booster in the detachment must be down.

"Phone," he said to the first person he came to.

"Use that one," the nurse said, "Dial nine for an outside line." She pointed briefly without looking up from pulling glass from a colleague with tweezers. Darren picked up the phone and dialed dispatch.

"Dispatch," he said. "SB 4, checking in. Status?"

"Ten-four, SB 4, four units have checked in by phone. No radio is available."

"Ten-four," Darren tried not to breathe too deeply. He tried not to break into tears.

105

"We need a full emergency response. The airstrip has been compromised but the heliport at the hospital is intact. Multiple explosions, probably from car bombs. Hospital is damaged but functional. Other areas, unknown. We have limited capacity to respond for aid to our citizens."

"Ten-four, SB 4, Initial team is enroute, ETA is 40 minutes. Will advise as more responders become available."

"Warn responders that further attack is possible. Repeat, attack is possible. Suggest they come in full gear and prepared."

"Ten-four."

He dialed another number. "Spruce Bay Fire," the answering machine responded. "If this is an emergency, please dial 911. Leave your message and Chief Harvey will return your call as early as possible."

"Hey," he waved down a nurse, "do you still have the old radio system for the fire and ambulance?"

"In the back room there. It's on the shelf. Darren forced himself to walk into the room. He switched the radio on and dropped into the chair. That may have been a mistake. He didn't think he'd be able to stand up again.

"Spruce Bay detachment to Spruce Bay fire," he said, "Please respond."

"What the hell is going on?" Chief Harvey's voice crackled through the speaker. "We're at the airstrip and it looks like a war zone here."

"Any survivors?"

"We've found two, they're enroute to the hospital now." Darren heard the approaching siren outside the hospital. "One gunshot wound to the shoulder. Serious, but stable. another burn victim, critical. I don't know if she'll make it to the hospital."

"Return to town," Darren said, "Let the fire go, we have several bomb attacks at the town center. Call out everyone who has any training and get them here."

"God almighty," the fire chief said. "I'm on my way, the crew will follow."

One more call. He changed the band on the radio.

"Spruce Bay to Rangers," he said, "Spruce Bay to Rangers."

"Rangers here,"

"We have a wide spread emergency here with multiple sites and casualties. We need all the help we can get."

"We heard, Spruce Bay, we're already on our way, ETA in 10."

"Go up top Rangers, the hospital is damaged but functional, access is clear."

"Ten-four, we have full gear."

He looked up to see a nurse standing in the doorway. She looked concerned.

"You're bleeding. Let me look at you."

Darren couldn't stand up, but he swiveled toward her.

"There are people hurt worse," he said.

"Just one so far, and he's in surgery." She came and pulled his jacket open to look at him. She gasped and Darren looked at what had upset her.

A branch sticking out of his ribs.

"Shit," he said. "I thought I'd broke something."

The nurse was yelling for a stretcher and a doctor.

Cam ran in the door as they helped Darren onto the gurney.

"Darren, Pat and Amber are up top starting the rescue work, have you heard from Staff? What do we do?"

"You'll have to run the show along with Pat and Amber for a bit. Help is coming. I'll be there in just a few minutes."

The nurse snorted at him. As they wheeled Darren into the emergency OR, Cam run back out of the hospital.

Chapter Twenty

Dust and cries floated in the air. The gymnasium that always seemed so large while running up and down playing basketball, now was small and crowded.

"I think a role call is in order," Mr. McRoy said to Georgia. She coughed and nodded her head.

He walked through the gym talking to the teachers, the teachers started counting heads. Some of the high school classes were present, others, she hoped, took other shelter. She hadn't heard any explosions from the high school side so they were probably safe. It didn't make her feel any better that Brad wasn't anywhere in the gym.

"All the sevens and eights are here, as are Mlle Dupuis and Mr. Roberts. The sixes appear to be all present except for Ryley. I haven't seen him today, so we'll pray he's at home. The three/fours are here with Mrs. Dalrymple. Understandably Mrs. Dalrymple is distraught and her class are caring for her, but Sandra took a count. Mr. Jackson is present with his entire class. Mrs. Hall is missing. None of her students can say for sure if any of their class is absent. Thank God, the Kindergarteners don't come in until the afternoon." He sat on the floor beside her and groaned slightly. "The high school side is less clear, but there doesn't seem to be any damage on their side. It has been suggested we move into the cleaner air of the hallways."

"Good idea," Georgia said, "Let's start with the younger kids. Match them up with the older ones so we don't lose track of them. It will make it easier for the teachers."

Mr. McRoy nodded and pushed himself to his feet again.

"Georgia." Anna came up to her. "There are some scrapes and bruises. One maybe broken arm from falling ceiling. That seems to be it."

"Mrs. Hall is missing, so is Ryley, and has anyone seen Ms. Taladut?"

"I saw Ryley going with Ms. Taladut after yard this morning. He looked like he was in trouble again." Georgia looked around and saw Paul, "Thanks kiddo, Mrs. Hall isn't here. Do you know where she went?"

"Jake had gone to the bathroom, when Maria came. She brought us here, but I think Mrs. Hall went to look for Jake."

"OK," Georgia rubbed her head. She'd never had a headache before, but now her head pounded and all she wanted was to crawl under the covers and go to sleep.

"Mr. McRoy said we are to take the younger kids in the halls of the high school. There haven't been any explosions for a while so it's probably safe."

Alastair looked at her. When did he start looking younger than she felt? He had a cut on his face and looked horrible. "I'll take Paul with me."

"Thanks, Alastair. Tell Mr. McRoy Mrs. Hall might be in the washrooms with Jake."

"OK." He walked across the room to where they'd opened the door to the high school and fluorescent light beckoned with a promise of normality.

"Tom, Steve," Georgia called and hoisted herself upright. "I know it's foolish, but I want to see if we can get to the primary washrooms and check on Mrs. Hall. We also need to look at the office. Ms. Taladut has Ryley with her."

"The main doors are blocked," Steve said, "I already checked. We could try the dressing rooms."

"They go to the Seven/Eight end of the hall."

"Maybe our end of the hall will be clearer. It's where the office is anyway."

"OK then," Her vision swam for a moment and she had to lean on Tom. "We don't touch anything. Nothing. Moving the wrong thing can bring the whole place down."

"Are you all right?" Tom put his arm around her. "Anna," he said quietly, but she turned her head instantly. "Georgia's hurt, get her to fresh air." Anna came and wrapped her arm around Georgia, Maria took the other side. They half carried Georgia toward the light of the hallway. Georgia wanted to protest, but the

109

world started spinning. She dropped to her knees and puked all over the floor. Fortunately, most of the kids had left the gym by now. The girls waited until she was stopped then picked her up between them and carried her the rest of the way.

"Mr. McRoy," Maria called when they got to the hallway. "I think Georgia's got a concussion. They put her down where she could lean against the wall. Georgia looked at her sweater and made a noise of disgust.

"Boys," Anna picked out some of the closest and biggest boys. "Make a circle around Georgia with your back to her. She needs privacy. The boys formed a wall and cut off the curious faces of the other kids and the light piercing her eyes.

"Sweater, off," Anna ordered her. Maria helped her take off the fouled sweater. The air felt cool on her skin, but she couldn't just sit in her bra. What if Mr. McRoy came? What if Brad did? She lifted her arms to cover herself, but Maria put a t-shirt over her head and helped her put her hands through the arms.

"Thank you," Anna said to the boys, "you can sit down." They sat in place forming a protective wall around Georgia. She saw Alastair was missing his shirt. It must be his she wore now.

"Here's some water," Steve said, "The whole hall on our side is blocked. We found a water bottle and filled it for you."

Georgia took a sip and washed the taste of dust and puke out of her mouth.

"It appears to be all clear," Mr. McRoy said, "Some of the high school boys have gone to help with the rescue efforts. The rest of us have been instructed to stay here unless there is an injury needing medical attention. I believe a head injury would meet the criteria." He knelt and spoke very quietly to Georgia.

"I don't know by what means you knew what was coming or how you had a plan in place, but if it wouldn't get me fired, I'd kiss you. You and your friends have saved a lot of lives today. Go get yourself looked at and I'll take it from here."

Georgia managed a tiny nod. Alastair and another boy from his class had a stretcher.

"It's kept in the equipment room," he said, "Hank sprained an ankle last month and we had to use it."

"We'll walk with you," Anna said, "but let me go find you a coat."

"Stay sitting upright. I fell when we lived in Mexico. My head had a big bump on it and I got sick when I tried to lie down. You'll be fine." Maria steadied Georgia as she sat on the stretcher. "We should have two more boys," she said to the boys, "Not that you aren't all strong, but it is a long walk and she needs to be kept steady."

They finally decided on six boys, one for each handle and two to spell off anyone who got tired. They lifted Georgia as she sat on the stretcher and Maria walked beside her. She felt strange, like she was play acting. Georgia clenched her hands together to stop from waving to the other kids. The little kids waved to her and she tried to smile for them. Anna met her at the door and wrapped a bright pink coat around Georgia.

The sunlight was painful but the cold air made her feel better. It was easy walking along the path to the hospital entrance. Georgia felt a lump in her throat when she saw the damage to the doors and windows, but people moved in and out as if everything was normal. The boys walked up to the desk and Maria spoke to the nurse on duty in rapid Spanish. The nurse nodded and asked a couple of questions which Maria answered.

"This way." The nurse led the way to a gurney that sat in the hall. "You will have to wait." She took Geogia's pulse and then her blood pressure. "But Maria will stay with you. If there is any change, she will let me know. Try not to sleep. Come," she herded away the others, "I have work for you to do." They waved at Georgia then followed the nurse.

"Mi Madre," Maria said, "If you don't mind I will sit on the bed with you and we will be out of the way. You can lean on me if you need to." She climbed up on the gurney and sat beside Georgia, put an arm around her and held her close. Georgia liked the warmth of the other girl beside her. She had her friends, but they didn't hug or hold each other. Maria was nice.

"So, I will talk and you will listen and make noises *mmmhmmm* like that to show me you are awake. If you sleep I will have to pinch you."

"Mmmmhmmm" Georgia said.

"You are blessed, so I am blessed to be your friend. You are smart, and brave, and very beautiful. I know. That Alastair he'll never wash this shirt again because you wore it. He is smitten, my

111

friend. He had his eyes closed tight when he gave me his shirt because he was afraid if he peek; you would be angry. But he wanted to. He would have carried you too, but I told it him too cold without a shirt."

Maria chattered on and Georgia let her words flow over her like a balm.

Chapter Twenty-one

Cam worked with Fire Chief Harvey to coordinate rescue efforts focusing their efforts on the mall. Somehow the children had got away before the explosions brought most of the elementary school down.

The people in the mall weren't as lucky. The car had gone through the door and made it almost to the Library before it exploded and brought down the entire back half of the mall. Another car had hit the detachment - the explosion destroyed the detachment and laid open the council chambers. A team from the Rangers picked their way through the rubble to check for survivors. Cam didn't have much hope.

Pat and Amber were clearing the Food Store with another team of rescuers, these ones made of fire fighters and whoever had had mine rescue training. People who could walk were sent to a tent the Rangers had provided. First aiders checked them over and made notes for when there was time for doctors to do their work. People who couldn't walk were loaded onto the backs of pickup trucks and driven around to the hospital.

He heard helicopters. Help was coming and not too soon. Three of them flew over the scene. One broke off to land at the heliport by the hospital and the other two found space in the school yard. People boiled off the helicopters and ran toward the mall carrying their weapons and looking like they expected a fire fight at any moment. As soon as they were clear the choppers took off again and headed south.

"Who's the officer in charge?" One man asked. He had Sergeant's bars on his uniform. He looked military rather than police.

"I guess I'm the closest thing to someone in charge until our Staff gets out of surgery."

"I'm Sergeant Fredericks with the Reserve in Thompson. We'll worry about chain of command bullshit later. What do you need us to do?"

"We have people in the mall," Cam waved behind him, "Our first job is to get them out. We have no count of how many, so we need to work carefully and not miss anyone."

"What about there?" Fredericks pointed at the school.

"Word is the kids got out before the blasts took the place down. There are four missing, two teachers, two students." Cam pulled out his note pad and scribbled a map. "A teacher and a young kid are in this area, the primary washrooms. Her name is Mrs. Hall; the kid is Jake."

Fredericks waved over four people and handed them the map. "Two possibles in this area. Use caution, that doesn't look stable. We want rescues, not more casualties."

They ran toward the far end of the school where they stopped and pulled gear from their backpacks.

"The other pair will be in that area." Cam pointed to a pile of rubble. "We can't tackle it without machinery. We're working on that." He walked toward the mall drawing another map. "The mall is C shaped, this entrance shares a wall with the school on the right. On the left is the food store. The pharmacy is on the corner, then there is a coffee shop, an empty store, then a general store, clothes, crafts, you name it. The next corner is where a special task force set up shop. Then another few empty shops. Across from them was the detachment, the Council Chambers, then the arena running along the back wall to the library. The hospital is off this corner, but there's no connection between the mall and the hospital."

Fredericks sent more people to help Pat and Amber then the rest of them started going through the wreckage.

"Casualty!" one called, "marking location." They marked several more bodies before they reached someone alive - one of the clerks in the Town Office. Cam remembered her as always having a smile on her face. They dug her out and carried her to the parking lot where they loaded her on the ambulance. The paramedics checked her out as the vehicle moved even though it wasn't a one minute ride.

The rescuers couldn't go any farther. The entire back roof had come down

"Are there any service corridors?" Fredericks asked, "We need a way to get into those stores."

"I don't know," Cam said, "The Fire Chief would." He went to find the Fire Chief. The Food Store had been cleared and they were trying to get into the pharmacy, but they ran into the same problem. The mall had collapsed and movement was impossible. The Fire Chief Harvey showed Fredericks and his people the corridors. They found some open spaces and pulled a few more survivors out.

Cam heard the rumble of equipment. Ruth Cassidy was driving a front-end loader while Joe McCrey had a back hoe. A flat-bed truck carried a couple of bobcats.

Fredericks directed them to start on the pile where Cam thought Ms. Taladut and Ryley might be. The four who had been sent to find Mrs. Hall and Jake had found them huddled in a corner of the bathroom. They'd suffocated under the weight of the collapsed roof.

Cam wanted to tear into the rubble and throw it aside, but it was slow delicate work. Each time they lifted a piece out, they chanced the entire pile shifting. Teams braced and reinforced as they worked. Slow as it was they made progress. Every ten minutes Fredericks had all the equipment shut down and he shouted into the rubble. They waited for an answer before starting again.

"Cam," Pat stood at his elbow. "You need to see this." She led him away toward the road leading into the parking lot. It was lined with cars, trucks, and people.

"I thought we sent all the non-rescuers home."

"We did, these are people from the reserve. They've come to help."

Mike Tremblant came up to Cam.

"You and the rescuers can't work on empty stomachs. We have food, water, blankets. You're our neighbours, and we're not sitting back while our neighbours suffer."

"Thank you," Cam had to swallow before he could continue. Why don't you set up right here? Just leave a road in and out for us." He turned to Pat. "Put together a team of people to go through town, knock on doors, find out who's missing. Let people know we're here. We want to make sure there aren't any casualties out there from heart attacks or the like."

"Yes, sir," she said.

"You and Amber both have more years than I do. Why am I in charge?"

"You're the one giving orders." She patted his arm. "And so far, they've all been good ones. We'll let you know if you get out of line." She walked over to a group of woman and started organizing people to go door to door.

Cam took a deep breath and turned to go back to work. Mike handed him a bottle of water.

"Drink," he said, "We'll bring more to the rescuers."

"We have a tent of people who have minor injuries…"

"I'll send food, water and blankets to them." Mike waved another man over and gave a few instructions. "Ron will take care of it."

Mike walked with Cam back to the mall. Cam introduced him to Fredericks.

"Good," Fredericks looked up at the sun. "It's time to eat and start taking breaks. Tired and hungry rescuers make for more injuries." He sent a first shift to eat and rest before they went back to working on the pile of rubble.

"Cam," Amber tapped him on the shoulder. "Darren is out of surgery. His injury wasn't as bad as they thought, but he won't be working for a few days. Staff Sergeant is out too, but he hasn't woken up yet. They're putting a good face on it, but they're worried. The Deputy Minister is hanging on by a thread. She was badly burned. The helicopter took her to Thompson and they'll fly her to Winnipeg. None of the rest made it. They're out on the airstrip lying in the dirt. I want to take a team out to recover their bodies before the animals get to them."

"We're rotating through rescuers here, Amber, I don't want to lose any more, but maybe some of Mike's people can help you. Just make sure you tell them they're going to have nightmares about what they see."

"Mike?" Amber asked.

"Tremblant, the chief from Spruce Bay Cree Nation."

"OK," Amber said. "I know him. We'll get it done."

116

"One other thing, Amber. Keep your eyes open. Someone shot Staff and set explosives on the gas depot. They may be waiting for someone else to show up."

"I'll be careful." She headed toward where her truck was parked. Cam turned back to the rescue effort.

Chapter Twenty-two

Ms. Taladut tried to relieve the cramp in her legs, but the tiny space didn't allow it. She closed her eyes and slowed her breathing. She didn't know how long she'd been there. It felt like she always been there, under her desk.

She'd worked very hard at not taking her humiliation out on the children. She knew they didn't like her. What they didn't know was she was doing her best, just out of her depth. It was so easy to have an opinion. Even more tempting to act on it. Before she knew it she'd become a raging lunatic abusing teachers and terrifying the children. She should have quit, but somebody had to do the administration. Maybe she could fix it.

She'd seen Ryley arguing with a boy on the school yard. It didn't look like a big deal, but it was an opportunity.

"Ryley," she said, "Tell me what's wrong."

"Angry," Ryley had said, "Not stupid."

"Nathan," she said to the other boy, pleased she remembered his name. "Tell me what's wrong."

"Ryley was looking at my car and broke it." He showed Ms. Taladut a toy car with a wheel broken off.

"Ryley sorry. Fix?" He held his hands out and the other boy put the car and the tiny wheel in Ryley's hand. The bigger boy peered at the car and poked at the wheel. Ms. Taladut could see where the plastic had broken.

"Maybe it needs some glue, Ryley." Ms. Taladut said.

"Glue," Ryley said and nodded his head.

"Nathan," She smiled at the boy. "you go and play while Ryley and I try to fix your car." Ryley followed her into the school with the car and the wheel in his hands. They got to her office and put the car on her desk. She had a tube of crazy glue for fixing a mug she'd broken.

"Fix cup," Ryley pointed to the mug. "Georgia fix Ryley's cup."

"Where is it now Ryley?"

"Wendigo break, wendigo smash because Ryley not wolf, not kill."

"Oh dear." She put her hand on her heart. "He wanted you to kill?"

"Ax," Ryley said, "but Ryley choose, not wolf, not kill."

"I'm very glad you did Ryley. You are very brave."

"Mom brave." Ryley ducked his head. "Ryley broken, but Mom fix. Love is glue."

"Yes, it is." Mrs. Taladut blinked back a tear. "You are smart Ryley."

Ryley grinned at her and shook his head.

Ms. Taladut opened the glue and tried to glue the wheel back onto the tiny bit of plastic on the end of the axle.

"Did you hear something?" she asked Ryley, but he was concentrating on the wheel.

"Broken." He poked at the car. "Ryley sorry."

"Let me try again." She put a tiny ball of glue on the end of the axle and held the wheel in place. She held her breath and focused everything on that tiny black wheel. Somehow if she could help Ryley fix this car, then everything would be OK. She knew it was ridiculous, but still she focused and prayed.

Then there was an explosion and the whole building shook. She fell to the floor and dropped the car. Ryley screamed. Ms Taladut saw the car under her desk. The second explosion hit as she gripped the car and pulled it out in triumph. The ceiling fell in but Ryley pushed her back under the desk before the building collapsed on top of them.

Ms Taladut sat in the black under the desk. In one hand, she held the car, in the other she held Ryley's hand. Tears ran down her cheeks. *All the children*, she imagined them buried like Ryley, slowly cooling. She didn't know why Ryley had pushed her under the desk. He could have dove past her and saved himself. He chose to save her.

She cried until she had no more tears and her throat burned from sobbing and dust. Time passed and she had no idea of how long. She wondered if she'd died, and this was punishment for

119

letting her ambition turn her into a mean and conniving woman. If so she was prepared to take it. Ryley's hand had gone stiff now, but she still reached out to hold it, as if he could feel her presence where ever he was.

Then she heard the equipment working. Hope hit her as painful as thawing fingers. She yelled, certain her throat bled, but no answer came. Just the slow grind of steel and concrete.

The air grew thick and she had trouble breathing. Dust clogged her nose. They were closer. She heard their shouts the last time they stopped. She yelled in response, but didn't think they heard. It would be a suitable punishment if they missed her location and she stifled so close to salvation.

Then the grinding noise became unbearably loud and suddenly light made her cover her eyes. She must have screamed, because she heard shouts above and hands moved smaller pieces before the machine lifted the last big piece off the desk. They lifted her out and passed her hand to hand until she was safe.

The sun lit the scene with a golden glow making destruction horribly beautiful. Leigh stood with a question in her eyes. Ms. Taladut couldn't say the words, instead she fell to the ground weeping. The only words she could force past her tongue were *It should have been me. I wish it had been me.* She refused to leave the site until it was dark with the moon making harsh shadows and they brought out Ryley's body.

Leigh fell to her knees beside her son and wailed her grief.

All Ms. Taladut had left was a certainty it should be been her lying there cold and blue. She swore to herself, to God if he was listening. Somehow she would give this sacrifice meaning.

Chapter Twenty-three

Jim sat in his chair and tried to type left handed. The sling was a nuisance, but not as bad as the pain if he took it off. He sat in an office in the old industrial district of Spruce Bay. The building smelled musty with walls in various shades of gray. They had no internet. TV was gone too. They had both come in through the Mall.

Typing and swearing at the pain was better than seeing the hole in the community where the mall used to stand. Makeshift offices filled old buildings down the hill from the town. They felt disconnected from the people. Even the graffiti artists hadn't bothered to come here.

Jim struggled to report how they had misjudged the danger so badly. Because of that mistake more than fifty people died, including the Deputy Minister who gave up the fight just that morning. He wanted to smash something. He wanted to find who was responsible, shoot them, then bring them back so he could shoot them again. He wanted to read one more story to Ryley before tucking him into bed.

Jim sobbed and then cursed as the pain hit him. He tried to wipe the tears away with his free hand, but just smeared them across his face. Nobody needed his report. He was here because it was less painful than seeing the grief etched on Leigh's face. Damn it they were supposed to save that kid!

Not just Leigh, Jake's family and Mrs. Hall's, the families of all the other dead. Too much grief for the small town to hold. Every time he saw someone, he felt he'd failed them.

"Staff," the radio on his desk sputtered to life, "you'll want to come see this. Amber should be outside to pick you up."

"Ten-four, Cam," Jim didn't bother saving the half dozen words he'd taken all morning to write. He put his coat on and walked out to the truck where Amber was waiting.

"Where are we headed?" he asked as he did up his seatbelt.

"Airstrip," Amber said. "You aren't going to believe it." She wound through the industrial district. Jim saw where Derek Smythe had set up a temporary grocery store in a storage shed. The pharmacist had been killed so people had to order prescriptions from Thompson. The Horate's had set up a Mexican food and Coffee Shop across the way in what had been dealership of some kind.

The road took them past the mall sitting crumpled and gaping; surrounded by fence Cam had found in some shed. Snow drifted down on the memorials lining the fence. Jim turned away before he started tearing up again. The road out to the airstrip was rough, it hadn't been maintained. The plow's driver had been drinking coffee when the attack came.

Jim saw the airplane before they reached the strip. It was the biggest plane he'd ever seen. Dozens of figures in white camouflage scurried about unloading gear. As he watched a transport truck drove down a ramp and turned toward them. As Amber pulled onto the runway he saw the wreckage of the burned-out airplane had been pushed to one side.

"We cleared the runway the day after," Amber said, "I figured someone might want to use it. That's when we found the other bodies."

"Other bodies?" Jim knew she'd said something to him at the time, but the last week was a fog.

"Zeke Hamilton and Ted Hadstadt were in the equipment shed. They'd been shot at close range with a shotgun and dragged there. They probably came on the terrorists setting the bomb on the fuel tank and been shot for their trouble. Since bodies would have given away the attack, they were put in the shed."

"The shed was locked."

"That's right, we had to cut the lock to get the equipment out."

"Why lock the shed and not lock the gas depot?"

"Why do any of this shit?" Amber said, "None of it makes sense."

"I guess." He tried to reach across to open the door, but couldn't. Amber climbed out and walked around the truck to let him out. By the time he'd maneuvered himself out of the truck a man had walked over to meet them.

"Sergeant Anthony Creeley," the man said, and Jim saw the bars on his sleeve. "The Colonel's compliments and he would like to meet with you."

"That's what we're here for," Jim said, "Lead on."

Sergeant Creeley spun and walked away toward the only person not wearing white gear. He was dressed in full uniform. Jim wondered how he hadn't frozen to death without coat, hat or gloves. The answer was a radiant heater plugged into a generator. Jim felt over heated as soon as he reached the Colonel.

"Colonel," The Sergeant saluted. He nodded at Jim and Amber before heading off to yell at a group trying to get a bundle of crate off the plane with a crane.

"Colonel Clayton Stone," the man introduced himself without shaking hands.

"Staff-Sergeant Jim Dalrymple and Constable Amber Mouski," Jim said. "I don't want to sound inhospitable, but we don't have supplies or space for this many people. No one informed me you were coming."

"No one knew we were coming. If I'd told you I was bringing my people here it would have been all over the news and we would lose our opportunity. We brought our own supplies. We are completely self-sufficient, Staff-Sergeant. We can't count on people rolling out the welcome mat when we arrive. We have a good location here to set up HQ. I'll get one of the techs to give you a dedicated radio so we can keep you informed of anything we may need you to do."

"We are busy," Jim fought hard to keep his voice from shaking, "We have thirty-nine dead from our own town. We don't have time to run around helping you out. We didn't ask for you."

"Understood." The colonel looked away from Jim and something flashed across the man's face. Guilt? Anger? Jim couldn't say. When the man looked at him his face held sympathy. "You folks have suffered a grievous loss. I won't be asking you to do much more than stay out of our way. I should be asking you what we can do for you."

"Nothing, unless you have a building big enough for the entire town to meet."

123

"Quartermaster." The Colonel didn't look around.

"We can spare it," The woman holding a clipboard flipped through a few pages. "It's on that truck." She pointed to the transport which had just come off the plane.

"See to it."

The woman nodded and headed over to the truck.

"Tell the Quartermaster where you want it set up."

"The school yard," Jim said. Amber shrugged and walked off after the Quartermaster.

"Did any of your people engage the enemy?"

"The closest we came to engaging the attackers was Constable Darren Little almost running one of the cars off the road. He probably saved the hospital."

"I would like the opportunity to debrief the constable at his earliest convenience."

"He was injured, but he's back on light duty." Jim breathed slowly to push the pain away. "I will ask him to make himself available to you when he comes on duty. Someone can come to show you around town."

"I have maps." The Colonel nodded and pointed off the side to a rack holding tubes. "But a tour would be very welcome. I see you were also injured in the action. I won't keep you. Someone will deliver the radio before nightfall." He turned back to watching the unloading proceed. Jim took it as dismissal and trudged to the truck. He climbed in and waited for Amber. She arrived a few minutes later and they drove back to town.

"I understand his desire for security." Jim ground his teeth. "but it would have been helpful if we'd been alerted."

"I'm guessing there is a complete blackout on the military presence here. It wouldn't be good for people to know we are fighting a war on our own soil."

"A war?" Jim's shock outweighed the pain momentarily. "Isn't that a little melodramatic?"

"What would you call it, Staff?"

Jim wasn't sure, but what he did know he wanted nothing to do with living in a war zone.

Amber dropped him at the new detachment building and he went to his office to think. He looked at the maps on the wall and other things he'd put up to make it look like a detachment. His office was bigger than the old one, there was a garage in the back with space to park three trucks; in many ways a better space than their detachment office at the mall. He hated it. It felt like a betrayal of Carol who had died with their old detachment.

"All units," he said, "we will meet at 1830 to discuss the military's arrival. Staff out."

"Ten-four," came the responses. The main radio they had used to stay in contact with provincial dispatch had gone down in the blast. Jim dispatched them out of his office. He only needed one arm for that. Darren took over for the night shift. None of them had a night off in the week since the attack.

He went back to trying to write a report. That would keep him from thinking too much before the meeting.

At 1830, his four constables sat with him in the area Jim had designated as the staff room.

"Colonel Clayton Stone has arrived with about a hundred army regulars and some support staff. All I've been able to turn up on him is he served several tours in Afghanistan and was on peace keeping missions before then. This is a full military response to the attack on Spruce Bay. No one is talking about this response. The people higher up are using a very heavy hand to keep this quiet. I do not want to be the person responsible for turning this into a media circus.

"It is clear he is taking over. I was told our job is to stay out of his way. I expect that will be expanded to keeping the population of Spruce Bay out of his way too. Suggestions?"

"I hope he is going to keep a tight rein on his people," Pat said, "If any of them cause trouble I will bust their asses."

"That's going to be a problem," Cam said, "I grew up beside a military base and the MP's always assumed their jurisdiction took priority over anything else. The local force spent a lot of time gnashing their teeth."

"I'll keep an eye on it" Jim made a note to look up regulations.

"We'll need to let the people on the reserve know a whole lot of people will be tramping around on their land.," Darren frowned.

"I don't think the Colonel will be happy with that," Amber said.

125

"The people of Spruce Bay Cree Nation were the first people here to help us. They are our neighbours, not a security risk."

"We will hold off on broadcasting anything to anybody for the time being," Jim held up his hand. "I don't want this Colonel to be angry with us from the start."

"I don't like it, but I don't have much choice." Darren shrugged and sat back.

"I wouldn't say things like that around the Colonel." Cam shook his head. "I don't think he would approve of sympathy for the enemy."

"The Cree are not the enemy," Darren scowled and crossed his arms.

"No," Jim met Darren's eyes, then Cam's. "They aren't, and yet the people who attacked us may have been Cree. We haven't recovered any identities from the bodies of the attackers. We're guessing it has something to do with the arsons at the lodges and Dupreis is Cree. There were at least five other people involved who may or may not have been Cree or First Nations."

"You will have a chance to scope out the Colonel for yourself. He's requested the chance to debrief you. Unless you have a good reason for not cooperating, I expect you to report to the airstrip at the start of your shift. Take Pat with you as backup. He's less likely to be offensive if there is a witness."

"I guess I need to show him at least one Cree is on our side." Darren grimaced. "There goes my relaxing night of driving around waiting for the next attack."

Chapter Twenty-four

Colonel Clayton Stone hated working around civilians. It was his sworn duty to protect the country and its citizens. He just didn't like them very much - a result of spending most of his life in the army, and most of that deployed in one zone or another. In a war zone, things are clear. His people did what he expected of them and there wasn't any confusion about purpose.

He'd had an illuminating chat with Constable Little. From what the constable had shown him the car could only have come from an area along a mostly abandoned road. Possibly from the mine at the end of it. A mine site would be a perfect location for a terrorist camp. They would be free from surveillance and could build whatever they wanted in secret.

"Colonel," Lieutenant Mary O'Neil stood at the door of his tent. "Come," he said.

"I have the results of the search you asked for." She stood at ease. "There are no reported large thefts of explosive in the last six months. There are many reports of smaller thefts from mines and constructions sites across the country. It is difficult to correlate data about First Nations since almost all those sites have First Nations employees. The turnover rate is high enough even for non First Nations that coming up with a name or list of names is impossible at this time. I could find no one person or small group of people present at each of the thefts."

"Is there a change in frequency or severity at any time?"

"There may be a slight bump in the frequency of thefts in the last three months. It is small enough to be statistical noise."

"So what you're saying is theft of explosives is a constant across the board."

"The lower the effectiveness of the explosive the less control is exercised. Until we do an analysis of the site of the explosions, we won't be able to determine the nature of the material used."

"The locals haven't done this?"

"Permission to speak frankly, sir."

"Go ahead,"

"I'm surprised the locals are able to function at all, never mind organize lab tests. They are civilians unused to the idea of attack. They have thirty-nine dead in a population of less than a thousand including the people on the reserve just outside of town. We can't expect much aid from that quarter, and any intelligence we do get may be suspect."

"Yes," The Colonel rubbed his forehead. "So we don't have any idea of where he got the explosives, what he used, or how much he still has on hand."

"Sir, we have no intelligence he is involved."

"It has his fingerprints all over it. Fortunately, they are focused on this Dupreis fellow. Let's see if we can keep it that way." The Colonel picked up a pen and examined it closely. "If theft is as pervasive as you say, Lieutenant, we should be looking into companies which have not reported any theft. See if there are any connections."

"Yes, sir," she said. He waved his hand and she saluted and left him to think.

They'd spent months, years trying to dig the insurgents out of their caves. Rivers would know the value of such a defensible position. Damn him anyway! He was part of the team. The Colonel took it as a direct insult that the man had vanished only to return like this. There would be no court martial for Rivers this time. When they caught him, the Colonel planned to carve out the man's heart personally.

He picked up the radio on his desk.

"Strategic meeting in 10." He didn't bother waiting for acknowledgments. They were military. They would be there.

Ten minutes later he looked at his command team. Lieutenant O'Neil was the youngest and only had one tour under her belt. Captain Hugh Banning had been with the Colonel the longest. The Colonel had recruited him out of Officer's Training to put together his first team. Captain Al Raffin had joined them during their first tour in Afghanistan.

"The camp is secure," Capt. Raffin reported. "I have people doing wide sweeps and snipers on several rises."

"The equipment is down and checked and ready for operational use," Banning said. "Being short one shed, I have some under tarps with men posted guard."

"We won't be here long before the word gets out." The Colonel leaned forward. "so I intend to make use of the time we have to act without people watching over our shoulders." He unrolled a map. "The constable stated the car he chased came from this direction. There is an abandoned mine at the end of this road. It's in poor shape and is mostly used by hunters with quads or four-wheel drives. It should be usable by our equipment. I want a convoy out there by dawn. That means it leaves in four hours."

"It's what we're here to do," Banning said. "The men are ready."

"Excellent." The Colonel pulled another map out. This one a satellite photo of the mine in question. "As you can see there are several buildings which could house the enemy. It is possible they are underground, but unlikely. They would lose mobility and response time. None-the-less, I want the mine sealed. Anything underground is going to stay there. We hit the buildings and flatten them. You know who we're looking for. I want a positive I.D. on the man, preferably of him in a body bag.

"Captains, you will draw up the battle plan and choose the teams to execute it. Take whoever you need and whatever equipment. I don't want this coming apart because we decided to be cheap. Ottawa wants this quick and clean. They want to be able to report the people responsible have been dealt with before it turns into a circus and other people start getting ideas. We are here to stop this action here and now."

"Yes, sir."

"Get to work,"

The captains saluted and left. Lieutenant O'Brien hung back.

"Yes, Lieutenant?"

"If you are sure Rivers is behind this attack, I would like permission to set up surveillance on his family and known associates. I'll keep it passive for now, but he needs to be getting his information and support from somewhere."

"Very well," the colonel said, "but keep in mind he will be expecting you and will have counter-measures in place. Double check, hell, triple check anything you find before suggesting we act on it."

"Yes, sir."

The colonel heard the rumble of gear moving out. They hadn't brought tanks, but they had modified LAV III's. The soldiers were the most experienced he had in his unit. They would get the job done and not make any mistake about it.

Rivers was good at what he did, but he was working with amateurs. He didn't stand a chance.

Even with that assurance, the colonel wasn't able to sleep after the last APC left and the camp returned to silence. He wondered if the Lieutenant was asleep. Only one way to find out. He got dressed and slipped out of his tent. He took his radio with him. Some rules he didn't mind breaking, but he never let himself be out of communication.

Chapter Twenty-five

Private First Class Davidson drove the APC with active night vision. He was so used to the night vision he wouldn't drive civilian vehicles at night. He didn't feel safe unless the world lit up in green and black. Private Levesque used the infra-red. The night was cold, maybe minus ten, but that just made it easier to see heat traces, even old ones. Neither of them saw anything.

They ran on minimum electronics - just in case the enemy had some surveillance to detect their signal. It wasn't like they could get lost. There was only one road.

The trees were strange, like toothpicks with Christmas trees stuck on top. They cut off vision and yet allowed enemy movement. They couldn't see very far into the forest, not with their ground-based infrared. Davidson would be happier with some air support, but choppers made too much noise. They'd have to do without.

Nothing. No people, no bombs, not even any wildlife. There was lots of space up here. That meant space for the enemy to hide. Davidson hoped they were holed up at this mine like the brass thought. They could deal with the enemy and get back to where it was decently warm.

They reached the edge of the woods and Davidson paused while the scouts offloaded and walked around the perimeter. Even with the new gear, they showed up brightly on the infrared. He watched them explore then wave him on. They didn't see any movement or light. Levesque pointed to his display. The buildings glowed with heat. He waved the captain up and showed him.

"Very good, private," the captain said, "watch for individual traces. I want a number."

"Yes, sir."

The captain sent a runner to inform the other LAV's. When she got back, they edged forward into the clearing.

"Be ready to bring up full electronics," the captain ordered them, "The building we are taking is marked in TechNav."

"Yes, sir."

The last LAV cleared the woods behind them.

"Let's go." the captain had strapped himself in so Davidson gunned the engine and the vehicle roared forward. He kept carefully in the center of the road. They had a straight run until they got to the fence. Intel was that inside the fence was rock and gravel. He wouldn't bog down in the few inches of snow covering the ground.

They went through the gate without even feeling it and Davidson headed toward the building flagged on his Nav system. They had talked about the best way to subdue the buildings and settled on the most direct. They would circle the building and fill it with gunfire from their turret guns. Then the foot guys could go in and mop up.

Davidson reached the target building.

"Mark," he said, and the gunner lit it up. Plywood splinters flew and the steel of the walls turned into swiss cheese. He completed the circuit and they cracked the doors. Six soldiers carrying almost as much firepower as the LAV kicked through what remained of the door.

Davidson could see the captain's screen showing the cameras from the six person squad. He tried to remain focused on his screens, but he also wanted to see the action. He loosened his straps a little and contented himself with stealing quick glances.

"Clear." They shouted as they went through room after room.

"Clear."

"Shit, trip wire," he heard, then the flat thud of a grenade.

"Clear, no injuries,"

"Stay alert." the captain ordered. "Slow down."

Davidson heard another explosion. He thought maybe a grenade from another building, but the sound was wrong. He scanned with his camera.

"Holy, Mother of God," he said, "Captain, get them out of there. Get everyone out. They've blown the mine head. He heard more explosion and saw the puffs of smoke from them. The huge structure started its slow fall to earth. The footsteps of the crew clattered on board and he gunned the LAV backward. The mine head accelerated, he wasn't going to make it. Then it hit the ground with a horrific rumble and kept hitting the ground. He drove blind, just going straight backwards. Dust and debris flew at them and clanged off the front of their LAV. Somehow they were still alive.

He felt the right rear hit something. He didn't know what. It didn't matter. It slewed the LAV to the side and it flipped. Davidson hoped everyone had strapped in. He was thrown back and forth and he felt things in his body give way. Pain became his only reality.

They stopped rolling on their left side.

"Call out," the captain ordered, cool as ever.

"Squad's good," Sergeant Cooper reported, "Fitz has a busted leg."

"I'm good," Levesque said.

Davidson tried to say something, but his voice wasn't working. It took him a second to work out he couldn't talk because he wasn't breathing. He tried, but the message wasn't reaching his lungs. He heard Levesque checking him out, but couldn't feel anything.

"Shit," Levesque said, "Davidson's gone."

***

Captain Banning surveyed the damage. They'd lost three LAV's and twenty-three soldiers. They had two LAV's to get the remaining seventeen back to base.

They hadn't seen a single enemy. The buildings were warm because heaters had been hooked up to generators and left on. They'd been sucker punched, that bastard Rivers had known they would come here first. It was too damn logical. He and his people were still out there. He had no idea how many or even who they were fighting.

"Load up and let's get out of here," he said.

He rode in the point vehicle and Captain Raffin rode at the rear. It was just pure dumb luck neither of them were buried under that rubble. *No,* he thought, *not luck, Davidson, the poor beggar.*

He'd given them enough time to get clear. Life wasn't fair and war even less so.

The sky lightened in the East as they limped back into camp. Banning thought about the report he had to make to the colonel and just for a moment thought wistfully of being dead and buried under tons of wood.

Chapter Twenty-six

"He suckered us," Colonel Stone said when Banning made his report. "I should have known it was too easy. I trained Rivers and I forgot my own training. We won't make that mistake again." He played with the pen on his desk. Banning didn't know what it was with that pen. Stone had it since before they met and where ever they deployed he brought it with him.

"I want a full team to go to the mine site tomorrow, put it together, then get some rest. I want you back there with a full team for security. We need analysis of the explosive used. Bring back anything they left behind. We know they were there, let's see what we can learn from the site."

"Yes, sir," Banning saluted and walked to his own field office where he called in the sergeants.

"We're going out tomorrow on a retrieval and intel mission," he said, "I need people who can do the work without getting distracted. I will also want a perimeter team to maintain security while we are on site. I want those people hand-picked. They have to be able to assess and respond immediately to threats that may not be familiar."

They looked thoughtful and left to make up their teams. Banning pulled the files on the soldiers they had left behind. He started writing the letters to their families. With each letter he wrote, he got angrier. More of his people had died in one night than had in all their tours in Afghanistan. He had a pattern for the letters he followed, though he hand-wrote each letter. He refused to do a death notification with a form letter.

Only when he had done with the last letter did he allow himself to go to bed to rest. He knew he must have slept because he woke with visions of a massive building falling on him.

He went to see the colonel before they headed out.

"Sir," he said, "I would like to get aerial support. Either some drones or choppers. We need people in the air to find Rivers and his people."

"Understood, Captain," the Colonel said, "Ottawa wanted to keep this operation small and quick, but I think now that's wishful thinking. We can't afford wishful thinking. This is our own backyard. I will not allow this to drag out indefinitely. I am calling in more men and equipment. We will expand our base here to make room for them. Lieutenant O'Neil is coordinating with the Quartermaster. In the meantime, Captain Raffin is setting up a check point on the road out of here. His team is also marking the trails and closing the ones we can't control. I will not have Rivers and his people moving easily in and out of town."

"That's not going to be a popular move."

"I'm not here to win a popularity contest, I'm here to shut down Rivers before this war can spread. He's a cancer and we will cut it out."

"Yes, sir" Banning went to join the team headed out to the mine site. They had the LAV's and some conventional vehicles. He just hoped they didn't get stuck. The ride out was boring and exhausting. Without any air support, they could only see a few meters into the forest. He expected an attack, but none came.

At the site, Banning sent the perimeter people out.

"You are watching outwards. You won't get much warning of an attack and it may not look like anything you expect. Use your heads and stay in touch. Keep up the radio chatter. They'll know we are here. I don't want them thinking we're afraid of them. The LAV's are to keep a roving perimeter inside yours. Call on them for support if you need it."

He watched them get into position, then sent in the recovery people. They had heavy machinery brought on a flatbed. They checked the wreckage for more traps before they started digging for bodies and evidence. The work was slow and emotionally draining. Each body they found a reminder of their own mortality and weakness. Not a safe thing for a soldier to spend a lot of time thinking about.

The short day ended and Banning had them sleep in shifts in the LAV's. It wasn't comfortable, but more secure than tents. They had a tent for the bodies of their comrades. The work started

136

again in the morning and continued through the next day. It started snowing heavily. Banning worried about the vehicles getting stuck on the trail. He radioed base to check on the status of the weather.

"Weather services is calling for a major winter storm," Lieutenant O'Neil said.

"How long do we have?"

"It's here now, and it is going to get worse."

"I need the trail cleared or we'll get bogged down before we get five kilometers."

"We don't have a snow plow with us."

"The town must have one. Borrow theirs."

"I will discuss the matter with the colonel."

"Thanks, Lieutenant, Banning out." He sighed then picked up the mic again. "Banning to perimeter, tighten the circle, watch your GPS and don't wander. This is going to get worse before it gets better."

They worked hard to find the last few bodies under the heaviest rubble. Banning had some people start loading the recovered bodies onto the trailer they brought to carry them. They also placed several mangled generators and heaters in the trailer.

"We're done," he heard from the recovery team. "We're coming in now." Banning watched the slow progress of the machinery toward the flatbed. It was practically swimming in the snow. He'd called in the roving LAV's since he didn't want them bogging down.

They struggled to get the equipment loaded and the convoy lined up.

"Base to Banning," the Lieutenant said, "A snowplow is on its way to your location. Their regular driver died in the attack, but the Staff Sergeant found a person who would drive. The driver suggested you wait on his arrival. If you bog on the trail there may not be room to extricate you."

"Roger that," Banning said, "will wait for the snowplow's arrival."

It was already dark, but it was black night by the time they saw the lights of the snowplow come slowly across the clearing to them. The driver climbed out and walked over to the LAV's. Banning put his coat on and went to meet him.

137

"I want to thank you for your help," he said to the plow operator. The man had the same bronze skin as Rivers, Banning tried not to let it bother him.

"I suggest you put the most important vehicles in the front," the man said, "the road is soft and each vehicle that drives on it breaks it down more. I don't have the equipment to pull you out if you get stuck. We'll go slow but steady. I'm not going to stop if I don't have to and neither should you."

"Sounds reasonable, let's get out of here," Banning said.

The driver walked back to the plow and drove in a circle he came as close as he could to their position before he started back down the road.

"Follow, keep a spread," Banning ordered the drivers, "maintain movement at all times."

The LAV's rumbled forward, the first one pulled the trailer with their recovered dead. The other two came after. The big rig with the heavy machinery came after that.

When Banning ordered his drivers to maintain momentum he didn't realize how long the drive was going to be. They moved even slower now than they were on the outward drive. They had a visible enemy now. The snow fell ever thicker and at times making it impossible to see the vehicle in front or even the trees to the side. The drivers kept going long past the time when Banning thought they would drop. He wondered at the stamina of the driver of the snowplow. The man was making the trip back to back with no rest.

Banning didn't know they were back until the lights of their base appeared through the snow. The snow plow circled again and waited until they all passed before pulling out and returning to town.

The sentries looked annoyed the driver hadn't paid them any attention, but Banning told them it was fine, this time. He sent his team off to a well deserved rest and went to report to Stone. He could hardly call being rescued by a snowplow from town a victory, but at least no one had died this time.

Chapter Twenty-seven

Jim looked out his window. The white of falling snow blanked out everything.

"The view isn't going to change anytime soon," Joe said. "Don went home, but he did a great job of getting us home from the mine. I'm glad you suggested having two drivers. From what I could see through the storm that old mine had been blown all to hell. They had three of those armoured vehicles, one pulling a trailer and a flatbed rig with a back hoe and a bulldozer. I think they were looking for something there and got caught by the weather."

"I don't think they're used to functioning in this climate," Jim sighed and turned away from the window. "Maybe the Rangers can help them."

"I don't know," Joe shook his head and leaned against the wall. "They didn't look like they'd be happy getting advice from an auxiliary reserve. Their boss looked like he'd bit into a lemon when he saw me. Polite enough, but…"

"You look like the people they think are the enemy," Jim said with a sigh. "Darren said the same kind of thing. I hope it doesn't get to be a bigger problem."

"This country can kill you if you aren't prepared," Joe didn't move, but his shoulders tensed. "Even I would think twice about going out in this kind of weather. It is easy to get turned around and GPS and compasses don't always work right."

"Zeke Hamilton said something like that." Jim walked over to the map and looked at the area Zeke had pointed to. He'd marked it lightly in pencil. "Said it was in this area."

"That would make sense," Joe walked over to peer at the map. "The spirits of that area are unsettled. It's the place Fran's father went looking for evidence of the Vikings."

"Did he find any?"

"Not that I know of." Joe went back to leaning. "But there are stories of Vikings in our ancestry. I had a cousin who had blue eyes. His dad thought the mom had cheated on him, but kohkom set him right and told him the kid was a spirit child and a descendant of the Vikings."

"What happened to the kid?"

"He died in a house fire along with five other people. His dad killed himself a year later." Joe looked at Jim. "No one can say life on the reservation is nice. It's hell, I came within a hair's breadth of becoming my father. All it takes is a tiny push one way or the other. I'm worried this thing will be the push into destruction. What does death mean when you barely believe you are alive in the first place?"

"So let's work to keep that from happening," Jim said. "I can't do anything about the attack on the town. The army folk have taken it over and they won't appreciate interference. We can look at the deaths of Zeke and Tim."

"I thought they were killed in the attack?"

"That's what the timing suggests and Amber has a good theory about it, but there is something which just doesn't sit right with me. I'm going to look into it and see what I can dig up."

"Sounds like you're just trying to find something to justify your existence."

"Maybe."

"All right then, how can I help?" Joe's mouth quirked at Jim. "Don't look so surprised. Remember I grew up trying to justify my existence, I found my reason in my family."

"I should too…" Jim took a deep breath and looked out the window.

"I've seen this on the rez," Joe said, "A family loses a kid and they fly apart. They just can't contain the grief and they can't let it go."

"How do you survive this?"

"Don told me Leigh asked for a sweat before all this came down. There is an elder coming down from the North to do the sweat as a favour for Don. You should go."

"I'm not sure I have the time to drop everything for three day for a sweat."

"You're dropping all the important things already, Jim."

140

"Damn it!' Jim went back to looking out the window. "Darren can run the show while I'm gone, but sweat or no sweat if something really important comes up, I'm gone."

"OK," Joe put his hand on Jim's shoulder, "So ask yourself, what is more important than Leigh?" He went and put his coat on. "I'll get Don to set it up."

"Soon." Jim picked up a pencil, then put it down, "The sooner the better."

"Sure thing," Joe closed the door behind him as he left.

Darren came in later and Jim was still looking out the window.

"Is it shift change already?" Jim asked.

"Go home," Darren said, "I've got it from here."

"Home," Jim said, his chest tightened at the thought. *Coward, you'll willingly face a gun, but you can't face your wife's grief. God, what must she think?* He picked up his coat and almost ran out the door. He drove up the hill to his home. He'd find Leigh sitting in the dark staring at the TV that had been turned off.

He came in and hung his coat on the back of a chair and kicked his boots off. She was there, where he'd left her every day this week. Today he didn't pretend everything would be fine. He sat beside her and put his arm around her. It was like hugging a store mannequin.

"Don is arranging a sweat for us," he said to her. "Joe just about ordered me to go. I spent all day staring at the snow. I thought about how I'd been there for you when you first got sick. I had no idea what I was doing, but I knew I had to be there. Leigh, I still don't know what I'm doing. I don't know how to help you, but I'm done running away. I'm going to be here. Somehow, I'm going to be here for you. I'm going to be here for us."

Leigh didn't say anything, but she suddenly relaxed and leaned against him. They sat like that until his stomach growled. She laughed and it was a shattering sound.

"Let's make supper." She picked a casserole out of the freezer and put it in the oven. She moved randomly around the kitchen rearranging things.

"I was so far away," she said, "so far even the whispers couldn't reach me. I knew you were there, but there was a million miles of glass between us. I don't know how, but you touched me through the glass. I'm back, but I'm afraid, what if I go away again?"

"Where ever you go, I will go." Jim put his hand over hers. "Remember your sister read that at our wedding. I thought it was nice, but until today standing watching the snow I didn't know what it meant."

"It hurts so much," Leigh clutched his hand. "I see the TV and it's like a knife in my heart all over again."

"Joe was sure the sweat would help."

"Have you been on one before?"

"Once when we did our training."

"Supper won't be ready for a bit," Leigh said. "Let's go for a walk."

"Sure, walking in a blizzard must be good for the soul," Jim grimaced and Leigh swatted him. For a second it almost felt normal. They put boots and coat on along with all the gear they needed to stay warm in the storm. Jim followed her out the door.

"You know this is ridiculous. I'm glad you suggested it." He took her hand as they walked into the wind and snow stung their faces. The cold blew through them and feelings they didn't know they had brought tears to froze to their faces.

"Time to turn around," Jim spoke through chattering teeth. "Before your nose freezes and fall off."

"You're one to talk," Leigh turned around. Jim saw Georgia. The girl wore an old coat and had wrapped up in so many layers Jim didn't know how he recognized her. Georgia was trying to say something, but she couldn't seem to be able to put the words together. Finally, she gave up and flung herself at Leigh and held her tight. Jim could see the girl shaking with her sobs. He wrapped his arms around both of them and they stood in the storm.

"Come back with us," Leigh took Georgia's hand. The three walked along the street with the wind pushing them toward the house.

When Jim opened the door, the house smelled like home again. Leigh and Georgia followed him in.

"I've never been in your house before," Georgia looked around as if the house was strange territory. "I thought there would be more books."

"They're in my office." Leigh said. "Come and look."

Jim set the table for three while he listened to Leigh and Georgia talk books and learning. They came out of the office and Georgia stopped when she saw the third plate.

"Oh no, I can't,"

"You walk in the door when supper is coming out of the oven, you sit down and eat." Jim pointed at the table. "Or at least you're welcome to."

"Let me call my parents."

After a quick phone call they sat down and ate. Jim was content to let Georgia and Leigh carry the conversation.

"You know Ryley used to stand outside my house," Georgia said, "Way back when he was a wolf. I was never afraid of him. Somehow I knew he was guarding me. Even when he moved in with you, he watched over me. I never felt freakishly smart around him. I could just be me, and he was content to be himself." She looked at Leigh with tears on her cheeks. "I miss him, Leigh, I look out my window hoping to see him."

"I miss him too, Georgia," Leigh said. "He always seemed to know what to do when I had a bad day. He'd come up and say *Ryley help* and he did. It seems right the last thing he did was save someone's life."

"Why was he there? Why wasn't he in class?"

"Ms. Taladut told me he'd accidentally broke Nathan's car. So, she took him to the office to try to help him fix it. The explosions hit and…"

"I'm sorry," Georgia dropped her head. "I had kids run to every class room along the hall, but I didn't think of the office."

"Georgia." Jim reached over and lifted her chin with his finger. "You and your friends saved a great many people, but you can't save everyone. Sometimes things happen and you grieve and learn to live with failure. As long as you never stop trying, you will be OK."

"Can I tell you something?" Georgia blinked. "You have to keep it secret."

"I can't keep something secret if it's against the law," Jim said.

"I don't think it he broke the law. He was trying to help, and now he's missing."

143

"Who?"

"Brad," Georgia blushed when she spoke his name.

"When was the last time you saw him?" he asked slipping into police mode.

"I think he was at school the day of the attack." Georgia wrinkle her forehead. "but I'm not sure. I was kind of out of it."

"I heard you'd hit your head hard," Leigh said.

"A piece of ceiling must have fallen on me. I really don't remember. I just had this mad headache and started getting sick. They took me to the hospital and Maria talked to me all day to keep me awake."

"You haven't seen Brad since then?"

"No, I went looking for him to thank him for his help, but he wasn't at any of the places he usually hangs out."

"Some families left town," Jim buttered a slice of bread.

"His family is still here, but they won't talk to me. His mom just told me I was too young and would get him in trouble."

"He's in High School?" Leigh half smiled at her. "I have to agree with his mom."

"He was waiting for me. That's what he said after I kissed him."

"I see."

"He told me people were watching him. He warned me something bad was going to happen. We had our arms around each other like we were making out. I thought a kiss would make it look more real…"

"It was a bit more than you expected?"

"A lot more!" Georgia turned red. "I couldn't stop thinking about him, about the kiss. I wanted to see him again and say thank you, because we wouldn't have been ready without his warning."

"Are you sure he's missing?"

"As sure as I can be without looking in his bedroom."

"I think I know who you mean." Jim closed his eyes. "He hangs out at the old equipment shed."

"Yes," Georgia nodded. "You know about that place?"

"Oh yes, but they aren't doing any harm there, so we leave them alone. What's Brad's last name?"

"I don't know," Georgia hung her head again. "He hangs out sometimes with Jaimie's brother."

"Ah, OK, I do know who he is. I'll get the members to keep an eye out for him. I expect he wouldn't appreciate the police getting too interested in his whereabouts."

"Thanks, Sergeant," Georgia sighed. "Mrs. Dalrymple, I should get home now."

"OK," Leigh said, "but I want you to call me Leigh when you visit here. It will have to be Mrs. Dalrymple at school, but I'd be pleased to have you as a friend. I hope you visit any time you need to talk."

"It's more like anytime my parents need to talk," Georgia stood. "It's so hard on them, trying to figure out what they are. Matthew, the reporter guy was a big help, but it is still hard."

Leigh gave Georgia a hug and they watched her walk down the street. Georgia waved from the corner, a vague shape in the blowing snow, then she vanished and Jim closed the door.

"Bedtime," Leigh leaned her head against Jim. "I think it's time I got to work to organize a memorial for our dead."

"Why is that your job?" Jim asked.

"Because no one else has done it yet."

Chapter Twenty-eight

Leigh woke in the morning with Jim's arms around her. The pain of Ryley's loss hit her, but for the first time she thought she might survive this. There were others hurting like she did. Time she did something to recognize the wound to the community.

She started by making coffee and putting toast on for Jim. The snow had stopped and he'd be going to work. He appeared in the kitchen looking rumpled and wonderful. She walked over and gave him a hug.

"Thanks, love."

"Do you need me to stay home today?"

"I'll be fine." She poured him a coffee. "You have work to do, you promised Georgia. I have work to do too."

"OK then." Jim sipped at his coffee and spread peanut butter on his toast. "Call me if you need anything." He finished his coffee, then with a kiss and a hug, he went out the door. Leigh didn't look at the TV, but went to her office. She'd start with Jake's mother. She was a single mom who stayed in town because she didn't have anywhere else to go.

"Hello," Leigh said, "I doubt you'd remember me, I'm Leigh Dalrymple. I'd like to talk to you about putting a memorial service together for the people who died in the attack."

"I don't know what to do," the other woman spoke in a flat tone.

"Why don't you come here and we'll talk about it?"

Ten minutes later, a girl who didn't look much older than Georgia came to the door.

"I'm Lyane. I don't know if I can help, but anything is better than sitting at home missing Jake."

"I know, but I don't think we can just sit and miss our kids for the rest of our lives."

"So what do I do?"

"I don't know," Leigh rubbed her eyes. "But I thought we could start by having a proper memorial time for our children and the other people who died. I wrote out a list and I'd like to talk to all of them, but I'd like your help."

"Why me?"

"I had to start somewhere."

"So give me some names," Lyanne pulled out her cell phone. "and let's get to it."

Somehow after each call they ended up inviting the person to come to Leigh's to help. The house was packed with people in every room. Some crying, some talking, some hugging the criers.

"Usually when there is a death in the community, we have a service and we gather around the family." Leigh stood in the kitchen trying to talk so everyone in the house could hear her. "Now there are so many people hurting we don't know how to react. I think we need to have a service. We need to tell our stories and cry our tears. It will help the other people with their loss to. Every single person in Spruce Bay is in pain. Let's do something to help the town move forward."

"We can't just forget!"

"No, we can't, but we don't want to remember by stopping everything either."

"Where would we have this service?"

"The army put up a huge shed on the school yard," Leigh said. "It's big enough to hold the entire town."

They kicked around ideas and then, by ones and twos they left to go home. Leigh sat with Lyanne at the kitchen table. "Wow," Lyanne heaved a sigh. "I didn't think talking would be that much work."

"Some are harder than others."

"I don't want to go home. There's nothing there for me now Jake's gone."

"Stay here for a while then," Leigh said. "I don't mind the company. I'd better get started on supper though." She picked a casserole from the freezer and put it in the oven.

"You have everything cooked ahead of time?"

"With both Jim and me working it is just easier. I cook on the weekends, then we eat all week."

147

"Maybe if I could cook, my boyfriend would have stayed, but probably not. He wanted to get off the reserve so bad. He was furious when I told him I was pregnant. We were just in high school. He bailed. I think he's in Winnipeg, but I haven't heard from him in years. I dropped out of school to have Jake. All I did was take care of him for all those years. He was a smart kid; he would have done good."

"I'm sure he would. So, what are you going to do now?"

"I'm not going back to the reserve. I don't know if I want to stay here. It isn't like I have any job I'm good at."

"Why not go back to school?"

"I suppose, it would be better than sitting looking at Jake's room and wishing I was with him."

"I'll help you," Leigh put her hand out. "If you decide to go back."

They talked until Jim got home and then talked until long after dark.

"I'm sorry," Lyanne put her coat on. "I should go, but I don't want to. I'm so alone at home."

"You're welcome to spend your days here." Leigh said, "Until we got some kind of school going again, I have little to occupy me."

"Let's drive her home," Jim picked his keys off the hook again. "It's a cold night for walking."

Leigh put her coat on and her mitts and hat. Lyanne stood with her shoulders slumped in a thin coat. She had her hands in her pocket.

Leigh reached in the closet and handed her a good pair of mitts and a hat.

"If you're going to be walking here you'll need something warm for your hands." She pushed the coats out of the way and pulled out an old coat. The first winter coat she'd bought for herself in university. She told the pang in her heart it was foolish to keep it. It hadn't fit in years.

"You can borrow this for the time being," she said. Jim looked at her with an odd expression on his face, but he didn't say anything. Lyanne caressed the coat like it was fine fur and put it on. For a moment, her face lit up and Leigh saw again how young she was.

148

They walked out to Jim's truck and Leigh saw Lyanne wore thin canvas running shoes. She squashed the impulse to run back and root through their winter boots. Lyanne climbed in back and Leigh sat beside Jim. He drove into the Grid and pulled up in front of a trailer roughly divided into two. Leigh let Lyanne out of the truck. The girl gave her a quick hug and ran to the apartment and let herself in.

Leigh climbed back into the truck.

"OK, what are you going to tell me about that poor girl?"

Jim shook his head, then put his truck in gear.

"It isn't going to help her to have a police truck in front of her place." He drove in silence for a while, weaving through the streets. Leigh realized he was patrolling. He had his cop face on. Leigh didn't see it very often.

"So Staff-Sergeant Jim," she said, "how much trouble am I in?"

"None, yet." He flashed her a brilliant smile. She hadn't seen one since he took over as Staff. "But if you really want to help that girl, you need to know what you're getting into. We've had quite a few calls to her place. We always send a woman member or go with two of us."

"She didn't look that dangerous."

"She isn't dangerous," Jim frowned, "She's a vulnerable kid people have been using for years. Anne told me about her the first time I had a call to her place. She talks about a boyfriend who ran off and left her, but even Carol..." he paused to take a deep breath, "even Carol who was here longer than anyone else couldn't every remember one boy who hung around with her. She started turning tricks when at twelve, maybe thirteen. It was her and her mom at that point. The consensus is her mom pimped her out. Lyanne was fourteen when Jake was born. I expect the mom was annoyed he wasn't a girl. The mom was killed a few years later by a drunken customer. Lyanne just stayed in the apartment and took over the family business. We've watched Jake very carefully and he showed no signs of being anything other than a normal, happy kid if you can call living in that kind of poverty normal. In the last couple of years, the calls to respond to her house have dropped some too."

149

They wove through more streets and Leigh wondered how she hadn't known about this area of extreme poverty. Houses were boarded up, some leaned off kilter, graffiti covered them, and yet there were snowmen in the yards and cars parked in some of the drives.

"This isn't really even the Grid," Jim said as if he were reading her thoughts. "It is a corner where the Company dropped some cheap housing when the town ran out of space back in the boom. When the mine failed, they never took the houses away again and people moved in and stayed." They drove out of the poverty stricken area and were back in the Grid. Jim pointed out a house as they drove past.

"Brad Beauchamp's home, he's Jamie's cousin. The father has some significant gang connections. He's not a very nice person. The mother is so beaten down she won't even look at us for fear Bo will think she's talking to the police. Brad's older brother is doing time down south; his sister ran away and is probably living on the street in Winnipeg.

"There are a lot of things that make Spruce Bay a very hard place to live. The gangs don't help, but they give cohesiveness to people who are still dealing with the fallout of the residential schools and the foster system. If we don't give people a community that cares, they will find one.

"You need to know what you are getting into if you're going to help these people. I'm not going to tell you not to help, in fact I plan to do what I can to support you. God knows this community needs something. Just be careful, don't come down here alone and don't carry anything you couldn't stand to lose. If someone tries to rob you, just give them everything you have."

"Thanks, Jim," Leigh said. "I knew something was wrong with Lyanne, but you've put it into perspective for me. I'll do some research and see what has worked other places."

"I'll look into space for you to work. I heard there was a huge crowd at the house. It's not that I don't want people there, but if the number of people increases, there won't be space for them."

"It needs to be somewhere people can walk to easily," Leigh said, "and while we are talking space, who do I check with about using the huge shed on the school yard?"

"I guess that would be me," Jim sighed. "The town council and most of the employees died on the attack. The one girl who survived was flown to Winnipeg. We've been running most of the stuff through our office."

"Who do you have doing the clerical work?"

"No one at the moment," Jim said. "We need to get permission to hire someone and they have to do their security checks. We just haven't had time."

"Well, while we are in the advice mode," Leigh poked his ribs. "I suggest you put the request in, then put someone in on a temporary basis, at least to answer phones."

"I will talk to Division tomorrow. It's hard with the radio down."

"Maybe the army folks can rig up something for you."

"Probably, but I'm nervous enough about having them here without getting them more involved. Some of those folks have a similar outlook on life as the gangs do, it's just they joined the army instead of a gang. I don't want them wandering through town - that's trouble waiting to happen."

Jim drove them home and they went to bed, for the first time in a week it wasn't grief over the loss of Ryley keeping Leigh awake.

Chapter Twenty-nine

Leigh woke with tears in her eyes. She'd been dreaming of Ryley. Instead of the boy, he'd come as a wolf to sit outside her window. She didn't know why she was sure the wolf was Ryley, but she'd run outside in her bare feet to greet him, but he'd shaken his head and growled. Not a threat, but a warning. That's when she woke feeling his loss again.

Her feet ached as if she really had been running in the snow. Leigh slid her feet into slippers and wandered through the house. The walking slowly reduced the ache. Walking past the kitchen window she couldn't stop herself from peeking through the window out into the night. The snow had stopped and the moonlight broke through the clouds. A car sat across the street she didn't recognize. She thought there was someone sitting in it, but it was hard to tell. Then, just as she decided it was worth telling Jim about the car started up and moved on.

Leigh thought about Ryley growling in her dream. *There's trouble coming, as if we hadn't had enough.* She went back to bed and thought about Ryley. This time he remembered him in the cell in the old mine access. He fought the wendigo because he refused to kill. He'd saved her life. She fell asleep with the thought in her mind.

In the morning, she made coffee and saw Jim out the door.

"There was an odd car watching the house last night," she said. "I couldn't see it very well, but it drove off as I watched."

"I'll go look," Jim walked across the street and looked around, but Leigh could tell he didn't find anything. He walked back.

"I'll look into the shed and the meeting space," he said. "Call me if you need anything."

As he drove off, Leigh saw Lyanne walking up the road. She stayed at the door until the girl got to her. She wore the coat, hat and gloves Leigh had given her, but her eye was purple and swollen.

"Come on in," Leigh said, "I'll get some ice for your eye."

Lyanne sat in the kitchen. She put her gloves and mitts in the coat pockets but still wore the coat. More than that, she huddled in it like it was a shield.

She put the ice on her face and groaned.

"You didn't ask what happened."

"I'm married to a police man. I have a pretty good idea what happened. If you want to talk about it, I'm here." She poured a coffee for the girl and put sugar and milk on the table.

"You hungry? I'm just going to make toast."

"Sure, thanks," Lyanne said. "Bo didn't like that I'd spent the day here. He was going to take your coat and sell it, but I told him you just loaned it to me and it would be trouble if it vanished. He gave me this black eye for talking back, but he didn't take the coat."

"Did he hurt you anywhere else?" Leigh poured coffee for herself.

"Nah, he wasn't in that mood last night. I think he was pissed about something else. He didn't really have his heart in the beating."

"Does he beat you a lot?"

"He says it keeps me straight, and the guys who visit me, they aren't interested in my face."

"Oh, Lyanne."

"I've been a whore since my ma sold me to a man for the night when I turned eleven. I came home crying and she slapped me and told me the men don't like girls who cry. I found some of them like it. Mom ran me and took all the money, so I figured I'd get some business for myself. The boys didn't have as much money, but they didn't beat me neither. Ma did when I got knocked up. She tried everything to kill that baby, but Jake, he was tough, He wanted to be born.

"When ma finally died, Bo took over from her. I told him if he ever touched Jake, I'd kill him. I had a knife to his throat, so he took me serious. As Jake got older I got to trying to be a better mom. With him dead, Bo figures I should be happy to go back to work. There aren't many girls stay in this town. Most go to the

153

'peg. It isn't any safer, but the money's better." She looked at Leigh and even with the ice held to her eye she looked determined. "I'm not going to remember Jake, by going back to whoring. Bo can kill me, but I'm not going back."

"It's going to be hard," Leigh said. "I won't lie to you. There are people who aren't ever going to trust you."

"Leigh," Lyanne shrugged and wrapped her hands around her mug. "Nobody trusts me now, no one 'cepting you, and I figure you just haven't heard what I am yet."

"What you are is a woman trying to make a change in her life. What you did then was what you did then. I'm not going to hold that against you."

"Thanks, Leigh," Lyanne said, "but I really just come to give your coat back. Then I'm going to go spit in Bo's eye and let him kill me. At least I'll be with Jake again."

"If you're going to spit in Bo's eye," Leigh put her hand on Lyanne's, "how about we do some real damage to him."

"You want me to talk to your old man."

"Why not? Bo can't kill you any deader, and maybe you can find a way forward that doesn't involve dying. I'm sure Jake will wait for you."

"But living hurts so much without him!" Lyanne put her head on the table. "I miss him every minute. I just want to be with him again."

"I had a dream last night that Ryley was a wolf and watching over me."

"Really? My kohkom told me those were spirit dreams. I used to have them."

"Maybe Ryley and Jake will keep each other company while we do what we need to here."

"I'd like to think that. Jake liked wolves. He had this t-shirt with a cloud that looked like a wolf howling." She lifted her head and looked at Leigh. "So when do we talk to your old man?"

"Let me call him and set it up." Leigh picked up the phone and dialed Jim's cell.

"Hi, Jim," she said, "I have someone who would like to talk to you. It has to do with spitting in Bo's eye. Yes, I thought it might interest you. OK, we'll do that."

"Looks like we're going grocery shopping, Lyanne, and there's some office space I want to look at to organize this memorial. The house can't stand many more people than we had yesterday."

They got dressed up and walked out to the garage where they climbed into Leigh's car. They pulled out and Leigh watched the door close behind them.

The drive to the new location of the grocery store took a few minutes and neither woman spoke. Leigh watched in the rear view and saw the car she expected. It always amazed her when Jim's paranoia played out. She drove like nothing was wrong and parked at the grocery store.

"Come on. I need some milk." They walked into the store and more than one person looked askance at Lyanne, but no one said anything. Lyanne kept her chin up and didn't try to hide the black eye. Leigh wanted to hug her, but it would have spoiled the effect. She took a basket and started up and down the aisles occasionally putting items in the basket. She saw a man enter the store – a big Cree wearing a leather jacket. Leigh saw him peering down each aisle.

"In here," Amber waved from the doors leading to the back. Leigh followed Lyanne through into a dark, cool space. Skids filled the area. Amber walked through them to a tiny space set up as a lunch room. She waved Leigh and Lyanne in and closed the door.

"Hi Lyanne," Amber said, "Nasty looking bruise, Bo again?"

"Yeah, he figured with Jake gone I could be turning more tricks again. I want out. I don't want to be making a living fucking guys who should be home with their old ladies."

"I hear you," Amber nodded and took out her notepad. "So, Leigh said something about spitting in Bo's eye?"

"What do you want on him?" Lyanne grinned, "There's this for a start," She pointed at her eye, "but we both know that's small potatoes. He's selling drugs out of his fancy house of his, but he doesn't keep most of them there. He's got a safe room under the place next door to me. I don't know that you'd be able to get him for it. The place is empty now, but he had a buddy of his there until they went up to the camp."

155

"What is this camp?"

"This place these tough guys are going to learn how to fight back. They're going to kick the settlers out and mine their own shit and be rich. Least that's how Bo described it. He was drunk though. Sent his poor bastard of a kid up there 'cause he was hanging with a white chick."

"So Bo knows where the camp is?"

"Nobody knows where the camp is. You go and walk for a day with a bag on your head. Then it's snowmobile or quad from there. Bo wanted me to go up there, said I'd make a fortune, for him anyway. Told him I wasn't leaving Jake."

"Anything else?"

"Some fat ass white man paid Bo to learn when the attack was going down. Don't ask me who he was, I never seen him before. The only guys I ever saw in a suit were the teachers, and he wasn't no teacher."

"You get that Staff?" Amber said and Leigh saw the little bud in her ear. "OK, sure." She looked back at Lyanne, "Staff-Sergeant wants to know what you need from us. We can get you out of here and keep you safe as a material witness, or we can put you in a more secure place here in town. We'll come up with a good excuse so no one comes after you."

"All I want is to say goodbye to Jake," Lyanne wiped her eyes. "After that I don't care."

"OK then, place in town it is. We don't want you in your old place; there's too much risk to you. Is there anything you need from there?"

"Nah, it's just shit, burn it down for all I care."

"We're done here," Amber put her notepad away. "You go with Leigh back to her place. We'll find you there when we need you. If you're with Leigh, Bo should leave you alone, but we're going to keep an ear on you anyway."

"What are you going to do with Bo?"

"We're going to get him to talk, then we'll see." Amber shrugged. "You know the game. We'll try to get him sent up for a few years. Long enough for you to be whoever you want to be."

"Ready?" Leigh asked.

"Let's go finish our shopping," Lyanne stood.

"Bo's out front frothing, so pick up a few more things. Don't get drawn into a fight, we want to give him a little rope before we bring him in. We don't want anyone connecting you to the bust." Amber handed Leigh the earbud and a tiny microphone she clipped on her collar. "We're going to hear everything you say for the next little while, so don't be talking about what you're buying me for Christmas."

"Thanks, Amber."

Leigh walked out the door and they wandered the aisles and picked up more food. Leigh could see Bo standing outside staring at them. She stood in line to pay for the groceries and looked at magazines. She made fun of the headlines and soon had Lyanne in giggles. They picked up their bags and walked out of the store toward Leigh's car.

"What are you doing, bitch?" Bo moved close to Lyanne's face. "I told you to stay put."

"Do I know you?" Leigh peered at Bo, "I'm sure, I've seen you before."

"Get out of my face!" Bo put his fist up to Leigh's face. She heard a horn beep and Bo looked to see a police truck turning to come back.

"This isn't over, white bitch. I know where you live." He ran to his car and drove over the curb. Amber winked at them as she drove past.

Once in the car, Leigh let out a long breath. "Jim," she said, "you know someone should tell him when he's in close he's vulnerable to the old fashion knee to the balls. I was sorely tempted…No dear, when I knee someone, they stay down, it's all in the follow through."

Lyanne giggled all the way to Leigh's house. They unpacked the groceries and Leigh made tea.

"We didn't get to look at the office, maybe tomorrow."

They sat and drank tea as they talked until there was a knock on the door.

"Sorry to interrupt ma'm," Cam said when Leigh opened the door, "but they told me at the grocery store Lyanne Grasnie left with you. Is she here?"

"Yes, constable," Leigh stepped back to let him in. "Is there a problem?"

157

"It seems there was a fire at her residence, we need her to come with us."

"Holy shit!" Lyanne laughed in delight. "A fire? For real? I'd like to see that. Bo will be pissed!"

"I think I'll come with you to give emotional support."

"Seeing as she's so broke up about it," Cam winked at them.

Leigh and Lyanne sat in the back of the truck while Cam drove them to Lyanne's apartment. Sure enough, the fire department was there hosing the house down, but flames were visible through the window and smoke poured out through a hole in the ceiling."

"Sorry, miss," Fire Chief Harvey said when he came over. "The fire was too far gone to save the building. We did manage to save one thing for you." He handed Lyanne a tiny plush wolf. Lyanne put it to her face for a moment, then they sat in the car and watched the house burn to the ground.

Chapter Thirty

Matthew stared in disbelief at the words on the computer screen in his office beside the news room. The official explanation for the Deputy Minister arriving in Winnipeg to die of her burns, was the plane had crashed into the mall causing the death of an unspecified number of members of the community. No names had been released pending notification of the families. Matthew thought the story sounded a little strange at the time, so he called Georgia.

Georgia told him about explosions and the building collapsing, but since she was in the gym she wasn't an eye witness to the attacks. Matthew tried to get permission to go to Spruce Bay and do the story if nothing else it was a huge human interest story. The bosses had said no. Reluctantly, mind you, but the answer stayed.

Rumours abounded. There was a terrorist attack. The plane deliberately crashed into the mall. The entire town was dead. The government had sent elite troops there to annihilate the First Nations people. Matthew guessed from his brief conversation with Georgia there had been an attack and the reason he wasn't allowed to go to report on the news was the government had responded in force and was trying to keep a lid on it.

Then he saw the posting on his screen - a press release from a radical group claiming the government had declared war on the First Nations people.

'We are a group taking our name from the spirit moose bringing the message that enough was enough. It is time and past time for the original people of this land to rise up and reclaim their rightful place. For centuries, the governments of Canada and the United States have signed treaties with the Nations of Turtle Island. That these treaties have not been fulfilled is a sign these governments never intended peace. The policies of residential schools, the welfare system, the reserve system are policies of genocide. The clan of the White Moose has struck the first blow in Spruce Bay against the instruments of that genocide.

We call on our brothers and sisters of the First Nations across this continent to rise and strike back. They have been fighting a war against us since they arrived on this land. It is time they felt the pain of the destruction of family and peace. The war has been fought for centuries. Now we fight back.'

A video accompanied the release claiming to show the army moving to attack what looked like an old mine. Armoured vehicles circled buildings and fired into them. There was no return fire. At the end of the segment, the mine head exploded and fell on the army, crushing man and machine.

He sat back in his chair and swore softly. He had a flag on any mention of Spruce Bay, but when other people started seeing this, it could be chaos. He picked up his phone and called his boss.

"Ralph," he said, "I'm sending you a link. Watch it and call me back." He forward the link, then started looking for response to the call to arms. The comments began predictably with questions about the validity of the post and the video, but soon other less skeptical people started posting their support of the people in the video.

"F***g well about time," one said, "I'm loading my gun and going to shoot the next white face that shows up on our land."

"Doesn't surprise me," another posted, "those people have been living off our taxes for years. Any Indian tries anything around me, they'll be dead. Maybe it's time we put a bounty on them again."

It got worse from there with people threatening each other and increasing the nastiness of the racial slurs. A couple of other blogs had picked up and reposted the link, some in support and some with a call to step back and avoid violence.

Ralph phoned him back.

"Get to work on this. Talk to the government people and get their reaction. You said you had a source in that town. Talk to them and keep me posted."

Matthew called up Hannah in research.

"I need everything you can get me on the treaties with the First Nations people. How many have been filled and what ones still haven't been settled. Just send me stuff as you get it."

"People write books about this stuff," she said. "You'll need to be a little more specific.

"Anything on claims of genocide then," he said, "I remember something a while back, with the Human Rights Museum. Anything that connects the treaties with the genocide."

"That I can do." Hannah hung up.

Matthew called Aboriginal and Northern Affairs and got the expected delays and run around. He was trying the Army people when his computer beeped at him. He read a story about a group of young native men who had attacked a business which was the subject of controversy in the communities in Northern Ontario surrounding the reserve. No one had been hurt, but the mining office burnt to the ground and a crude white moose had been spray painted on the owner's car.

Another beep, two First Nations boys had been severely beaten after they were caught spray painting a white moose on business with a reputation for refusing service to natives. That was in New Brunswick.

He pulled up the material Hannah was sending him. It was sadly familiar with its tale of abuse, sickness and isolation. He wove in the stories of the growing number of incidents connected to the White Moose' call to arms. He wasn't going to wait for a government response, but a press release dropped into his computer calling for calm and for people to wait while the government took the appropriate action.

Too bad whoever wrote it didn't stop to think that telling First Nations people who were angry at government inaction to wait patiently while government decided what was best for them.

The number of incidents increased exponentially.

"We need to get on this." Ralph walked into Matthew's office. "Somehow we need to get a balanced report out there before it turns into a blood bath.

"I can go on now with what I have," Matthew said as he dialed the phone. "I'm hoping to talk to the Grand Chief and get their opinion. With luck, she will call for moderation." He swore when he got a message. He left a quick request for a call back.

161

"Go then," Ralph waved him out of the room. "Everything else stops when you start. I'll try to put a panel together to join you."

Matthew ran to the newsroom and they did a rush job on his face before dropping him at the desk. He took a breath, looked at his notes and the director signaled him, three, two, one…

"Hello Canada, we are at a crossroads in our history. A radical First Nations group calling themselves the White Moose are calling for all-out war against the settlers. It is at times like this we need to think carefully about who we are and what we aim to be. Some background now before we talk to someone at the Assembly of First Nations to get their reaction….

Chapter Thirty-one

Jim had always wondered how it would feel to be an arsonist. Now he knew, it was exhilarating and terrifying. Also more work than he expected. He wanted the house to be destroyed enough Lyanne would have to move, but not so gone they couldn't accidentally discover the cache in the other half of the home.

He thought he got the balance just about right. Fire Chief Harvey had no objection to simply letting the place burn. He'd long been an advocate of bulldozing the houses that were next to derelict and moving the people to the apartments sitting mostly empty. Jim just hoped Harvey didn't decide to follow Jim's example.

They found the cache easily enough. It was there on the assumption the police wouldn't search a property without due cause, but with the fire and looking for its cause, the extra door was opened and Jim and his people were called in.

Jim's first thought was it looked like Tanist's den of sin which had also sat below an abandoned house. It had the same stench of corruption. The shelves were partially filled with drugs, but there were also weapons, ammunition and pornography. A bed with a camera pointed at it suggested some crude porn was made locally. Jim looked through a few of the pictures sitting in neat piles on a shelf. What he saw made him feel like hunting down Bo and shooting him on the spot.

Jake was there in various degrees of nudity as well as other children Jim vaguely recognized from school. He looked through them, trying to focus on the face to put a name to the child. He counted four other children besides Jake. There were a few different adults as well, both white and Cree. None of their faces showed. Maybe something would come up in the movies.

"Pat," Leigh said when he climbed out of the hole. "There is some nasty porn we are going to wrap up and send to the task force at Division. We will keep copies of face only shots for identifying victims. Once we've finished processing that evidence, the others can catalog and process the drugs and weapons. I want a car out front and we'll work around the clock to clear this out." He grimaced and just stopped himself from trying to spit the bad taste out of his mouth.

"I want Bo picked up and kept secure. Charge him with assault for now, but more will be pending."

Pat passed the word on to the other members then followed Jim down into the basement. She had to come up again to vomit against a wall before steeling herself to return to the hole.

They worked all night bagging evidence and recording it. They ended up with half a dozen file boxes.

"This looks relatively new," Pat loaded the last box into the back seat of the truck. "Maybe the last six months. I remember Amber talking about the appearance of the pink polar bear shirt, because she had a sister send one up for Chelsea. I wonder if Bo was trying to raise money for something."

"Or someone," Jim said. "We have a connection between him and the camp. It takes money to put together the kind of operation that attacked us."

"But using children from his own people?"

"Those are all children from vulnerable families. They are poor, or involved in gangs. Mostly both. They used what was at hand."

"We're going to stop them, aren't we?"

"Damn right," Jim clenched his fist. "They aren't helping anybody."

They drove to the temporary detachment and locked the boxes in a room. By then Jim had heard Darren had picked up Bo outside Jim's home. Jim ground his teeth on the way down to the makeshift interview room. He stopped outside the door and did some slow breathing until he thought he could enter the room and not kill Bo. He left his gun with Pat and walked in.

Bo sat, leaning back in the chair. He had a grin on his face.

"Howdy, sheriff," he said, "I was thinking I needed to get arrested again. It's time to boost my street cred."

Darren leaned against the wall. He was working hard at looking bored, but Jim could see the tension in him. Probably Bo could as well, and was trying to get a case for police brutality. Not today, though Jim hoped a good beating was in the man's future, he didn't plan on soiling his hands on the punk.

He ignored Bo and fiddled unnecessarily with the video camera in the corner. It was already running, but they wouldn't use anything until the bastard had been properly warned, again.

"Bo," Jim put on his official voice. "You have been arrested on a charge of assault. You have the right to remain silent and the right to retain counsel. We have a phone you can use to talk to the duty counsel if you wish."

"Yeah, yeah," Bo's grin didn't slip. "I know my rights, you fuckers have told me often enough. I'm untouchable. The little bitch will never testify against me so you have no evidence to hold me. I'll just be going then."

"Sit," Jim pointed at the chair. "While you've only been charged with the assault at this time there is the matter of a substantial amount of drugs and weapons the fire department discovered in the course of doing their work."

"If you don't have a search warrant, you can't use them."

"The fire department doesn't need a search warrant to look for the cause of a fire. When they found your little cache, they called us. We had reasonable cause to check the illegal items there and determine who they belong to. We only need a search warrant if we are going to search your home or vehicle in the course of an investigation, but we appreciate your confirming you are the person who put the cache in place."

"Wait," Bo's grin faded. "I didn't confirm anything."

"Well maybe not." Jim shrugged. "But it hardly matters given your fingerprints are all over the place. You'll get to meet with your bro's in prison for a while. What may make that meeting a little less friendly is the considerable evidence of the making and distributing of child porn we found."

Bo jumped to his feet and sent the chair flying against the wall.

"I'm no childfucker," he screamed. "I have nothing to do with that shit."

"Not how it looks to me," Jim said. "I'm expecting a warrant by the time we finished talking here to take some photographs for comparison purposes. I'm afraid you will find the process

165

somewhat undignified, but you know how it is. In the meantime, the child porn was out in plain sight with the drugs and guns so it would be hard to explain how you didn't know it was going down."

"That piece of shit, two timing," Bo walked around waving his arms, "Johnston McCrey has been running the cache. I wanted to be out of the picture, plausible deniability your political fuckers call it. He must have set it up." He dropped his pants. "Take you pictures you won't see this cock in any child porn."

"Pull your pants up," Jim had to fight off laughter. "We'll get to it in time. So, this McCrey, where do we find him?"

"He's gone to the camp," Bo leaned over the table. "He's supposed to take money and shit up there and we get future favours."

"What kind of future favours?" Jim raised his eyebrows.

"I've already talked too much." Bo leaned back looking truly scared. "I'm a dead man."

"Pity." Jim dropped the folder on the table and pulled five photos out of the folder. They'd been cropped to just the face, but he could see the fear in their expressions. "How about you tell me who these kids are."

"That brat is Lyanne's, she's probably in on this. She's been a whore since she was born. This girl, she belongs to a girl I have in the reserve. I'm not sure about the others."

Jim put the pictures away.

"Hold tight. We'll be back with a camera."

He left and Darren followed him. They locked the door behind them and moved down the hall to where Bo wouldn't be able to hear them.

"He sounded genuinely pissed there was child porn." Jim frowned and look back down toward where Bo waited. "We'll get the picture, but I think we'll find there's no match. I've identified at least three adults. Two are white and one probably First Nations. The First Nations had what looked to be a rather painful tattoo. It wasn't on Bo. I want a warrant out on this Johnston McCrey, and whatever we have on him. If he's Bo's second, I'm sure we have something. If we get McCrey, we may be able to get the names of the whites who are involved."

"What do we do with Bo?"

166

"We have the assault charge and the weapons and drugs charge. We transfer him to Thompson for a hearing and let the Crown take over. If we let her know what else we're working on, I'm sure he'll get remand. While we're waiting for transfer, let's keep the pressure on and see if we can get more out of him. He talks too much when he's angry, so let's keep him angry and off balance. Get Pat onto identifying those kids. Ask Leigh and the other primary teachers. Find the parents and put some pressure on them too. I hate to say this, but we need to bring Lyanne in. Jake's involvement is a huge question mark. Call Leigh and ask her to come in with Lyanne."

"Got it, Staff." Darren slapped Jim's arm. "It's good to have you back."

Jim went up to his office and put the folder in a drawer and locked it. Guns, drugs and porn, all connected to this camp Bo and Lyanne mentioned. He looked at his map. Assuming the one day's walk followed more or less a straight line. He drew a circle on the map of about twenty kilometers in radius. He couldn't imagine walking much further blindfolded.

A knock at his door interrupted his thinking.

"Come in," he said.

Pat brought in the owner of the grocery store.

"Staff, Derek wanted to talk to you. I'm off on patrol." She waved the radio at him. He nodded and turned his attention to the grocer.

"Hi, Derek," Jim said, "I appreciate the use of your back room."

"Anything to keep those bastards out of my store," Derek said, "but that's not what I'm here about. My shipment from Thompson came in. The driver told me some guys in army uniforms stopped and searched his truck. I lost some product because they moved around and it fell. Made a huge mess in the back of the truck. The driver's pissed because he has to clean it out and it's going to slow him down."

"Interesting," Jim made some notes. "I don't recall them informing the detachment they were going to block the road. I didn't think they had that power."

"The guns they have, they can do whatever they want," Derek frowned. "We're up here and isolated. If the internet goes down, you can be sure there's going to be big trouble. It must be like those movies on TV where they kill a bunch of people to get power to do what they want. No one saw who was driving those cars did they?"

"I'll talk to the Colonel," Jim met Derek's eyes. "In the meantime, I suggest you watch some different movies."

"You just wait and see," Derek waved his hands. "They're going to take over and there will be nothing we can do about it. This is what comes of paying taxes."

"Thanks, Derek."

"One other thing, Staff-Sergeant," Derek waved his finger at Jim, "the driver said there's a lot of traffic on the road, all of it northbound and all of it in army green. They're getting ready for an invasion."

He left and Jim sat and thought for a while.

"Pat," he said over the radio, "have a mosey to the south and see what's on the highway out of town."

"Ten-four, Staff."

Darren came in just after he finished his call to Pat.

"Bo was kicking the door. He's demanding his phone call to his lawyer. "

"Get him a phone. There's a phone jack in the room. No games, he gets privacy for his phone call, but make sure you take the phone away when he's done. Better get him something to eat as well. He going to be here at least a day or so until we can arrange transport. We're short enough without losing someone for the day driving him to Thompson."

"OK, Staff. By the way Leigh called to say they were coming in. Should be here in a minute."

"Thanks, Darren." Jim went down the stairs to meet Leigh and Lyanne as they came in. He wasn't looking forward to this conversation.

The women came in just as he reached the front foyer.

"This way." He led them to another office.

"Did you arrest the prick?" Lyanne asked.

"That's part of why I needed to talk to you," Jim said. "We found the drugs and some guns where you told us. We found some other things that were very disturbing." He took out the photos of the four children whose pictures were in the room along with Jake's. "Do you recognize any of these children?"

"This is Susie, she's Amy kid. Amy's one of Bo's bitches. He keeps her in the reserve to try to hide her from his old lady. Fat chance, she's scared, not stupid. Gracie is Andie's kid, Andie watches Jake for me once in a while. That's Mika, he's Andie's boy a year younger than Gracie, the last one is belongs to another one of Bo's girls, Tina's her name, I don't remember the kid's name."

"That's very helpful, Lyanne," Jim put the pictures back in the folder after making notes on the back of each."

"How long has Andie been watching Jake?"

"First time was maybe six months back. A john got a little rough and Andie offered she'd take Jake for the night, let me recover without worrying Jake."

"We have reason to believe those four children and Jake were being used to make child porn."

"That bastard!" Lyanne screamed and pulled her hair. "Where is he? I'll kill him myself! Just wait until I get my hands on Andie. You'll need a baggie for what's left of her when I finish. My poor Jake! What did they do to you?" She collapsed weeping on the desk and Leigh sat beside her.

"Darren," Jim spoke into the radio, "pick up Andie McCrey, you'll need to take someone with you to take custody of her two children. Joe McCrey would be good. Bring Andie here and let Joe take the kids. Instruct him to listen to the kids, but no questions."

"Lyanne," Jim put his hand on her shoulder. "As much as I'd love to let you beat Andie to a pulp and rip Bo's nuts off, I can't do that. You understand?"

"Yeah, the law protects fuckers like that, but not kids like Jake."

"I suspect Johnston was the one making the porn. Bo was almost as pissed as you."

"He's still dead," Lyanne snarled. "He's as close to Johnston as he is to his own hand. Johnston wouldn't do anything without Bo's word."

169

"Think back six months," Jim crouched to see her eyes. "What changed? For some reason, somebody needed money bad enough to get into the child porn business."

"I can't think of anything," Lyanne dropped her head into her hands. "If I do, I'll let you know. So now what?

"You and Leigh finish planning the memorial for the town. We need it. Then we wake up the next day and deal with that."

"Do you have permission for us to use the shed?" Leigh asked.

"Whenever you need it,' Jim said, "just tell me when."

"Today's ten days after the attack." She gazed up for a moment. "I don't want to drag it out. Let's hold it in two days. Everyone is welcome to be there and we'll talk about the dead, and the living."

"Two days," Jim made a note. "I'll get some people to set it up for you. Ask the families to bring pictures and we'll set up tables across one end for them."

"Thanks, Jim," Leigh said, "I'm going to take Lyanne home for now."

"We're working on getting an apartment for her, but she'll need to spend the night."

"I'll be fine," Leigh led Lyanne out. Jim went up to his office to wait for Darren to report.

"Darren to Staff," the radio came to life while Jim was looking at the map again.

"Go ahead," Jim said.

"The house is cleared out. Clothes are gone, there's not much food."

"Thanks, Darren. I'm going to go have a chat with the Colonel as soon as Pat returns."

She came in just before shift change so Jim updated all four of them on what he'd learned.

"I'm thinking the money for this attack, and whatever other plans these people have, came from gang money. It seems to go back six months or so. That means they planned the attack before the spirit moose was killed. The moose just gave them a recruiting tool. If the gangs are financing this thing, then the word will be out there. If you know someone who might have loose lips, now's the time to have a chat with them. This camp has been mentioned

170

several times. I'd like to have an idea where it is. What we have on it so far is it is a day's walk blindfolded then you travel by snowmobile or quad."

"The blindfold suggests it isn't a straight walk," Cam said. "There must be some significant landmarks they don't want people to see.

"Good thinking," Jim nodded at him. "So try to come up with some ideas about where they could hide a large number of people for months at a time. They'd have to feed them and make sure the camp was sanitary enough people didn't get sick."

"Probably there is only one fixed part of the camp," Darren said, "and the rest of the people are nomadic. It would be harder in the winter, but it is not as easy to find a lot of small groups. If they started six months back, there could be a big cache of food."

"Right," Jim said, "but a lot of these people aren't going to be skilled at living off the land. Maybe we need to look for some traditionalists who have those skills."

"I can't imagine any traditionalists who would advocate the kind of murder these people are about," Darren frowned. "The First Nations aren't the only people with survival skills."

"What would be the draw for those other people?" Amber looked around at the others. "There would need to be a convincing reason for them to get involved."

"What if they were promised an end to government interference?" Pat said, "Some of those survivalists are radical anti-government."

"OK." Jim put up his hand. "Now we need to investigate. Talk to the people and keep your ears open. Find out who else has vanished from town. I'm going to talk to the Colonel. Darren, go home, but stay ready to advise if necessary. Cam, Amber, patrol, but be careful."

Jim left them to do their work and climbed into his truck. He drove out to the military base. Derek was right about one thing - there was a lot more equipment and people there. The massive airplane had left, but metal huts lined either side of the runway and there a fence surrounded the whole compound. He saw a sentry standing on the top of a cherry picker.

171

Jim was met at the gate by two sentries who waved him through after checking with someone on their radio. Another soldier rode with him to the tent set up as the Colonel's office.

"Come in Staff-Sergeant." The Colonel stood as Jim entered. "I was going to ask you to come here for a report soon anyway."

"Would you have explained the road block and searches?" Jim asked. "My grocer in town was very upset your people made a mess of his shipment."

"My apologies," the Colonel said and nodded at a woman standing to the side with a clipboard. "I will speak to the men about being more careful in their search. Someone is supplying these people and if we can cut their supplies it will help our cause."

"It may be easier said than done," Jim parked himself in a chair. "I've learned these people have been raising money for at least six months. It appears they've been using gangs as sources of income. The gangs stand to make a good deal of money from the chaos. We've uncovered a large cache of drugs and weapons as well as a brand new child porn ring. The person involved is allegedly at the camp with the attackers. His family is there and I know of at least one prostitute who they tried to recruit."

"Really?" the Colonel's eyes widened. "You've been busy."

"Anecdotal evidence suggests the camp isn't too far from here. Less than a day's travel by snowmobile or quad. New people are walked for a day, then transported from there. They are blindfolded while they walk incidentally."

The colonel pulled out a map of the area and looked at it.

"I think we can safely say they aren't south of us, but I've sent choppers to do flyovers anyway. We have infrared sensors on the choppers. Once we know where they aren't, we can cut them off and isolate them."

"I suspect they have a substantial cache of food," Jim refrained from pointing out the size of the search area. "And even in the winter it is possible to harvest a lot of food through ice fishing and hunting. We're speculating they are cooperating with people who are survivalist and anarchist in temperament. It is also important to remember the First Nations had trade routes across the country well before we built road and railways. It is going to be hard to contain them that way."

172

"Noted, Staff-Sergeant," The Colonel didn't sound pleased. "Is there anything else I should know?"

"The town is planning a memorial to those who died in the attack. It will be in two days' time. This will be the first gathering of the whole town since the attack, and it may be a target for another attack."

"I will arrange for security for your memorial."

"Far enough away that my people aren't caught in the middle of a fire fight while they try to grieve."

"Of course." The Colonel picked a pen and fiddled with it. "Do you have any other advice for me?"

"A couple of years back someone tried to take over the town using gangs. He staged his actions from an old mine site here. There is just one building and few deep holes. If I were planning an attack on town, I might use that as a staging area. The building closes off access to a mine which never got fully developed, but the tunnel goes back a hundred meters before it stops." He tapped on the map where the mine was located.

"I see, thank you, that will be very useful." The Colonel stood and walked Jim to the door of the tent. "I will make sure my men on the blockades are more careful. If I may ask, how did you get this information you've passed on?"

"We arrested someone in connection with some of the illegal activities that may be funding this thing."

"Would it be possible to speak to this individual?"

"It would be highly irregular for me to allow him out of police custody. I'm waiting for Thompson to send someone up to transport him south."

"That might be a long wait?"

"It could be."

"What if I made some of my resources available to transport him? I have some Military Police here, and a secure vehicle. It is, unfortunately necessary in a camp this size."

"This man's a drug dealer, a pimp and a general all round bastard," Jim said, "but if he has one bruise on him when he arrives in Thompson there will be hell to pay."

"Staff-Sergeant." The Colonel shook his head. "Torture is both crude and ineffective. We will care for him as one of our own. I'd just like to have a chance to ask one or two questions."

173

"I will make arrangements with Division. If they approve, then you can transport him."

"I appreciate it, Staff-Sergeant."

Jim left with a strong feeling Division Headquarters would get a call from high up in Ottawa. Fine. Let them take the heat if it went sideways. He wasn't sure what made him think of the old mine, but it made sense, and he rather the army went in than him.

Chapter Thirty-two

The town packed the shed. There weren't enough chairs, so people stood in rows and only the families of the dead had seats. Tables crossed the front covered with pictures. Children's school pictures, family gatherings, fishing and hunting photos all showed the lives of people who they'd lost.

Leigh had decided not to invite any dignitaries. She didn't want this to turn into a media frenzy. It was a family service. The media would get their turn, but not here, not now. Each of the families had been given a chance to speak, to tell a story about the person. Most had agreed.

It was cold outside, but the air in the shed was already stifling. Leigh hoped no one fainted. She walked out to the center of the tables and picked up the microphone.

"Welcome," she said. "I'm glad you are here. This isn't going to be an easy service, but I ask you to be patient. If you need to sit down, please sit. if you need to walk around, feel free. There will be time for you to look at the pictures, and talk to the families about your own memories. I wish we could have a meal, but there is no one who could cater to the entire community. We had no idea of how to choose an order for those who are going to speak, so I'm going to ask them to come up as they feel ready. Don't talk for too long, we have a lot of people to honour, but tell your story. We are listening.

"I'll go first, since I'm already here and I know what I want to say." Leigh took a deep breath and then continued.

"Ryley was part of the wendigo's wolf pack, as he called them - children who were manipulated into becoming killers. At the end, when he was ordered to kill me, Ryley refused. He suffered greatly because of his choice. If he died then, he would have died a hero. He lived and came to stay with me and my husband Jim. We learned he was a strong and gentle soul. He had

175

his problems, we all do, but he was a boy who loved deeply. He died and his final act was to save another person. Ms. Taladut, who was helping Ryley repair a car. Nathan put the car with Ryley's picture on the table. I will miss Ryley. I will miss him every day, but every day I am richer because I knew him."

Leigh put the mic down and went to her seat. Macky stood up next.

"My sister, Alecia was a Librarian. Most of you knew her. She was the person who could always find the perfect book for you to read. The only person who never once got angry at me, no matter how annoying or hyper I got. If I get to do half as much as she did, I'll be happy."

So it went, person after person, some very brief, some took longer, some broke down in tears halfway through and sat down. The crowd rustled, but remained silent. Leigh could sense their regard for the speakers. Lyanne went last.

"I'm Jake's mom," she said, "He died with Mrs. Hall, because she went to find him. I will forever be grateful he didn't die alone. He spent too much time alone. Most of you know me, you know what I am. I didn't choose my life. I'm not a whore because it's fun or good money or any of that shit. People made me this. Jake was freeing me. Because of Jake I was a mom instead of a whore. I got to go to parent teacher night. I even made cookies for his class once. I didn't tell him I burned four batches of cookies before I got it right. He was taken away from me, like all these people were taken from us. Only I have my memory of him, his smile, the way he hugged me. Because of Jake I get a second chance at life, and this time I'm making my own choices." She put the mic down and went to her seat.

Leigh stood up again and picked up the mic.

"Please stay and talk to the families and each other and look at the pictures—" She was interrupted by the sound of distant gunfire. "I afraid I'm going to have to insist everyone stay here and stay calm until we hear what is going on. Keep the doors closed. I know it is stuffy, but it is just safer that way. My husband and his people are out there protecting us. Let's not make it harder than it needs to be.

***

Sergeant Creeley shivered under his snow sheet. He knew his suit was designed to maintain his body at optimum temperature, but damn it, his body told him he was supposed to be cold. He huddled under a white sheet which reflected his heat down and lay on another to insulate him from the snow underneath. Eight other men and women were hidden in a similar way around the clearing. They would have liked to have people in the building and tunnel, but it would leave signs in the snow. Their source told them as far as he knew, there was only one way in or out. He should know, he spent his youth exploring the place. Creeley just hoped this Joe wasn't playing them.

There were other people further back in the woods. A bombardier held more people and had a fifty-caliber mounted on the roof. It was back just far enough any advanced scouts for the enemy wouldn't likely see it. As soon as they engaged it would arrive. The rest of the soldiers formed a loose line surrounding the town. They would stop any attack from another source. Creeley didn't make strategy decisions, but he was sure the Colonel was right. There would be an attack today, and they'd kill a bunch of the fuckers.

He saw movement in the woods across the clearing. Men in white camo scanning the woods across the way. Creeley didn't think they would find him unless they stood on him. Apparently, he was right because more men came, some carrying guns, but most didn't appear to be armed. Maybe the guns were in the mine. One of the men crossed the clearing and opened the door. It looked like he disarmed a trap. The entire group filed through the door until just two men were left standing watch. These two had guns.

They stood on either side of the door and watched the woods. Orders were to wait for the people to come out. They didn't want to have a siege situation and they didn't have anything big enough to blow the mine. Let them out, then take them down. The fuckers wouldn't stand a chance. It was a good plan. The only part Creeley didn't like was the order to take prisoners. Prisoners were a pain.

The guards looked nervous. One constantly jerked his gun back and forth. Creeley half expected him to shoot his partner.

The partner had frozen. He had his back to the wall and stared straight ahead. Creeley didn't think the man blinked.

A rabbit hopped out of the woods and the jerker blew it to bits. The other one started shooting at random into the woods. Creeley heard the roar of the bombardier approaching. He swore and put a bullet into the second man, someone else took out the jerk. Someone from inside came to check what was going on. Creeley shot him too, but not before he shouted.

"Squad one, take left. Squad two right. I'll fire cover down the hallway. We don't know what shit is in there, so don't take chances. Squad four, hold back, I don't want to give them a target, but be ready. Three move forward and cover the line, stay low. If these guys are all this stupid, they will fire high."

His people moved like the well drilled team they were. Creeley fired a steady stream of bullets down the hallway. With luck, it would keep the enemy pinned at the back.

Someone at the back of the hallway started to return fire using a fifty cal and they weren't shooting high.

"Grenade in the door," Creeley ordered. Two grenades were thrown in the door and the fifty-cal stopped. Creeley moved away from the danger zones. "Four, move in and cover that door, one and two be ready to move on my mark."

The bombardier moved in and the fifty-cal on the roof opened up on the hall.

"Hold, four," Creeley ordered them, "one and two move, let's clean up. The eight people ran into the hall, taking turns kneeling and providing covering fire while their comrades cleared the rooms on the way back to the mine tunnel.

The constant gunfire made it hard to know what was going on, but his people were the best at what they did. They were trained to break into guarded urban environments. This wasn't much different except for the snow, and the rocks, and the trees.

One of his people came to the door and gave a hand sign, *all clear*. Creeley stretched and safetied his weapon before walking to the mine to see what kind of mess they'd made.

The hallway was clear up to twenty meters where the fifty cal shooter lay filled with shrapnel and bullets, beside him lay another man who had been holding a RPG. Creeley was really glad the guy hadn't got to pull the trigger. More bodies littered

178

the side rooms. Those rooms were stacked with guns; a mix of hunting weapons and more military looking guns. Crates of ammunition too. Further back they found military grade gear. Another RPG in a case. A fifty-caliber waiting for someone to use it. The door to the mine tunnel had been blown to pieces. In the tunnel were snow machines and quads with weapon mounts on them. A couple of the quads had mortars mounted on the back. Somewhere someone was supplying serious equipment to these people.

All the men in the tunnel had their faces painted in one way or another. Creeley pulled a picture from the pocket of his coat and started comparing faces to the picture. Whoever the guy in the picture was, he wasn't here. Creeley didn't expect him to be. Someone that smart sent other people to die for him.

Creeley was happy it was the other guys dying today. He went outside and called it in to the Colonel.

"To be on the safe side," the Colonel ordered him. "Clear your people out of there and wait for our techs to get there to assess the situation."

"Yes, sir," Creeley said. "OK, boys and girls, we wait outside for the brains to come and tell us who we killed. Wrap it up and clear out."

They had just settled themselves into their holes to wait in warmth, when a thump came from inside the mine. Dust blew out the door and the ground rumbled. The techs weren't going to get much to look at. It looked like someone was monitoring the radio frequencies. Their good luck whoever was listening was slow on the button.

They stayed alert until the techs arrived. The mine had collapsed and the only thing they recovered was the bodies of the two sentries. Those were bagged and loaded, then the entire crew headed back to base.

We're even now, but it won't stay that way for long. We'll be coming for you.

Chapter Thirty-three

Sam Cranston hated his name. That's why he liked being an MP. People just called him Sir. He was paired up with Betty, who didn't like her name much either. Most people didn't know they were in counter intelligence. As MP's they got to hear some interesting things and plant information in useful places. Today they were transporting some guy named Bo to Thompson.

Their orders were to question Bo about the camp and any other intel they could get out of him. Questions only; the Colonel didn't trust intel that came from pain. People would say all kinds of shit when they were hurting. Sam knew this, he'd spent time in the field watching assholes trying to beat the truth from captives. They never got anything he'd call useful.

Sam liked mind games. It made him useful to the Colonel. They were also a lot more fun.

"The file says he's charged with drugs and weapons as well as assault. There are allegations of child porn too. He's a gang banger, so tough is his way of life. But gang bangers like to brag."

"So we start as sympathetic listeners, and we'll tighten things down when we get some leverage."

That was one reason Sam liked to work with Betty. She didn't need a lot of explanation. It also helped that she was easy to look at. He figured it would help grease this Bo's mouth.

The driver was private Bill Hacket. Sam instructed him to drive and nothing else. If he didn't listen he couldn't get into trouble. The fourth in their crew was another private named Baily Simpson. Sam had worked with him before. The man knew how to keep quiet. Sam didn't even have to pay him much.

Sam had thought about taking an armoured truck, but he wanted Bo to be more comfortable than was safe for him. They took an officer's car. Bill up front with Baily. Betty and Sam would be on either side of Bo.

They picked him up at the detachment in town. The towns people were gathering for a memorial and Sam wanted clear before it started. He didn't want to soil the service with Bo's presence. The Staff-Sergeant and a woman officer brought the prisoner out and handed him over.

"Tell the Colonel we appreciate the help," Jim said, "We're short -handed and don't have the secure facilities we need to hold a prisoner."

"Our pleasure," Sam set the prisoner between them and fastened the man's seatbelt.

"Let's go," he told Hacket.

The car rode like a dream and Hacket was a good driver. Sam let the beginning of the trip pass in silence.

The checkpoint stopped them briefly and reviewed their orders. Sam could have arranged to drive through without stopping, but he wanted Bo to get a look at the soldiers and their weapons. They had their rifles and a 50-caliber machine gun mounted on a jeep. Bo looked thoughtful.

The drive to Thompson took four hours on a good day. Hacket had been instructed to drive a little slower than necessary to stretch that time. As Sam expected, Bo broke the silence.

"Why are you guys transporting me? How much did you pay the pigs to give me to you?"

"We're just helping out," Betty sounded like a movie star. Sam wondered if she was overdoing the sexy a bit, but guys like Bo didn't do subtle.

"Sure," Bo rolled his shoulders, "we get around the bend and you start in on me, I know what you're like."

"Why would we do that?" Betty wriggled to get more comfortable. "You're just some punk the Mounties want out of their hair. We drive you to Thompson, we pick up coffee and donuts for the Colonel and everyone is happy."

"I'm not just some punk," Bo puffed up as much as he could in handcuffs. "I run the trade in town."

"Yeah," Sam said, "small town, small trade."

"Fuck you," Bo angled himself to look at Betty.

"They told us you were going down for assaulting some girl. You beating your mistress?"

181

"The little bitch wouldn't do what she was told. She knew she had it coming. You know how it is."

"Let me guess, she said she wasn't going to spread her legs for you anymore."

"I could have made a lot of money for both of us if she'd just listened. Now she's a dead woman. I have friends."

"Seems like a lot of trouble for a woman." Sam watched the scenery pass outside the window.

Bo tried to turn even more, but the seat belt wouldn't let him.

"I provide an important service," Bo said. "Warriors need willing women to keep them happy."

"And you provide the women and make sure they're willing." Sam shrugged and made sure Bo felt it.

"It's the way the world works. The strong use the weak. We're going to run the North and all the oil and money is in the North. You white fuckers are done."

"So you're going to be part of the new order?" Betty tilted her head, her voice like honey.

Damn she's good. This guy's going to have a hard on all the way to Thompson.

"Damn straight." Bo shifted in his seat trying to get comfortable. "The cops think putting a whore in the apartments will keep her safe. But she knows what she is and as soon as she goes back to being what she was born to be, someone will get to her and bang, that'll be it. They can't pin the other shit on me. There wasn't any legal search."

"So you go free and you can get back to making the kiddie porn," Sam said.

"That was fucking Johnston and when I get hold of him he'll wish he never fucked with me. I don't do kids. It's bad for business."

"Not to mention it puts you in a bad light with your loser friends in prison." Sam laughed. He'd practiced that laugh. People told him it was like being whipped.

"I told you, I'm not going to prison. I'm too important. I'm the only person the Chief trusts with the location of his camp. You could look between the lakes for years and never find it."

"So how come you're so important to this Chief?" Betty stroked her finger along Bo's leg and he shifted again. *That's what you get for wearing those tight jeans.*

"We're related," Bo said, "He told me so hims-"

A bullet hole appeared in the windshield and Bo's brains spattered across the back windshield. Hacket started to swerve to make any more shots impossible, but the second shot hit his shoulder and the car went out of control. Baily reached across to take the wheel, but it was too late. The car left the road and slammed into the rock face.

Sam heard Baily's neck snap. Hacket was breathing, but he didn't sound good. Sam tried to kick the door open, but a shot hit him in the side and he slumped against Bo. Betty undid her seat belt and kicked out the window. The sniper must have been reloading because she got out of the car without being shot.

Then Sam heard someone talking to Betty. Something about being taken back to camp to work. He recognized the next sounds. He sparred with Betty enough to know the sound of her fist on flesh. People underestimated her because she was beautiful. Whoever she hit was either dead or dying. If she could get off the road she had a chance. More bullets smacked against the car, but the sniper kept shooting. He'd missed his best chance

Go girl, Sam thought, *Go*.

***

Betty dodged and wove through the sniper's shots. She had to be unpredictable, or she was dead. Salvation came the shape of an eighteen-wheeler that made the corner, but then either the driver panicked or the sniper shot him, because the truck pancaked into the rock face. The car and the bodies in it were flattened, but Betty hadn't stayed to watch. The truck blocked the sniper's line of fire and she ran around the car and into the woods even as the shriek and crash of twisting metal stopped.

They should have just stood back and filled the car with bullets, but they wanted her body, and it killed one of them and if Betty had anything to do with it, it was going to kill the other one too. They'd screwed up because they got horny. She wasn't going to complain about their stupidity.

She found a track which ran parallel to the road and jogged along it as quickly as she could without exhausting herself. At

183

least the temperature was only minus ten or there abouts. If she didn't get a bullet in the back or die of hypothermia, she would be safe from permanent damage to her lungs.

She came on a line of shorter trees hanging heavy with snow over the track. Betty knocked snow over her footprints as she went, then went to the end and knocked snow down as she came back. Just where she would have stepped into the new snow she jumped as far as she could off the path and threw snow to cover the last of her tracks. She breathed deeply to increase her body heat and waited. If the sniper came before she got too cold, if there was only the one more person, she'd have them.

Betty was beginning to think she'd misjudged her opponent when he came along the trail holding his rifle at the ready and moving cautiously. He seen her crush his partner's throat. He stopped when he saw the disturbed snow. Betty watching him sight down the path with the scope and held her breath in case it betrayed her. She was slowly letting the air out of her lungs when he lowered the gun and continued along the trail. He moved even slower and looked like he was checking for traps. Betty wished she knew how to make traps. If she survived, maybe she would learn.

She waited until he was just a little past her before she jumped back to the trail. In the movies, they always screamed when they attacked. She thought that was foolishness. She stayed silent, and the sniper died never knowing she was there.

He was bigger than her, but she stripped off his gear and put it on. He carried a knife as well as the big sniper rifle. The rifle didn't make a good weapon for what she needed to do. She removed the bolt and put it in her pocket. Too bad he didn't have a pistol, but with his cold weather gear and his knife, Betty figured her chances of survival went up to better than even. She tried to remember how far they'd travelled since they passed the checkpoint. A long way, maybe too long. Maybe someone would listen to the tape from the bug in the car and send help.

Maybe pigs would fly. She had to get out of this mess on her own feet. Betty walked out to the road and set herself a steady pace to get back to the checkpoint.

Chapter Thirty-four

"There is a mole in your organization," the Colonel glared at Jim. "Someone let the enemy know this Bo was being transported by us. I don't care if he's dead, but I have three dead, and a very good Military Police Officer who is still recovering from the experience."

"That doesn't make the mole one of my people," Jim reined in his anger. "Your people picked Bo up in front of the detachment. No one attempted a covert action. As for how they knew he was being transferred, Bo called his lawyer. At least he said it was his lawyer, but he didn't change his actions after the call. I think he called his friends at the camp and told them what was going on. It's standard procedure to transfer prisoners to Thompson. Even with the old detachment, we didn't have the facilities to hold people for very long. The sniper and his mate could have been waiting for any vehicle going south, or someone watching the transfer might have let them know what vehicle he travelled in."

"None the less we still have the problem of leaks of information from town. We have no way of knowing what these people's sympathies are."

"The first people to come to our aid were the Cree people of the Spruce Bay Cree Nation."

"They may have wanted to see the effect of their attack."

"They were helping. The Rangers, who are a trained auxiliary of the army, spent hours looking for survivors and days recovering bodies. The people from the Reserve fed us and kept us warm. Historically, we have looked with suspicion on people whose only crime was to look like our enemy."

"I'm not here for a history lesson, Staff-Sergeant," the Colonel frowned.

"So you are going to repeat the mistakes of the past and make the situation worse."

"I'm not suggesting a quarantine of the First Nations people, Staff-Sergeant. I am telling you to look at your own people and make sure you know where their sympathies lie. I am tired of losing people."

"I trust my team with my life," Jim said. "I will back them up against any charges of being the source of the leak. Keep in mind this has been in planning for six months and the person behind it apparently has military training. You may very well have moles in your own organization."

"Who told you this leader has military training?" The Colonel stood up and leaned over his desk.

"I'm a police officer, Colonel. The evidence points toward military training. You just confirmed my suspicions. It might be a good time for you to fill me in on what you know."

"And why would I do that?"

"Because the only useful intelligence you have so far has come from my office. If we knew what we were looking for, we could do even better."

"OK," The Colonel sat down and suddenly looked exhausted. "We had a man named Rivers Beauchamp in our unit. He was fully trained in counter-terrorist tactics - explosives, weapons, group dynamics, the psychology of recruiting and training and more. One of the best we had at what he did. He was with me through two tours in Afghanistan. Then something happened. I still don't know what. He went off the grid and was gone for two years. We had rumours he was seen in terrorist camps, but nothing substantive.

"Then there was a rumour he was in Canada. We looked for him, but no luck. Our intel suggests he, not Dupreis, was the one who killed the hunters. It was similar to the action he took just before he went AWOL."

Jim just sat and looked at the Colonel. The silence broken only by the sounds of people and equipment moving around outside.

"I will pass any information we get along to you." The Colonel fiddled with his pen. "We've been trying to track the explosives, but if they are buying explosives, it may make it more difficult."

"They will still need to buy through a legitimate business," Jim said, "but between construction and exploration up here, almost everyone uses explosives. I'm sorry about your people. If I find any connection between my people and the terrorists, I will take suitable action."

"That's all I can ask." The Colonel put the pen down.

Jim stood and left the tent. He didn't think the Colonel liked admitting he trained the leader of this terrorist group. There had to be more the man was holding back. He drove back to the detachment and sat in thought for a while.

Jim didn't like the idea of a mole in his organization any more than the Colonel did, but he needed to check it out. The lack of internet and TV made it hard to know what was going on. In his grief, Jim hadn't thought about checking with people on the outside. He suspected it was the same for most of the people. *In far too many ways, we are completely isolated from the rest of the country.* He picked up his cell phone. Maybe it was time to start breaking the isolation.

"Hi, Anne," he said when the retired Staff-Sergeant picked up her phone, "how is retirement?"

"Boring," she responded, "but I could get used to boring. What do I owe this call to?"

"What have you heard about Spruce Bay these days?"

"Fires at several lodges up in the area, and the children went on strike to support a teacher. Leigh, I'm guessing. Things went silent after the Deputy Minister and her staff were killed when their plane crashed into the mall on the way home. Then this clan of the White Moose claimed they were declaring war on Canada and things have blown up. It is just a matter of time before people start getting killed. It doesn't help that nothing is coming out of Spruce Bay. People are making up the news as they go along."

"I realize it's a mess, but I need your help. It has something to do with this White Moose group." Jim said. "I need your input on a Rivers Beauchamp, the name suggests he might be from this area, but it could be misleading. He did a stint in the Army in Afghanistan. Are there any connections to people up here? The usual things, jobs, relationships that kind of thing. Do you remember anything about him?

"I'll have to think about it. I'll call you back. In the meantime, you stay out of trouble."

"Way too late for that, Anne," Jim said. "I'll be in touch."

Jim didn't like the complete news black-out on events in Spruce Bay. The violence in the rest of the country was only going to get worse unless they could get a handle on what was going on here. He wondered how long the government would be able to maintain the secrecy, and what would happen when it broke. Jim didn't think it would be good.

There was a knock at the door and Darren stuck his head in the door. "How did it go with the Colonel?"

Jim hated that his first instinct was to hold back information. Darren had worked with him for almost two years.

"The Colonel came clean with a name," Jim said. "Rivers Beauchamp. Bo claimed just before he was shot that he was related to the man. Have you heard the name in any of your conversations?"

"No, but I can ask around."

"No, let's keep it away from the community for the moment. I don't want the man knowing we're looking specifically at him. Just keep your ears open. Pass the word to the others. Listen, but no questions. The other thing I want to investigate is who was around to see Bo get into the car."

"You think someone tipped them off."

"It is a possibility," Jim said. "If we can put together a list of people who were around, it might be helpful."

"I'll get the others to work on that too," Darren said. "Have you considered there might be a mole in the organization?"

"It has crossed my mind."

"It would be hard to stay under cover in this small community, but if there was someone in Thompson feeding them information…"

"The possibility remains that Bo signed his own death sentence," Jim sighed and leaned back. "See if you can find out what number he called to talk to his lawyer. He may have put in a call to Rivers thinking this supposed relationship would get him out of trouble."

"Right," Darren nodded.

"What did the Colonel say about the other action the day of the memorial?"

"Not much," Jim said. "They put a team down by the old mine the wendigo used and took out about twenty men. They were in war paint, but someone blew the mine and buried most of the evidence."

"Did they back track the trails of the incoming people?"

"Apparently, they met up a kilometer or so north of the mine. Past that, there are twenty different trails. He has people following each of them, but no report yet, at least nothing he passed on to me."

"Not the trusting type, our Colonel," Darren grimaced.

"Can you blame him?" Jim said. "He's after one of his own people, that has to make you doubt everyone around you."

"His own people?" Darren stood up straight with wide eyes.

"This Rivers was trained in counter-terrorism by the Colonel himself."

"That's got to suck."

"Yeah, but it also means we're up against someone who knows what he's doing. This is no amateur who got lucky a couple of times."

"Thanks for filling me in, Jim," Darren leaned against the wall. "It would be easy to assume because I'm Cree I'm a sympathizer."

"We may have to work with that," Jim couldn't meet Darren's eyes. "If the Colonel can't find this camp, we'll be looking at planting a mole of our own."

"Shit, Staff, I hate winter camping."

"I'm hoping it doesn't come to that."

"I'll start putting a plan together just in case."

"You do that, and we'll pray we don't need to use it."

189

Chapter Thirty-five

The last of the scouts returned frustrated. All the trails they had followed had simply vanished after several kilometers. The trails led no one direction other than vaguely north.

The Colonel looked at the map and thought about one day's walk and then travel by machine. Outside the circle of that blindfolded walk they didn't have to bother to cover their trail. Either Rivers didn't think they could find a rarely used trail in such a large area, or there was enough traffic in the region to make any one trail fade into all the others. They had a cache, or probably several, but they would still need to get specialized supplies in - things that weren't predictable.

He pulled out a smaller scale map and looked at the larger region. There were several communities in Saskatchewan which might be staging points for goods headed for Rivers' people. He made a note to get Lieutenant O'Neil to check on gang activity up that way. There were also communities to the North. How far could one travel on snowmobile?

Where ever they got their equipment, they had to be hiding somewhere, and if people were out there, then they gave off heat. Perhaps it was time to send out the choppers to look over the region. It gave Rivers more information than the Colonel wanted to, but they needed to push this thing. They were taking too long already. The media blackout of Spruce Bay wasn't going to last much longer. There would be hell to pay when it came out the leader of the White Moose had been trained by the army. They needed something to show the army response was effective and moderate.

The choppers went out in the morning. They had three of them. They had orders to stay low enough to be effective in scanning the countryside, but not so close they were at risk. The Colonel hadn't forgotten the RPG's at the old mine. He didn't want to think about what Rivers' had planned for them, but they would have devastated the people inside the shed if they'd struck.

The choppers returned without reporting anything new. They fueled up and went out again. They had to search hundreds of square kilometers. It would take time. In the meantime, they needed to do some specific training for the terrain. Rivers had the advantage of home territory. The Colonel didn't trust the Rangers to be free of enemy influence, but the Staff-Sergeant's people would be safe enough.

"Betty," the Colonel called, "Bring my car around, I'm going to go pay the Staff-Sergeant a visit."

She met him outside the tent a few minutes later. He climbed into the back seat and she drove toward town.

"I'm going to suggest the RCMP folks train with some of our people. We need to get a feel for this country. While I'm talking to the Staff-Sergeant, I'd like you to scope out some possible locations. I'd get Lieutenant O'Neil to manage it, but she's tied up with the choppers. I want this training to happen soonest."

"Yes, sir," Betty said, "Do you want a variety of terrain, trees, buildings, open country?"

"That would be best, and if there is a central location to debrief it would help."

"I will ask around."

"Thank you." The Colonel climbed out of the car, "Do this well and I could make your career take off."

"Yes, sir," Betty saluted.

The Colonel walked into the detachment wondering if there was a way for him to spend some time with this MP without O'Neil getting jealous. He put the thought to one side for the moment and reviewed his arguments in preparation for another jousting match with the Staff-Sergeant.

"I can see it being a useful exercise," the Staff-Sergeant said to him when he'd explained what he wanted. The man kept surprising him. He'd expected to have to convince him of the value of the training. "You might want to get your people to look at the old ski lodge. It is close to town, but isolated enough no one will wander into the training and get hurt."

"When can we put this together?" the Colonel asked.

191

"We can start tomorrow if you'd like, but it will take several days to go through the issues your people will face out here. We've worked with the Rangers and can give you an overview of the main things. How many of your people do you want involved?"

"I was going to get the Sergeants to train with you, and they can pass the essentials to their squads. So, eight people, ten if the Captains decide to join in."

"That'll work well," the Staff-Sergeant made notes.

"Let's say tomorrow at dawn." The Colonel stood. "If you say the ski lodge is good, that's enough for me. Oh, one more thing, I'd like the MP who survived the attack on our transport to take part."

"That's fine." The Staff-Sergeant stood and walked him to the door. "You send me the people and I'll train them. We have some paintball gear we use."

"I'd like to use live fire training rounds, essentially paint balls in standard cartridges. That way we're using the weapons we're used to. We'll supply the same for you."

"I've heard of those. It would be interesting. We all use nine mm ammunition."

"Excellent"

The colonel decided to join the Captains and the Sergeants for the training exercise. Lieutenant O'Neil was up to her neck tracking the choppers and their search. He had his radio so he could react immediately to anything that came up.

The ski lodge turned out to be an A-frame building with a small balcony up high off an interior loft. It had a big deck on the other side of the building. To one side of the building was a shed that probably stored equipment. Another small building set near the shed. There was a large open space bordered by the lodge and out buildings on one side, forest on two sides and a sharp downward slope on the fourth side.

The Staff-Sergeant and his people met them inside the pleasantly warm Lodge.

"Here are the training rounds." Sergeant Creeley held up a box. "For safety reasons, I'm going to ask that you leave all lethal rounds here in the lodge. We'll put them in this box. This way no one accidentally loads the wrong round and kills someone. It's

192

bad for morale." He handed out boxes and watched the Staff-Sergeant and the constables unload their guns and put the lethal rounds in the ammo box.

"Thank you," he said, "the next thing is safety. These are just fancy paintball rounds, but like paintballs they hurt. They can do damage if you get shot in the face or at close range, so be respectful. I'd hand out goggles, but they'd just fog up. Instead I'm going to trust you to not shoot each other in the head. Since we'll be wearing winter gear the rest of our bodies will be safe enough. I have training whites. They go over your gear so we can see when you're shot. That's it for me. Over to you, Staff-Sergeant."

"It seems a little unwieldy to keep calling each other Sergeant when most of you are Sergeants. Call me Jim, this is Darren, Cam, Pat and Amber."

"I'm Tony," Creeley held up his hand, then pointed at the others. "Bob, Mike, Gretta, Oscar, Sandy, Paul and George,"

"I'm Hugh, and this is Al," Captain Banning said. "Everybody knows the colonel was baptized *Colonel*. The Military Police Sergeant is Betty."

"Let's get started then," Jim said. "You guys know about snow and cold weather. What we have up here to make life confusing is really deep snow, and trees. Fortunately, it's early yet and the snow isn't more than half a meter deep. But it's plenty to slow you down. It's the trees that will confuse matters. Forest will range from impenetrable bush, to fairly wide open. We have a little of each here."

Jim handed out some maps.

"These are the trails. They used to be groomed and packed, but we haven't had the money to do the work for some years. Look at the red trail. That's the shortest one. What we'll do is this. You will head out on the trail from the sign marked near the back door of the Lodge. We'll go the other way on the trail. When you see the other team, take them down."

They loaded up their guns and went out on the trail. The Colonel had his sidearm as the Captains did, but the Sergeants had C7's. The Sergeants formed up front and back with the officers in the center. As the Colonel expected, it was chaos when

193

the teams met. The only person standing at the end was Betty because she was observing and not a target.

"That was fun," Jim said. "Though I have to admit it is strange using my real gun to shoot friends. Now we're warmed up, so to speak, the next thing is a chase. Darren is going to start; we'll give him two minutes then go after him. I have given him no instructions, so I don't know what he has in mind, but I can assure you it won't be what you expect."

Darren started off and Jim timed the two minutes. The Colonel found he was shivering at the end of it. The heat of the first battle had worn off. Jim fired his gun into a nearby tree and the Sergeants led off. They formed a wedge with Bob a few steps ahead. The Colonel and his Captains followed a little way back with Betty observing again.

It was ridiculous easy to follow the trail in the snow - the footprints were clear and Darren didn't seem to be moving quickly. They should have him in a minute or two. Then the Colonel felt a shot between his shoulders and saw the red paint on the Captain's backs as well. Darren also picked off two of the Sergeants before they turned around. They shot at him, but must have missed, since they took off after him. The Colonel got to his feet and followed. They got him in the end, but the Colonel wondered if he'd allowed them to catch him.

"It is tempting to think the snow tells you where your enemy is." Jim grinned at them. "But it only tells you where they have been. The forest lets you play all kinds of games with people." The Colonel saw Betty nodding in agreement. "The other challenge in heavy forest is staying on a straight line. We're going to get you to just walk from one side of this bit of forest to the other. Don't depend on your GPS, you can't count on it working all the time out here."

The Colonel walked through the forest and was shocked at how quickly he got off the straight line. It was instructive. He had no problem when he followed the GPS. He didn't think there was a way to jam the satellites, so he didn't give much credence to the notion they couldn't depend on the technology.

They kept up the pace through the day. Each time the Colonel thought there wasn't any twist for the Staff Sergeant and his team to pull on them, they did something to make his head spin. They climbed trees, hid under snow banks and generally made the lives of the Army people miserable.

"OK," Jim said as it started to get dark, "That's it for the day, I'd like to invite those of you who can take the time to join us at my home for supper."

"I'll take the duty Sergeants back to base," Captain Raffin said, "You go enjoy yourselves."

The Colonel surprised himself by thoroughly enjoying the evening. The Staff-Sergeant's wife, Leigh and her friend Lyanne, made sure they were all well fed and watered. It felt much later than it was when they headed back to base.

"What did you think?" he asked Betty as she drove him back.

"They took it easy on you," she said, "especially Darren. I had the feeling he could have gone through the entire day without a mark on him. We will need to remind the men that the alternation of action and waiting puts them at particular risk of hypothermia. Jim watched us carefully for signs. He had us in the Lodge frequently to warm up. He's a good trainer, our people hardly noticed they were getting their asses handed to them all day."

"I think I'll stay at base tomorrow," the Colonel said, "I'm not used to this and I'm getting stiff."

"Understood, sir."

Damn it, just what did she mean by that? He tried to find a comfortable way to sit in the seat but his pants were just too restrictive.

195

Chapter Thirty-six

He forgot about his discomfort when O'Neil met him in his tent.

"We may have found them, sir," she said without preamble. "There is a region north of us between two fair sized lakes within possible travel distance. The choppers saw some heat signatures and what might be trails."

"Are they sure the heat signatures are people and not moose or something?" The Colonel stripped off his outer layers and laid them to the side for his aide to clean and put away. He decided to switch to his customary dress blues for the strategy meeting he was going to call immediately.

"The sensors are calibrated to human temperature," she said. "Oh for goodness sake, let me take care of that. You won't be able to concentrate in the meeting. He felt her cool hands down the front of his base layer. She gripped him hard.

"We don't have time for this," he said.

"It isn't like it's going to take long." After a few seconds, he shuddered with release. She was right on both accounts. It hadn't taken long and he felt much more capable of concentration. O'Neil fixed the minimal amount of lipstick she wore and left the tent. The Colonel finished getting changed and walked briskly to the HQ tent where he was sure she would already have the command team assembled.

The map was posted with a layover showing the area in question. It was still a big region to search, but much smaller than what they had been looking at.

"Suggestions," he said.

"The space there is still quite large," Captain Raffin peered at the map. "We'll need to split our offensive into several teams and coordinate by radio. The radios are encrypted, so the enemy won't be able to listen in.

"Use GPS to mark and track locations of the teams. That will let us give support and orders from here. I suggest we hold back the choppers until we engage, they don't have an unlimited amount of fuel."

"I can load the topo maps into the men's GPS units," Lieutenant O'Neil said. "We can check with the locals, but I doubt the ice will be strong enough to support the men, never mind any equipment."

"I don't want any word of this offensive outside this room." The Colonel frowned at his people. "Whether the leak is in the detachment or not. If they don't know we're moving, they can't pass it to the wrong people."

"Perhaps the MP you had observing today could take a different squad to the training with the RCMP. That would keep them occupied and out of touch for the day. We could say the Sergeants are training their squads and sent these people out to get hands on experience."

"Very good." The Colonel grinned briefly. "See to it."

"Captains, we will need to get a large number of soldiers out to the area, preferably without tipping off the enemy."

"There is a road travelling in the direction of the offensive before bending west. We could truck the soldiers to the bend, then utilize the bombardiers to transport the rest of the way. They will give us heavy weapons support. We have four of the bombardiers on site and can fit twelve in each if we crowd them in." Captain Banning pointed to the map. "We move then in along these four routes and we'll effectively have a loose line we can move North."

"Very good." The Colonel nodded and tapped on the table. "There is no guarantee we will find anybody, but the chance to operate in winter conditions will be good for the soldiers. Be sure they understand the importance of proper gear and awareness of the temperature."

***

Well before dawn, fifty soldiers loaded onto an assortment of trucks and bombardiers. They wouldn't pack in like sardines until they'd gone as far as the trucks could take them. Two soldiers would stay with the drivers to secure the trucks. The rest would cram into the Bombardiers, fortunately they had sleds to

197

put their gear on, so they weren't sitting with rifle barrels up the ass.

Creeley thought about the little training exercise he'd taken part in the day before.

"Mark this point on your GPS, boys and girls, if everything goes sideways, this is the place you want to be. Don't get cocky out there. You are well trained, well armed, and well paid, that puts you three points ahead. What the enemy has is home field advantage. They grew up fucking around in these woods. So stay sharp, don't make stupid assumptions and you just may get home again. It is damned cold out there, so don't fondle your weapon with your bare hand. You've been issued a pair of thin gloves. Keep them on at all times."

They rode across rough terrain and Creeley harangued them the entire way there. The driver slowed and stopped.

"We're at the mark, Sergeant, I'll be behind you at a walking pace. We're Bravo team, Alpha team's ten k west and Charlie is ten k east." She opened the doors for them.

The squad climbed out of the machine and grabbed their gear from the trailer. Creeley had them unhook it. If all went well they would retrieve it. If not, it wouldn't matter and it might get in the way. The ten soldiers spread out and started walking north in their snowshoes. It was awkward at first, but they fell into the rhythm and stayed in line and ready. All they needed now was someone to shoot at.

Creeley wasn't sure if he wanted to meet the enemy or not. He felt a great need to hand out some ass whupping, but he also knew there was terrible potential for disaster in every battle plan. *Shit, that's why they pay me the big bucks.*

He kept an eye on the formation. They needed to be spread out to cover ground, but not so far individuals were vulnerable to attack without support. They'd done this before, just not in the snow.

They kept up chatter on the radio.

"Nothing."

"More nothing."

"If I see a moose, can I shoot it?"

"Only if you plan to carry it home."

They'd been walking for an hour when they came on the trail. Everybody paused while he went to look at it. It looked fresh to him, but what did he know? *Let's follow it and find out.* It made as much sense as what they were doing. He called them in and gave them their new formation. They would parallel the trail on either side while two people walked on the trail.

"Pay attention, people. GPS says we're well clear of Alpha team, but keep checking. No fuck ups today."

They walked for another hour. Creeley kept looking at the trail, but it was better than randomly walking through the wilderness. This country was so empty!

The radio chatter continued.

"Nothing,"

"Clear,"

"Snow and trees here."

"Look, there's a rabbit."

"If it isn't armed, ignore it."

"Movement!" Green on the far end of one wing.

"Hold silence," Creeley ordered them. "Close in and support Green. If this is a bad call, you're buying a round, Green."

He heard shots being fired. They sounded strange, maybe the cold air messing with his ears.

"Report!"

"He took a shot at me, and buggered off. He missed. I'm in pursuit."

"I'm on your nine o'clock, don't shoot me by mistake."

"Nah, if I'm going to shoot you, I'll mean it."

The soldiers formed a new line with Green at the center. The trail was easy to follow. They chased the enemy with him stopping to take occasional pot shots. None of their return fire hit.

"He's leading us somewhere," Creeley said. "Keep your eyes open, because I don't want to walk into a trap." He heard gunfire at a distance and grinned. One of the other teams had found themselves some action.

His caution proved well founded as more enemy appeared and started shooting. The bombardier was trying to find a way through to their location, but this part of the forest was a tangle of fallen and burnt trees. Creeley's group was pinned down and had to pull back.

199

"Bravo to Alpha team," Creeley switched to the command channel. "We have enemy pinned at these coordinates…"

"Roger that, Bravo," the reply came. "We're on our way."

He switched back to his squad channel.

"Petersen," he said, "drop back and see what's keeping the bombardier. We need their guns."

"Copy that," Petersen slipped out of the line. Creeley heard him request the coordinates from the driver. He took a second to input them into his own unit, then went back to the fight.

They exchanged fire with the enemy, but Creeley couldn't tell if they were doing any damage. The trees meant they could barely see who they were shooting at. He heard more gunfire approaching from the west. Alpha team was here.

"We're going to try to push them out of this shit to where you can see them," Creeley informed Alpha team. "Be advised the enemy is wearing similar whites. Try not to shoot us."

"Copy that."

Creeley sent his people to flank the enemy and maybe close the circle with Alpha team. "Talk to each other people, do not shoot your own people." They closed in, but the enemy had stopped firing.

"Careful," Creeley said. "Watch for trip wires. They didn't lead us here for nothing."

They closed the circle in and found three bodies, but nothing else.

"I was sure there were more than three positions firing at us," Creeley said to the Alpha team leader.

"At least four we engaged." She pivoted to examine their surroundings.

"Where the hell did they go?" They couldn't find any trails leading away. "Shit." Creeley said. "OK, let's rendezvous with the bombardier and get back to work. Stay sharp, people, those assholes didn't just vanish."

Alpha teamed moved off while Creeley called the bombardier.

"We're coming back to your last location. Stay put."

"Copy that,"

He looked at his GPS and led off toward the machine. They walked for half an hour and didn't find it. Creeley checked his GPS and saw they weren't anywhere close to where he'd thought.

"Petersen," he called, "where the hell are you?"

"I don't know, Sarge," Petersen responded. "I'm at the mark the bombardier gave me, but they aren't there."

"Get back here," Creeley said, "Follow the gun shots." He detailed one person to fire every thirty seconds and called the Alpha team.

"The GPS is fucked up," he said, "I didn't believe it was possible."

"So that's what the shooting is about, I thought you were after a squirrel."

He called the bombardier again. This time he got no response.

"SHIT! It looks like the bombardier is out of commission somehow."

"So this whole thing was about about cutting you off from your ground support."

"Looks like." Creeley clenched his fist. "the Colonel is going to have my ass for this. Petersen. We're joining up with Alpha, get your ass back here."

"On my way," Petersen said.

"Alpha, hold your position and report to command. We'll join up with you as soon as we get Petersen back."

"Copy that."

Petersen arrived and they formed up.

"The GPS isn't working," Creeley said to his crew. "We'll follow Alpha's track and join up with them. I'm sure the enemy isn't finished playing with us."

They followed the other team's trail and met up with them within the half hour.

"Command has recalled us," the Alpha team leader reported. "Stay with us and we'll put you in the trailer. It won't be fun, but it will get you home."

Chapter Thirty-seven

The Colonel was angrier than he could ever remember. The incursion into the area where they thought Rivers hid out had been a failure. The White Moose had posted video of the action and the army people looked ridiculous. At the end of the video they showed the driver and gunner from the captured bombardier. The statement they released with the video made a big deal about them not mistreating the prisoners.

It is not us who are brutal and uncivilized.

The Colonel called up his superiors in Ottawa.

"We need to release information on the original attack," he said, "We should have done it from the start."

"It was your request to keep it quiet," the person on the other end replied. "Now if we release the information, they will claim we created the attack to discredit them. We have no direct proof they were involved. We both know they were, but that won't carry any weight with public opinion."

"I need better air support." The Colonel ground his words out. "There is just too much territory up here to try to find these people with ground troops."

"I saw the video," The voice was terrifying in his mildness. "You can't give them any more material to strengthen their cause. Expect your air support to arrive within the day. Use it wisely."

The Colonel seethed after he hung up. The brass was hanging him out to dry. Whatever happened, his career was done. Well if he was finished, then he'd take Rivers down with him.

He looked at the map. It was hard to determine exactly where the action had taken place. The GPS marks were all over the place. Somehow that terrain interfered with their technology. They did know people were there, and in large enough numbers to be able to create a trap for his people.

The trap was another source of irritation. That damned Staff-Sergeant was right, there was a leak in his organization. High up too, because those people were waiting. They knew exactly what they needed to do. The Colonel was tired of being blind to the actions of the enemy. But with a mole in his ranks, he couldn't consider sending one of his own people. It would be a death sentence.

The Staff-Sergeant had the perfect person to put in place. All the Colonel needed to do was convince him without letting a whiff of his plan escape to betray his spy.

"Betty," he called her on his radio, "bring around my car." He walked over O'Neil's office tent. She worked at her desk. Every folder aligned exactly, her notes as clear and readable as the print on a computer screen. It amazed him that she was so unrestrained in other areas.

"Colonel." She looked up from her work.

"I'm heading into town to talk to the Staff-Sergeant," the Colonel said, "He mentioned at the training GPS weren't always reliable I want to find out what else he knows about it."

"I will research the question as well, Colonel," she said. "Is Ottawa sending the air support you wanted? I will need to find a place to put them."

"They are supposed to be here within twenty-four hours. Let me know your plan for housing them."

"Very good, sir." She went back to work and the Colonel walked out to meet his car. He had no complaints about O'Neil's work, or her less legal contributions to his comfort. He just wished he understood her better.

Betty drove him into town in silence. The Colonel wondered if he had made her angry at him. He was a fool around women and he knew it. He tried to stay away from them whenever possible.

"Betty," he said, "have you done any work tracking down moles in the military?"

"I have some experience," she said as she pulled up in front of the detachment. "You think we have a mole in our camp?"

"I'm afraid we have one high up in our command structure," the Colonel rubbed his forehead. "I hand-picked those people myself, I'm not entirely objective on their abilities. If you looked into each of them, it would give me fresh eyes."

"I will do what I can."

The Colonel climbed out of the car and headed for the detachment door. Betty pulled out and headed back toward the base. He wasn't sure why he'd asked her to investigate. Maybe because of her experience on the attempt to transport Bo. She'd also been the one to suggest bugging the car and taping the conversation for later analysis. She felt like someone with unknown depths.

It didn't help that the Colonel kept fantasizing about some of those depths. He shook the thought away as he stepped into the detachment. One of the constables worked at the desk.

"Good morning, Colonel. I'll check to see if Staff is free." She came back a few seconds later and escorted him to the Staff-Sergeant's office.

"Good morning," the Colonel said, "I came for a couple of reasons. The first is to get whatever information I can from you about the effect of certain regions on our GPS units."

"It was something an old prospector mentioned to me." The Staff-Sergeant waved the Colonel to a seat. "unfortunately he died at the time of the attack."

"Many good people died when your mall collapsed."

"That's true, but this man and his pilot were shot and left in the shed on the airstrip. The theory is the people who set the explosion on the fuel tanks shot them and hid them there."

"You don't sound convinced." The Colonel sat and tried to relax.

"There are some things that don't add up," the Staff-Sergeant said, "but we aren't in a position to investigate right now."

"The penciled circle on the map is where he thought the affect would be found?"

"Approximately," the Staff-Sergeant looked closer at the map. "I drew the circle myself. He was complaining that someone had messed with his mine claim markers. When we put the map up I marked the area. I wondered if his claim was there. A friend of mine told me it was an area of uneasy spirits."

"Now it seems those uneasy spirits belong to a group of terrorists."

204

"Do we have any information on how many people are involved?"

"Other than we've killed maybe twenty or so of them, no. It could be hundreds; it could be thousands." The Colonel stood and walked over to look out the window. The view was depressing. Just white snow and black trees with a few grey buildings in the foreground. "We need to get a person on the inside. I'm sure you've seen the news of the unrest across the country. If we don't get in under control soon, it will tear the country apart." The Colonel turned away from the window and looked at the Staff-Sergeant. "You were right about the mole. They're someone in my command structure, but it means I can't try to place a man myself. It would be a death sentence."

"But if I put someone in," the Staff-Sergeant said, "they won't report to you."

"No, it has to go through you. I don't want to know any of the details, I may let something slip. It is going to be hard enough on your man as it is."

"I will talk to him." The Staff Sergeant sighed. "But it is up to him."

"I understand. I will leave it in your hands."

The Colonel left the office and walked out on the street before he thought to call Betty. He saw a small restaurant and decided to sit and have a coffee, then he would call. He didn't like the idea of leaving something as important as planting an agent in someone else's hands, but he didn't trust himself. Someone he'd chosen had betrayed him. It reopened the wounds of Rivers' betrayal.

Rivers always had a bit of arrogance. As he ran missions and became more effective at his work, the arrogance had grown. Then he'd trusted the wrong person and his team had been shot to pieces. The review placed the blame squarely on Rivers' shoulders. He made the call against the advice of other people. The Colonel's superiors decided Rivers should not be put in command of any further missions. Rivers had reacted with fury. He'd gone AWOL. The man who betrayed Rivers' team was found hung and gutted from the rafters of his own home. The family was all dead, their throats cut.

205

He'd tried to track Rivers down, but the Colonel was always a step behind. Now being a step behind was killing people, the Colonel's people. If one of his own people was betraying him, what did it say about the Colonel's ability to command?

Chapter Thirty-eight

"So." Darren closed his eyes and leaned against the wall. "It's time, is it?"

"The Colonel believes he has a mole in his command. He wants someone who is completely separate from his people to infiltrate the White Moose."

"And that person needs to be me?"

"You do have a unique qualification the rest of us lack," Jim looked ashamed to be stating it, as if recognizing Darren wasn't white was a social gaffe.

"I'm Cree, and so I could be one of the enemy."

"Unfortunately yes, I don't like it, but if you are willing, we do need to get information from inside the organization."

"I won't be able to just walk up and join them. Anyone from here will know who I am."

"I think you're going to have to snap in a big way, something to make the news and give you credibility."

"I'm afraid to ask."

"Lyanne suggested the gangs were involved in a big way. We'll find an excuse to make a move on one of the gangs. You accuse us of racism and resign."

"It needs to be more than just an argument," Darren crossed his arms. "I need to kill someone so it is clear I can never go back."

"That would be hard on your partner."

"I have a few of those training bullets left. I could make it look real enough if we don't give them time to examine the body."

"I think we'll need a new recruit for you to shoot. Someone irritating enough we won't miss them when they're gone."

"Do you have someone in mind?"

"I'm thinking we get Cam to play dress up. He should be able to pull off the annoying part. We let the sparks fly in public a few times, then you go to do a bust and do your thing from there."

"How am I going to report? I can hardly carry a cell phone or send you an email."

"This is one of those new GPS units that allow you to send text messages through the GPS satellite. You won't be able to report regularly or in depth, but anything about numbers or position will help." Jim pushed it across his desk.

Darren left the office with a pit in his stomach. They'd touched briefly on undercover work at the academy, but this would be harder than just putting on a persona for a drug buy. He was going to have to leave his own feelings about non-violent solutions behind. Even if the murder to get him started was faked, the other crimes he would commit wouldn't be.

Someone had to go, and it might as well be him. He had no serious relationships. His family had almost disowned him when he became a cop. The only life he would ruin was his own.

He looked at the GPS Jim had given him. Jim having it at his office meant he'd been thinking about this seriously before the Colonel came in. They both had, they just didn't want to put it into action. He'd have to have a cover story for the GPS, maybe he could program in the coordinates they used for the failed ground attack. It would explain why he had the thing.

The next day Constable Fred Hawkings made his appearance. He'd been sent up with the new air support choppers which arrived at the base. The man was as much an asshole as possible to be and still have human DNA.

Damn, Darren cruised through the town showing the 'new guy' the ropes, *Cam is enjoying himself way too much.*

"So you just let these indians off the reserve anytime they feel like it?" Fred said as they walked through the grocery store.

"These *First Nations* people live here too," Darren didn't bother to hide his annoyance. "They were the first people to respond when we needed help."

"Sure." Fred rolled his eyes. "They were the ones who caused the problem. I think they have the right idea when they say all the Indians should be rounded up and put back on the reserves. We should fence them in and keep them there."

208

"I don't know how you graduated with that attitude, asshole." Darren snarled, forgetting it was all an act. "but you'd better change it quick."

"Didn't you hear, Tonto? They sent all the Indians home from the Academy." Fred laughed as Darren just stopped himself from decking the man.

To make matters worse, they worked the same shift and Pat was designated to watch the shop. Darren couldn't escape.

The call to the reserve didn't come soon enough. Darren dreamt about not changing the bullets for the fake ones when he shot the bastard. Joe would be nearby visiting a relative and make sure no one got too close a look at the body. Darren's gut churned with nausea.

He arrived in his truck to find Fred already there in his. Constable Fred had the people, men, women and children lying on the ground in the snow and below freezing temperature.

"Nice of you to join me Tonto," Fred waved at Darren. "I've got this in hand. We'll charge them all with whatever we can and ship them off to jail. At least they can't kill anyone there."

"Not all these people are guilty of a crime," Darren silently apologized to the people in the snow.

"They're here, they share a house with the dealer. They're guilty. If they don't want to be guilty they should have reported his drug dealing ass."

"He's family," Darren gritted his teeth. "They don't operate that way."

"Well, they'd better start. In this country from now on, they will play by our rules."

"And what rules would that be?"

"This country belongs to us. They better get used to it. If they don't like it too bad," Fred kicked the drug dealer. "or they die and get out of our way."

Darren pulled his gun and emptied into Fred. He hit the vest with the first few shots, then shot the man's arms and legs. He heard screaming and swearing behind him as the people ran away. He ejected his slide and checked his rounds, one left.

He walked up to the cop lying in the snow. Fred glared at him trying to talk.

209

"Save yourself the effort. I've decided to retire, give my regards to Staff." He shot Fred dead centre in the forehead.

"Shit," someone said behind him, "Have you gone crazy?"

Darren turned with his gun still in his hand. The speaker backed up quickly - Johnston McCrey, Bo's second in command. Darren had to restrain the urge to shoot the man on the spot.

"No, I've just got sane." Darren took his uniform coat off and threw it on top of the body. His hat, shirt and shield followed. "Someone is going to come soon. I'd better get out of here."

"Follow me," McCrey led Darren around behind the house. There were two snowmobiles there. McCrey started one and pointed to the other. Darren climbed on and started it up. He followed McCrey onto a trail and away into the bush heading north east. He figured they were heading to a rendezvous point. He hoped it wasn't too far. It was too cold to be out in just his base layer and vest.

They drove for an hour and pulled up in front of a cabin.

"Come on," McCrey pushed him in the door. "I'll get a fire going. There's blankets and some extra coats. Help yourself. Stay here until I get back. If you try to leave or follow me, you're a dead man - the War Chief's rules. You don't argue with the War Chief twice."

Darren wrapped a scratchy wool blanket around himself and sat down. It was done now, as far as anyone in the rest of the world knew, he was a cop killer and a traitor. Darren shook violently, and not from the cold.

He fed the fire and kept waiting. The light faded until it got black night outside. When he started getting hungry, Darren searched the cabin and found some jerky and granola bars. He returned to his seat and watched the fire burn in the little stove.

The sound of approaching snow machines woke him. The fire was down to embers, so he put some wood in and waited. The machines stopped and seconds later the door opened and Darren saw maybe four men come into the cabin, hard to tell in the dim light of the embers. One of the men used a flashlight to find and light a naptha lantern.

Darren recognized Roger Dupreis from the photos of him. McCrey was back, he was the one to light the lantern. The other two Darren didn't recognize, but they held shotguns and stood on either side of the door.

"Johnston tells me you shot your partner."

"That's right."

"So why would an apple like you, suddenly go ape-shit and shoot a cop?" Roger crossed his arms and glared at him.

"I joined the force to make things better for my people. It didn't work. That asshole just clarified things for me."

"You made the evening news." Roger waved at the cabin, "This is luxury where you're going. Are you sure you're up for it?"

"Something tells me either I go with you, or I get left for the ravens. I'm going with you. If I change my mind later, I can always shoot myself."

"Speaking of which," Roger said. "Maybe you'll put your gun on the floor and kick it over?"

Darren unclipped his holster and pushed it across the floor.

"It's empty. I have a spare clip if you'd like." Darren pulled it from his belt and tossed it to Roger.

"Put some warm clothes on." Roger stuffed the gun and clip into his parka pocket. "It's a long ride."

Darren kept his ballistic vest and his flashlight. He ditched the uniform pants and put on some wool pants that looked as old as he did. A flannel check shirt went over the vest and a coat over that. He found a toque and mitts.

"I'll do. Let's go before you change your mind."

"You're not going to change yours now, are you?" Roger came right up in his face. "That wouldn't be healthy."

"I shot my partner in the face." Darren didn't budge. "No one's taking me back."

"Then I guess we're done here." Roger walked out the door, Darren followed him. He heard one of the shotgun wielders putting the cabin back in order.

"Johnston," Roger yelled through the still open door. "Burn the pants and anything else that shows our ex-cop was here. Head back to the rez, and try to stay out of fucking trouble."

"Sure, Roger," he shouted from inside the cabin.

They climbed on the snow machines and rode into the night. Darren had never seen the point of riding a snowmobile in circles

211

and calling it fun, but he discovered he was enjoying this ride. They wound along a trail barely wide enough to let the snowmobile pass. When they got to lakes they went around. Darren guessed it had more to do with the track they'd leave behind than the thickness of the ice.

The moon had risen when they pulled the machines into a lean to covered with snow. From above it would look like the ground.

"We'll sleep here," Roger tossed Darren a sleeping bag. Darren stripped down naked and hung his base layer up to dry, then got into the sleeping bag. It was cold for a few minutes but soon warmed. In the morning, he shook the ice off his clothes and got dressed.

"Glad to see you haven't forgotten everything;" Roger nodded at him.

"I grew up on the Rez," Darren said.

"I know," Roger said, "I know a lot about you. Grew up on the Rez, brothers went into the gangs. Two of them dead, one in prison and a sister who's still on the Rez popping out babies. Your dad was pissed when you went cop. said you'd gone apple. You almost got thrown out of the Academy for pushing the old man's teeth down his throat. Then you got posted to Spruce Bay, the asshole of the North, and everybody forgot about you."

"The only thing you got wrong was the teeth." Darren shrugged and walked around to warm up. "The old man wore dentures."

"Well what we're looking at here is the way it should be. No rez, no white man's laws. We take care of ourselves and everybody else stays out of our way. You got a problem, you deal with it. You can't deal with it; you take it to the War Chief and he deals with it. He deals with a problem it stays dealt."

"I'll keep that in mind."

"Just remember, you used to be a cop." Roger pointed his finger into Darren's chest. "You aren't any more."

"You poke any harder, you're going to break that finger."

"You want to go at it right now?"

Roger seemed to be working himself up, none of the others paid any attention.

"I don't think it would make a good impression if I showed up dragging the War Chief's second by the dick." Darren picked up his coat. "So let's get a move on."

Roger laughed and turned away, then he lashed out with his knife. Darren gripped Roger's knife wrist, pulled and twisted. Roger ended up on the ground while Darren held the knife.

"Not bad," he said, "but you forecast your move with your feet. It's a mistake a lot of people make." He put out a hand to help Roger up. "Are we dancing or are we traveling?"

Roger took his hand and Darren pulled him up. He flipped the knife in his hand and offered it back to Roger. The other man took it and put away in its sheath.

"Snowshoes from here. I hope you haven't forgotten how."

"It will give you something to laugh at," Darren bent down and fastened them on quickly. His cop boots weren't the best, but they would have to do. They started out again with Roger breaking trail.

"We never use the same trail twice," one of the other men said, "unless we want to leave something for the whites to follow."

"If we're going to be calling them names, wouldn't pale faces be better than whites?"

"Huh." The man rolled his eyes. "I don't want to be talking like some damned movie."

"True," Darren said, then saved his energy for keeping up. They trained regularly in snowshoes and carried them in the trucks, but short training walks were different than walking all day. His legs burned and he figured he'd be sore tomorrow. On the other hand, at least he didn't need to break trail. Roger and the other two men took turns.

The arrived at a rocky outcrop, but instead of going around, Roger walked through a gap in the rocks and entered a cave much larger than Darren would have thought from the outside.

"Welcome to Valhalla," a voice said from the back of the cave. A man walked out into the light and Darren immediately was glad Roger had the knife and not this man. He wasn't especially big, he would have fit in without a second glance at any pow wow, except for the cold blue eyes. He was dressed in a similar outfit to the others, but this was the War Chief.

213

"Isn't Valhalla a Viking thing?" Darren asked.

"This is a Viking fort, or at least what's left of one." He walked around Darren. "So you're the cop turned cop killer."

"I'm not the first," Darren stood at ease, not trying to follow the man with his eyes.

"Or the last I expect." The War Chief put his hand out and Roger gave him Darren's gun and the clip.

"I like to see a gun properly maintained." He slid the clip home, pulled the slide and shot Darren in the chest in one smooth motion.

Chapter Thirty-nine

It was like getting sucker punched. Darren went to his knees and gasped for air.

"I wanted to make sure they were real bullets." The War Chief put out his hand and Darren gripped it. He couldn't believe the casual strength this man had.

"My name is Rivers," the man said, "when we're just bullshitting. When we're talking business, you call me War Chief."

"Yes, War Chief," Darren said. Rivers put the safety on the gun and handed it back to Roger.

"Follow me." The War Chief walked back into the darkness and around a corner. Stopping to turn a lantern up he led Darren along tunnel to a room lit with more lanterns. "These Vikings were smart," Rivers sat on a bench and waved for Darren to find a seat. "They have this whole place built so the air stays fresh. It makes it a bitch to heat, but we don't wake up dead in the morning. You'll be staying here with me and a few others. The rest are spread out on the land so we don't leave obvious trails for the Army."

"That's what we figured," Darren stretched out his legs. "Never thought about tunnel and caves. They make infrared useless."

"There are other ways to fool the infrared. You can't become too dependent on technology or you get weak."

"I've seen that," Darren said.

"Good."

Rivers seemed content to just sit in silence, so Darren used the time to review his options. The GPS might work, but he didn't think so. He'd find another way to get a message to Jim when he needed to. His first task would be getting to know this War Chief. He didn't have the charismatic fire Darren was used to thinking about when looking for gang leaders and such. If anything, he was quieter than the people around him. Darren guessed Rivers had a deep spiritual side his followers either didn't know about or didn't understand.

"I like a man who know how to keep silence," Rivers said after a long time. "Most of my people would have grown impatient by now. I think you will do just fine.

"What do you need me to do?" Darren asked.

"What are you good at?"

"I was a damned good cop."

Rivers laughed.

"I can believe it," he said. "Some of our people, they become cops, they are worse than the settlers. All that power goes to their head. My boys, all they have for you is respect. You didn't bust their asses unless you needed to. I can use you as my right arm. I need someone to help keep the peace around here. Too many of the people think being Cree or Anishnabe or Dene or whatever means no law, just the rule of the strong over the weak. I'm going to educate them, but until it happens, your job is to keep them from killing each other."

"How do you know you can trust me?" Darren asked.

"I don't trust you," Rivers said, "but it doesn't matter. If you are really joining us, you will do what I ask because you believe in it. If you are a spy, you will do what I ask because you'll want me to trust you. Either way, I get a little peace."

"So, if I'm going to be enforcing your rules, you'd better tell me what they are."

"The first thing you need to understand, is that it isn't about rules. You are trained in the police and me in the military. We had to learn books and books of rules - who to talk to, how to talk to them, which people you could shoot, which you couldn't. Here, it isn't about rules, it's about the community. Anything that damages the community needs to be avoided, and the solution is not to find out who's to blame but how to repair the community.

"Sadly most of the people here have been brainwashed into the white man's idea of rules and justice. Many have been in jail and learned about obeying and breaking rules. They don't know how to resolve their issues without fighting, or they come running to me to get me to judge for them. We need some elders, but the

216

elders don't agree with what we're doing. So we must make our own elders and our own society.

"You are going to teach these people how to mediate with each other and deal with their shit. It's going to be a thankless and dangerous job, but like I said, you have no choice. I'm not really sorry about that. You made your choice when you came here."

"I didn't have much of a choice." Darren shrugged, then rubbed his ribs.

"Don't bullshit me." Rivers met his gaze. "You're smart, but you aren't that smart. If you'd shot a man point blank in the head with a nine mil his brains would be all over the place. I saw the video someone took. No brains, no blood. It was a good move throwing your jacket over him, but it was a play, a set up."

"Then why didn't you kill me?"

"Because I need you and it would be a waste to kill you. You are smart enough and brave enough to take on a really shitty job. I don't hold that against you. No one else suspects and because I'm going to accept you, they will too. Blind respect for authority has been beaten into them for generations."

"What are you?" Darren asked, "I expected a madman raving against the evil whites and calling for blood and death. Instead you want me to teach your people peace and wholeness."

"I don't hate the whites," Rivers stared up at the ceiling. "I hate what they're doing to us, what they've always done to us. It is hard to stop becoming what I hate. I need you as a balance. The Vikings used to have one person who was required to argue against war and violence. It was his job to try to find a different way of resolving the conflict. You're my designated man of peace."

"So what if I argue against more attacks on the Army? Am I going to get taken out and tuned up by all these out for blood warriors you've recruited?"

"You are supposed to argue against violence," Rivers sounded annoyed. "Pay attention. That's your job. How you deal with the bloodthirsty warriors is your problem. If you don't like it, don't do your job and there will be no voice of reason in the circle."

"I'll have to think about this," Darren's head spun.

217

"Good." Rivers flipped his hand. "So go think. Let me know when you're done, but I'm not waiting for you. We have a War Council in the morning. Be there." Rivers got up and walked out of the room, leaving Darren sitting on the bench. He leaned back against the cool stone wall and tried to bring order to his thinking.

Rivers knew he was a plant and didn't care. For some reason that terrified Darren, not that Rivers would change his mind and kill him, but that the man was confident enough he wasn't worried about a spy at his right hand.

Darren found himself drawn to the idea of being the peacemaker. Rivers, damn him, knew it too. It was what made Darren a good cop. He could follow his natural inclinations and not get called on it. He didn't need to play at being bloodthirsty.

If Darren was honest with himself, he was a little disappointed.

A Cree woman came and showed him to an alcove carved into the rock. It had cedar branches for a mattress. A blanket covered the branches another one lay folded at the foot of the 'bed'.

"Anything you value," the woman said, "keep with you at all times. Anything left behind is assumed to be public property."

"Thanks," Darren said, "What do we use for toilets?"

"If you go to the entrance cave, look to the right. There's a room with buckets. It's cold. We don't have much toilet paper so go easy." She turned to leave.

"What's your name?" Darren asked as he folded his coat into a pillow.

"You can call me Dianne," she said, "and thanks."

"For what?"

"For not assuming a woman here must be a prostitute."

"Why would I assume that?"

"Everyone else does." Dianne left him in by the alcove. He decided to use the buckets before he went to bed, and it would give him a chance to see the layout of the fort. The tunnel was one of four branching off the central room. One of those led to the outside. He found it by the cold air flowing through it. He used the buckets and returned to his alcove. He stripped naked and crawled in between the blankets leaving his clothes spread on top of him for extra warmth and so they could dry overnight.

It took him longer than usual to fall asleep. He heard the sound of moaning from further up the hallway. Someone was enjoying rigorous sex. He tried to ignore both the noise and his body's reaction. They finished and Darren heard light footsteps pass him in the dark. He eventually slept.

A hand shook him awake and he trapped the hand and sat up before he came completely awake. Dianne was looking at him with wide eyes. A lantern sat on the floor.

"Sorry." He released her hand. "Reflexes from years of living with older brothers."

"They will be serving breakfast soon. It is easy to sleep too long because the tunnels are always dark." She walked on down the tunnel. He heard a soft conversation, and concentrated on getting dressed before the woman came back with the lantern. He didn't want to carry the coat and outdoor gear, so he buried it under the cedar. He decided that is was less risky to keep his flashlight and other gear he brought with him on his belt. It would make him look too much like a cop, but he had no other way of carrying it. The GPS fit in a pouch that would have held handcuffs if he hadn't left them at the cabin.

Finding breakfast was easy. He just followed his nose. One of the other tunnels running off the central room led past storeroom to a room with a fire pit and a crack in the ceiling. One of the men who'd been with Roger handed Darren a bowl.

"Are there spoons?" Darren asked.

"The guys carve their own," the man said, "Some are better than others. If you can't carve, there's always fingers."

"Thanks," Darren took the bowl. "My name's Darren."

"Mack," the man said, "as in truck." He handed Darren a chunk of wood. "Birch, makes a decent spoon if you're patient."

Darren nodded, the man looked as big as a truck. He took his bowl back to the central room and ate with his fingers. When he'd finished he took the knife from his belt and unfolded it. He hadn't whittled anything since he was a kid, but his hands remembered. He soon had something looking like a cross between a paddle and a spoon. He put it in his shirt pocket and carried the shavings back to Mack in the bowl.

"Where do we do dishes?" Darren asked. Mack pointed to a pile of bowls.

219

"I'll heat water later and do them up. Most of the people who are here will be gone by the end of the day. I enjoy the cooking and washing."

"I'm always willing to help," Darren said.

"I'll keep that in mind," Mack put Darren's bowl on the stack and fiddled with the fire. Darren went back to the common room and waited for someone to tell him where the meeting was.

Rivers walked into the room and sat down. Other men and a couple of women joined them. Neither Rivers or anyone else said anything. Roger arrived last and sat in the last opening in the circle. Darren saw him struggling to stay silent, but it was a short struggle.

"We need to attack again," Roger said.

"Why?" Darren asked.

"Because we're warriors, and warriors fight. I'm tired of waiting in the cold. We should push them out of town and take over," Roger glared at Darren.

"How are we going to do that?" Mack asked. "There's more of them on their base then we have here. Even if we brought everyone in, we wouldn't have enough."

"We put out a call, there's people all across the country who are fighting the whites. They'll join us." Roger swung his arms as he talked and the people beside him had to duck.

"What makes our fight more important than theirs?"

"Look if you're a coward." Roger pointed across at Darren. "I don't care, but let the real warrior fight."

"Real warriors know what they are doing." Darren ignored Roger's insults. "They don't fight for the sake of fighting. Let's say we attack the base. We do a surprise attack at night and come from a direction they don't expect. We kill a lot of white soldiers. Then what? We have to get away, they have choppers and bombardiers with machine guns mounted on them. Are we going to out run those? How many will get back here? Who will lead the revolution then?"

"I'm not afraid to die!" Roger pointed his finger at his heart like a gun. "I'll take ten of them with me."

"Of course you will," Darren said. "No one doubts you, but they can lose ten or a hundred or a thousand, and just bring more people, more guns."

220

The others around the circle nodded while Roger almost frothed at the mouth.

"So we just sit and wait?"

"We need a plan, Roger," one of the other men spoke up. He looked vaguely familiar. Darren wondered if he'd arrested a brother or father of this man. "A plan to hurt them and make them buzz like wasps, but with no one to sting.

"Pfah," Dianne said. "if you want to hurt them, break their toys."

Some of the others nodded and Roger looked thoughtful.

"We don't have the weapons from the mine anymore," the vaguely familiar man said. "How are we going to damage their machines without the big weapons?"

"We have the bombardier," one of the ones who hadn't spoken yet said. "Can we use it?"

"What, just drive up to their gate and start shooting?"

"Bait," the War Chief said. "We use it for bait, they come after us and then we have them." The others started nodding like so many bobble heads. It had a better chance of success than a full on attack.

"If we take or destroy more of their equipment," Darren said, "and let them walk home with their tails between their legs, it will hurt their morale. These people are used to winning. It's a weakness."

The bobble heads were going again, except for Roger. He staring at Darren. He wanted blood. In many ways, he was more dangerous right now than Rivers.

Chapter Forty

Betty suspected everyone. They'd trained that way. She dropped the Colonel off at the Detachment and drove back to base. She drove carefully, but her mind concentrated on how to investigate the command team without tipping them off. Nothing annoyed a superior officer more than discovering they were the subject of an investigation.

What made things harder was the base formed an isolated community with minimal contact with the outside world. There was no possible way she'd be able to do anything without O'Neil finding out. O'Neil was the perfect ice cold bitch in public, but Betty had caught the Colonel a couple of times regarding the woman with a little too much warmth. She didn't particularly care about their relationship. It didn't appear to be affecting their work, but it wasn't the kind of thing an ambitious Lieutenant wanted to be made public.

Betty needed to get off base for a few days. Her brain acted before she knew she made the decision. Just a little too much steering, a little too much gas and the car slewed out of control across the road and into the deep ditch. The front end slammed into a rock and airbags slapped her head.

Blast, there goes my cushy job as a driver. She looked in the mirror, but didn't appear to be injured enough. *This had better pan out, or I'm going to be really annoyed.* Loose glass covered her and the seat. She carefully picked up a larger piece and embedded it in her brow above her left eye. She had to bang her head a few times to get it to stick. By that time, she had no problem sounding shaky as she radioed for assistance. She decided being passed out might be a good play, so she put her head back and let unconsciousness take her.

***

Betty woke up in a military hospital. She had no idea which one, but it didn't really matter. She waited for the doctor to show. While she waited, she made plans.

"Awake, I see," The doctor walked into her room. "I'm going to assume you had good reason for jamming a chunk of glass into your face, so I'm not going to ask. I am also not putting it in my report." She held Betty's wrist and took her pulse. "Don't look so surprised, I worked intelligence before I got this job. I can give you a few days of rest before I'll need to send you back or write a more detailed report on your status."

"A few days should be enough," Betty said. "Can I get a mirror?"

"Don't worry." The doctor smiled at her. "you chose a good location, there won't be a noticeable scar."

"Thanks, but I also need to look injured enough to have been in an accident."

"You'll have a real enough black eye." The doctor took Betty's blood pressure. "And a real enough headache to go with it. You're lucky you didn't give yourself a concussion. I'll leave the nurses a note to give you ibuprofen on request."

"Thanks, but none of this will help if I don't get access to a secure system."

"I have a system in my office secure enough for your purposes. I will have to do a psychological assessment of your mental state considering the previous incident. The Colonel was quite insistent you get top drawer treatment."

"That will work well." Betty closed her eyes. "I wouldn't mind one of those pills now and maybe we could have that talk this afternoon."

"I'll see to it." The doctor left the room and Betty wondered at the luck of getting a doctor who had experience in intelligence. Betty didn't believe in luck, but she wasn't going to waste the opportunity.

A nurse came into the room and gave her some pills and a glass of water.

"If you feel up to eating," she said, "lunch will be by in about an hour. Dr. Mahd has asked for you meet in her office to determine whether you will need a full psych assessment. You can do that after lunch."

223

"Thank you," Betty leaned back on the bed. She worked on the bio-feedback exercises she had been trained in and the headache faded into the background. She'd have to be careful as they also left her feeling more detached from reality.

Lunch turned out to be soup and a dry sandwich, but it was filling and she felt better for the nutrition. The nurse fetched her and walked her down the hall to the doctor's office.

"We like to accompany patients the first time or two they walk, just in case there are surprises. You're doing well. You don't need to call us unless you feel the need."

She knocked on the door and the doctor opened it and let Betty in.

"Here you are, try not to take any more time than I would in looking you up. The system doesn't track whose files I access, but it does track the amount of time I spend. Making sure I'm not looking at pictures of cats on Facebook I guess."

Betty sat behind the desk and pulled up files on Captains Banner and Raffin and Lieutenant O'Neil.

"You worked in Afghanistan or former Yugoslavia?" Betty tapped commands into the computer.

"Yugoslavia, there was a mess. People who'd been neighbours for years were suddenly enemies again. Nobody really knew what was going on."

"Sounds rough."

"I was glad enough to get out and go back to just being a simple physician."

"Hmmph," Betty scanned through the files as they came up. Banner, as she'd expected, had large amounts of his file redacted. She wouldn't try to access those parts or she'd set off alarms. What she wanted was further back. He'd grown up in Ontario in some small town. Gone to school and done ROTC which put him straight into the field. The colonel had snapped him up out of training.

Raffin hailed from the East coast. Halifax to be exact. First generation from Romania. His last name was an anglicization. It was too long ago for his parents to have been involved in any of the ethnic troubles. They had fled the communist regime; no flags then or since.

Lieutenant O'Neil came from Manitoba. She'd been born in a small town outside of Winnipeg. Gone to university in the city. She signed up for the Army a few years after she'd graduated. Never been married, never been north that Betty could tell from the records.

She pulled financial records on all three of them. Nothing extraordinary there either. None of the three showed any recent changes in finances. No debts or sudden increases in purchases.

"That's long enough for today," Dr. Mahd said. "Come over here and sit down."

Betty closed out her queries and went to sit across from the Doctor. She took a longer look at the woman. She looked like a nice, just passed middle aged woman. It wasn't obvious from her facial features that she came from the ethnic region former Yugoslavia, but Betty was sure she'd fit in. Maybe her parents came from the region.

"My father," Dr. Mahd said, "was ethnic Muslim, he got out years before the troubles started again. He met my mother in Canada and I was born here. Now, tell me about yourself."

"I was born in Toronto." Betty said, "I have no idea where my parent's family came from, we were just Canadian. Boring when all the other kids had exotic names and came from places all over the world. I wanted to see those places. I wasn't going to be able to afford that on whatever salary I could make as an accountant or sales clerk. I signed up for the reserve at eighteen and ROTC when I went to university. I could have gone to university without it, but I would have had big debts to pay off. My parents had split and neither hell or high water would make me live with either of them."

Betty shook off the memory of the groping hands of various men who'd lived with her mother. Her father's insistence she not lock the door when she had a shower was worse. She'd roomed with an older woman through university. The rules were strict, but Betty never had a problem with them.

"I did psych in university and wandered toward criminal psychology. They put me in counter intel training out of university and then set me up as an MP wherever there might be a problem. No one suspects the blonde bombshell of being a spy.

I partnered up with a guy the last few years, but he got killed when they killed our informant."

"I gather they tried to kill you as well."

"They tried some other stuff first," Betty said. "I took one out when he tried to grope me. A tractor trailer drove through the scene and crashed giving me a few seconds to get into the woods. I killed the second one when he came after me and didn't pay enough attention."

"How did you feel, having to kill two men?"

"I don't like killing." Betty frowned. "But we're trained to kill and how to live with it."

"And how do you live with it?"

"Personally, I choose to accept the guilt. I killed this person. I'm a murderer, so I'd better make my life count. The first time I had to kill someone he was in the middle of trying to rape me. I don't have any sympathy for rapists in or out of the military. He's why. This last pair weren't much better. They wanted my body. It killed them. I haven't lost any sleep over them, but I didn't enjoy it either."

"OK," Dr. Mahd said, "that will do for now. We'll talk more later."

"Thanks, doc."

Betty walked back to her bed not sure where Dr. Mahd was going with all this. She figured if she didn't come across as a pyscho bitch she'd get a clean report and be back on duty in no time. She'd always been careful. Most of the people she'd removed from this life had looked like accidents. She loathed rapists and their like. She felt no compunction about ending their lives and the damage they did. She just had to be careful around this doctor that she didn't slip up and give away her hobby.

After supper, she watched TV. The news was full of argument and speculation about the First Nations' Rebellion as they called it. The Chiefs were almost unanimously against the violence breaking out across the country. They were smart enough to know they would lose in the long run. Others were more radical, who talked with their faces covered about taking the war to the places of governance. They sounded like young recruits Betty heard talking about how they were going to be the ones who made the difference in the war. She'd been there herself. Now she knew better. The only difference she made was a tiny scratch in the surface of the problem of violence. Might not be even that significant.

Several reserves had been attacked by gangs of whites trying their own 'final solution'. The death toll on both sides rose. Police and military were stretched trying to keep people from killing each other.

Betty thought about Dr. Mahd saying how neighbours had re-discovered they were enemies. That's what was happening here as people who had lived together in uneasy peace turned away from it. She didn't know how it was going to end. She didn't think it would be pretty.

She turned the TV off and went to sleep.

The next day was a repeat of the first, Dr. Mahd came by to check on her. She ate mediocre food. That evening she left the TV off.

"Don't complain, Lil," one nurse said out in the hall, "at least the military paid our tuition, we'll be out in three years with no debt. My sister paid her own way and she's still paying her school off six years later."

"I don't know," another nurse, probably Lil, said, "I don't like the thought of being even slightly involved in action against the natives. I grew up with friends from the reserve who came to our school. I don't want to choose sides."

"We don't get to choose sides," the first nurse said, "We just care for the people they send us."

"Still, my grandmother was native," Lil said, "I could have applied for status and got my school paid."

"Then what?" the first one responded, "you'd be nursing up in some little hospital with old equipment and not enough doctors. Just do your job and be happy to have it."

Betty's headache was coming back. She pushed the called button and waited for the nurse to come.

The girl was probably just out of school. Betty could see she had a little First Nations. It was in her black, straight hair, but if she hadn't been looking, she wouldn't have given it a second thought.

"I could use some ibuprofen," she said to Lil. "a friend of mine is thinking about school and wants to apply for status. How would she do that?"

"How?" Lil looked confused, "oh, you heard our conversation, please don't tell the Unit Manager, we aren't supposed to talk in the hall."

"I won't," Betty said.

"Your friend just needs to prove she has First Nations' ancestry. A grandparent or parent who is status."

"So the band keeps track of who's status?"

"Yes," Lil said. "Though the government has a record too. Now some people are saying all the status people should be put back on the reserves."

"I'm thinking it wouldn't be much fun for people who've worked hard to get off reserve."

"You're not kidding."

Betty let the young nurse go and lay back to think. O'Neil had a university degree and no debt. She was young enough she should have a debt. Betty wondered who paid for the Lieutenant's education.

Her head ached slightly when she woke up, but Betty didn't bother asking for painkillers. Instead she asked if she could talk to Dr. Mahd again. The nurse came and told her Dr. Mahd had a few minutes to talk now if she was up to it.

"Come in," the doctor said when Betty knocked on the door.

"I need to check something," Betty said as soon as the door closed. She sat by the computer and called up O'Neil's records. She looked for a record of the woman's status. She had a treaty number and was a member of a band just outside Winnipeg near where O'Neil had grown up. A little more digging showed O'Neil was her mother's name and she'd been adopted. Between high school and university O'Neil had tracked down her birth family and applied for status. Her birth family's surname was Dupreis. Roger Dupreis was a cousin.

"I need to get back North," Betty said.

"I have a question about how many people you've killed Betty."

She looked up and saw Dr. Mahd with her hand in her pocket. Betty was sure there was a gun or something equally lethal in her hand.

"I promise you, I will answer all your questions," Betty said, "But I need to report to my Commanding Officer, in person."

"I can give you two days," Dr. Mahd said, "then I will flag your name. I can understand what you think you are doing, but it has to stop."

"And if I promised you I would stop?"

"I wouldn't believe you."

"Two days?" Betty kept her eyes on the doctor's hand. "Then I'll come back and answer your questions? What gave me away?"

"I've been following your career," Dr. Mahd grimaced. "It is no accident I'm your doctor."

Betty nodded. She didn't believe in luck.

Dr. Mahd discharged her and Betty used her connections to get on the next flight up to Spruce Bay. Before she left she sent a coded message to her superiors, just in case it took longer than forty-eight hours to convince the Colonel his lover was the leak. In a way, it made sense. O'Neil probably knew her actions would cloud the Colonel's judgement.

The flight landed her in Thompson and she grabbed a seat on a chopper bringing supplies north. They'd never bothered opening the road. It was already late by the time they hovered over the cleared area on the base. Betty left them unloading the freight and went looking for the Colonel. She'd used up most of her first day in travel.

He wasn't in his office, nor in his quarters. His aide tried not to look like he was covering for anything. Sometimes the Colonel went for a walk in the evening. Betty knew she should wait, talk to him tomorrow, but the time limit terrified her. Her head pounded but she didn't have time to wait.

She went to O'Neil's quarters. She had a tent set up conveniently at the end of the row of women's tents. Betty's was at the other end. There was a space between officer's quarters and the enlisted. It also made it easy for the Colonel to slip in and out without being seen. Betty wondered how long the affair had been going on. How long had O'Neil been passing information to the enemy.

229

She stood outside the tent and listened. She could hear them. Probably the women in the next tent over could hear them too. They were talking.

"We need a clear cut offensive," the Colonel said, "It has been worse than fighting in Afghanistan and never knowing where the enemy was hiding or if this village was for you or against you today."

"I've found out there are supplies coming in from across the north. Accounts with names of people we're sure are in camp have shown up in several northern communities in Saskatchewan and Ontario." O'Neil sounded just as she always did.

"We can't move on them until we're sure of our own secur-" the Colonel cut himself off.

"What are you saying?" O'Neil said, something in her voice Betty didn't like.

She opened the front of the tent and slipped in. She didn't have a weapon, Both the people in the other half of the tent had sidearms. Betty picked up a letter opener from O'Neil's desk and entered the other half of the tent. From their voices, she'd expected them to be sitting talking, maybe drinking coffee. They were nude and the Colonel was on top of O'Neil and still moving inside her. He looked up at Betty like a kid with his hand caught in the cookie jar.

Her moment of hesitation gave O'Neil the chance to pull the long pin holding her hair in the tight bun she always wore and stab it several times into the Colonel's neck. He put his hand to his neck which spurted blood across the tent. Betty ran toward O'Neil. O'Neil pushed the dying Colonel off her and rolled away toward the Colonel's uniform. She came up with his side arm just as Betty reached her. The bullets tore through Betty and she knew she was dead, but she had enough time left to put the letter opener in her hand through O'Neil's eye and into her brain.

Betty heard shouting from the rest of the camp. People were going to burst in and see the total fuck up she'd made of this thing. Her last thought was relief she wouldn't have to answer Dr. Mahd's questions.

Chapter Forty-one

Captain Banner came awake with his knife inches from the neck of the terrified private who had just shaken him awake.

"Next time, kick the foot of the bed and stay clear. I'd probably regret killing you." He rolled out of bed and started getting dressed. "Brief me while I dress," Banner said to the private who was trying to sidle his way out of the tent. "I don't have time for shyness."

"One of the women privates heard shots from her tent. She went to investigate and found Lieutenant O'Neil and the Colonel…"

"Spit it out, boy," Banner said. "I need information, you can be embarrassed later."

"They were both naked, sir," The private straightened and stared at the tent wall. "She had a knife through her eye into her brain. The Colonel's driver lay on the floor with several bullet holes in her chest. She was dressed, sir. The Colonel was bleeding profusely from being stabbed in the neck with a long needle. Neither the driver nor the Colonel are expected to live, sir."

"Bloody hell!" Banner paused in his dressing. "Any idea of what was going on?"

The private turned beet red.

"Besides that, private," Banner pushed passed the boy. "Have they been flown out yet?"

"They've been taken to the hospital in Spruce Bay." The private he chased after Banner. "The medics didn't think either one would survive transport any farther."

"Captain, sir," Sergeant Creeley stepped in front of the Captain. "Your presence is requested in the command tent."

"You know what is going on, Sergeant?"

"I've heard," Creeley said.

231

"What could be more important than dealing with murder within our base?"

"The missing bombardier has been spotted by our scouts. It is heading toward Spruce Bay and is shooting the hell out of anything on the road. It's going to reach the reserve in twenty and Spruce Bay in forty."

"Damn," Banner stopped to think. "Find Raffin and get him to command, then I want you to go to the Spruce Bay Hospital. Take a squad and make sure nothing gets to them. Grab a couple of RPG's, just don't lose them." He headed over to the command tent without looking to see how the Sergeant dealt with his orders.

Raffin ran in a few minutes later still straightening his uniform.

"I've sent a squad to the Hospital," Banner said, "and two squads up the road to meet this thing. I want your input on putting the choppers in the air."

"Having the choppers and their lights would be handy and if we send a loaded one, it will blow the thing sky high. But if they have another RPG, we could lose the chopper. My guess is if they had one, they would have used it on the bombardier instead of losing three men to take it and the prisoners. Go with the chopper."

"Two," Banner said into the radio, "you're a go. It's a bear hunt."

Seconds later they heard the chopper overhead.

"What do you think they're up to?" Raffin asked as he looked at the map.

"What do I know?" Banner stalked over to the map. "None of this makes sense. You don't start a war with your own people when you're outgunned and outnumbered."

"Happens all the time," Raffin said calmly. "Once in a while they even win."

"Not this time they aren't." Banner said, "not on my watch."

"The enemy has turned and is fleeing back up the road," the chopper gunner reported. "Action?"

Banner looked at Raffin, who shrugged.

"Take them out, Two, but be careful."

"Copy that."

They listened to the chatter between the pilot and the gunner, then the big machine guns on the chopper.

"They should have used a missile and got out of there," Banner said. He picked up the radio, "Two, go high and use the birds."

"Copy tha-" The gunner broke off into cursing. "They unmounted the fifty cal, Base, taking fire. We're high and buggering out, but we've taken damage. We'll go down in the first open space we see." The radio tailed off into static.

"Do not land on a lake," Banner said, "Repeat, do not land on a lake, the ice won't handle it."

"Land vehicles, send a team to recover the chopper crew. Use extreme caution. The rest of you proceed with caution, but stay on the road. Enemy has a fifty-caliber mounted on something other than the bombardier. Don't get chewed up."

"Raffin, did that machine have a mortar?"

"I don't believe so." He looked at Banner and raised his hands. "OK, I'll call the garage and confirm." He went over to the other side of the command tent and spoke quietly on the field phone. Not so quietly Banner didn't hear him order someone to go wake someone else up. It was that kind of night.

"Ground crew," Banner said, "enemy may have a mortar in their possession. Proceed, but don't leave yourself open."

"Copy that," the answer came back from Gretta, second to Creeley. Banner stared at the radio and willed himself to step back and stop giving advice. He would just get in the way.

***

Gretta wished Banner would shut up and let her do her job. She wondered where the Colonel was. She'd heard something was up, but before the grapevine could swing into action she and her squad had been sent out with two others to stop the enemy from driving through town with their fifty-caliber blowing the hell of everything.

Oscar was junior so he got sent to pick up the flyboys. She and Mike drove up the road in LAV's with their gunner's fingers on the triggers. At least the machine was down, so whoever was left out there was on small equipment or on foot. The gun was heavy; they wouldn't be moving it far. They came around the corner and saw the burning wreck of the bombardier. That was when one of their wheels hit the bomb buried in the road. The explosion wasn't big enough to blow the armoured vehicle, but it pushed them toward the ditch and the LAV rolled onto its roof.

Mike followed far enough back he could stop. The fifty-caliber started up in the trees banging into the side of his LAV.

The rounds banged against the side of their LAV. She didn't think they would penetrate, but she didn't want to sit around and find out.

"Lights down, engine off," she ordered, "let's look dead. Get clear of the door and kick it open. I haven't heard anything from that side yet, but it doesn't mean they aren't there. If they shoot stay on the ground and try to get a shot back at them. Otherwise we bail out and head back up road around the corner. Then we'll come back and thump whoever has the big gun. Questions?"

She waited a few seconds.

"Kick it and get clear." The door swung open, but no one opened fire on them. "Fast now, out."

They moved out of the LAV and into the woods in seconds.

"We need to be back far enough the stray shots don't kill us," she said quietly, "Move."

They fought their way through knee deep snow past Mike's LAV and back far enough Gretta thought it was safe to cross the road.

"One at a time," she ordered them, "low and fast. If someone starts shooting, we shoot back and get cover. Go" They crossed the road without incident. Gretta started to wonder how many people the enemy had out there. There were probably two working the fifty-cal, and maybe another couple to plant the bombs in the road. It didn't have the feel of a full squad or double squad. She'd have put people along the road to stop just this kind of action. She shrugged, no use complaining about the enemy's mistakes. She led her people toward the gun.

They were getting close when they heard it jam. What she didn't hear was any cursing or trying to unjam it.

"Let's get close but don't touch." Gretta led them to where they found the fifty-caliber mounted on the back of a snowmobile. No one was there, but there was a trail leading away from the machine.

"Fuckers aren't going to escape," Bobby said and headed toward the trail.

"Stop!" Gretta yelled at him, but too slow, he hit the trip wire and the grenade blew him to pieces.

"Anyone else hurt?" she called through the ringing in her head.

"I'm hit, but not bad," Kurt said. The rest were fine.

"We leave this here," Gretta said, "Kurt, you OK to set our own trap?"

"Sure thing." He pulled the antipersonnel mine out of his pack. He carefully placed it where prints showed it should be safe, then brushed snow over it to hide it.

"Mark it for our guys," he said and read the GPS coordinates off.

"Let's get back to the road. Mike, we're coming down on your three o'clock. Appreciate it if you didn't blow us up."

"Folks," she said, "Stay off the road, and watch for more wires."

They got back to the road and Mike had his LAV backed up and turned around. They headed back to base driving and walking carefully in their own tracks. They met up with Oscar who had the soaking wet and shivering pilot and the gunner from the chopper. The co-pilot had taken a round and gone through the ice with the chopper.

He put some men out of the LAV and took Kurt and the flyboys back to base quickly. Gretta and her crew walked while Mike's LAV followed behind and covered them. They didn't see any more of the enemy. Twenty minutes later a truck from Base picked them up.

"I don't get it," one of the guys in her squad said, "They wasted a bombardier for nothing."

"Not quite nothing," Gretta said. "They took out a chopper and rolled the LAV. We'll have to sweep the road clear before we can retrieve the LAV assuming the assholes haven't rigged it in the meantime."

"We'll just come out and get them again." The guy puffed out his chest. Tim was his name.

"Yeah, we will, and they will have some other sneaky fucking trick to poke at us and get away. I used to work under this guy and he is one nasty piece of work."

"So how do we beat him?" Tim asked.

"We get nastier," Gretta answered.

Chapter Forty-two

Matthew didn't pay any attention to his new office. He hadn't had time to do more than stack the boxes against the wall. Fortunately, the tech people had set up his new computer and made sure all his information was transferred over. Matthew wasn't going out into the field to report. Now he had people across the country he could call on to send in tapes and reports of what was happening.

He would have hated it, but it would be a waste of energy. He determined somehow to make a difference by the way he reported on the First Nations' Rebellion. Journalists weren't supposed to get involved in the news. But as far as he could see, no one else was even trying.

He looked at the latest call for peace from the Federal government. After more than a week of violence the government's attitude still seemed to be one of the First Nations should calm down and wait for the government to decide what to do. The First Nations members of Parliament frothed at the mouth, but paternalism appeared to be the order of the day.

He read through the listing of the latest police actions.

Police in one city broke up and arrested a group of First Nations elders leading a drum circle in a prayer to end the rebellion. Matthew guessed it was easier to face drums than guns.

Another group of police blocked an attempt at an armed attack on a reserve where some white lumber workers had decided were contributing to the rebellion. No arrests, though several shots were fired.

A third group dealt with some young warriors blockading a bridge by sealing off either end and waiting for the warriors to surrender. They were still waiting.

The response from the Assembly of First Nations seemed to be rational. They begged their people to refrain from violence, but because they also named the crimes the Canadian government perpetrated against the First Nations, the officials in Ottawa viewed them with suspicion and refused to talk. Surrender first, talk second was the message out of Ottawa and even the Chiefs were getting tired of being told to surrender.

"What more do we have to surrender?" the Grand Chief said, "We surrendered our autonomy, we surrendered our lands, we surrendered our children. What's left?"

The only bright point in his day was the quick check in with Georgia and her parents in Spruce Bay.

"Hi Matthew," Georgia said, "nothing is happening here. I told you about the service we had, and there was gunfire close to town. We hear helicopters coming and going all the time, but there is nothing else. We are trying to get some kind of school set up in the big shed, but it isn't heated and there is nowhere else really big enough. The kids are bored and that makes for trouble. Mlle Dupuis, our French teacher and Mrs. Dalrymple have reopened the old ski lodge, and we can ski or snowshoe, but that's it. The TV is still down; the internet is down. The only thing we have left is cell phones and you know what that's like.

"Still it is better than the reserve. They don't even have cell phones there since someone knocked over the towers. They can't drive to town now because the road is all dug up. No one is explaining anything to us so we just have to sit and wait."

"Hang in there, kiddo," Matthew said, "You stay safe up there. It is such a mess out here I wish I could come up there where it is quiet. I'm supposed to be on in ten minutes with an hourly update. I could sum it up by saying the people in charge are being blind and stupid and refusing to listen to the only folks who have a chance at sorting this mess out, but it would get me fired."

"So you're saying it anyways, with bigger words and clips of other people saying it," Georgia said.

"You got that right," Matthew laughed. "Say hello to the folks for me."

"Right," Georgia said. "Talk to you tomorrow."

Matthew went and did his hourly update which went as Georgia had described. He decided he needed a break so he signed out and walked down the street to the coffee shop.

"Black with sugar," he said to the girl behind the counter.

238

"Are you that reporter who does the special reports on the Rebellion?"

"That would be me," Matthew dug in his pocket for change.

"Well I want to know why you're so soft on those Indians. They should just go back to their reserves and stay there."

"There isn't enough space, for one thing, and even if there was, not all First Nations people were born on reserves." He handed over his money.

"Well what do they want anyway?"

"Pretty much the same thing you want," he said, "a chance at a fair life."

"It isn't fair if my taxes go to support their lazy asses."

"Forget the coffee," Matthew said. "I'm sure it would be too bitter for my taste."

He turned and walked out the door and headed back to the station.

"Who do you think you are coming in to our coffee shop and being rude to Alice?"

Two men planted themselves in front of Matthew.

"I don't want any trouble, gentlemen," Matthew's heart pounded.

"Well you found it Indian lover," one man swung a haymaker at Matthew and he stepped back to avoid it. Someone caught his arms and held him while the two men pounded him. An approaching siren sent them running and Matthew fell to the street.

"What's going on?" The voice appeared to be attached to a pair of black boots.

"I know him." A voice came from boots on the other side of him. "He's that reporter who thinks the police are being too hard on those poor First Nations kids. You know the ones who shoot at our cars as we drive past."

"Right," the first pair said, "well here's a message from your friendly police." The boots kicked him in the ribs.

"Talk about how the police are over reaching their mandate again, and we might have to look you up," the second pair of boots said. "We can always find a way to arrest the people who cause us trouble."

They walked away and he heard them drive off.

239

Matthew laid on the street trying to find the strength to get up. A gentle hand turned him on his side.

"We have this trouble in my country," the man said, "I came here to get away from it." He helped Matthew to his feet. "I'm beginning to think I should go back home. It isn't far from hating your First Nations to hating blacks." He walked Matthew to the station. "You not so bad, you lucky they don't really know how to beat someone. They learn though. They learn quick. You better to stay inside." The man walked away and Matthew pushed his way through the door.

"Good God, man!" The station manager ran over to him. "What happened to you?"

"Some critics of my news reports." Matthew winced as he took stock of the damage.

"You go home for the day. Get some rest."

"Like hell," Matthew said. "I've got a show to do."

"You can't go on air like that!"

"Just watch me," Matthew went to his office and started working on the script for his next update. True, he learned some police were being shot at while they drove. No one had been injured yet, though it was just a matter of time.

The makeup woman was horrified at Matthew's appearance.

"I don't think I can cover that up."

"I don't want you to," Matthew said, "It's time people started to see the face of the choices they are making."

He walked out to the set and took stock of the shock on the studio crew's faces. They counted him on.

"Hello." Matthew looked into the camera. "Here is your three o'clock update on the First Nations' Rebellion. I've learned some police in Winnipeg are being shot at as they patrol the city. The assumption is First Nations people are at fault and given the last week it appears to be a likely assumption. I was told about this problem by two police officers who chased away the men who were beating me for being too lenient on the people they blame for all this trouble. I couldn't thank the officers for their information and help since I was lying on the road trying to breathe at the time. I still lay there when they left. I suppose I was lucky, I might have been arrested for blocking traffic.

240

"The truth is people; we are all at fault for the violence besetting us. The so-called warriors are at fault for not knowing enough about their own culture to know what they are doing is acting like is a gang, not warriors.

"The government is at fault for ignoring the problems faced by First Nations people and ignoring the recommendations of their own people going back decades suggesting a lot of the exact same things for which the First Nations leaders are asking.

"Those same leaders are refusing to hold their people to account for the actions which are harming everyone.

"And you, dear listeners, are at fault because you are content to sit with the same bigotry and ignorance which brought us to this place. What is going to stop the violence if we can't be bothered to learn a little about each other? It isn't the army, or the police, or our leaders who are going to stop this travesty. It is people like you, who arm yourselves with compassion and knowledge and refuse to let this country descend into violence, racism and stupidity."

The station manager stood on his toes like he wanted to charge at Matthew and add to his collection of bruises.

"If the people upstairs hadn't told me to let you have your head," he said when Matthew walked over to him, "I would have pulled the plug right at the start, but I'll be standing there watching when they fire you."

"It's a good thing I didn't unpack my boxes then. I'm going to see if there is any ice in the kitchen."

Chapter Forty-Three

"Going hunting right now is not a good idea," Joe could see the boys weren't convinced. Hell, at their age, he wouldn't have been convinced. Tom and Steve looked at him with a look letting him know they were hunting, whether he liked it or not.

"OK," Joe said, "Go to the east of town. If you follow the riverbank there is a big open area the moose like to winter in. There's lots of willow for food and thick bush for shelter. Take the radio with you. If you shoot a moose, you'll want some help with it."

The boys high fived each other.

"If you see one of those helicopters, stay out of sight. You don't need that kind of trouble."

The boys went off to get their gear ready and Joe sighed. What he really wanted was to go with them. He wanted out of this town, but if it was risky for the boys it would be twice as dangerous for him. The army was looking for people who looked like enemies. Joe looked like the people the army hunted. He went to find Jenna to tell her. At least they could share the worrying.

In a surprisingly short time he heard the snowmobiles head out. He could follow them in his head. They would be passing by his fishing shack, then to the track along the river. He could trust them to stay off the water. They knew the ice was treacherous. A track followed the bank. They weren't the first or last to head up to that meadow to look for moose. They'd get near to the open marsh and find a sheltered spot to put up their tent and bury it with loose snow. The next day they'd scout on snowshoes for tracks and sign. It would come down to how well they waited for their game to show up. If they were patient and quiet enough the moose would come.

He played with Joshua, his youngest son. The weather stayed cold and clear. Not the best weather for hunting, but better than a winter storm. He wished they could find some way to get the school going again. The kids were getting bored of their unexpected holiday, especially since most of the parents didn't feel it was safe in the woods.

The helicopters flew almost constantly again. Joe didn't think they would find anything. There was a lot of country out there and choppers could be heard for miles. They would be easy to avoid.

At first, Joe had sympathy for the army people. He'd even taken a night to help them out, but the longer they stayed the more uncertain he became about their presence. He'd heard the equipment going out at odd times and heard not so distant explosions too. This battle wasn't going well for the Army. Frustrated people were dangerous.

It would be better if they just left and stopped giving those idiot warriors a target. Stirring up the country like a hornets' nest wasn't a good way of making change. He wanted change as much anyone else in his nation, but he didn't like what little he heard about what was going on in Canada.

The next day, the wind increased. It would reduce visibility, but if the boys stayed downwind, it could be useful cover. He resisted the temptation to check in with them on the radio. It was still early in the morning; he didn't want to spook a moose. The choppers headed out and one flew along the river bank. Joe watched it until it disappeared behind the trees. Maybe he should get Jim to inform the army people there were boys hunting in the area. Reluctantly Joe climbed into his truck and headed over toward the detachment.

"Hi Pat." He smiled at her. "Is Jim busy?"

"No," she said, "Go right in."

"Thanks." This being sociable with the police still felt odd for Joe. He kept expecting them to remember the kind of person he used to be, but Jim was the only RCMP member left who knew Joe when he was often drunk and always trouble. Jim and Leigh were a lot of the reason he got sober and back with his family. He pushed the door open to see Jim at the desk filling out paperwork. Jim looked up and pushed the papers aside.

"Hi Joe." He waved to a chair. "I haven't seen you for a bit, I wanted to check with you about the sweat you mentioned."

243

"Sorry, Jim," Joe said, "I'd forgotten it. I sent the word out to some of elders east of here, but I haven't heard back."

"So what can I do for you?"

"Tom and Steve went hunting. One of the choppers went over their direction and I hoped you'd let the Army people know the boys are out there."

"Sure," Jim picked up the radio on his desk. As he picked it out the radio in Joe's pocket came to life.

"Dad," Tom's voice said sounding panicky, "Dad, the helicopter just blew up a bunch of people. They were coming to visit," his voice broke. "Steve was with them. They're all gone, Dad. Oh shit, they're coming back -" a thump cut off his voice.

"There's snowmobiles down stairs," Jim said, "Let's go!"

They ran past Pat and Jim yelled for her to let the hospital know there might be casualties coming in. Jim tossed Joe a warm coat and a helmet.

The police snowmobiles were big and fast. They had extra large fuel tanks and spare gas with them. Joe put the helmet on and fumbled the gloves on. He started the machine and took off at full throttle with Jim behind them.

He'd never gone so fast over the snow. Even when they'd drag raced across the lakes he hadn't gone this fast. The trees blurred as they passed, and he had to use his whole body to steer on the trail. Every time he thought about slowing down, he thought about Tom's voice on the radio and kept his thumb tight on the throttle.

Even at full speed it felt like an eternity to get to the meadow. It normally took two or three hours. Joe thought they made the trip in less than half the time. They burst out of the trail onto the meadow and saw the chopper sitting on the snow and figures with guns who spun and pointed their weapons at them. A siren wailed from behind him and the guns lifted. They reached the crew. A man sat with his head in his hands in the open door of the chopper while three other people, Joe thought two men and a woman walked around.

"You can't be here," the woman said as soon as they pulled up.

"Gretta," Jim said, "We got a call from Joe's son. He was here. We're not leaving until we find him.

"Shit, the second shot was over there." She pointed up the meadow. "If anyone survived it will be there."

Joe took off to where the army women pointed. He left Jim talking to her. The blast had destroyed one tree and knocked over several others. A hole in the ground steamed in the cold air. He saw the twisted wreck of what used to be Tom's 30.06. He felt sick, but he forced himself to think. Tom wouldn't have been this far out in the open. He would have set up further back where the trees would hide his shape. Joe got off the snowmobile and walked back into the trees. Pieces of wood had been embedded in trees. He found Tom's trail. He'd been wearing his snowshoes. One of them was stuck in a tree above Joe's head. A boot dangled in the harness. No blood on the ground so it was just a boot. He looked further in that direction and found Tom. The boy was burned badly and it looked like at least one piece of wood stabbed him. It had been so long. If those damn fools had looked they would have found him. Joe saw a bubble of blood form on Tom's lips and burst. He wanted to pick his son up and run to the snowmobile. Instead he left Tom there and ran back. He picked up the radio and hoped it worked.

"Jim," he shouted, "Jim, I've found him. He's hurt."

"Joe?" a woman said, "This is Pat. Where's Jim?"

"He's with the army people. I found Tom, but he's hurt bad. I need help."

"I'll tell Jim. Just hold on."

Joe saw Jim jerk suddenly and look toward Joe. He pointed up to the end of the field and appeared to be arguing. Then the woman soldier climbed on the snowmobile behind Jim and they roared up the field toward him. The other two people climbed back on the chopper and it lifted off and flew in his direction. It landed just as Jim and the woman arrived. Two people jumped off the helicopter with a stretcher. They followed Joe back to where Tom lay in the snow. The tiny delicate bubbles still formed on Tom's lips. The men carefully transferred him to the stretcher and carried him back to the helicopter. It took off as they returned to the field.

"Let's wait here," Gretta said. "They'll be back as soon as they've dropped your boy off."

245

"What about the others?" Joe pushed his anger down. He wanted to strangle her. "My cousin was with them."

"The other group took a direct hit. It's a miracle your son is alive. There is no other miracle. I'm sorry."

"What the hell happened?" Jim asked.

"I'm not at liberty to discuss that." Gretta's face closed up.

"I'm going to assume you commanded the helicopter and no shots would be fired without your order."

"I told you, I can't discuss that."

"Fine," Jim pulled something from his belt. "Sergeant Gretta, I'm arresting you for reckless endangerment causing death. We'll determine the number of counts when my team is done with the site."

"What the hell?" Gretta started to move away, but Jim had already put the cuffs on her. He sat her down on the snowmobile.

"Move, and I may just shoot you myself."

He picked up the radio on the snowmobile. "Pat, I'm at the moose meadow off the river. The army fired on civilians. I need a full rescue team here. Get the Rangers if you can. They'll need tarps and body bags and a lot of sleds behind the snow machines. Joe will be here waiting for them." Jim looked at Joe with a raised brow and Joe nodded slightly. "They'll need full investigation gear, but recovery is key."

Jim fastened the cuffs to the backseat rest of the snowmobile, then headed back with Gretta staring daggers at Joe as she rode facing the back of the machine. Joe took his machine back down to where they entered the meadow. If it was as bad as the woman said, he didn't want to see it.

He heard the chopper return and moved back into the woods and buried himself under the snow. It circled the field once then flew away west. He climbed out of the snow and brushed himself off. He sat on the machine and waited for the people from town to come.

Chapter Forty-four

Jim walked Gretta into the room they'd reinforced for holding people and removed everything from her that could be used as a weapon. It made a substantial pile.

"Don't cause any trouble," Jim said, "I'm going to talk to Division. If you're expecting your army friends to come and sweep you away, I would suggest you don't make any more work for them than you already have." He pointed up to the corner. "Video camera. It feeds to a computer here on site. Do anything stupid and we'll have it on tape.

"Don't I get a call to a lawyer?"

"Sure, when I can arrange a secure line for you. The last person to talk to a 'lawyer' from here," Jim made air quotes when he said lawyer, "got himself shot on the way to Thompson."

"Is that a threat?"

"Just a warning, some people value silence over friendship." Jim locked her in and went to his office.

"Acting-Staff Sergeant Jim Dalrymple, in Spruce Bay," he said after he finally got a real person to talk to, "I need to talk to whoever is liaison with the military."

"What is it about?" the voice on the other end didn't sound sympathetic. "We aren't going to force the MP's to give you someone back so you can charge them with drunk and disorderly."

"How about the murder of about a dozen civilians?" Jim's rage bled into his voice. "I need to talk to the liaison, not some cheeky person in reception." After a huff on the other end he was cut off. He was sure whoever would claim it was an accident. He decided he didn't have the patience for Division. They would probably kick it up to Ottawa anyway. He phoned Ottawa and played with the phone tree until he got a real person.

247

"I have an Army Sergeant in custody for the death of a least a dozen civilians," Jim said to the person on the other end. "I need to talk to someone about the situation before I'm forced to make a statement to the press."

This time he got passed through to someone who introduced herself "Deputy Commissioner Gregs."

"Deputy Commissioner," Jim said, "I'm Staff-Sergeant Dalrymple in Spruce Bay, Manitoba. A helicopter crew fired on a civilian group near to town. They killed an undetermined number of people and there is one survivor in critical condition."

"This is a military matter," the DC said.

"Not if it means they are going to white wash it and refuse to give information to the families of the victims. These people deserve to know what happened."

"You will turn your prisoner over to the Army." The DC's voice gave no clue to her feelings. "She will be tried by them. I will try to work through channels to make sure you get your information. You need to remember your area is effectively a war zone."

"That should mean greater care around civilians." Jim's knuckles were white on the phone. "not less."

"I'm not saying I don't agree with you, but things are a mess out here too and they don't look like they are going to get better soon."

"So even more important the people in charge take the death of civilians seriously."

"These were Cree people?"

"Yes," Jim said, "The boy in the hospital is the son of a friend of mine."

"I will do what I can." The DC almost sounded sympathetic. "Try not to aggravate the situation any further."

"The law still applies in Spruce Bay until I hear otherwise."

"Don't push it Staff-Sergeant."

"Yes, ma'am." Jim hung up and felt like kicking something. He wasn't sure what he expected. Sympathy perhaps. He should have known better. He picked up the radio connecting him with the Base.

"Staff-Sergeant Dalrymple to Colonel Stone," he said into the radio.

"I'll get the Captain for you," the voice on the other end responded.

Jim would have argued, but the person had probably gone already.

"Captain Banner here," the Captain was obviously angry, "Make it quick Staff-Sergeant, I have a person to find."

"Would it be Sergeant Gretta?" Jim said, "I'm sorry I don't know her last name. She is in my cell charged with reckless endangerment causing death. I've been advised this is a military matter so if you send a couple of MP's I'll release her into your custody."

"That was a military operation, Staff-Sergeant," the Captain apparently struggled to stay coherent. "You have no right to involve yourself."

"Civilians died." Jim snarled back at him. "Children. Their only crime was being Cree when your chopper flew over. I listened on the radio as the chopper circled back and fired a second time at a child who was talking to his father."

"The crew stated they were being fired upon. I saw the fucking bullet holes myself."

"Whoever was shooting at them wasn't these people. There's a lot of ground out there. Are you going to kill everyone out in the woods if they look Cree?"

"If I have to," Captain Banner said, "I have a war to win."

"I thought the Colonel was commanding," Jim said.

"He was, until the mole your bloody Indian friends planted killed him. Your fucking incompetent doctors let him die on the table. I will have people there to pick up the Sergeant and her gear. Tell your people to stay in their homes."

"This is Canada still," Jim protested, "They have rights."

"Not any more," Captain Banner shouted. "I'm declaring martial law under executive order from the Cabinet. No one is to leave the bounds of the town or the reserve. As soon as my people get there, go home. You don't have a job anymore."

Jim fumed while he waited for the army people to show up. They handed him a document detailing the Commanding Officer's right to impose martial law if they deemed it necessary for the security of the nation. Jim didn't think this situation qualified, but it had gone well above his pay grid. When they led

249

the Sergeant out of the detachment she had all her gear and was clearly not in custody. She walked over to Jim.

"You shouldn't have fucked with us. Now stay out of the way, or I'll find an excuse to lock you up."

Jim didn't say anything. He walked back into the detachment and handed the document to Pat.

"Fax this to the Division and to Ottawa, then call the others and tell them to stay home until further notice. Once you've done that, lock everything up, give me the keys and go home."

He walked up to his office and sat thinking for a long time. A soldier with an arm band reading MP came into his office.

"Sir," she said, "you were instructed to go home."

"So, you're going to keep peace and order in town?" Jim asked. "Don't you want to know anything about the town."

"No sir," she said. "Instructions will be given to civilians to stay indoors. Any attempt to move about town will have dire consequences."

"You're going to shoot people for going grocery shopping? Or maybe you'll just threaten them for visiting their friends."

"Sir, I will not ask you a third time. You no longer have jurisdiction."

"I will tell you something, kid." Jim stood and looked her in the eyes. "These people aren't going to pay attention to you, or your threats. Someone will be hurt or die because you don't know your ass from a hole in the ground. When it happens, I will make sure it is your face plastered on the news so people can say. *It was her job to stop this, and she failed.*" He walked past her, locked the door and pocketed the keys.

"You will surrender the keys to this facility."

"You know, that paper gave you the right to declare martial law. It did not give you free access to the files and records in this detachment. I read it. Did you? The paper has been faxed to Division and Ottawa. They won't intervene, but they will be watching. They'll be looking for some excuse to take you down a notch or two. Go ahead, give them reason."

Jim walked out of the detachment and locked the front door. "Are you planning to spend the night in there?" he asked. She stepped past him and he pushed the door closed and locked it. When he'd done that, he drove home. He put the keys to the detachment and all the files away behind some books in Ryley's room. Leigh must still be out at a friend's.

Shortly after Gretta pulled up to the house in an army jeep she walked up to the door and banged on it.

"You open this door or I shoot the lock off and come in anyway," she shouted.

Jim picked up his phone and walked to the door.

"Good evening, Sergeant," he said, "and no, you may not enter my home."

"Fuck that!" she shouted.

"Do you know who is on the phone?" Jim asked, "District Commissioner Gregs, do you wish to introduce yourself?" He handed the phone to the Sergeant. He could hear the voice on the phone explaining to the Sergeant that Martial Law still meant law and the she couldn't do whatever she pleased or he would personally see to it a military review committee looked at every decision she made for legality and more importantly to the military, just how bad she made them look.

The Sergeant handed the phone back, and Jim wondered if she was trying to decide if she could get away with shooting him. She spun and walked off. Jim closed the door and sagged against the wall.

"Thanks, Cam," he said. "You sounded convincing enough. We'll hope they don't check back up the chain."

After he hung up he called every friend of Leigh's he could think of. She wasn't at Lyanne's or at Jenna's. He found out from Jenna a couple of helicopters had returned and chased Joe and the others away. He was at the hospital with Tom.

He located Leigh at Fran Dupuis' and she agreed to stay the night there.

Jim didn't sleep much, but in the morning, Leigh showed up at the door, not much the worse for wear.

"What is going on?" she asked.

"The military screwed up and killed a bunch of people," Jim said. "Steve Beauchamp was one of them, Tom is in the hospital. My guess is they saw a group of people and they shot them. It looked like some kind of missile. Now they've declared martial law and are forbidding people from going out."

"They can't do that, can they?"

251

"I don't think it's defensible." Jim shrugged. "I'm hoping in the morning light they will reconsider, but I'm not holding my breath. Apparently, there was a murder on base and the Colonel is dead. Captain Banner is in command and he seems much more volatile than the Colonel."

There was a knock at their back door and Jim opened it to see Georgia standing there.

"Get in, before they see you." He pulled her in the door.

"Those morons?" Georgia said, "they're just driving around shouting through the PA on their cars. Most of the kids are out and about, but the people in the jeeps will never see them. We could move around and you couldn't see us, and you know the town."

"All it takes is for one of them to get trigger happy and we have another tragedy on our hands," Jim said. "Don't push your luck.

One of the jeeps went by and they listened to the message.

"Spruce Bay is now under martial law. No one is to leave town without permission from the Military Police. Movement through town is forbidden after dark. You are not to gather in groups of more than three at any time."

"Idiots." Georgia rolled her eyes. "Half the families in town have more than three people."

"Don't underestimate them." Jim rubbed his eyes. "They have guns and they are certain they are right. I don't want you killed too."

"Who have they killed?" Georgia turned pale and sat down. "You wouldn't be like this unless they already killed someone."

"I know Steve is dead, and Tom is in the hospital." Jim sat across from her. "There were some other people who had come to visit."

"Steve?" Georgia's eye's widened, "I thought he and Tom had gone hunting."

"They did, and they were fired on by the military. They claim someone shot at the helicopter. They might be right, but they attacked the wrong people."

"I've got to go see Tom." Georgia wiped her eyes.

"I'll drive you there." Leigh picked up her keys. "It will be safer if you weren't seen with Jim. He's not popular with the military right now."

She drove Georgia to the hospital and called back from the nurse's desk to say Tom was still alive, but only barely. The doctors wanted to fly him out to Thompson, but the military refused, saying it was too much of a risk.

Jim sat down and started making notes. When this was all over, he wanted to be sure he had all the details correct.

Chapter Forty-Five

Georgia leaned forward in the seat as if it could make the car go faster. The ugliness of the shattered mall didn't depress her as it usually did. She was too focused on getting to Tom. The glass at the front of the Hospital had been repaired with plywood. She ran into the hospital and saw her mom.

"Why didn't you tell me Tom was in the hospital?" she said.

"I'm not allowed to, Georgia." She hugged her. "As much as I wish I could."

"Where is he? I need to see him."

"He's in ICU, or the closest thing we have to one. He's in bad shape Georgia."

"I still need to see him."

"I know, if you need to talk afterward, come and find me." Her mother gave her a final squeeze and sent her off in the direction of the room.

Tom's dad sat outside the room. He didn't look like he'd slept in days.

"Hello, Mr. McCrey," Georgia stood in front of him.

"Hi," he said, "call me Joe. I'm never sure who this Mr. McCrey is."

"I'm sorry about Tom. Is there anything I can do?"

"I really don't know." Joe looked lost. "I don't really know much. Some people came by, they wanted to charge my Tom with being a terrorist. The doctor sent them away. The only people Tom ever terrorized were his mom and me."

Georgia had trouble breathing. For a moment, she wondered if she were sick, but then she knew that she was angry. Angrier than she'd ever been. Even the wolves had been more objects of pity. But this travesty filled her with rage. She felt like she should be able to shoot lightning bolts from her fingers.

"Tom is one of the nicest and bravest people I know," Georgia said, shocked at how calm she sounded.

"Thanks." Joe went back to staring at the wall. Georgia went into the room. Anna sat beside Tom. She held his hand and watched him breathe.

"This is more than I can understand," Anna spoke without turning her head. "We were going to get married. He was going to be a police officer and I was going to heal like my kohkom taught me. Now what can we do?"

"Remember the tree that broke off behind the school?" Georgia didn't know where her words came from. "One of the branches started growing up and in a few years, it will be a tree again."

Anna started to cry. She made no sound, but tears ran down her face. Georgia took some tissues and dried her friend's face.

"I can sit here and think all kind of horrible things," Anna said after a bit, "and I have no problem. As soon as I think about something hopeful I just lose it. I have to be strong for Tom. How can I be strong if I'm afraid of hope?"

Georgia wrapped her arms around Anna.

"You will find a way. Remember what your kohkom taught you and it will come to you."

Anna sat silent for a long time. Georgia was used to it. Anna talked as little as Georgia talked a lot. Georgia looked at Tom wrapped in bandages with IV's and cords coming from all kinds of places on his body. A monitor beeped quietly. If she hadn't known it was him, she wouldn't have recognized him.

Anna started singing in Cree. It was quiet but strong. Georgia thought her friend could sing for hours. Still, she needed help. Georgia didn't know much about Cree medicine, just what she guessed from things Anna let drop, but she knew it needed a community.

"I'm going to find some people to help you." She ran out of the room and waved at Joe. She found her mom.

"I'm going to find some people to help Anna sit with Joe," she said. "They're going to sing or drum or whatever, please make it OK with the hospital people."

"The only thing they can't do is smudge," her mother said. "I'll talk to people. It will be all right."

255

Georgia ran out of the hospital and immediately felt her throat burn in the cold. She forced herself to walk. It would be no good finding people if she couldn't talk to them. She headed down to Anna's uncle's place. He sat in his living room. The shades were pulled and the TV off.

"Mr. Beauchamp." She took his hand, ignoring the tears on her face. "Anna needs help with the healing medicine at the hospital. I don't know much about it, but I know she can't do it by herself."

He seemed to shake himself and looked at Georgia as if he'd never seen her before.

"I can go sing. Go to Ella Dupreis. She'll help too."

"Thanks." Georgia left the house and walked across the Grid to the Dupreis' home. The house was filled with people and Mai sat in a corner weeping. Georgia went to her.

"I'm so sorry about Steve," she said. Mai just nodded. Georgia saw Steve's kohkom sitting in a corner. She went over to her.

"I'm very sorry about Steve, but Tom needs your help. Anna is singing to him, but she can't do it alone."

"No. she can't." The old woman pushed herself to her feet and walked over to her daughter. They talked for a moment before she came back to Georgia.

"I will go help, but you will need to talk to my son. He's chief at the Reserve, but he's here in town with the Rangers. He's staying at the apartments. Georgia nodded at her and headed across town to the apartments.

"What are you doing?" One of the jeeps pulled up beside Georgia and the man at the wheel looked at her suspiciously.

"I'm visiting friends," Georgia felt the rage that had hit her in the hospital burning hot, but she pushed it down. She wouldn't be a help in jail.

"Fine," the man said, "just be in by dark."

Georgia nodded and walked on to the apartments. Mike Tremblant was in an apartment on the second floor.

He answered the door and stared at her.

"Your mother asked me to come here." Georgia would have continued but a fit of coughing paralyzed her vocal cords.

"I would be at the house," he said, "but I don't want to poison the place with my anger. I knew something like this would happen."

"I know." Georgia gasped in air. "but Tom needs you. Can you put your anger aside to help him?"

"I will. I'll get my bag. There's some tea on the stove, drink some of it before you go out again." She watched him leave with a large green duffel bag. The tea was an herbal tea somehow warm and cool at the same time. Since she was here, she decided to go check on Lyanne. They'd met a couple of times at Leigh's.

Lyanne didn't come to the door immediately and when she did she looked like she was in pain.

"Sorry. I thought it was … someone else."

"Who's been bothering you?" Georgia looked around.

"It's nothing you should worry about," Lyanne she hunched in on herself, "I've done it before, I just forgot how hard it was."

"The army men have been here," Georgia's rage burst into flame. "Those self-serving bastards! You can't stay here. They'll just be back. Come with me and you can stay in my bedroom. No one should have to put up with this."

"No really," Lyanne held her hands up.

"Look." Georgia grabbed Lyanne's hand. "My friend is probably dying in the hospital. I spent all day feeling useless because I can't help him. You, I can help. Pack what you need and we're going." Lyanne put some clothes in a bag and they started off toward Georgia's house.

"Where do you think you're going?" It was the same soldier in the jeep. "Go home."

"Why?" Georgia said, "So you can go by and fuck her again?"

"She didn't say *no*," the man sneered.

"No, she wouldn't would she?" Georgia stepped between him and Lyanne. "You're twice her size and you have a gun. How many of your friends visited her too?"

"She's a whore, kid." The man leaned out the door of the jeep. "and she's going back home."

Georgia pulled out her cellphone and pointed it at the soldier.

"What are going to do, post a picture of me on your Facebook. Maybe you want some too?"

257

"I'm uploading a video of you to the internet." Georgia spoke coolly as if she threatened men with guns all the time. "I have a friend named Matthew who can make you famous. Just keep talking."

"Give me that phone, bitch." The man started to climb out of the jeep.

"This way!" Georgia pulled Lyanne with her and ran between the houses. She heard the soldier yelling behind her, but he didn't follow them. Georgia ruthlessly forced herself not to cough as she led Lyanne through the back trails to her house.

Once they reached the house Georgia doubled over with coughing while her dad rubbed her back. Paul brought her a glass of water. It helped enough she could sit down and just breath until the urge to cough passed.

"You shouldn't have made him angry." Lyanne said.

"It was make him angry or just let him keep using you," Georgia said in a rasping voice. "Call Leigh and let her know what is going on."

"Smart to use the video to scare him," Lyanne took out her phone.

"Yeah, but service is so slow here it would take ages to upload the video."

"Too bad."

"Yeah."

Lyanne talked with Leigh for a while, then she talked with Jim. After she hung up, she came over and sat beside Georgia.

"Thank you, I don't want to be that person anymore."

"My friend is staying in my room tonight, Dad," Georgia said. Lyanne looked confused for a second but shrugged it off. Georgia liked her even more.

"I'll set out another plate for dinner." Georgia's dad went back to the kitchen.

"Dad?" Lyanne whispered.

"Long story," Georgia said, "I'll tell you later."

They ate supper and Georgia's mom arrived in time to sit with them.

"A whole lot of people came to Tom's room," she said. "Some sang in Cree and there was at least one drummer. Mike

Tremblant danced. It was beautiful. I just wish they didn't need to."

"Thanks, Mom." Georgia said.

After supper, she took Lyanne up to her room.

"Whatever you need, just ask. I don't know if anything I have will fit you."

Lyanne stroked the bed with her hand.

"I never had any girl friends. They all hated me because I was a slut. The boys just wanted to do me. You're at a dangerous age, Georgia. You think you're still just a kid and no one is interested in you. I was your age when my mother sold me the first time. That soldier would have hurt you if he'd caught you. He'd have treated you worse than he did me, because you're younger. Never let yourself be alone with someone like him."

"OK," Georgia said, "now I have some calls to make. I don't mind if you listen in, but I'd rather you didn't talk to my parents or other adults about it."

"Sounds like you are planning something dangerous," Lyanne put her hand on Georgia's shoulder. "Just remember what I said. These men will do more than just yell at you."

Georgia dialed Maria.

"Hi Maria, it's Georgia."

"Hola," Maria said, "thank goodness I can talk to someone other than Marc, He is making me crazy."

"I believe Marc could drive you crazy. If I had to watch Paul all day, I'd be crazy. Do you have a cell phone that takes video?"

"Sure, don't all phones? What about it?"

"What I want you to do is start videoing the soldiers. Don't be obvious. They'll get really angry."

"I don't want to make them angry. They scare me. They're like the polizia in Mexico. Dangerous. I have an old phone. It has video too. Maybe Marc can help."

"That might be good, but it's really important no one knows you are recording them."

"So what do we do when we have these videos?"

"You have a memory card? Put the videos on them. I'll see if I can get them out to a friend who will be very interested in what is going on. I have to go. Thanks"

"Very dangerous," Lyanne said. "How can I help?"

259

"I'll think of something." Georgia nodded absently at her. "But you are in even more danger than the rest of us."

She called Alastair.

"Hi, Georgia," he said, "I just got my cell phone back from my mom. I've been talking to the soldiers. I want to go into the army when I get old enough."

"Neat, Alastair," Georgia said. "Are the soldiers all different or are they from the same group?"

"The ones here are all in Gretta's squad. They worked in Afghanistan together. I don't think they like it here very much."

"I see, I'm always interested in learning new things. Call me if you learn something interesting."

She hung up and had to stop herself from throwing her phone against the wall.

"Boys!" she snarled. "He thinks the soldiers are cool."

"I doubt they are telling him about their visits to my apartment," Lyanne grimaced. "but it sounded like you managed him well."

"He had this massive crush on me," Georgia said, "but no matter what I did, all he noticed was how I looked in my sweater or t-shirt or whatever."

"Well, he could hardly comment on what he was really looking at, could he?"

"I don't have any," Georgia looked down at her chest, "not really."

"I'll bet the sweater he likes is tight," Lyanne grinned at Georgia.

"You're right," Georgia grinned back.

"You know what a man is like by whether he looks you in the eyes or not."

"Brad looked in my eyes."

"Brad?"

"A boy, his dad is dead now, but he didn't like that Brad was talking to me. Brad disappeared a while back."

"You have lots of time," Lyanne said, "I'm sure you'll see Brad again."

"I'll put out some towels and stuff for you." Georgia changed the subject before she started bawling. "Then I'd better get ready for bed."

"Thank you, Georgia." Lyanne smiled sadly at her. "Do you think you could sleep in here? I don't like sleeping by myself."

"Sure, I'll bring in a foam mattress from our camping stuff."

Chapter Forty-six

"… and now the army are slaughtering any First Nations person who wanders out into their own traditional land. Don't sit back and let this genocide continue. Fight back! Where ever you are, whatever you are doing. Fight back, and let the colonial oppressors know we aren't dead yet. Join the Clan of the White Moose."

Rivers shut the satellite phone off and walked back to Darren.

"I notice you didn't mention the people shooting at the helicopter," Darren followed Rivers into the trees. It was a three hour walk back to the fort. He might get some answers from the man. Darren still hadn't decided what Rivers was about. He seemed serious about a return to First Nations' law and traditions, but he had no problem spinning a horrific situation to his benefit.

"The idiots are supposed to be able to hit the broad side of a barn," Rivers said, "but I hoped to knock out at least one chopper before this happened."

"You knew this was coming?" Darren fought to keep up with Rivers and to keep his voice even. He didn't know what it was about this man that made him go macho.

"It was inevitable," Rivers didn't have any trouble talking in spite of the stiff pace he set. "Create a frustrating enough situation for the army and someone is going to pull the trigger too quickly. In Afghanistan, the biggest danger wasn't the Taliban, but the troops from the other countries."

"So now what? Roger is going to want to strike back."

"Of course he will." Rivers led the way into some very tight brush. "It will be amusing to watch you two circle each other. You are like dogs fighting over a bitch."

"Roger is going to get a lot more people killed." Darren ducked under a branch and followed him.

"When he does, I will use it to push the people who think living under the thumbs of the colonialists is OK."

"But those are your own people." Darren stopped to glare at Rivers. "I know those kids."

"Sorry, if I am breaking your fucking heart." Rivers turned to look at Darren, "but it wouldn't be much good if it was white kids and elders. No one is going to fight because their enemy took a hit. The white people are out there congratulating themselves there are a few less indians for them to support."

"Not all of them," Darren said.

"No, but all of the ones that matter." Rivers started off at an even harder pace. Darren followed and had no breath for talking. It didn't stop him thinking. He noticed Rivers started swearing when he was trying to cover up how upset he was over something. What Darren couldn't figure was if the anger was directed at the army for killing the kids, at himself for using the tragedy, or at Darren for continuing to question the tactics of the rebellion.

They walked in silence the rest of the way to the fort. Mack had supper ready. Roger and Dianne weren't anywhere to be seen. Darren rolled his eyes. They were as horny as teenagers. When they came for supper Dianne had a black eye. Darren's cop instincts kicked in as he watched the way Roger hovered possessively around the woman. Darren wondered how he'd missed it before. *Damn there's nothing I can do without blowing my cover.* Then he accused himself of cowardice. His cover was already blown with Rivers. He'd been given the job of maintaining peace according to native tradition and law. He was certain coerced sex was frowned upon by the tribe. He'd need to come up with a plan that didn't involve fighting Roger to the death. He had no doubt he could handle the man, but he didn't feel like killing. It left him with too many nightmares.

"War council," Rivers said after supper.

They met in the circle, though with just the four men and Dianne it made a much smaller circle.

"We have to do some major damage to those bastards," Roger made no pretense at silence, "and yes, coward, I know they outnumber us."

"It isn't being a coward to think," Dianne said.

"Shut up, woman." Roger glared at her.

263

"She's here at the council." Darren damped his anger. "She has as much right to speak as you do. Just because you can beat her up doesn't mean you can shut her up. She's a Cree woman and has the right to make her own decisions."

"You stay out of what goes on between me and my woman."

"If she was your woman, you wouldn't have to hit her. You shame yourself and this Clan."

Roger lunged across the room at Darren. Darren blocked the other man aside and into the wall. He waited for Roger to bounce back and gave him a calculated blow to the face.

"Now you have a black eye to match Dianne's." Darren stood relaxed and ready. Roger pulled out his knife and went at Darren again. The man was predictable. Darren took the knife arm and chopped at Roger's forearm. The knife fell to the floor and Dianne picked it up. Darren pushed Roger back to his seat.

"That's twice you've pulled a knife on me, Roger," Darren held Roger's enraged gaze. "If you try a third time you will regret it."

"Are you going to just sit there and let him get away with this, Rivers?" Darren watched as Rivers looked at Roger as if the man were something that he'd stepped in."

"War Chief," Darren said, "I believe we were talking about retaliation for the helicopter attack."

"Yes, we were. What do you suggest?"

"I think we should strike at their base."

"Sure," Roger sneered, "We're going to just walk up and start shooting. Fucking brilliant." Rivers frowned slightly. He didn't like profanity at his War Council.

"I'm thinking more of using the back door." Darren leaned forward in his seat. "And taking out equipment more than people. If we do enough damage they'll have to call in more reinforcements. it will hit their pocketbooks and we know how much the government loves to spend money."

"Good," Rivers said, "how many will you need?"

"I will need one other person," Darren said, "This attack is about stealth not blunt force."

"Take Dianne." Rivers looked at Roger. "I am not going to trust you to keep yourself under control. Attack someone in my

War Council again, and I will kill you myself." He stood up and left the room.

"Get some warm clothes ready," Darren said to Dianne, "we're going to be roughing it for a few days." He ignored Roger's scowl and went to get his own gear ready.

They walked to the lean-to hiding the snowmobiles. Darren put Dianne on ahead of him and put extra gas on the back. It would be crowded but he didn't want to run two machines. He set off to the east for a good ways before he turned south. As he hoped they met up with the river. He followed the river south until it got too dark to ride safely. He found a spot where an overhang made a natural cave - small and surprisingly warm. He made sure they would have good air through the night and lay down to sleep. Dianne cuddled up against him.

"I thought you slept in the nude," she said.

"Usually." Darren rolled onto his back and wrapped an arm around her. "The best way to be cold at night is to wear damp clothes to sleep. We don't have any blankets or sleeping bag, so this will have to do."

Dianne stripped off her clothes and laid her coat on the floor along with a blanket she'd carried wrapped around her waist. Darren shrugged and took off his clothes too. He laid them out to dry as much as they could in this snow cave. They lay on the blanket and put their coats on top of them as blankets.

Dianne kissed him and let her hand wander across his stomach.

"I thanked you for not assuming I was a prostitute, but that's exactly what I was. I came here to make money. I'm not sure where I thought a bunch of men in the wilderness were going to get money. Roger ended up claiming me. He was going to make me rich. There's some mine he has interest in."

"You don't have to give yourself to me." Darren caught her hand gently. "I didn't take you from Roger, I made you free to make your own choices."

"This is my choice." Dianne kissed him again. "I want to know what it's like with a real man."

"I'm a little out of practice," Darren felt the heat travel up his face.

She laughed and let her hands wander further.

265

"Your body remembers."

He stopped trying to convince himself he was being stupid and just gave himself over to enjoying sex with her.

They woke tangled together in the morning with cold air blowing across their naked arms and legs. It only took a few minutes to get dressed and they were on their way again. Darren stuck close to the bank and hoped the ice stayed thick enough. They had no trouble and passed Spruce Bay. He found another overhang and they spent another night keeping each other warm.

In the mid-morning the following day, Darren turned up a creek that flowed into the river.

"This will take us to the south and east of the Base." Darren explained. "We'll come at night and cut through the fence from that side. There will be guards, but not as many as the north side and where the road is." They stopped at a spot where trees leaning over the creek bed made a roof. He pulled the snowshoes off the snowmobile. "We'll wait here until it gets dark."

They didn't have long to wait. They nestled into the snow and kept out of the wind. Darren watched the wind and decided it worked in their favour. With luck, it wouldn't die as the night progressed.

At about nine o'clock he signaled Dianne and they climbed out of the creek bed after they put on the white suits he'd brought. With the blowing snow, he figured they'd be just about invisible to the naked eye and hard to see even with night glasses or infrared.

"Stay low, and don't move in a pattern. We want to use the drift to cover ourselves. They started out toward the glow of the base. Darren figured they had to cover a few kilometers. They followed the low places of the land and moved slowly enough they didn't generate a lot of heat. It took them a couple of hours to reach the fence. He could see the helicopters parked on the runway and some of the other equipment as well. People moved around them. Getting them ready for their missions tomorrow, Darren guessed.

There were steel sheds set up around the base as well. Some had light shining from windows and the sounds of people. Others were dark. He kept looking until he picked out a shed not far from the helicopters. It was guarded too. The mechanics would walk to the shed and it looked like they were doing paperwork

Paperwork in this weather suggested weapons. That's what he wanted. He took out a pair of pliers and went to work on the fence while Dianne watched for people coming in their direction.

No alarms went off; nobody came running to investigate. Darren heaved a carefully silent sigh of relief. One barrier down. He cut just enough for them to roll under the fence. Still no alarm. The wind got stronger on the runway and it was hard for them to see anything, but they stayed on the ground and moved very slowly toward the building. It felt like hours before they were close enough to hear the murmur of voices at the front. They settled down for another wait.

The night became bitterly cold, but buried in the snow, they stayed mostly sheltered. The wind drifted snow over them and covered their tracks. When a guard did walk past between them and the fence, they didn't see anything wrong. Darren listened for the voices and the occasional clank of tools. He didn't know what time it was when they tailed off. He waited a while yet. The guard walked past again, walking the other way with their face down to protect themselves from the wind.

Darren started moving along the wall toward the front of the building. He reached the corner and peeked around it through the drifting snow. Dianne wasn't far behind him. The guard beat their hands against their side and shifted from one foot to the other. They kept looking at their watch as well. Darren guessed the replacement was due soon. He let the snow drift over him again.

He didn't have long to wait. A shadow appeared out of the drifting snow and saluted.

"I'm relieving you," the shadow said. "One stupid joke, and I'm freezing my ass off out here."

"Your ass isn't frozen yet," the guard first replied. "But it will be soon enough." He took something from around his neck and gave it to the other man. "You're supposed to put it around your neck."

"Yeah, like I need something steel around my neck." He put the thing in his pocket. "If I get busted, I'll know who's to blame."

267

"They won't hear from me," the guard said. "I wonder if I can transfer to Sergeant Aspen's squad. I heard they get a warm welcome from some of the people in town."

"Warm welcome or not, you won't catch me anywhere near that psycho bitch."

"That would be Sergeant Psycho Bitch."

The two men laughed and as if that were a signal the first guard walked away toward the buildings which still had warm light coming from the windows.

Darren listened to the new guard's complaints and attempts to find a way to stay warm. He took to walking up and down the front of the building. Half the time he faced into the wind. The other half he had the wind at his back. He also worked up a sweat which would just make him feel colder. Darren watched him walk several times. Nothing else moved. The next time the guard approached, Darren waited until he'd just turned his back. He moved silently and had a choke hold on the guard before the man knew what was happening. He struggled a few seconds before succumbing.

"Aren't you going to kill him?" Dianne asked as Darren pulled the key from the guard's pocket.

"No need," Darren handed her the key. "Open the door and I'll bring him inside." Seconds later they crouched in the heated building with the door closed behind them. Darren took a flashlight from the unconscious guard and found some cable to tie the man up. Darren guessed after what he was planning the man would prefer to be dead. Too bad, Darren didn't plan to kill anyone tonight.

He used the flashlight to take a quick look through the shed. It was organized very carefully and logically as Darren had expected from the military. He found the RPGs quickly enough. He put one near the door and went to the back of the shed. Crates of ammo were stacked to the ceiling. He put a grenade against the back wall and weighted it with some boxes of fifty -caliber. Pulling the pin left the grenade in place but ready to explode if jarred out of position. He picked up the RPG and three rockets. He took a moment to load it and make sure he knew what he was doing. Then he handed a regular grenade to Dianne.

"This is safe enough as long as you don't pull the pin." He put the flashlight out and let his eyes adjust to the wind.

That was when he heard someone banging on the door.

"Morris, you cretin," the someone shouted. "You can't guard the armoury from inside."

Darren pushed Dianne to one side of the door. He stood Morris up and held him.

"Open the door," he said quietly. Dianne threw the door open and Darren heaved the unconscious Morris on top of whoever was on the other side of the door. The other man went down in a heap and Darren heard laughter. *Too close, damn it.* He hoisted the RPG to his shoulder and aimed at the helicopters. He hoped it worked like in the movies. He pulled the trigger.

The noise just about deafened him, but the rocket streaked out to hit the central helicopter. It exploded in a spectacular ball of flame. Pieces of helicopter started falling as he loaded again. He tried not to imagine people with machine guns opening fire on him. A second rocket flew to add to the fire. Other helicopters and machinery started to explode as the heat set off their ammunition. Things fell on the roof of the shed. Darren didn't know if the missiles on the choppers would explode and he didn't want to be near to find out.

"Let's go." He ran out of the shed. The man had pushed Morris off him and started to stand up. Darren kicked him and ran to the corner of the shed they had crawled up. He heard guns firing past the back end of the shed. The wind was much stronger now and snow swirled in mini-tornadoes. Darren aimed the last rocket somewhere between him and the gunfire. He fired it off and the explosion rocked the building.

"Shit," he shouted, "run!" He grabbed Dianne's hand and bent over to run as fast as he could toward the fence. Bullets came through the turmoil from the last rocket, but nothing hit him. Fire, snow and wind mixed in a mad dance. Darren felt like laughing but he kept his energy for running. He pushed Dianne down and she rolled through the gap and he followed. He heard a shout from the other direction. The shooting stopped, but Darren knew it wouldn't be long before they shot through the fence at them. From the sound of explosions, he didn't think they'd be chasing him with anything mechanical.

269

Just as he rolled under the fence the armoury blew. He couldn't hear anything now, but he crawled through the snow as fast as he could. Dianne moved well ahead of him. They reached the small depression leading off toward the creek.

Shots came from the Base, but Darren didn't think they were anywhere close to them. They crawled and squirmed until the lights of the base were out of sight. The snowshoes still lay back at the fence so they had to push their way through the snow. Even with the deep track they left, the wind filled it up behind them.

They found the snowmobile and Darren got it started. He drove them down the creek to the river as fast as he dared. They followed the River north. He drove with the river bank just visible on his left. When the sky started getting light he found an overhang and hid the snowmobile under it. He and Dianne crawled into the tiny space that remained.

"Are you OK?" Darren asked.

"Fine," Dianne said. "you sure know how to show a girl a good time! But what am I supposed to do with this?" She held up the grenade he could just see with the light filtering in past the snowmobile.

"Keep it, you never know when it will come in handy."

"Date night and a gift," She cuddled up beside him. "If only we had just a little more space." Seconds later she fell asleep in his arms. Darren held her gently and let himself drift off to sleep.

Chapter Forty-seven

"You can't trust anyone," Sergeant Gretta Aspen said, "especially the little fucking kids. We had a kid come in with cookies for our unit. We wouldn't eat them; you know what it's like over there. Some moron American scarfed the whole plate. Next thing he's in the hospital with crushed glass all through his guts."

"Oh, come on," Creeley said, "you don't think a little kid baked the glass into the cookies?"

"I don't care who baked the cookies, but they were meant to harm. People use kids to get past our defenses. There are no noncombatants anymore. Everyone is suspect."

"That's got to be a hard way to live."

"Better than dying," Gretta decided maybe she'd had enough to drink tonight. In a few minutes, she'd be crying in her beer. She hated drunks who cried in their beer. Honestly, she hated everybody and no one more than herself. She often told the story about the glass cookies. She never told about what happened the next week. A bomb went off and her squad was sent in to check it out and render assistance. She'd gone in with her heart hardened against the bloody bodies and body parts. She hadn't been prepared to find the same kid with a chunk of glass embedded in her gut. The girl was still alive and crying for her parents. Her father had been the bomber. He'd brought his family to watch him blow himself up. The kid died while Gretta watched.

"I'm heading for my tent," she said. "I don't want to get lost in the storm on the way."

Creeley shrugged. Gretta wondered about him. He'd never once tried hitting on her in all the years they'd worked together. Then again, maybe she should be wondering about herself.

She opened the door and the wind slapped her in the face. She put her head down and walked out into the night. She heard some laughter by the armoury. That idiot Morris getting into even

271

more trouble. Gretta sighed and headed over there. Time to tear Morris a new one. She tried to think of a duty worse than guarding the armoury.

The first explosion knocked her to her knees. She fought her way to her feet and started shouting at the privates who stood in stunned horror as the helicopters burned. A second rocket left the shed and more helicopters and equipment were swallowed by fire. Guards ran toward the armoury and Gretta saw two shapes run out the door and around to the back.

"Go around back and fill that space with lead!" she shouted. The guards changed course and seconds later she heard gunfire as they obeyed her. She ran to stand behind them. The wind and snow was so bad she couldn't see if the bullets hit anything. The nose of an RPG poked around the corner and it streaked toward them. By luck or the enemy's stupidity it hit the ground fifteen feet away from them. Hellfire filled the space between the armoury and the fence. She saw shapes running toward the fence.

"Start shooting again," she screamed, "by the fence." They sprayed the area with gunfire, but it would take a miracle for them to hit anything. They swore, running after the enemy, but Gretta's gut twisted.

"Back," she yelled, "everybody back." They were so used to orders they immediately turned and ran. Gretta joined them. She saw Captain Banner standing by the command tent. If her gut wasn't right her career was over.

The armoury exploded and kept exploding as grenades, ammunition and mines went off. The blast knocked all of them off their feet. One of the men stayed down as the others dragged themselves up.

People shouted all over the camp. The choppers still burned while pieces of sheet metal rained down around them.

"Back," Gretta said hardly able to hear her own words. "We're still in the danger zone." The guards picked up their comrade and they ran far enough that the deadly rain missed them.

"What happened, Sergeant?" Captain Banning didn't appear to notice the cold or the wind. He stood in his shirt and tie staring at the disaster.

"Enemy incursion, sir," Gretta said.

272

"How did they get in?" the Captain suddenly shook himself and walked back to his tent. Gretta heard people fighting the fires and checking on casualties as she followed him.

"I'm guessing through the back fence," Gretta stood at attention. The Captain waved at her.

"Stand easy, Sergeant," he said, "I thought you were off tonight."

"Yes, sir, I was headed for my tent when I noticed a disturbance by the armoury. I went to sort it out and then someone fired an RPG from inside. It took out several helicopters. A second shot took out the rest and probably rendered most of the equipment inoperable. I saw two people run out of the shed so I had the guards shoot through the gap between the armoury and the fence. The enemy fired the third rocket and was able to run to the fence before we could start firing again."

"You were already running before the armoury blew."

"Yes, sir, my gut told me the enemy probably rigged the armoury to explode. It's what I would have done."

"I see," the Captain said, "I doubt one more person is going to salvage anything from this mess. I suggest you go to bed. Oh, one more thing," he said before Gretta reached the door, "your squad is patrolling the town?"

"Yes, sir."

"Keep your ears open," he said. "It is my experience these attacks don't come out of the blue. Someone knew about it. I want that person here. Understand?"

"Yes, sir."

She made it out the door this time and hunched her shoulders to try to stay warm.

"How's the Captain taking it?" Sergeant Bob Dickson asked. He was duty Sergeant tonight.

"Like you'd expect," Gretta said, "He ordered me to bed. I'm going to be collecting intel tomorrow."

"You think someone in town knew this was going down?"

"The Captain thinks so." Gretta shivered and tried to hold on to the last bit of warmth. "That's good enough for me." She walked off toward her tent in the middle of the line, slightly sheltered and with the heater and venting system, bearable even

273

in this weather. She stripped off her clothes and laid fresh out for the morning.

It took a long time for her to get to sleep. She had to come up with a way to find a person for the Captain to question. A random person would do no good. There needed to be a connection, a reason they would be part of an attack like this. Just before she fell asleep, she saw the face of the man who had been with the Staff-Sergeant where those idiots shot up a bunch of kids and old people. He had a good reason to hate the army. He'd be easy to find too. Gretta would bet he was still at the hospital.

She woke up in the mood to cause some serious hurt. That seemed appropriate for the day she planned. She dressed and headed to the canteen. The armoury and the choppers were just black, twisted wreckage. There was a pile of shrapnel. The guys had probably been up all night collecting the shit. Better them than her.

She didn't pay much attention to what she ate. - just made sure she had good strong coffee. After breakfast, she headed to where their jeeps were parked. Fortunately, well away from the freaking disaster zone. The morning guys were there already and had the jeeps running warm.

"OK." She gathered her people around her. "This is the drill this morning. Any chance that someone knows anything, and I mean anything at all about this fuck up, we bring them in. Make sure they're scared and ready to talk. I'm heading to the hospital to pick up a guy who looks good. I'll want Jones with me for back up. The rest of you be visible and get in people's faces. We aren't here to make friends. I want to find out who did this and nail their asses to a wall."

She climbed into the jeep and Jones got in the passenger seat. The road to town was full of drifted snow, and even with the four-wheel drive it was tricky. The roads in town weren't much better. *Nobody gives a shit about anything in this place, serves them right if it all gets blown to hell.* The road around to the hospital had been plowed so it was easy getting there. She parked the jeep beside the doors and went inside with Jones.

"The guy whose son was hit by the missile strike," Gretta said to the first nurse she saw. "Where is he?"

"He's with his son. They're keeping him in isolation to lower the risk of infection."

"Fine, take me there."

The nurse didn't look happy, but Gretta wasn't moving and Jones was the biggest guy in her squad.

She heard the racket as soon as they left the stairs. Someone was wailing and banging on a drum. The sound set her teeth on edge. She strode up the hallway to where a group of natives gathered in the hall outside a room. In the room a man in deerskin and feathers with his face painted danced around the bed.

Gretta saw the man she wanted. He stood a little to the side with a woman she figured to be a wife or girlfriend.

"You." She pointed at him. "You're coming with me. The Captain has some questions for you."

"I need to be here with my son." The man didn't even look at her.

"Listen," Gretta got up in his face. "You come, or I get a squad here and the whole damn lot of you come, and you," She pointed at the dancer who had stopped and looked at her with obvious rage. "I see you with warpaint on again, I may just shoot you."

She nodded at Jones and he took hold of the man Gretta wanted. For a moment, she thought there was going to be a fight and she went on her toes, ready, but the man slumped his shoulders and walked out quietly with her. Jones pushed him into the back seat and climbed in beside him. Gretta started the jeep and headed back to the Base.

Nobody spoke on the way to base. Gretta pulled up to the command tent and climbed out.

"Let's go." Her adrenaline spiked like she expected a fight, but he simply climbed out and ignored her. He looked around at the devastation and Gretta was sure she saw a smile twitch at the corners of his mouth. Maybe she was wrong. She could never read Rivers either. Like he was the ice man. Well if this fucker wanted to be ice man, she'd melt him quick enough.

She walked into the tent with the man behind him and Jones behind him. The Captain was looking at reports and frowning. He was not a happy man.

"That was quick." The Captain walked around the desk and pulled out a chair for the man. "So what is this person's name?"

The man stayed silent.

"His son was one of the kids hit by the chopper strike, sir." Gretta said.

"And you figured he'd hate us enough to help someone blow up our base." He sighed and pulled up a chair across from the man. "It's a start."

"What's your name?" the Captain asked the man.

He still stayed silent. Gretta kicked his chair and the man looked at her. She stepped back and dropped her hand to her gun. She'd never felt hate from someone as strongly as she did from this man.

"Answer the Captain." She kicked the chair again.

"Sergeant," the Captain said, "restrain yourself." Gretta ground her teeth and stepped back.

"It is difficult to have a conversation with someone when you don't know their name. I'm Captain Hugh Banner. You have met Sergeant Gretta Aspen and Private Jones." He leaned back in his chair and looked at the man. "I truly regret the incident which injured your son and killed others of your people. It is unfortunate, but in war these things happen more than you would think."

"How many people died?" the man asked.

"Pardon?" Captain Banner his brow wrinkled.

"How many of your people died last night?"

"We had four people who we flew out for treatment, but as of this time, no one has died."

"If I'd been involved in that attack," the man said, "you wouldn't be able to count the bodies."

Gretta's anger flamed up and she stepped forward and slapped the man across the head. She hoped he would attack her, she'd take him apart. He just looked at her with rage burning behind his eyes. His hands stayed relaxed on his knees.

"Sergeant." the Captain snapped at her. "If I hear so much as a hint you have used force on any prisoner I will have you arrested and court-martialed. Dismissed. Jones, perhaps you would drive the Sergeant back to town to resume her duties."

Gretta saluted and marched out of the command tent. Ice ran through her. She thought the Captain understood. The man was a criminal. All his people were. No one was innocent.

"I need to walk to clear my head," Gretta said. "Wait by the car. I will only be a few minutes. She walked toward the wreckage and walked around the taped off exterior of the armoury. The choppers had also been blocked off and they looked even worse. They laid on their sides and one on its rotors. They reminded her of birds that used to hit the window of her home when she was a kid only to flop helplessly until they died. The LAV's were in slightly better shape. They might even be drivable. One of the bombardier's lay on its side and gear spilled out of it. Snow drifted over it. Abandoned, like Gretta felt. She saw a case with just a corner sticking out of the snow, but she recognized it immediately. She drew breath to call someone to have them put it in a secure location, but then she thought of another use for it.

Tonight, she'd move it. If it was still there it would be sign she was supposed to use it.

She walked back to Jones who waited patiently at the car.

"Let's get back to work."

Chapter Forty-eight

The videos her friends gave her were undeniably boring. The only bit even slightly incriminating was the bit she had of the one soldier threatening her. Even that when she looked at it with fresh eyes wasn't enough. Georgia needed something which would make people yank the military out of here so they could get on with rebuilding their lives.

Her phone rang.

"Hello."

"Georgia," She recognized Alastair's voice, "I know you and the others are taping the MP's. They think it's cute. But something has got them upset today. They were asking me who might be in contact with this Spirit Moose Clan. Someone attacked their Base last night. I heard the explosions. Leave the games alone for a bit. I don't want them to have any excuse to hurt you."

"It isn't a game," Georgia said. "It's a war, and the war is on us. All of us." She hung up on him and was going to throw the phone against the wall, she stopped herself. If the soldiers were upset, then they might make mistakes. But they needed a different plan if they knew they were being taped.

She looked at her phone and dialed a number. It went straight to voice mail. like it had for the last few days.

"Matthew, it's Georgia. We're still under martial law and being pushed around. Someone told me the Base was attacked and they are looking for a person to blame. I'm still trying to get you a video you can use. I don't know what's happening to you, but I hope you're all right."

She hung up then went to talk to Lyanne. Maybe it would distract her enough to come up with a different idea.

Lyanne was watching a DVD, some kid's movie. Georgia thought it might be one of Paul's. Paul sat beside her and they were laughing at the movie. Georgia changed her mind and went out. She'd go down to Leigh's place and talk.

The wind had dropped, but it was still gusty enough she put her hood up to shelter her face. That's why she didn't see the soldier until she almost walked into him.

"Out walking by yourself is dangerous," the soldier said. "Maybe I should drive you to wherever you are going."

"No thanks," Georgia kept walking.

"That's not very nice," the soldier grabbed her arm and spun her around to face her. "Some of the girls in Afghanistan were younger than you."

Georgia thought it a ridiculous statement, of course there were girls younger than her. Then it clicked that he meant a particular kind of girl. She tried to pull away, but he was far too strong for her. She took a breath to scream and the soldier stuffed his glove in her mouth.

"Get in the car and I promise not to hurt you," he said. "I just want to talk."

"You can talk to someone else." A voice rasped behind them.

The soldier whipped his head around and the Staff-Sergeant stood, hand at his waist where his gun would be. Georgia pulled away and took a few steps back.

"What do you think your Captain would say if he knew you were trying to pick up young girls while on duty? It would be an interesting conversation I'm sure. I may just drive out there and find out."

"Don't try to fuck with me." The soldier dropped his hand to his gun.

"I'm a cop." The Staff-Sergeant didn't budge. "I'm just doing my duty. I suggest you go do yours before this gets ugly. Every house on this street has someone watching you, so you go ahead and pull that gun."

The soldier jumped into the jeep and drove off.

"Georgia," the Staff-Sergeant said, "it is too dangerous for you to be out alone."

Georgia tried to say something but instead she threw up on the ground, almost on the Staff-Sergeant's boots. He didn't even back up. He just patted her on the back until she'd finished.

279

"Maybe you should come to the house," he said. "Leigh will get you some tea."

She took his arm like she was some lost little kid and let him lead her to his house. Leigh greeted her with a hug and took her coat that was covered with puke.

"I'll throw this in the washer, be right back."

"Sit down at the table." The Staff-Sergeant pointed. "I'll pour you some tea."

When he put the cup in front of her, she felt like crying. Georgia tried to shake herself out of her funk, but she felt like a little kid. Then she felt Leigh's arm around her and she gave up the battle and just let the tears flow.

"I'm sorry," she said when she could talk again, "I'm acting like a stupid kid."

"Your body has a better idea of how much danger you were in than your head does," Jim said. "If Leigh hadn't sent me out to check on you, it could have been very different."

"But they are supposed to be protecting us!" Georgia said, as if she hadn't been trying to prove how badly they were behaving.

"Not really," Leigh looked at her husband, "they are supposed to keep us out of their way while they fight their war. Only they don't have anyone to fight, so they come after us. It isn't even all of them, just a few, but even a few is too many."

"I think the Captain put this Sergeant in charge of the town to spite me." Jim sat across from her. "I doubt he knows what all is going on. As long as we're quiet and out of his way, he has no reason to care."

"Drink your tea, Georgia, and when your coat is dry, Jim will take you home," Leigh said, "as much as I enjoy your visits, I think it would be better if you stayed inside where you are safe."

"And don't think you can sneak the back trails anymore." The Staff Sergeant frowned. "I've seen them walking through the trails as well. It isn't fair, but the safest thing right now is to be invisible."

Jim drove her home and she saw him sitting and watching her until she went in her door. Georgia took a deep breath and pushed all the fear and uncertainty aside. She wasn't going to let anyone see how shaken she was.

Georgia sat in her room and looked at the phone on her desk. It didn't do her any good there. Of course, if they knew she was videoing them, it wouldn't do any good anyway. They would just take it away. She put it in the drawer with her old phone. She'd just take the Staff-Sergeant's advice and stay inside and away from trouble. She walked over and sat at her desk. Her hands wanted to shake, but she wouldn't let them.

She heard her phone ring. Probably Alastair again, treating her like a kid. She decided to answer it anyway. It might be someone else. She ran over to the drawer and picked up the phone.

"Georgia," Matthew said, "I'm sorry I didn't get back to you. I've been off work for a few days. They pretended it was because I got beat up, but the truth is I crossed the line and got a whole lot of viewers angry at me. The only reason they didn't fire me was almost as many viewers supported me."

"You got beat up?" Georgia gasped, "Are you OK?"

"Yeah, I was stupid and went out alone."

"I know how that feels, fortunately someone came along and saved me."

"I'm glad they did. Be careful. I'd hate to hear that you got hurt or worse. I listened to your messages, can you be a little more detailed about what is going on?"

"Not really, one of my friends heard explosions from the Base and he said the soldiers were upset. He figured there had been an attack."

"Right, it makes sense." Georgia could hear the scratching of a pen as Matthew took notes. "You said the military fired on some civilians in one of your messages."

"That's right. Anna told me the military claimed the boys were shooting at the helicopter, but it had to be someone else. The helicopter fired a missile at a group of elders and one of the boys. The other one was further away. It came back and tried to kill him too. He's in the hospital. He hasn't woken up yet. He's terribly burned. They still aren't sure if he's going to live."

"I would think they'd have flown him out."

"The military won't let them; too much of a security risk."

"The White Moose Clan released a statement condemning the military for firing on innocents. The military hasn't

281

responded. You are the first confirmation anything happened. Do you think you could get pictures of the boy?"

"I can try, but remember it takes a long time to upload here."

"I'll pay whatever costs you have," Matthew said, "I'll send you a number to use just for uploads. It may be faster. It is a dedicated server. It will alert me if anything comes through."

"It won't be today," Georgia looked out at the already dark sky, "I'll try tomorrow."

She hung up her phone and stared at it. Maybe what she needed was a decoy. Something to give up if they demanded her phone. The soldier knew she had the new phone so it would have to be the decoy. The old phone didn't have a bad signal, slightly better than her new phone, but the battery on it was weak. She wouldn't have much time to upload anything.

She remembered the trick she showed Brad. She went down to the basement and found some wire and needle nose pliers and took them up to her room. She carefully made the extra antennae. Now her old phone had almost five bars. She pulled the charger out and plugged the phone in.

She went downstairs and brought her coat upstairs. She wrinkled her nose at it. She couldn't smell it, but she couldn't get the idea of the vomit out of her mind. It was done after this. She cut a hole in the front pocket, just big enough for her old phone to take video through. She wouldn't get a lot of time, but it would be better than nothing.

Now she was almost ready for tomorrow. All she needed was the courage to step out the door.

"What are you doing?" Lyanne asked as she came into the room.

"Setting up something to record video that won't be as obvious as holding the phone in my hand."

"What's the wire for?"

"It gives me a little better signal. I just wish I had a better battery. This phone might go dead before it uploads anything. It's the best I can do."

"Risky stuff," Lyanne said. "Please don't get caught."

"I can always ditch the phone and come back for it," Georgia said.

"Assuming they let you go back. These people play for keeps."

"I know, but I can't just do nothing."

Lyanne gave her a hug, then they went downstairs to have supper and watch silly movies with Paul.

Chapter Forty-nine

"I still say you shouldn't have let him go," Captain Raffin said. "You have no idea if any of the stuff he told you is going to check out."

"If I need him, I know where to find him," Captain Banner didn't like being questioned and opposed on everything. Technically he was the senior officer, but Raffin argued about everything.

"So we just go looking for a drug dealer in the reserve and he's going to give up Rivers?"

"Joe is cousin to this dealer -"

"All the more reason not to trust him. These people hold to family come hell or high water."

"Not when their actions are getting your kids killed," Banner said. "Creeley is going to do a sweep through the reserve tonight. Joe told me the places his cousin usually hangs out. If he isn't there, I'll get Aspen to do a sweep through the community for him."

"She's a loose cannon," Raffin shook his head.

"She knows this kind of work," Banner frowned. "She did this kind of thing in Afghanistan several times. She'll keep it professional."

Raffin snorted, but didn't say anything. Banner didn't know how the Colonel worked with the man, or perhaps he was just getting worse, like all of them in this pressure cooker.

"We get Rivers' location and we send a strike team. We do it quick and quiet. Then this thing will be done."

"What I'm afraid of, Hugh," Raffin stood up and shrugged his coat on. "Is that we'll get out of here only to discover the whole damned country is at war with itself. I hope I'm wrong."

"So do I."

Banner walked to his tent to catch what sleep he could. He'd given Creeley instructions to wake him if there was anything to report. He saw someone over by the wrecks and thought about confronting them, but to be honest. He knew how they felt. He had a hard time believing they were that vulnerable. He thought about what Joe had said. Who goes to all the trouble to attack and doesn't kill anyone? It didn't make sense, and Banner was uncomfortable with things he couldn't explain. He turned and went to his tent and left whoever it was to make their own peace with mortality.

The Sergeant woke him at six to report they had not been able to find Johnston McCrey. The few people who would talk to him suggested he preferred to operate out of the town.

"Very good, Sergeant," Banner said, "Go get some rest."

Now that he was awake, he went to the canteen to get coffee and breakfast. Aspen would be in for her briefing and he would be very clear about what he expected.

***

"We'll meet in the parking lot beside the Mall," Gretta told her team. "We're all on deck today, make sure you're fully loaded." She climbed in the car and spun the tires on the way out of the Base. Jones was wise enough not to say anything. She banged her hand on the steering wheel until the pain in her hand overwhelmed the pain in her head. He wanted the town swept for a known terrorist sympathizer, but they had to be polite, gentle. How the fuck were they going to root out terrorists by being polite and gentle? She pulled into the lot and parked in the corner away from the shed. The rest of her squad showed up. They looked like a pitifully small crew to shake down the entire town.

"This is how it is going to work," she said to them when she was able to force the words out, "We will start in the half of the town with all the squirrelly streets. Be polite, but be firm. We are looking for someone who is aiding the terrorists. Don't force your way into any homes, but squirt me the address and we'll deal with them later. Tell the people to stay in their homes. Anyone who is caught wandering around we'll stuff them in the shed until we're done.

285

"I'm going to stay here and coordinate. I'll watch for anyone who tries to slip past the net. I'll take Jones and do the hospital as well. Get on it, this is the easy part, so let's not waste time."

The squad went off in pairs to start at the far end and try to make sure any runners didn't have anywhere to go but past Gretta and Jones. While they were getting into position, Gretta stormed into the hospital.

"We need to search the hospital," she told the nurse, "tell everyone to stay out of our way."

"I can't do that." The nurse crossed her arms. "This is a hospital; we treat patients who have depressed immune symptoms. You can't just walk through the hospital carrying infection from one room to the next."

"We're looking for a terrorist," Gretta growled the words at her.

"There are no terrorists here." The nurse didn't move.

"What about the guy in war paint in that kid's room?"

"We have no terrorists here," the nurse said again. "That man is a native healer. Since you people won't let us transfer our patient out we have to do whatever we can here."

Gretta's hand fell to her gun.

"Don't get in my way -"

"You can shoot me if you'd like, but the answer is still no."

Gretta ground her teeth and got ready to bull her way past the nurse.

"Sarge," Jones said, "Just get them to go into lock down and we'll deal with it later."

"That I can do," The nurse relaxed slightly. "no one will leave the hospital until your search is complete."

"They can't come in either -"

"I am not turning away anyone who needs treatment." The nurse tensed again.

"Sarge, we got work to do."

"Later," Gretta said to the nurse. She spun and walked out of the hospital.

"Jones if you ever pull that shit on me again, I'll pound you into dust myself."

"We need you here, Sarge, not arguing with some bitch nurse."

"Don't push it." Gretta led the way back to the lot.

As she expected some people refused to let the teams go through their house. The cop was one, but most meekly let the soldiers check quickly and move on. No one was reported on the move and faster than she expected they met back in the lot.

"The next part we do different," Gretta said. "I don't want this guy to get lost in the confusion, so we clear the area. Everybody gets sent here. We'll confirm their ID and put them in the shed while we finish the sweep. No violence unless someone else starts it. I don't want the Captain busting my ass. Don't take any shit either; these are terrorists or sympathizers. They walk here too, it's a warm enough day, they don't need heavy coats. I don't want to be wondering what's under them. Tony and Mike, you stay here with me. We'll need the extra guns to keep people under control. Teams One, Two and Three, I want you to maintain a line between the two halves of town, no one crosses into the area we already swept."

The teams went off again and soon a line of angry people started showing up shivering and complaining. Many of them were supporting elderly parents. They didn't argue with the soldiers and their guns. Once again the teams were pushing people toward the center of town. It was all going well until a woman showed up with a big carafe of coffee and some food.

"What the hell are you doing?" Gretta asked.

"You have our neighbours standing in the cold with no coats and only that drafty shed. I'm bringing them food and drink," the woman said.

"Fine, take it in, but you can't leave."

"These are my neighbours," the woman repeated, "I'm not going to leave them."

She pulled her car up near the shed and soon people were coming to get drinks and food.

The woman came back to Gretta.

"I've run out. I need to go get more."

"No," Gretta said, "You can't leave."

"These people are cold -"

"I don't care." Gretta raised her voice like she would with a new private. "This is a security sweep, not a tea party."

"Don't raise your voice to me, young woman," the woman said. "Your salary is paid by their taxes."

"Get out of my face you old biddy!" Never in all Gretta's career had anyone talked back to her. The woman glared at Gretta and walked back to her car. Gretta put her attention back on the growing number of people who were showing up. More of them young people with attitudes, and only the obvious weaponry of the soldiers kept them in line. The shed and the area around it was getting rowdy and Gretta called in Team One to help keep order.

That was when more people started arriving with cars. Gretta ran over to them.

"What the hell are you doing?" she shouted at them, "Go home!"

"Ms. Taladut called us," one of the woman said. "She needs more food and some blankets too.

"Team Two, Team Three," Gretta said into her radio. "What are you doing?"

"No one is going into the clear zone," one man said.

"You're letting all these people into the area."

"You didn't tell us not to," the same man said, "If you want us to stop them we're going to need support. Half the freaking town is heading this way."

"Shit," Gretta threw the radio down. Now what the hell was she supposed to do?

"Young woman," it was that annoying woman again.

"What!" Gretta shouted.

"Some of the older people and the children need to use the washroom. There are none in the shed. What are we supposed to do?"

"Nothing," Gretta snarled at her. "Tell them to hold it, to shit in their pants. To go in the corner, they're probably used to that."

"Young woman," the woman said. "Don't take that tone with me. These are people, our people and I will not see them abused."

Gretta pulled her gun without thinking and put it to the woman's head.

"Get out of my face, you old bitch, or I'll shoot you right here."

"I'm only here because one of those people's children died to save me." The woman didn't move. "I'm not going to let some spoiled brat with a gun abuse them."

"GET THE FUCK OUT OF MY FACE!" Gretta screamed.

"My dear, didn't your mother raise you better than that?"

Gretta didn't know if it was an accident or deliberate that her finger moved a fraction of an inch on the trigger. Her gun fired and the woman fell to the ground with a disapproving look still on her face. People screamed. Some ran away from her, but some ran toward her. Three boys jumped one of her soldiers and tried to take his gun. Gretta fired again. The others were shooting as the mob tried to escape.

Gretta heard shouting behind her and realized Team One and Two had come in to support. She tried to tell them to contain the crowd but it was impossible.

"Let them go," she yelled. "Cease fire, cease fire damn it!" The shooting stopped and Gretta looked at the carnage. There were at least a couple of dozen bodies on the ground, some of them still moving.

"What a fuck up!" Jones said. "What do you want us to do?"

"Get some weapons and put them in those people's hands," Gretta ordered. "Get pictures of them. We were attacked and defended ourselves. Understand?"

"Clear, Sarge," Jones went and started talking to the others. Gretta was shaking. She never had the shakes. It didn't matter how intense the action, but this … she looked at the woman. A kid lay next to her, maybe high school age, another woman, younger with a baby lying beside her. The baby wasn't crying. Not with that bullet hole through it. Gretta knew it didn't matter what she did, she was fucked. Her stomach cramped up and she puked up on the snow. That was her life right there. When she straightened up she saw a young girl. One of the ones who thought it cute to video the soldiers at their duty. She had a phone in her hand.

"Her!" Gretta shouted to her squad. "Catch her and bring her to me. Make sure you have her phone. The girl took off like a scared rabbit with Jones and Mike after her. A couple of others jumped in a jeep and drove around to cut the girl off.

289

"Forget this," Gretta said to the ones who were left, "Go report me to the Captain. Blame me for everything. I went crazy, whatever you need to save yourselves. I'm going to the squad room. Just tell Jones I'm there, then you're clear. You don't know anything from here on." She climbed into her jeep and drove away.

Chapter Fifty

Georgia came with her Dad and Paul to bring blankets for her friends. She set the phone recording as soon as she got there. She had maybe twenty minutes of battery time even at the minimal quality she set the video at.

She watched Ms. Taladut confront the Sergeant. Georgia was impressed. She wouldn't have the nerve. The army woman terrified her even from a distance. Then the Sergeant shot Ms. Taladut and the world went crazy. People screamed, some boys tried to attack the soldiers. She shot them. Then she shot a mother and her baby. Georgia wanted to run, but her feet wouldn't move. People died in front of her and she stood like a statue.

It was over and the Sergeant gave orders to the soldiers. They started putting guns beside the bodies and taking pictures. The Sergeant threw up in the snow. Georgia didn't think soldiers would react like that. Then the woman looked at Georgia and pointed her finger.

The paralysis broke and Georgia ran. At first she didn't have a plan, but as she ran she knew in minutes if not seconds, her lungs would betray her. She went through a line of trees onto a path, pulled the phone out and sent a video text to the number Matthew had given her. The antennae was gone, she'd forgotten it at home. She didn't know if the phone would upload before it ran out of battery but she had to try. The phone took her attention so she didn't see Alastair in time. She crashed into him and they both fell to the ground. Georgia dropped the phone and saw the big soldier and the one who tried to abduct her coming after her. She cut through the trees and tried to get away between the houses. A jeep skidded to a stop and cut her off, then the creepy soldier tackled her.

"So." He leered at her. "We're going to get to have that ride after all." He pulled her to her feet. Georgia kicked and screamed, but the big soldier punched her in the stomach and it was all she could do to breath. They pushed her into the Jeep and they drove away. The creep lay on top of her and she could feel his hands on her even with her heavy coat.

"Help me get her coat off," the soldier said.

"Leave her alone," the big soldier said, "or I'll break you in half, right now. I have a sister her age."

"You should introduce me sometime."

The big soldier grabbed the other by the throat and kicked open the door. He pushed the soldier out onto the road.

"Too hard," the big one said. "I was hoping you'd run over him."

"I can go back and try again." The driver slowed a little.

"Nah." The big soldier closed the door. "He ain't worth the gas."

They drove down to the old industrial area where the new grocery store and detachment were. The jeep pulled up in front of a building at the end of the road with a Jeep in front of it already.

"Sorry, Jones," the driver said. "Sarge said to drop you here and bugger off."

"Right, go save your skin then." Jones slid out of the Jeep and casually tossed Georgia over his shoulder. She watched the Jeep driving away as she was carried into the old building. Coffee cups and half eaten snacks littered the table. He walked past the mess to a room in the back. He put Georgia down and leaned against the door of the room.

"Give me the phone," The Sergeant said.

"I don't have it." Georgia's voice shook.

"Jones," The Sergeant had barely spoken and the man's hand clamped her arms. The Sergeant went through the pockets of her coat and found Georgia's new phone.

"I don't like liars." The Sergeant slapped Georgia, and her head spun. The Sergeant fiddled with the phone. "Where's the memory card?"

"I don't have one," Georgia said, and the Sergeant slapped her again.

"Once more." The Sergeant glared at her.

"I told you -" The blow crunched into Georgia's face and she wondered if her nose had broken.

292

"So, we do it the hard way." The Sergeant spoke as if nothing had happened. "Jones, you have ties?"

He pulled zip ties from a pocket and fastened Georgia's hands behind her, then her feet together. Gretta pulled a knife from a pocket and snapped it open.

"What about your sister?" Georgia asked.

The big soldier shrugged. "She has a big mouth, like you. I can't let Mike talk about her like that, but this is business. You'd have been better to tell the truth." He stepped out the door and closed it behind him.

"You'd think I'd remember to do this before I had him tie you." The Sergeant unzipped the coat then ran the knife up the arm and cut it off her. She searched the coat, cutting open each pocket and seam until it was just a pile of rags on the floor. The hat received the same treatment, then her boots and socks.

"You know this is a nice sweater on you. I'll bet the boys really like it on you. Too bad." The knife cut up the side seam of the sweater and down the arm. "And here I didn't think you'd be wearing a bra yet. You girls grow up so fast these days."

The Sergeant's voice was friendly, even kind as she thoroughly destroyed the sweater. Georgia concentrated on remembering to breathe. She wondered if the creepy soldier would have been less scary than this woman who made pleasant conversation while she destroyed Georgia's clothes.

"You're thinking about Mike." The Sergeant looked over at Georgia. "He has his uses, but isn't patient enough for this. He doesn't think about what he's doing. Me, I know exactly what I'm doing. I'm going to find that memory chip and I'm going to destroy it. My career is down the toilet, but there's no reason to take the rest of the squad with me." She slid the knife up each leg of Georgia's pants and pulled the wreckage off. Georgia pulled her knees up to her chest.

"Such pretty panties. They didn't have anything like that when I was a girl, not that my mother would have bought them for me. She didn't have money for anything but booze or drugs. When she couldn't sell herself any more to buy them, she sold me. I disappointed her though. I ran away and joined the Army. They made a man out of me. The woman laughed, as if what she'd said was funny.

293

"Last chance to cough up the chip, girl."

Georgia just shook her head. She knew if she'd had it she would have handed it over. She also knew with an absolute certainty she wasn't going to survive this. Lyanne was right. She didn't know what she'd got herself into.

The knife cut through her bra and Georgia tried to hide her breasts behind her knees.

"Now, it's not like you have much to see, not like some. I can see why Mike likes you. He really is a pervert." She put the blade of the knife on Georgia's breast. "Open wide. Any tricks and I cut your tits off."

Georgia opened her mouth and the Sergeant peered in and felt around with her finger.

"Dear, dear a pity those memory chips are so small these days." She pushed Georgia onto her back and cut her panties off.

"This is going to hurt just a little," the Sergeant said, "go ahead and cry if you want. I did my first time."

Georgia bit her lip and refused to cry as the Sergeant's rough fingers invaded her.

"So maybe you were telling the truth." The Sergeant snapped her knife closed. "I have to do my job properly, you understand." She walked to the door and left. Georgia heard a brief conversation before the door closed.

"Anything?" the big soldier asked.

"Nothing," the Sergeant said, "I'll send Mike, but we have some people to kill. I want people to be screaming about the awful terrorists, not the Army."

They left and Georgia gave into her tears. She sobbed on the floor, then the tears transformed into screams of rage. When the rage was gone, she lay and waited for Mike to come and satisfy his desires before he killed her.

She waited and no one came. The floor was cold but she couldn't stand with her hands behind her back. She rolled on her back and curled up as tight as she could and managed to work her hands around to her front. She felt better now she could cover herself. The room was bare except for the pile of rags that used to be her clothes. She pushed herself over to the clothes and sat on them. Still cold. She eyed the door. Had they locked it? Maybe they didn't think their perverted friend would be this long. Maybe

294

they didn't think she'd be able to move her hands or get to her feet.

Georgia maneuvered herself to her feet and hopped over to the door. Locked. She felt like crying again. She could see the catch. Georgia looked at the pile of rags. There was some plastic in her boots. Hopping over to the pile she knelt and went through the pile with her fingers. There, she pulled out a small piece of plastic that used to be part of her boots. Pushing herself to her feet, she hopped back to the door. The plastic just fit. She'd seen this in a movie, even tried it for herself on the doors at home. It was much harder with her hands tied together, but finally the door swung open.

At first she didn't want to go out in the hall. What if someone was there? Then she shook herself. Her face hurt, her mouth hurt. She hurt in places she'd never thought of hurting. She wasn't going to let embarrassment stop her. Georgia hopped out into the hall and toward the front of the building. Where there was coffee, there might be a kitchen. Kitchens had knives and scissors. She found the kitchen and the only knife was a tiny paring knife. She held it in her teeth and sawed at the zip tie until it broke. Her arms screamed with pain at the sudden movement. She ignored them and cut the tie around her ankles. Now she could walk she went looking for a blanket or jacket or anything to put on. There was nothing. Not even a tea towel.

It was still light outside. Georgia had expected it to be pitch black. She went to the windows and peered out past the blinds. Cars sat in front of the little cafe Maria and Marc's parents ran. They weren't military cars. The only person who Georgia knew was coming here, was coming to rape and murder her. She'd rather freeze to death. She looked at the hundred meter walk to the cafe and thought freezing seemed a real possibility. Someone came out of the store and drove away. She thought she saw someone in the store turn a sign in the window around.

She ran to the door and pushed through it. The cold bit into her and made her gasp. The snow was painful on her feet. Georgia thought she would scream, then Maria's dad stepped out of the cafe and locked it up. She did scream. Georgia screamed and ran through the snow waving her hands. Mr. Horate looked in her direction and dropped his keys. He fumbled in the snow to find

295

them and unlocked the door again. Georgia ran past him and fell coughing on the floor. She heard breaking dishes then felt a table cloth wrap around her. Mr. Horate spoke rapid Spanish into the phone.

Georgia didn't care what he was saying or what he was thinking. The only thing she cared about was it looked like she might live through the day.

Chapter Fifty-one

Alastair picked himself up from the snow and watched the soldiers tackle Georgia and force her into the Jeep. He remembered the big one's name was Jones. He didn't seem to have a first name. The other one was Mike and Alastair didn't like him. The stories he told about sex, according to him, with girls of all ages who just spread their legs for him, made Alastair feel an uncomfortable combination of excitement and guilt. The guilt grew worse when Mike talked about what he'd do to the little bitch who stole the town's only whore away. Alastair knew he was talking about Georgia. He didn't want to speculate about what was under her clothes, at least not the way Mike did.

Fortunately, they had no interest in Alastair. The Jeep roared away and left him standing alone, still shaking after the riot and the bloodshed. He'd run away as soon as the Sergeant shot Ms. Taladut. Alastair was disgusted with himself; he should have stayed, maybe he could have helped with the wounded. Nothing on earth would get him to go back there.

A beeping from the snow made him look down. An older cell phone lay in the snow. He picked it up and saw the battery indicator showed it was low. Georgia was videoing the soldiers again and it got her into trouble. He'd warned her.

He wondered what was on the video. He put the phone in his pocket and headed for Georgia's house. The charger would be there and he'd be able to tell her parents the soldiers had Georgia. They'd know what to do.

Georgia didn't like him much since he started talking to the soldiers. Sure, some of them were creeps, but so were the kids at school. Most of them just did their job. A job Alastair hoped he'd be doing when he got older. He liked Georgia, but though she was a grade seven to his eight, she made him feel young. Her group of friends just automatically did whatever she asked. He made a suggestion, and they all looked at her to see if it was OK.

He still liked her. He had dreams which made him feel guilty when he woke up. They'd been getting more detailed after listening to Mike.

Alastair had reached Georgia's house. There weren't any cars in the drive, but he knocked anyway. Maybe someone was home.

Lyanne came to the door. She looked at Alastair with wide eyes and peered up and down the street.

"Come in, it isn't safe out there."

"I found Georgia's phone." He showed it to her. "She's trying to send a big file, but the battery's almost dead."

"The charger is upstairs in her room," Lyanne led the way upstairs. Alastair followed. "Everyone else is gone," Lyanne told him, "I told them not to go, but Ruth insisted and Paul had to go too."

She pushed a door open and he walked into Georgia's room. Neat and tidy. No clothes strewn about the floor like in his room. He had to kick underwear beneath his bed when his friends came over. He didn't think Georgia would be impressed. He didn't think she'd like him in her room even if her underwear wasn't scattered on the floor. He thought of the day of the attack at school and the tiny glimpse he'd stolen of Georgia in just her bra.

The charger sat on the desk. Alastair plugged it in. Just in time, the battery icon had been flashing. Now it went back to uploading, but it was so slow.

"She made this for it." Lyanne leaned over him and carefully plugged it into a port in the back. The reception improved and the upload became marginally faster.

"Shit, Lyanne," Mike leaned against the door. "I didn't think you liked them that young."

Alastair stepped between Mike and Lyanne. The soldier punched him in the gut and Alastair fell to the carpet. Mike kicked him.

"Don't get between a man and his woman." He kicked him again.

"Now, Mike, do you want to beat on that kid, or do you want some woman?"

Alastair saw Lyanne had pulled off her sweat shirt and stood in jeans and her bra. Her bra was much fuller than Georgia's. He felt guilty for thinking it. Mike threw himself at Lyanne and tore her bra off. He bit at the woman's breasts and fumbled at her jeans. She did something and they fell to the floor. She wore nothing under them. Now Mike fumbled at his pants and then pushed himself into her grunting like an animal. He grabbed Lyanne's breasts and twisted them until she whimpered.

"You know what I want, whore," he gasped.

She screamed and he closed his eyes tilting his head back. Lyanne kept screaming, but one hand felt behind her. It landed on the needle-nose pliers. She whipped her hand forward and buried the pliers in Mike's temple. He screamed and fell back away from Lyanne and twitched on the floor until his bladder and bowels let go.

"Fucking bastard," Lyanne dropped the pliers.

"Are you OK?" Alastair said. "It sounded like it hurt."

"He liked to think he was hurting me. He was a sick fuck that way. I just gave him what he wanted."

Alastair realized his pants were wet.

"Oh shit," he said and to his horror he started crying.

"Come on now, kid," Lyanne lifted him to his feet. "Bathroom's this way. You can have a shower and get cleaned up." She walked him to the bathroom and peeled off his clothes. He stepped in the shower and the hot water washed tears and grime from him. He felt Lyanne step in behind him.

"I need to wash the stink of him off me." She didn't seem to care that Alastair stared at her. He tried to cover the reaction of his body, but she touched his face.

"It's OK," Lyanne said. "You're Alastair, right?"

Alastair just nodded. He didn't trust his voice.

"You tried to stop him," she said. "I appreciate that. Don't feel guilty you couldn't. He's a soldier."

"And I'm just a kid, right?"

"You didn't act like a kid." Lyanne stepped out of the shower and dried off. She handed Alastair a towel. "Dry off."

In the hall, she handed him a pair of sweat pants and a t-shirt. "These are Georgia's, but they should fit."

Alastair dressed quickly, breathing easier with clothes on.

299

"When can I see you again?" he asked.

"You're young yet, you want a girlfriend, someone like Georgia. I'm too old for you."

"I don't mean that," Alastair turned red. "I want to get to know you. I don't want to be like him. I don't want to use you."

Lyanne kissed him gently on the forehead

"You're sweet."

The phone beeped and Alastair was distracted from Lyanne's scent. He walked through the room, carefully not looking at the soldier's body, and picked the phone up.

"The upload has gone through," he said, "wherever she sent it." He played with the phone for a minute to start the video. It started with handing out food and blankets. Then there was shouting and the camera turned to show Ms. Taladut confronting the Sergeant. He watched her murder and the carnage that followed. It didn't last long, but he could see the bodies on the ground. Then the soldiers started putting guns beside the bodies and taking pictures. The Sergeant was puking, then looked straight at the camera. The picture went crazy for a few seconds before it stopped.

"They are going to cover up the massacre," Alastair said, "and blame it on the people. I can't let them do that."

"How are you going to stop them?" Lyanne stood beside him.

"I'm just a kid, right?" Alastair grinned at her briefly to take the sting out of his words. Lyanne was right; he had a lot of growing to do before he would be ready for her. "But I'm a kid with an uncle in high places." He took out his phone and looked up the number that had got him into deep trouble because his uncle had to answer and explain the message. He put the number into Georgia's phone and sent a video message. He put the phone back on the charger.

Alastair took a deep breath, then dialed the number.

"Uncle Frank, please listen to me. You can have Mom ground me forever, or I'll come and work for you for the summer. Whatever, but just listen."

"You have thirty seconds," Uncle Frank said.

"I'm sending you a video, someone died because of this video and my friend is in danger because of it. We have a big problem here and I need your help. You're the only one who can fix it."

"Stay where you are, Alastair. I'll call you back when I see this video." He hung up.

"I'm supposed to stay here until my Uncle calls back."

"But you're not going to?"

"Georgia's in trouble, I have to get help for her."

"Dressed like that?"

"I would go out in a pink tutu if it would help her."

"I'm coming with you," Lyanne said. They ran downstairs and put on their winter gear. "We'll go to Jim's," she said. "If anyone can help it will be him."

They ran. Leigh met them at the door.

"He's at the mall, doing what he can," she said. "The Captains are there along with a whole lot of other military."

"It's Georgia," Alastair said, "they took her. I think to their squad room."

"Let's go see," Leigh led them out to the car. "Get in and buckle up." She drove to the old industrial area. They turned the corner just in time to see Georgia run through the door into the cafe. Leigh parked the car and Alastair jumped out and ran to the cafe.

Georgia huddled on the floor coughing with a table cloth wrapped around her. Mr. Horate came out of the back with what looked like white clothes.

"My wife, she brings you clothes from Maria," he said, "They won't fit so good, but better than a table cloth. You wear these until they get here."

"What I'm wearing will fit her better," Alastair tossed his coat off and peeled off the clothes he wore to hand to Georgia. He heard the crash of dishes and Mr. Horate held a table cloth around him. Alastair nodded to him then pulled on the cook's clothes. He had to roll the pants and sleeves up a bit, but they worked.

"Why were you wearing my clothes?" Georgia's voice was barely a croak.

"Long story," Alastair sat beside her. "The short version is I took your phone to your house to make sure the upload went through. Things got complicated from there."

She looked at Lyanne and frowned.

301

"How complicated?" she said in a rasp.

"Well, you might want to call your parents to warn them about the dead man in your room." Lyanne shrugged and grimaced.

"Right," Georgia shook her head. "Full story later. I have to get to the Staff-Sergeant."

"The video went through," Alastair said.

"Good, but the last thing the Sergeant said before they left was they were going to kill more people."

"My car," Leigh said. "Sorry, Mr. Horate."

"Go, go," He waved his hands. "I will console my wife with stories of naked children in my cafe. But not too many details, eh?" He winked at Alastair and he grinned back.

They ran out to the car. Georgia swearing because she'd forgotten she had no shoes. Alastair rubbed her feet to warm them up.

"So what's it like?" Georgia whispered.

"What?" Alastair croaked.

"I saw how red you went before Lyanne jumped in to save you." She looked at Alastair. "I just want to know it doesn't have to be horrible." To his horror she had tears running down her face.

"We didn't." Alastair looked down. "I think I'm just as happy. You shouldn't have to hold yourself back. Georgia. I'll never be able to keep up with you. It will take someone special for that. But I'd like to be your friend, really your friend, without anything getting in the way."

"OK." Georgia grinned past her tears. "You looked cute in my clothes, and Mr. Horate wasn't quite fast enough with the tablecloth."

"That's OK." Alastair matched her grin.

Georgia leaned her head against him and he put his arm around her. She started to cry. Silently, but shaking like a leaf. Alastair held her tight, and didn't say a thing. Lyanne turned in her seat and gave him an approving nod.

Chapter Fifty-two

Jim wanted to be sick, but he didn't have time. The bodies were laid out in the snow, in bags now. Twenty-four people dead or injured, because the military didn't let him arrest that woman. The two Captains were subdued and deferring to Jim around every decision. Now they could go home, the people refused. They stayed to mourn their dead. Some silently and some with wails and tears.

Leigh's car pulled up, and Alastair, Georgia and Lyanne piled out of it. They walked toward him and he could see the urgency in spite of the slow pace. Georgia was in bare feet.

"Wait a minute, Sergeant Creeley." Jim ran over to the three. For some reason both Lyanne and Alastair were holding Georgia's hands. She looked like she'd been beaten. Her face was swollen and her nose might be broken.

"Jim," Georgia said, "I got picked up by the soldiers who work for the female Sergeant here in town. I had something they wanted. They thought anyway.' Jim saw her squeeze Alastair's hand. "The Sergeant searched me." She looked down, "She searched *everything*. She cut off my clothes and left me tied up and naked. But that isn't what's important now."

Jim's stomach dropped as he imagined what might be more important than the violation of a full body search.

"The last thing she said to the big soldier when they were leaving was they were going to kill more people."

"Pretend you're hysterical." Jim told her

She fell apart like he'd thrown a switch, wailed and wrapped her arms around him.

"How's this?" she asked between cries.

"Perfect," he whispered back.

"Sergeant Creeley," Jim said, "I need to take Georgia to the detachment and get a statement."

"I'll come with you." Sergeant Creeley glanced over at the Captains. "The Army needs to know what this girl's been through."

"Alastair, Lyanne." Jim said quietly, "I need you to find Joe in the hospital and ask him to meet me at the detachment. Don't go straight there. Give it a few minutes. He picked up Georgia and carried her to his truck. Creeley climbed in the other side. Jim drove to his house and grabbed the keys to the detachment, then they drove there drifting around corners. He skidded into the parking place.

"Tony," Jim said, "would you bring Georgia while I unlock the door?

The Sergeant picked the girl up like she was made of china and carried her into the detachment.

He put her on the desk. Jim handed her a pair of boots.

"From the lost and found. You'd be surprised at what people turn in."

"I was wondering where they went." Georgia laughed at Jim's expression. "Just kidding, but I have to, you know."

"I do know," Jim he sat across from her. "Tell me what you can about your experience."

Georgia told her story in a flat voice. She left out no detail. Jim could see Tony was as upset as him. He didn't know how she could sit here telling him what happened as she put boots on and tied them up.

Joe pulled up just as she finished.

"Alastair told me you wanted my help," Joe said.

"If you were a terrorist going to kill more people," Jim asked "Where would you do it from?

Joe stood and thought for a moment.

"Since they don't have any helicopters. They're limited to rifle or the like."

"RPG probably." Tony looked like he'd eaten something rotten. "Range about 300 meters, maybe a bit more if you stretch it."

"There's a rock that lifts above the trees north of the hospital." Joe nodded thoughtfully. "It's within the three hundred meters. If they weren't there either the trees would be in the way or they would be exposed." He took his radio off his belt, then put

304

it back. "She'll have one, I can't warn them without setting her off."

"I can," Georgia said. "Drop me off near the mall and I'll walk there and let them know."

"And if she chooses that moment to fire?" Jim asked.

"Then, I die, along with my friends." Georgia looked at him with tormented eyes. "I can think of worse things."

"If she's listening to radio chatter, what if she thought her target was going to get bigger?" Tony said, "Get the Captains to send out some teams to ask people to come to the field to help. It doesn't matter why, just that they are coming."

"OK," Jim went to a locker and pulled out handguns for Joe and him along with a rifle. "You're a better shot." He handed the rifle to Joe. "Don't do anything you can't live with."

"You'd be surprised what I'm learning to live with," Joe took the rifle. "I'll take Georgia to the mall and go on the west side. You take the east. Don't go soft."

"Let's go," Jim said.

They walked out to the trucks and climbed in. Jim watched Joe drive off with Georgia. He worried about both of them. It just meant he needed to do his job and not put either of them through more hell. He drove along the lower road close to where the track to the old mine started.

"We walk from here." Jim handed Tony a pair of snowshoes. "I'll go ahead, you follow far enough back, an ambush won't take us both." The Sergeant nodded and they headed into the woods.

After a few minutes Tony whistled quietly. Jim turned to look at him. He gave Jim a thumbs-up. Georgia got through. They kept going. Jim noticed tracks to his left and pointed at them, but kept going. He felt they were running out of time. The light was fading and the Sergeant wasn't going to wait until dark. He heard a branch snap and the big soldier called Jones jumped out at Tony. The Sergeant twisted and threw the big man against at tree.

"Go on," Tony said in a conversational tone. "I can deal with this bonehead."

Jones roared and rushed at Tony. Jim didn't stay to watch but started running along the trail. If the Sergeant had any hearing at all she knew her time was limited. Jim didn't think she was sane enough to back down. He heaved air into his lungs in long

305

painful gasps, but he forced himself to continue. At least it wasn't cold enough to do permanent damage. He saw the rock and Gretta standing on it. She had the RPG lifted to her shoulder. Jim drew his gun but the range was still beyond him. He forced his breathing to slow and aimed anyway. Then a single rifle shot fired and the woman crumpled and slid down off the rock.

Just a few minutes later, Joe came around the rock. Jim had moved the RPG away. Tony had arrived just after Joe's shot.

"The idiot refused to learn judo isn't about strength." Tony shrugged. "Then he had a collision with a tree. Fortunately, the tree survived the encounter. I called the Captain to send a recovery crew. I hear them coming now."

They rode back to the lot on two of the snowmobiles, leaving the recovery crew to manage with the other two. Jim noticed two of the four were police machines. When he got to the mall, the other members were there.

"We heard we're back on duty, Staff." Cam said.

"Good. Start by finding out what people need and coordinate with whoever's around to get it done."

"Sure, Staff," Cam waved at the other two members and they started walking through the crowd assessing and talking to people. It was almost full dark when he heard a helicopter arriving.

"It sounds like one of ours," Tony looked up into the night sky. "If ours hadn't been all blown to hell."

The helicopter landed in the field on the other side of the shed. The man who walked around the building into the lights on the lot moved with the absolute assurance of command. He was accompanied by a large staff already taking notes and talking on cell phones.

"Who's in charge here?" The man asked.

"That would be me." Jim lifted his hand. "Staff-Sergeant Jim Dalrymple."

"General Frank Downey," the man said. "Where's my nephew, Alastair?"

"He's fine," Jim said. "He should be in the hospital."

"Good." The General looked around the field. "So fill me in on this mess."

"I think we have it under control." Jim straightened, ready to defend his newly returned jurisdiction.

"Well that's good," the General said, "because the rest of the country is going to hell. Someone got a video of army personnel faking a battle scene. It's going to be down to armed combat in days if not hours if we can't make some sense of this.

Chapter Fifty-three

Matthew argued with the talking heads who all had different theories about what was happening and how to stop it. The only thing Matthew knew for sure was he had started it by showing the video. Georgia had sent it to him with no explanation, but he watched the woman's murder, the riot and its aftermath. He was so outraged he put the segment on air immediately.

He hadn't counted on the violence of the response. In some areas, the First Nations had retreated behind armed barriers. In others, people surrounded army bases and threw trash and insults at the guards. There were riots in all the major cities as people reacted against the atrocity. Not to mention the people who just took any excuse to make trouble.

Canada was burning, and it was Matthew's fault. Yet he couldn't have done anything but shown that video. The talking heads circled the same ground yet again. The government had to declare martial law. Martial law would spin the country into chaos and civil war. People should just be nice and go home. He didn't know when the people the country listened to became so ineffective. Maybe they'd always been and it had just never mattered before.

His phone buzzed and he picked it up.

"Matthew," he said after turning his mic off.

"Matthew, it's Georgia," he could hear a painful rasp in her voice. "The General told Jim how bad it is out there. I heard what he said. My video started it off."

"I put it on air," Matthew said.

"So you need to put me on air now. I'm stealing wifi from the general's people, but they're going to cut me off. Please, Matthew."

"Matthew," the producer yelled in Matthew's ear bud, "Focus. You have work to do."

"Right." Matthew looked at the disaster that was the pundits. "Look Georgia, I have to go."

"No." Even through the rasp, steel sounded in her voice. "I didn't go through all the shit I survived for people to burn the country down around their ears. Put me on now, and I'll never bug you again."

"You realize I'll get fired for this." Matthew hooked his phone into the equipment.

"Excuse me," he turned his mic on and interrupted the heads, "I have a report from the ground in Spruce Bay where this tragedy began just weeks ago. Georgia, you're on."

"My name is Georgia, and I live in Spruce Bay," She held the phone so it showed the burned-out mall and the crowd of people. In the foreground. "We were attacked and the mall that was the center of our town got destroyed along with our school. People trying to start a war. The government responded by sending the Army." She moved the camera to show the General talking to two Captains, other ranks stood around listening, but privates and Sergeants worked in the background. They passed out food and blankets. Comforting people. "The Army made some mistakes, but mostly because they came looking for an enemy. When you look for enemies, all you see are enemies and it breaks you. It was a broken person who did all this. One person, not the whole army.

"Look at what we can be, Army, First Nations, white working together to fix our mistakes, because we all make mistakes. All of us." She turned the camera around so people could see her tear-stained face. "I sent you a video showing a terrible thing, but it didn't show what happened next - what happened when people came to help to stand up for their community.

That's what you need to do. Stand up for your community. Stand up for your country. We'll work on the mistakes, but we can't do that if there is nothing left."

"Hey, what are you doing?" Matthew heard someone off camera yell.

"Oops, have to go." Georgia gave a last half smile, "Please." Then the feed ended.

Matthew looked at the camera and pushed himself to his feet.

309

"I'm standing up for my country," he said, "How about you?"

To his astonishment the talking heads stood too. The camera swung around the studio to show everyone on their feet, some embarrassed, some in tears. He looked at other feeds. More people were standing. It was slow. It wasn't magic. But it made him believe they might just survive this thing.

"When that kid runs for Prime Minister." He said before he realized his mic was still on, "I'm voting for her."

Chapter Fifty-four

Tom was breathing better. Joe was sure of it. He sat and watched the rise and fall of the boy's chest. Anna sat on the other side and held Tom's arm. Joe didn't know what he thought of her determination that she was marrying Tom. They were just kids. Yet she had been here every day since they brought him in. She sung healing over him until she lost her voice and her friends took over. If it worked out, Joe thought he approved.

"Hi Joe." He turned to see Ella walking into the room.

"Ella's here," he said to Anna. She looked up and smiled.

"The boy's getting better," Ella said. "He's strong like his father." She looked at Joe for a long moment before she sighed. "I hate to ask you," she said, "but I need you to take me to talk to this White Moose Clan. Anna will stay with Tom."

"They're flying him to Winnipeg today," she said. "I can go with him if you say it's OK."

"I must have slept through that conversation."

"You looked so tired," Anna said, "and sad."

"I will take you, Ella," Joe said, "but it will be hard."

"When is life not hard? I have what I need."

Joe sighed and put his hand gently on Tom's shoulder.

"I will come as soon as I can." Joe walked out of the room. He picked up the bedroll siting in the waiting area, and walked with Ella to the main doors. Jim was there talking to Brenda.

"Oh, hi Joe," Jim said when he saw Joe, "Where are you off to?"

"Ella wishes to speak to the White Moose Clan."

"And you are just going to take her to them, after the Army spent all that time not finding them?"

"They didn't ask me."

"True, they didn't ask about a lot of things. All this search and fuss was trying to find Johnston McCrey."

"He has a cabin north of the reserve."

"Yeah, I'm headed there now with Cam."

"I'm going up that way," Joe said, "I can back you up if you need."

"Always glad for the help, Joe."

"I'll meet you at the trail north from the Reserve."

Jim nodded and went back to talking with Brenda about the status of the riot survivors.

Joe helped Ella up into his truck and drove to his house. Jenna met him at the door.

"How is he?"

"Getting better." Joe smiled at his wife. "Anna's going with him to Winnipeg. You want to go, go."

"I'll pack now. Would you like tea?" she asked Ella.

"I'm fine, thank you," Ella said. "Pack."

Joe packed what he needed and put it in the back seat of the truck with Ella's roll. He loaded the snowmobile on the truck and they headed out to the reserve. Jim and Cam were already there with the police snowmobiles. Joe remembered the speed of the machines and briefly wished he could take one. It would probably get him killed.

"Let's go," Jim said. "Joe, officially you aren't here, but unofficially if you could circle around when we get there and cut off the trail North from the cabin it would be helpful." He looked at Ella who perched on the back of Joe's machine. "Will you be all right, Ella?"

"Fine. Tell Johnston I will come and talk to him in jail."

"That would be a great help," Jim nodded to the elder.

They headed North. Joe knew the trail well. He used to visit with his cousin before Johnston got heavy into the gangs and Joe got chummy with the RCMP. He thought his choices were better. Johnston had become a jerk, but he was family, so Joe hoped they didn't need to shoot him.

He left the trail and raced along the side of a lake. It would let him rejoin the trail beyond the cabin.

"Would you mind waiting here, Ella?" Joe asked.

"Unpack the stove and I'll make tea."

Joe left her filling the pot with clean snow and cruised slowly toward the cabin. He stopped just out of sight of the cabin, but where he could hear what was going on.

The police arrived and banged on the door. He heard Johnston's machine fire up and come toward him. His cousin came 'round the bend and stopped.

"Shit, Joe," Johnston said, "not you too?"

"Ella's just a little way back making tea."

He swore Johnston went a little pale. Jim and Cam came up behind Johnston and he put his hands up in surrender. Joe drove Johnston's machine back to the cabin and gave the key to Jim.

"I'll see you in a while."

"If you see Darren," Jim said, "Let him know he can come in. It's cleared with the brass."

"I'll do that."

He returned and had tea with Ella before packing up the stove and pot. They continued North. Joe had to stop several times to find the most recent trail, but they made good time. Early the next day they arrived at a lean to hiding three snowmobiles. Joe took a moment to make sure they wouldn't run, then they continued. It was harder following the snowshoe tracks, but he guessed where they were heading. He'd got turned around once and stumbled on the tunnels and caves in the rocks. A perfect place for the rebels to hole up. The trail just confirmed his direction.

They arrived in mid-morning.

"Wait here. I want to talk to them alone." Ella strapped her snowshoes on.

"I've got your back," Joe unwrapped his rifle.

"You are already carrying a heavy burden." Ella walked toward the entrance. Joe could see movement there. They knew she was coming. He watched through the scope on his gun. He didn't think there was another exit, but he listened for the sound of someone approaching him.

"Come out and talk," Ella said when she came in shouting distance of the entrance.

"And have whoever is with you shoot us?" someone shouted back, "No thanks."

313

"He will not shoot without cause," Ella said, "I come in peace. You have nothing to fear."

"Just come in here, and we'll talk."

"This place has an evil history. I will not enter, nor will I leave, until I have spoken to your leader."

"How do you know I'm not the leader?"

"You don't speak like a leader." Ella unstrapped her snowshoes and sat on them. She looked like she could comfortably wait a lifetime.

Joe settled down for a long wait. After a while he heard someone walking toward him. They made no attempt at stealth, so he didn't try to cover them with the rifle. He leaned against a tree where he could see Ella and the approaching person at the same time.

He wasn't surprised when Darren came out of the trees with his hands away from his side.

"Hi, Joe," he said.

"Hi Darren."

"Rivers asked me to check on the old lady's backup. I figured it would be you."

"Jim said you could come in now. It's been cleared with the brass."

"I appreciate that," Darren looked uncomfortable. "But it's complicated."

"Nice job you did on the base."

"Thanks, I hope no one was hurt."

"Not seriously."

"Rivers liked the video. He said the Army was doing his work for him."

"They've stopped that now," Joe glanced at Darren. "There's a General in charge who knows his ass from a hole in the ground."

"I didn't know they made those."

Joe didn't reply and the two men sat and watched Ella sit patiently as a stone.

"How long will she stay there?" Darren asked.

"Til the snow melts," Joe smiled.

"I know a woman like that where I grew up."

"Should let them run the place."

314

"That's a terrifying thought," Darren said, "but it would be better than this mess. I'd better go back and report to Rivers. He's the calm one. The loud mouth is Roger Dupreis. He's more likely to be the immediate danger. Rivers is a long term danger."

Joe nodded. Darren walked away and Joe settled in to wait again.

The sun hadn't moved far before there was motion at the mouth of the tunnel again.

Darren and a woman walked out and greeted Ella. The woman sat in front of Ella while Darren stood behind them but out of the line of fire from Joe or the tunnel.

Joe guessed the woman was part of the complication. She had respect for the elders, so that was good. More movement at the tunnel and Rivers walked out. Joe knew instantly this was another hunter. He didn't peer around or appear concerned, but Joe was sure he knew exactly where Joe waited in the woods. The last one to come out walked out like he expected to be shot on the spot. He looked all over except where he needed to.

"Welcome," Rivers said to Ella. "May I know your name?"

"You may call me Ella."

"What do you want?"

"I want an end to the violence."

"You don't want an end to the killing of our people? An end to hunger and sickness'?"

"I want that too." Ella said. "But a healer doesn't treat a patient by becoming sick with the same disease. They must master the disease and send it away."

"So you just give up?"

"I do not give up, but a healing dance is long and tiring. Sometimes it looks like failure. You have given up with your desire to become more violent than the white people. You have become what you hate."

"They won't listen to anything else!"

"They are hard of hearing," Ella nodded her head. "But some listen. The dance is having its effect."

"How long?" It was as much a cry as a question.

"How long does it take a sapling to split the rock?"

"Enough with this Yoda bullshit!" Roger shouted. "Send the old lady away, or better yet, kill her and her friend."

315

"Your friend is young." Ella didn't look at Roger.

"He is." Rivers agreed.

"What the fuck? I've had enough of this." Roger pulled a gun and pointed it at Ella, who didn't move at all. Rivers moved even faster than Joe could center the rifle on Roger. He grabbed the gun and twisted it away from Roger, but not before Roger pulled the trigger. Joe saw the exit wound in Rivers' back. River's hand blurred and Roger's head snapped back. He fell to the ground. Joe was certain he was dead.

"I apologize, grandmother," Rivers spoke quietly. "The sickness has spread beyond my power." He sank to his knees and bowed as if in prayer.

"Joe," Darren called, "he wants to talk to you."

Joe walked out into the clearing and put his rifle down before going to where Darren knelt beside Rivers.

"Witness my words," Rivers said. Joe saw the bullet had gone through the man's liver. This was a dying declaration.

"I hear you."

"and I," Ella said.

"I was impatient," Rivers said. "I tired of my people's pain. I regret I've added to their burden. It is time someone else became head of the White Moose. He will continue the cause, but not the murder." He took a breath and Joe saw him will himself to finish. "I tainted the cause by taking money from a white mining company. They financed our weapons in return for two deaths…"

Joe waited for him to take another breath to finish his statement, but it never came. They sat in silence for a long time, before Ella stood and fastened her snowshoes.

"So you're not coming back." Joe said to Darren.

"No," Darren took the woman's hand to help her to her feet, and kept holding it when she was standing. "There are more White Moose Clan around and I can't just let them go back to violence. They will need a strong leader."

"It would have been nice if he lived long enough to tell me what mining company paid him off," Joe said.

"Tell Jim to check out connections with Ellers," Darren said, "I expect he'll find plenty of connections."

"Enough to put the man away?"

"Perhaps not, but Jim's got more than one way to go after him. I heard Roger tell a story about a white prospector who had a very amusing injury. Amusing to Roger in any case. There might be sufficient cause for a warrant."

"I'll mention it."

"You still a cop, then?" A huge man walked out of the tunnel holding a carving knife.

"Undercover. so deep I may never be heard of again. It will be useful to have a direct route to Ottawa's ears."

"As long as you aren't leaving us," the man said to Darren. "I need someone to feed. Speaking of feeding. No peace was ever settled without a feast."

"I could do with a spot of lunch," Ella smiled up at the man.

Darren and Mack, the big man, laid Rivers and Roger out in the forest for the time being and Dianne brought a blanket to sit on and cover the bloodstained snow.

Mack was ecstatic because Ella praised his cooking.

"We'll be moving on from here. Let them know about this place and they can collect the bodies."

"You'll have to reattach the battery wires on your snowmobiles. Take it easy."

The three of them went into the caves and came out a short time later with their gear. Joe shook Darren's hand one last time and watched them walk into the woods.

"Let's go," Ella said, "You need to be getting to Winnipeg to see that boy of yours." Joe walked alongside Ella to the snowmobile and they headed away to the south.

Epilogue

Jim stretched and looked around. The formal part of the gathering wasn't until tomorrow. The rubble of the destroyed mall had been removed and machines prepared the ground for new construction. In the interval, offices had been set up in the parking lot from buildings from the disassembled Base. The shed was still there and there was talk about keeping it and retrofitting it into a useful town venue.

He and his expanded unit were in charge of security for the gathering. Pat, Amber, and Cam he'd made shift leaders with their own teams. Jim finally felt he had enough people to do what he was paid to do.

He saw someone he'd been looking forward to seeing.

"You know, Sergeant," Ralph Ellers said. "It feels good to be part of the revitalization of this community. I believed in it from the very beginning. That's why Ellers Mining will continue to have our head office right here."

"Yes," Jim gritted his teeth. "I heard you filed a claim right after the attack. Turns out it was the same claim Zeke Hamilton had."

"That's right." Ellers nodded solemnly. "Zeke knew he was onto a good thing. After his unfortunate death, I put a claim in so the ownership would remain in Zeke's community."

"I would think that a very fine gesture on your part if I didn't know you conspired to have Zeke killed." Jim tried not to smile as he watched the florid red leave Ellers' face.

"You can't prove it." Ellers blustered. "And I'll sue if you so much as mention it again."

"What I can and can't prove isn't the issue." Jim kept his smile. "Though you'd be surprised at what I've learned about you and your friends. It is interesting how Rivers and Dupreis both worked at your company."

"I'm sure they've worked at a lot of places together."

"Not really, but we're also following the trail of some money used to buy weapons and explosives. Very interesting, our forensic accountants are having a ball. But what I personally find very interesting is what Johnston McCrey is telling me about your sexual preferences."

"Nobody is going to take the word of a drug dealer over mine."

"Well, not just a drug dealer." Jim's grin widened. "He went into a sideline of selling kiddie porn. He didn't tell you he was taping you, so you didn't think about the scar you have. It's very clear on the tapes. It must have been very painful."

Ellers turned so white Jim worried he was going to collapse.

"My only question to you at this point is whether you'd rather be arrested for murder or for the abuse of little kids, most of whom survived the attack on the school quite nicely."

"What do you want?" All trace of bluster was gone.

You aren't going to complain when the Spruce Bay Cree Nation contests your right to the claim."

"Fat lot of good that's going to do without money to pay for the drilling."

"They already know where the ore is," Jim said. "Zeke sent the coordinates to me along with a request to make sure his friends got their share." The man deflated further. "You will plead guilty to all offenses and then you will keep your mouth shut. No bragging, no deals with the media, no attempts to spin the events."

"And what if I do decide to talk?" Ellers made one last play at bluster.

"There is no statute of limitations on child abuse. Do you know what the life expectancy of a child molester in prison is?"

Ellers bent his head and meekly walked ahead of Jim to the truck where Jim cuffed him and put him in the back seat. Jim saw Georgia walking hand in hand with Brad Beauchamp of all people. He resisted the urge to wave at her.

***

Georgia liked the feel of Brad's hand in hers.

"Is that Mr. Ellers getting arrested?" Brad asked.

"It looks like it," Georgia said.

"Good, he was friends with my dad, and my dad wasn't friends with any nice people."

"So what are you going to do now he's gone?" Georgia asked.

"Go back to school, learn enough to keep up with you," Brad answered. "I spent a lot of time on the street learning being tough wasn't going to get me far in life."

"I'd thought you'd gone North.," She looked up at him.

"I'd last even less time in the bush than on the streets," Brad said. "I'm going to ask Joe to take me out though. I need to learn that as much as the school stuff."

"Sounds like a good idea. I wonder if he'd let me come along and learn too?"

"Ask him." Brad squeezed her hand. "Then you can explain all the long words to me."

Georgia thought of Joe spouting off a string of polysyllabic words and laughed. It was good to be able to laugh without coughing.

"So the Prime Minister is coming tomorrow?" Brad asked after a while.

"That's what Matthew told me. He's meeting with Mike Tremblant and Ella."

"And you're going to be there," Brad didn't sound pleased.

"I want you be in the front row." Georgia swung his hand. "I don't want a circus about our friendship, but I don't plan on hiding it either. This is me, Brad. I do stuff, I try to change things."

"But if you're hanging around with Prime Ministers, you won't want to hang around with me."

Georgia stopped and pulled Brad around so she was looking in his eyes. Very nice looking eyes too, part of her said. *You're right* she told herself, *but let's stay on task here.*

"Brad," she said, "I'm twelve, closing in on thirteen. I would much rather hang out with a boy who takes the time to accept me, than an old man who has a hard time listening to anybody." She gave him a hug. She wanted to give him more, but it wasn't fair to him. They walked on further and she saw Alastair with Lyanne talking with his Uncle. She rather liked the General once she got to know him. He paid attention.

***

"Thanks for paying attention," Alastair said to Uncle Frank.

"I'm thinking that you and your fierce young woman did this country a big favour."

"Mostly Georgia. I just made sure her plan went through."

"And helped her use military wifi too." Uncle Frank said, "though I have to say I'm glad you did."

"I'm serious about the summer job too," Alastair met his uncle's eyes.

"I'm sure I can find something for you to do around the place," Uncle Frank smiled slightly.

"I have another favour to ask." Alastair steeled himself.

"Hmm, maybe two summers?"

"Listen first," Alastair said, "then you decide."

"Fair enough."

"Lyanne wants to go back to school." Alastair nodded at her. "But it's hard because her son was killed in the attack and because of what she used to be."

His uncle looked at Lyanne and Alastair saw her lift her face up and look him in the eyes.

"Not everyone gets to make their own choices."

"Very true," Uncle Frank nodded and looked back at Alastair. "So you want me to get her into a school. What does your friend want?"

"A choice," Lyanne said. "I want to be able to choose to go to school or to stay here, or maybe both. There is no choice if there is only one option."

"OK," Uncle Frank fixed her with his General's gaze. "So what do you want to do in school?"

"I don't know enough to know that yet." Lyanne held his gaze.

"So I'm guessing finish high school for a start, then decide from there?"

"That would be good."

"There is a private girl's school in Ottawa which takes in scholarship students. I can talk to them. Alastair's aunt is an alumni."

"Thank you, sir." Lyanne smiled. Uncle Frank pulled out his phone and wandered away to talk on it. "Thank you, too, Alastair."

"You know I want you to stay, but you need your own life. I don't want you to hate me because I held you back." Alistair said.

"Come and find me when you graduate, and we'll see how we feel then."

"I will -"

Lyanne put her finger on his lips.

"No promises, a lot can happen in the time between now and then. But whatever we become then, I will always remember you as a friend." She kissed him on the forehead then walked away.

Alastair watched her go and knew he'd done the right thing. He just wished it didn't hurt so much. He took a deep breath and turned away from Lyanne. The hospital was the only part of the original mall still standing. Scaffolds surrounded it as workers checked to make sure it was solid. There were rumours of an expansion.

Alastair didn't care about the hospital, but he knew just as if he could see through walls that Anna and Tom were struggling through much more pain than he felt.

***

"Damn, it hurts," Tom said. It hurt to talk too, but he was tired of not talking. Anna watched him and he knew if she could have taken all the pain she would have. He forced himself to move his other leg. The skin was tough and didn't want to stretch. He had to rub cream on it and exercise. It was the only way to get out of this room.

"You're doing good," Anna said, "One more and you set a new record." Tom moved the first leg again, then collapsed in the wheelchair the physio had behind him. Anna wiped his face with a cool cloth.

"I'll leave you two for today," Cher said. "See you tomorrow." The physiotherapist wasn't so much cheery as determined. She had such faith in Tom he couldn't bear to not to at least try.

Anna wheeled him over to the window so he could look out at the forest.

"Why did you tell them we were going to get married?" Tom said. The pain made him grumpy and he hated himself for taking it out on Anna. He was never grumpy with Georgia when she visited, nor his mom or even his dad.

"Was the only way they would let me stay with you." Anna put her hand on his shoulder. "I was so afraid they would send me away and you would die without me there to sing for you."

That was a different answer than she had given him the other times he asked - just about once a day since he woke up and his dad told him he approved of Anna. The other times she reminded him of the talks they'd had about what they would do when they finished school. The talks had become kisses, but nothing more when all this started.

He could see his reflection in the mirror. The right side of his head from his ear back had burned also most of the skin on his back - the cause of the painful stretching sessions. Even with skin grafts the scars were stiffer than the rest of his skin.

Anna put her hands gently on the sides of his face. He couldn't see the burn anymore. He looked like himself. Tears leaked out of his eyes, he couldn't stop them. This pain made him weak.

"You are still you," Anna whispered in his ear. "I love you as much as I know how. Kohkom told me once she was married at thirteen. I won't force you to hold to a promise made in the heat of the kiss, but I will not go away. I will be your friend as long as you allow."

Tom turned the chair so he could look at Anna. She was the same girl he known all his life. They'd played together since they could walk. They'd gone skinnydipping with their friends when they were much younger. She was just Anna, but not just Anna. He tried to imagine life without her near him. He set his jaw and reached out to touch her tears.

"I expect our parents will want us to wait until we finish high school."

She pulled up a chair and they sat together and looked out the window until the light faded. Anna kissed him gently on the lips and headed out to walk home to her uncle's place.

"She's going to marry me when we get older," he said to the nurse as she passed Anna to help him into bed.

323

"Lucky her." The nurse smiled at him.

"Lucky me," Tom said. It hurt. He hurt all over, but he knew Anna would be here tomorrow so he could live with the pain.

***

Jim watched the Prime Minister climb out of the car and wave to the people of Spruce Bay, not to mention all the media cameras. Jim had all his people scattered through the crowd and the Rangers in a loose circle around the town. The town was as safe as he could make it.

The Army had set up a stage and a sound system in the Shed, so people could listen and watch regardless of the weather. They'd had heaters going all night and it felt just a little warmer than outside. The wind was picking up, so no one minded using the Shed.

The politician and his aides walked into the Shed and up on the stage. The crowd followed and stood watching. There was just a small corner with chairs for elders.

"So," Leigh said from behind him. "Does Staff-Sergeant Dalrymple have a moment for a hug from his wife?"

"Always." He put his arms around her. "So what is going on in acting-principal Dalrymple's life?"

"As soon as we're done here, the Army has some insulating panels they are going to put up which should make the Shed bearable. We are putting in dividers too and we'll end up with a tolerable temporary school. Add in the portables for the High School and we'll be in good shape."

"Good to hear." Jim gave his wife an extra squeeze. They stood quietly and watched the formalities begin.

***

"Camera one on the PM," Matthew said into the headset. He tried to watch half a dozen live feeds at once and make a professional looking newscast. He was terrified. He loved it. "Camera two on the Elder, camera three stay on the crowd. Four, I want a close up of the Chief now." He worked the camera like a conductor worked with a symphony orchestra. The Chief smudged the table and someone must have briefed the PM properly because he didn't look at all awkward. Now they sat at the table and the PM addressed the people, and incidentally the nation.

"Camera one, close up on the PM, two stay wide, three I want a slow pan of the other people at the table." They were an odd collection of people. The PM with some of his staff behind him, the First Nations Chief, and the elder, they all made sense, but then there was the boy in the wheel chair, and the girl who stood behind him. They wore feathers in their braids that told anyone who knew they were special. There was a General who watched the proceeding with interest. The one the camera lingered on longest was a face familiar to anybody who watched the news. She had broadcast a brief plea for people to stand up and stand together for their country. It had gone a long way to quieting the worst of the unrest. Matthew hoped today would go a long way to finishing the job.

"…work together as people of this great nation to resolve our differences and find a peaceful solution to living together and sharing this great land…"

At least the PM hadn't put her foot in her mouth. She finished his speech and sat down. The Chief, Mike Tremblant, deferred to the elder. Ella stood up. She didn't move to the podium to speak, but they had microphones along the whole table.

"We've heard plenty of promises," she said. "We've been hearing the same promises for generations. I'm tired of promises. I'm tired of my children and grandchildren going hungry and uneducated. I'm tired of my sons filling the jails and my daughters the streets. I want to see change. I want to see our children have the same choices as your children. I've had people ask how my people could do such terrible things. Yes, they did terrible things, but how long would you suffer before you rebelled?"

"Yes," the Prime Minister responded when Ella had sat down, "but these things take time. We need to study the issues -"

"You have studies, libraries of studies," Ella interrupted him. "You've had time generations of time. It is time to act. We stand together as a people." She pushed herself to her feet. "We stand together, or we fail." The entire room stomped their feet, once. They were standing. The elders stood as they could, some with children holding them. Chief Tremblant stood and the General too. Matthew knew all across the country, people would be standing in silent agreement with Ella.

325

Georgia helped set it up. She'd had Matthew prime the people by reminding them of their standing for peace. He was sure she was right and they would stand now, for this elder. People across Canada had *Georgia for Prime Minister* bumper stickers. Matthew had one. There were Facebook pages and web sites about her. She had offers to speak from all over the nation.

Georgia stood and leaned over to the mic.

"In six years, I get the right to vote and run for office," Georgia said. "I suggest you get ready."

Acknowledgements

This is a book which came to life in the north. Many of the social issues discussed in the book are real and pervasive across communities in the north. There are also people who have dedicated themselves to improving their communities and making hope real again.

I'd like to acknowledge both the troubled and heroic people of the north in the creation of this story.

No book is released without some people taking time to read and critique its early incarnations. I need to thank my beta readers, Harry Hobbs, Elvier Brunel, Anna Pinette, Fernand Béasse, and Lucie Kuly. As well as Katrina Béasse for proofreading.

Lastly Alexandra, who allowed me the time to write, and puts up with disjointed descriptions of the plot.

About the Author

Alex is an author, editor and reviewer living in Winnipeg, Manitoba overlooking the Assiniboine River. He has two dogs who drag him out for walks, a wife who makes him read out loud and a scotch collection to celebrate the successful completion of his next goal.

About the Illustrator

Matt Kehler is a Winnipeg artist. His unique style of work convinced me I had to get him to do the cover for this book. See more of his work here: http://mattkehlerart.com/

Other books by Alex

The Regent's Reign
Calliope and the Sea Serpent
Wendigo Whispers
The Devil Reversed
Generation Gap
The Gods Above
Tales of Light and Dark
Like Mushrooms (poetry and photography)
The Heronmaster
Blood and Sparkles, and other stories
Princess of Boring
By the Book
Sarcasm is My Superpower
Playing on Yggdrasil
The Unenchanted Princess

Alex also has stories in:

Canadian Creatures
Song of the Axe
Words on the Rocks
Beyond the Wail
Collidor Stream Collection 2016

Read short stories and excerpts from his novels at
alexmcgilvery.com